Books by Ramona Stewart

♣

DESERT TOWN

THE STARS ABIDE

THE SURPRISE PARTY COUPLES

PROFESSOR DESCENDING

A CONFIDENCE IN MAGIC

KIT LARKIN

CASEY

CASEY

CASEY

by
RAMONA STEWART

LITTLE, BROWN AND COMPANY · BOSTON · TORONTO

Published simultaneously in Canada
by Little, Brown & Company (Canada) Limited

PRINTED IN THE UNITED STATES OF AMERICA

For my grandmother, Mary O'Brien Waugh

AND

my grandfather, James O'Farrell Waugh

We are a primitive people wandering wildly in a strange land, the Nineteenth Century.
— a literate Irishman in America,
according to George Potter

There are scarcely five thousand persons in New York City who have even a faint idea of the methods which control their local affairs, the secret channels of influence, and the devious paths leading to a hidden power which in effect is as potent as that of a despotic monarch.
— Matthew P. Breen

An Irishman is only a nigger turned inside out.
— Old New York saying

Author's Note

THE Irish Poor Law of 1838 set up workhouses for dispossessed tenants, paying for it by taxing the Irish landlords, and providing the gentry with their first lively incentive to promote emigration from a ruined and crowded land. Then in 1845 the potato rot appeared, and for the next five years there was starvation in Ireland, and famine-borne diseases. Great masses fled to the seaports and boarded wretched emigrant ships bound for North America.

In the port cities, without funds and unable to travel further, they went on public relief or simply sank into the slums where intelligence and industry rubbed together with ignorance, depravity, pauperism and drink. A floating population of travelers, immigrants and vagabonds mingled with the permanent residents. In New York, ten thousand homeless children roamed the streets. Crime statistics soared, as did admissions to the city's almshouse, prisons and insane asylums. The natives recoiled from the flood of poverty-stricken foreigners. But recoiling was no solution; they weren't going to go away. By 1860, 1,600,000 residents of the United States were Irish-born, and New York was the largest Irish city in the world.

Contents

THE TIGER

♣ 1 ♣

ANOTHER riot began that evening. It was not so bad as the riots of three years before when the streets were barricaded for days, City Hall was held by the mob, and the troops were called in. It was just another one of dozens of small local riots that rippled across the city in a year.

It did not begin over any of the real troubles — the NO IRISH NEED APPLY signs outside the factories, the tenement firetraps, their walls leaking ooze, garbage piled up in the hallways, rats attacking the children. It began vaguely and irrelevantly, in the way of so many of the riots, with a fight between two drunks.

When the police separated them, one of the drunks fought back. A club on the head quieted him. They sat him against a brick wall and when he came to, started walking him to the station house. But by then, the windows were open in the tenement above and as the women began yelling, bricks came hurtling from a rooftop. Part of a neighborhood gang showed up. Somebody shoved a cop from behind and he swung, pulling his gun. Somebody shoved him again so he shot and a dark, ragged man crumpled into the crowd. Above them, a woman started screaming. Then the weapons came out and the gang moved in just as more cops came running around the corner and the tenement emptied onto the street.

The fighting moved down the block and as it spread, there was the crash of glass as a grocery window was broken and a bin of apples tumbled across the sidewalk. The proprietor came to the door yelling but he was driven back. He returned with a gun but a brick hit him; the mob surged across him and began looting. On their way out, the store was fired and soon flames from two more fires were lighting the evening sky and the battleground spread to another block.

Tom Casey heard the fire bell as he was working on a locomotive at the Harlem railway shop at Thirty-second Street. He got down from the cab and made his way through the engine steam to an open doorway where he stood searching the sky. He was a burly young man about twenty, dressed in dirty work clothes, his face grease-streaked from the engines. Beneath the grease was an ordinary Irish face, the skin fair, the nose snubbed. Only the eyes were unusual. They were hazel with a hard glint, slightly hooded, set into the lids flat like a dangerous fighter's eyes. His chin was square and stubborn. He studied a column of smoke lit by a red glow several blocks to the southeast while the men piled up about him in the doorway.

"Thirtieth Street?" a man said. "The coal yard, is it?" There was a coal yard on Third Avenue.

"Near Second, by the look of it."

"By Jaysus, there's the fireworks factory on Second."

A hand fell on Casey's shoulder. "Let's go, boy!"

But as they began to push out the doorway, he turned and bored his way back past the crowd into the shop. He jerked a red fireman's shirt from a nail and buttoning it as he went, ran out the far door.

It was a warm evening with wind stirring the East River smell into the spring air. He marked the wind as he ran toward the spiraling smoke; it was southerly and fitful, a bad wind for a fire. For a block he sped along the flagging sidewalk past the tenements, ground floors filled with billiard parlors, saloons and grog shops, red and blue globes blossoming in the dusk. Then he collided with a drunken woman, pulled her to her feet and ducked into the street to make better time. He avoided an oyster cart, turned his foot on a cobblestone and nearly went down. But he righted himself and was off again at once, not bothering with his enginehouse — the engine would have left by now anyway — but heading for the fire itself.

A rich column of smoke was rising as he pressed through the crowds boiling out on the sidewalk before the red brick tenements along Second Avenue. He found his company's hand-engine, the Pacific, in the mob, the men hauling the ropes stopped and the Pacific stalled like a child's toy decorated with axes and brass-socketed leather tubing.

Turk, the enginehouse dog, dashed up. He'd been a stray till Casey found him and trained him into a grand dogfighter. He leaped with joy and excitement to see Casey and Casey gave him a friendly nudge with his boot, then turned to look over the situation.

Work had just let out and men from the shipyards, slaughter-houses, and ironworks to the south had come running so now nothing more could get through. The boy who ran ahead with the signal lamp had managed to wriggle a bit farther. But the engine foreman was surrounded, shouting through his silver trumpet while his runners tried to force a path.

Caught behind two butchers in bloody overalls, Casey could see the fire a block away sending up waves of gassy flame and cinders. It was larger than he'd thought, consuming two blocks of tenements. Silhouetted against it he saw men fighting and the precinct wagons drawn up with their horses rearing in fright of the flames. Already there were ladders up so he knew that other fire companies had beaten them to it. One was the Valley Forge Company's new steam engine with fire spouting from its top, come across town from Eighth Avenue. That was bad enough. But then he recognized Pretty Boy's engine, the Mutual, from near the Gas Works on Twenty-second Street.

At the sight of Pretty Boy's engine, he gave a shout of rage, grabbed hold of one of the butchers blocking his way, swung him around and hit him. When the second butcher went for him, he grabbed the brass knuckles from his hip pocket and slugged him too. In the instant that the crowd parted, he hurled himself forward to join his engine. Scanlon was there, who fought with him in the Arsenal Gang; there were only the two of them from the gang with the engine company but they knew what to do in a fight.

"Let's go!" he cried, and together they plunged forward ahead of the drag ropes and began laying about them. There was a commotion below him as Turk came up snarling and getting a mouthful of pants leg here and there. Then his own men moved forward in a wedge before the haulers. The crowd roared again, and next second the feeling around him changed. He could sense it — the drag of opinion like a current and a shout went up that told him the crowd was with them. There was a great cheer in mounting volume — a tiger — "Hei! hei! hei! hei!" The ropes tightened and the haulers began to inch forward.

They moved deeper into pandemonium. Women who had been hurling bricks from their supplies stored on the rooftops and the top-floor rooms now were moaning at their own buildings going up in flames. The scream of the injured and the wailing of children rose above the mob cries. A dead man with his head and shoulders charred had been leaned against a building. Worn chairs, pots and poor bits of bedding were piled on the pavement and guarded by distracted families. The chain fire escapes were up already, their spikes dug into windowsills, and as Casey's company came up a lad of ten was lowering himself down one of the chains with terrible slowness. For a few seconds the crowd watched to see if he would fall, but he held tight, moved again and then cautiously once more, and as he reached the ground a woman rushed to him. They were motionless a moment, their faces reflecting crimson. Then a policeman caught hold of them and hustled them to safety as the crowd sighed like a beast and engulfed them. Next second there was a sharp crack as a floor collapsed and the building sagged, belching sparks and smoke. The sound of the crowd changed to a cry half of pleasure and half pity for the dying still inside.

The children from the tenements were not staying with their mothers. Children of the poor, they were tough and active. Dirty, in handed-down clothing, some without shoes, wild with excitement, they ran in and out of the coils of fire hose, climbing about the police vans and pressing in on the firemen rocking the steel bars that forced the water up the hoses, so that every so often one of the firemen broke his stroke to turn and hurl a child back. They were only quiet when they tiptoed up to gaze with relish at the injured. Beside the dead man with the blackened head and shoulders a line of bodies was laid out — smoke victims, limbs charred, clothes burned off, faces gone. The injured were huddled nearby — a drunk with his shirt seared, three half-suffocated children. As Casey's company came up, the crowd was starting to load them into pushcarts and wheelbarrows to take them to Bellevue Hospital. The police vans were already packed with rioters. Tom saw two boys from the Arsenal Gang pushed into a van but he stayed with his company — he and Scanlon were on duty; they all understood about that.

And all the time he kept looking around for Pretty Boy. He was not manning the brakes with his company, so he was likely inside, stealing what he could lay hands on.

"Take her on up the block!" Casey's foreman shouted and Casey saw they weren't going to jump the Mutual and move in on their hydrant.

As the draggers pulled the Pacific forward, they passed Captain Speight of their precinct and he gave them a hard look. There was coldness between them since last week when he'd told the *Tribune* reporter that he had stopped another firemen's fight between the Pacific and the Mutual. He was a jackass, looking for honors, Casey thought, and if he kept on interfering, he'd be found in an alley.

Just then Captain Speight turned and went on talking with the man behind him and Casey had enough of a glimpse of the stranger to place him — the top hat, the coat, the white shirt bosom. He was one of the rich fire runners. There were a lot of rich men who ran after the fires. They swarmed in like squirrels to watch the Irish get burned out, standing around staring and poking with gold-handled canes at the poor belongings piled on the pavement and shaking their heads at the shiftless Irish. And then what a row if some dirty Irish child came up from behind and stole a handkerchief.

But even as he went past, slipping off his knuckles since he hadn't found Pretty Boy, the contempt slid off the top of his feelings and pride welled up that the rich man had come to watch him. It was a big fire with four companies present and more arriving. The fact that the swell was there made him more eager to find a hydrant and fall in line at the brakes.

Then suddenly he was hearing his mother describe the day of the donkey races back in the old village when the grand gentlemen from Dublin came down from the landlord's castle in their top hats and capes, and stood about watching while the tenants threw the strong boys to racing and wrestling.

"They saw something that day," his mother said, and her simple pride in the scene enraged him. She could never understand why he had contempt for the village wrestlers. He wasn't sure himself. But he went cold at the thought of the fine gentlemen in immaculate clothes looking down at the village boys struggling in the dirt.

"The night before, the same heroes had been hamstringing the landlord's ewes," he said. The landlord had dispossessed a family the week before the race and the tenants struck back by cutting the tendons in the landlord's sheep.

"Sure, an' the gentlemen knew that," his mother said. "They knew it as well as we."

"I don't care what they knew. If we was fighting them, we ought not get down in the dirt and wrestle for them."

"Ah, there's the cunning of it," his mother said, looking wise.

But already the part that bothered him had slipped away. And now it was back in himself, with his own surge of pride that the gentleman from a Fifth Avenue brownstone would see him fight a fire and be struck — by what? That they ran the stroke up to some record count a minute with maybe a building collapsing and burying them altogether for the general admiration.

"There's himself," Scanlon said, but Casey was pursuing the dark thread of his thought and did not see till Scanlon reached past the engine backboard and knocked his arm. Then he looked up at Big John Maguire.

In the instant, the thoughts of the Fifth Avenue swell deserted him before emotions sharper and more conflicting. Maguire was a sight to rouse a man's admiration. Six foot tall, blue-eyed and black-haired, with a broken nose from his gang-fighting days, he was made more glorious now by his years with Tammany. Maguire at thirty-seven, alderman, saloonkeeper and district leader of the Twenty-first Ward, in snow-white shirt with yellow diamond studs, carrying his gold dog-headed cane with the ruby eyes, plug hat pushed back on his dark curls, and accompanied by his captain, had arrived at the fire to relieve the poor.

But there was the rub. For only last fall Maguire had gone through the ward pledging his word that the rumors sweeping the city were false, that Tammany had not been taken over by the Native American forces. But the suspicions were too great. Every one of the thirteen governing Sachems of Tammany was a native-born Protestant. And the history with the Native Americans was too frightening. Gangs of nativist toughs and butcher boys assaulted Sisters of Charity in the streets, burning convents, wrecking churches. Only a line of powerful Irishmen had prevented the sacking and burning of the cathedral. An Italian archbishop had to be spirited on board the ship sailing him back to Rome to avoid the mob waiting for him on the New York dock. For a time, every Sunday a mob ferried into Brooklyn and battled the Irish neighborhoods till the militia was called out.

The Irish panic set in with the rumors Tammany had betrayed them and the pleadings of Maguire were met by darker suspicions still, that Maguire himself had gone over to the enemy. The poor Irish vote stampeded and voted Fernando Wood into the mayor's chair.

It was only then, with the deed done, that they woke, hungover, and began to wonder if they'd not been gulled. Wood was corrupt, sure, they knew that. His plug-uglies controlled the polls election day. The gamblers and prostitutes and thieves paid him to stay in business. He collected from the very prisoners in the jails to swell his campaign fund. But they'd voted for him in the years he'd been the Tammany candidate, and when he'd been driven from Tammany, it was the whispering campaign that made them follow him.

But the whispers could have come from Fernando Wood himself. That was what Maguire had warned at the time, though panic made them disbelieve him.

Then last month Tammany had made one of their own, an Irishborn Catholic, the next Grand Sachem. Though belated, it soothed them and then increased their feeling that Wood had fooled them. And now, watching the man they'd all let down, Casey felt his old admiration for Maguire mixed with guilt.

At the moment, Maguire was speaking to a shawly woman with four children. She was gazing up at him, her eyes wet with tears, and Casey supposed she'd been burned out. It would serve them all right if Maguire sent her packing, but even as Casey watched, Maguire dug into his pocket. The shawly woman snatched at his hand and tried to kiss it. So he bore them no grudge. Far from it, he put a great arm about her shoulders and rumpled the hair of one of the children.

It was then, as Maguire looked away over her head, that Casey saw how embarrassed by her emotion the man was. The bold Irish blue eyes were discomfited; Maguire's forehead was flushed. Suddenly, the years were bridged to when Maguire was in his early twenties, fighting the forty-round bare-knuckled club fights, when he staggered up from the sawdust and came on, and his heart made the Irish love him. For he'd been all of them, the immigrant poor and the desperate. He was the boy from Tipperary who couldn't read or write, the brawler and political rowdy who slugged and gouged his way to the top. It was their pride and love that had opened the Tammany door to him, furnished his saloon, and raised him to be boss of the Twenty-first Ward. Before the desertion at the last election, Casey had only seen a Herculean figure glittering with yellow diamonds who was as good as any Fifth Avenue swell. But as their eyes met, he felt the heat of the man as if he were seeing the great body stir on the sawdust, the shoulders bunch, the lips part for air. When the giant staggered to his feet, fresh life breathed into him by the tremendous passion, the Irish cheered wildly, for he always got up and came on, and when he finally won, each man felt he'd fought with him.

It was such a man they'd thought had sold them out to the Native Americans. And in their fear and dark suspicion, they had betrayed him.

Just then, when his vision was blurred with Maguire so he was no longer seeing the burning tenements or the police wagons drawing away with the rioters, Pretty Boy appeared. His company had come up and without bothering to ask, they'd grabbed hold of the Pacific's hydrant. The Pacific's shout brought Casey back. He had a fragmented glimpse of red shirts and black fire hats piling up at the hydrant, and then by the flare of the flames, he saw Scanlon rushing past him.

He cried out but before he could move, he was grabbed from behind and whirled about. For an instant he saw Pretty Boy's face, cold, fair and lordly. Then the flowerlike eyes flashed in Pretty Boy's showy way as he slugged Casey in the gut. When he doubled, Pretty Boy clipped him on the jaw and he went down.

"Holy Christ," he thought, outraged, "he's using knuckles!" His jaw felt broke. But all the same, Pretty Boy had missed knocking him out and his arm snaked in reflex about Pretty Boy's boots and he brought him down. There was no chance to go for his own knuckles so he went for his eyes. Pretty Boy knew that one too, though, and went for his at the same time, so they clung to each other's faces, nails inching up to blind. He could feel the brass knuckles digging into his cheekbones but he hung on and tried to knee him. Still Pretty Boy was too smart and rolled him over.

Odd bits flashed through him as he fought in a puddle of ashy water to save his sight. He remembered a fighting dwarf from Mackerelville who had brass eye-gougers that fitted to his thumbs. He thought of his friend Eddie Mencken, that he found last summer in the Fourth Avenue tunnel with his two legs cut off by the trains right after the trouble started with Pretty Boy's Gas House Gang.

He remembered Pretty Boy the time at the Eagle saloon. They should have known better than to go there. The Eagle was a hangout for the Gas House Gang, who were Native Americans. But it had seemed a fine act to invade the enemy's territory. They were all swinging away in a grand sweat when Pretty Boy had come up and shouted that Casey was wearing knuckles. When he raised his hands to show he was clean, Pretty Boy knocked him cold. He'd come to consciousness hearing the laughter, and it was that laughter that echoed in his head now. In a fury, he slammed Pretty Boy's head against the cobbles and jarred him bad enough to work his fingers up another inch. Snarling, Turk came streaking back through the crowd and hurled himself on Pretty Boy. Casey had a glimpse of firemen's boots around them like trees. Then a great blow on his skull seemed to crush him. With a rush, he plummeted into darkness, his last thought, in shocked surprise: "Can it be? Am I going down to hell?"

♣ 2 ♣

It surely appeared to be hell. He swooped down a slide like a coal
chute with red flames all about while fiery devils rose up shrieking
with laughter to torment him. Down he went and around till off in
the distance he saw a dark, ragged throng that strangely oppressed
his heart. All at once he recognized them. They were the fever-sick
and starving who'd come dragging into the village with the famine.
His mother was wringing her apron with pity. But when she
shoved him toward them, all at once he was a lad of six again, his
heart turned to a stone, shrinking in disgust and guilt.

But they kept coming on, a few at first, and then dozens, totter-
ing and falling in the ditches by the Cork road. He found himself
bent over, running under cover of the hedges. But a hedge melted
like mist and they saw him. Wailing, they surged forward and over-
whelmed him. Their weak, moist fingers plucked at his clothes and
as he lashed out in revulsion, an old man dropped with a crackling
sound and lay crushed like an insect. In horror, he lay about him
till the road was littered with their bodies. Then he fled till again
he was discovered and again fought them off. Exhausted, slick with
sweat, he stumbled and went down, hiding flat to the earth as he
listened to their cries. Slowly the air grew sick-sweet and he realized
that the fever was floating from them like a fog. He pressed his face
to the grass trying not to breathe and dug in beneath the hedge so
close he felt the long thorns piercing his head.

And with that, he awoke and found himself piled in a heap in a
moving wheelbarrow. His head hurt where he'd dreamed the

thorns of the hedge were stabbing him and he put up a hand and despite the jouncing, managed to touch it. He'd been cracked all right but the blood felt caked, so he tried to flail his arms to make the barrow stop. At that his head throbbed like it was going to burst but the barrow was set down and he held himself still until his vision cleared.

He was in an alley lit by the gleam of a gas lamp. Music was coming from the back of a saloon and he heard a fight breaking out in the rickety tenement above. He waved his arms again and Turk jumped up, his white teeth flashing, his paws on the barrow. Then Scanlon came into view, leaning over to inspect him. He was wearing his black fire hat and chewing tobacco grimly.

"That's more like it," Scanlon said. "I see ye've come to."

Casey gave him a sign and Scanlon grabbed his arms and helped him up. He felt sick and the alley seemed to be whirling but Scanlon caught and steadied him between a wall and a rain barrel.

"Where were you taking me?" Casey asked him.

"Well now, I'm not certain," Scanlon admitted and by the gaslight his broad face looked sheepish. "But a bit of bandage on that head wouldn't do no harm."

So it was Bellevue Hospital Scanlon had had in mind. He must look bad to make Scanlon think of that.

"I'm all right now," Casey said thickly.

"That's fine then," Scanlon said, but he sounded unconvinced.

"How's Pretty Boy?" Casey asked, trying to divert Scanlon from seeing his weakness too closely.

"Oh, he's flourishing. The last I seen him he was riding off in the wagon with half the Mutual boys and some of ours."

"Who got me?" Casey asked, hurting from the news that Pretty Boy was unscathed.

"Didn't he?" Scanlon said, surprised.

"He did not," Casey said, going hot that Scanlon thought he'd been beaten by Pretty Boy alone. "I was going fine, slamming his head on the street when there was boots all around and I come to in this barrow."

"Is that how it was? Well, there's no telling. A tremenjous army jumped us. Some unknown must of give you a hit with a brick." He

unhooked his thumbs from his pants pockets. "Do you want to
hang onto me and I'll help you home?"

"I can make it," Casey said, still put out. All the anger he'd felt
at Pretty Boy suddenly switched to Scanlon who was seeing him
sick as a cat and had had to help him. Scanlon had been his best
friend for years. They'd fought side by side against marauding
gangs invading the Fourth Avenue Tunnel, got drunk, rolled
drunks, swapped lies, and their first visit to the cheap Mackerelville
whores they'd made together. All the time Casey had been the
leader and Scanlon was glad to be his follower. But now Casey's
rage was channeled to Scanlon. The plain freckled face struck him
as smug and he wished he could pick a fight so he could hurl Scanlon down in the alley. But he knew he was too weak. After the first
shock at Casey's going for him, Scanlon would kill him. So Casey
kept his face stiff not to show his feelings and said: "Take the Turk
with you to the firehouse. I'll go home by myself."

"I'll just see you there," Scanlon said stubbornly.

And since he felt wobbly when he moved from the rain barrel,
Casey didn't argue. He just pulled his arm away when Scanlon
tried to help him. But Scanlon seemed to sense how he felt and
after shooting him one quick look, he didn't try to help again, only
lifted the handles on the wheelbarrow and pushed it along silently
before him. If they left it, it would vanish, and Scanlon had either
borrowed it or stolen it.

At the end of the alley, one of the pigs that scavenged the city
blocked the way while it dragged a meal from a garbage pile, but
when Turk snarled the pig sprang aside and let them through.

Passing the schoolyard on Casey's block, they stepped over refuse
outside the distilleries wedged in among the brick tenements.

Every time he saw his building he had a feeling of shame, which
he had no call to do in front of Scanlon, whose mother drank. She
sat in their two attic rooms all the day, dispatching the younger
Scanlons down with the growler while the old man lay about
shouting how he had to fight black niggers to get work on the
docks. Scanlon's building was worse, but still whenever he went
home he felt the way he did when he'd been bathing in the East
River and had to fight back his disgust at pulling on his greasy

clothes again. With no more than a nod to Scanlon, he turned sharply away and dove through the loiterers drinking from a pail about the door so he wouldn't hear their joking when they saw his head.

He flung himself past the ground floor saloon into the side door and in one long breath, took it into himself — the smell of backyard privies, sour babies, stale beer, boiling codfish, swept it into his lungs in a great yellow draft beneath the hall gas jet with the cracked globe. In the end, it was easier to do it at once. By the time he'd dragged himself over the cigar butts and potato peelings that littered the stairs, it felt like home and he no longer saw the walls scrawled at child height with KEP OB THE GRAS or the banister broken last New Year's when Professor O'Neill, the street astronomer, went into the horrors and hurled himself down the stairwell.

At the top landing he paused and waited for his head to stop swimming. In the front apartment he could hear the Bohemian cigarmaker shouting at his wife. The whole family made the cigars, father, mother and four children, and they'd be at it every night till after midnight to feed themselves and pay the rent. As long as they worked, the old man shouted orders and flew into rages. It helped not to understand Bohemian but the roaring was fearful. Luckily, their kitchen-sitting room was on the street while the Caseys' was on the back court with the bedrooms in between. If it weren't for the bedrooms, there'd be more trouble than there was between the nations. Though on Saturday nights when the Casey boys were drinking there was usually an exchange.

But tonight, after the fire and Pretty Boy, Casey let the shouting go. He turned down the hall, and finding the door ajar, pushed into the kitchen. His mother was standing with her back to him boiling laundry on the stove, and with luck he might have got past her to bed but that it was his sister's day off from the family she worked for in Union Square. His father was home in honor of her visit, and even his brother Frank had lingered, shaving at the kitchen table and gabbing before he left for his night streetcar run.

They all sat and stared as he walked in. He'd be damned if he'd speak first, so he just nodded at his sister, and as cool as he could, dipped his arms into the bucket by the door and splashed water over his face and hair to clean the gash on his head.

His mother turned round and he heard her draw in her breath as she saw him bloody. He set his teeth at the sound and went on sluicing.

"Tom!" she cried. "Holy God, Tom!" She came to him and when he felt her hands on his shoulders, he forced himself to shake her off gently but she came right back at him. "Who kilt ye? Who smashed yer lovely head?"

"Nobody," he mumbled, his face in the water.

"Nobody is it? Will you look at him?" she cried, swinging to the others. "Me own flesh, he's been murthered by the divils!"

"I'm fine," he said, groping for the sacking that hung on the nail above the bucket.

"Fine!" she cried with a little laugh, and he turned to see she was smiling blindly at the family in the way she had just before her face broke to pieces and she began to tear her apron.

He tried ignoring it all. "You're looking good," he told his sister.

"Tom!" his sister said, giving him a frown, and he saw there was no hope there. Mary loved a row. She'd sit like an angel of God in her silks and new hat, you couldn't tell her from a lady, and watch the clod of a brother put their mother in her grave.

"Keep your long nose out of it," he said.

"I'll not have ye yelling at yer sister," his mother said.

He didn't answer.

"Ye've been fighting," she said.

"I have not."

"Ye have. Running about with criminals, drinking and dogfighting."

"I was to a fire," he said.

"A fire! Ah God, the fires! With that fine company of yers, no doubt. A crowd of dirthy felons thieving and carousing and the Lord knows what goes on in those places at night." She meant the firehouses and there was more to her suspicions than he cared to get into.

"Keep it up and I'm leaving!"

"Go then!" the mother cried bravely. "Ye can't stand five minutes in a dacent house. Go back to yer Scanlons and firemen, the low dregs of the city. I tried me best but I had no help —" A blow at his father. "Washing, ironing, wearing me heart out," she cried in a relentless litany. "I sent ye to school with these two poor hands taking in strangers' washing."

"For a year! For one damn year you sent me to school and I've never heard the end of it," he said, his temper rising in spite of his resolutions.

And then the storm broke as his mother began to sob. She sank on a stool and threw her apron over her face, and though part of him twisted, another part was so mad with irritation, he felt like smashing furniture. But he managed to hang on. He knew it was no use slamming into the bedroom either as she'd only wail louder so he'd hear. And she'd end by following.

The trouble was there was truth in it. He did fight, he ran with a gang, he came home beaten up, he'd joined a fire company. Sometimes he got drunk. He was everything she hated. She loved cleanliness and order and longed for the quiet, steady rise to pride and property.

"If I had a garden," she used to say when he was still a child and she was in good temper, dreaming together over saucers of tea in the lean-to shanty his father had put together out of iron and board in the northwest reaches of the city. And when she was sprightly: "If I had a cow." Then looking out the open shanty door, the piece of board they dragged back and forth to shield them from the elements, he'd point out: "Ye have a garden."

They both would look out at the rolling, rocky terrain but they each saw something different. She, the discarded pots with holes in them, the rusting hoops from old barrels, the scrawny chickens scratching about the shanties down the hill, and filthy children with parents too drunk or too lazy to go to the river or to the collects with their water buckets. While he saw the green grass springing up about the rocks, the goats from a neighbor's herd, bells tinkling at their necks, and the blue sky with white clouds rolling, all colored with Old Country stories. He saw the vast green demesnes of the great Anglo-Irish families. He dreamed of castles

and fine blooded horses. They rose in the air from the weeds, a few
goats and geese, and an abutment of rocks.

"A garden," she said bitterly. "A dumpyard. We're squatters on
the city dump."

And the scald of it shriveled him. As it shriveled his father, his
brothers, and it shriveled herself. Till it seemed like a step up when
his father found a job in a carline stables and they began to pay
rent in the tenement on Twenty-eighth Street.

Outhouses in the backyard then, slime oozing from the soil till
they couldn't open the kitchen window. Water carried up five
flights from the backyard hydrant instead of the river. Pavement
everywhere, black-spotted pigs scavenging filth, great brown rats,
and neighbors jumping down the stairwell with the horrors. Girls
from a raided brothel moved to the floor below and soon they were
sending him to run errands for them. He was passing out their
cards on a street corner till his mother caught him. That's when
she'd sent him for the year of schooling by taking in the famous
washing. But it was too hard on her altogether; one night she was
raving so they feared she might follow his sister Anne to the lunatic asylum on Blackwell's Island. The next day he'd left school at
thirteen and was working for a mechanic at the Harlem shop.

One August he went back to find the old shanty. The rusting
barrel hoops were still there, the dirty bottles, a few sticks of a bed.
A crew of ragpickers had taken over their cabin; they'd added a
new lean-to room of sagging tin and board. Smoke was rising from
the stovepipe chimney. It was all she had said. And yet, he felt, if
she'd not taken it so hard, like a proud horse thrashing and kicking
down its stall — for there was air, and space, and a breeze in the
summer.

By '57, of course, the Depression was upon them with the stock
market crash and the banks failing. The bread riots began and in
their fear of the starving mob, the city fathers had made work for
the dangerous classes by laying out Central Park. His own father
and his brother had taken shovels in the amazing outbreak of land-
scaping. Trees were planted, bridle paths were made, grass scattered — and the shanties were pushed to the north. Their own lit-

tle cabin had gone then. So even if they'd stayed, it could not have been forever.

It had been true enough, what she said of the shanty. As it was true about his gang-fighting and the firehouse boys, just as the leaking outhouses were true, and the brown rats and vermin. But it seemed to have happened without anybody planning, an impersonal thing, simply part of the city, though she managed to put the guilt on Dan Casey or himself or his brother till she had him mad with shame and fury. Still, it was soonest over when he held his tongue.

"I try. I strive and strain and nobody knows how I try," was coming from the apron as he pulled a stool to the table and sat down by his brother.

"Yer all right then?" his father asked quietly from his chair by the window where he was rocking and smoking his pipe.

"I'll survive," Casey said, and though his father didn't smile lest the mother drop a fold of her apron and see him, his face lit for a second as he went on rocking. He had no beer mug with him, Tom saw, so he was still off the drink. Not that he drank bad. Sometimes he got silly and fell to giggling. But the mother had it in her head that a man's troubles with providing were always due to drink. The times he was working as a veterinary, he tried it anyway, but when he was idle it was best not. Since the Harlem stables let him go the week before, he was on the water wagon. Probably he'd been hoping for a taste in honor of Mary's visit but with all the furor, his chances were blasted. When Casey lifted the pail that stood by his brother's shaving water, he didn't pass it to the window.

"I paid for that," Frank said, scraping at his jaw before the looking glass.

"I'll buy the next," Casey said, after he drank.

"Yer too generous," Frank said.

"Drunken sons," came from the apron. They didn't let on they heard, though it was hard to carry it off while cries rose brokenly behind them. And all at once Casey was starving. He knew better than to ask if there was any supper left. It was even dangerous to ask his sister. He couldn't be sure what she'd do with the opening.

Still, he hadn't had food since noon and part of the ache in his head and the weakness might be due to that. So after another swallow from the pail, and with the beer expanding in him, he rose and without looking at his mother, went over and explored the back of the stove behind the boiling caldron of washing. He found two lumps of potato awash in slush in the pot and a bit of fish in a skillet. Nothing was hot and it was easy to hook them out with his fingers. As he set down the skillet and wiped his hands on his pants, he saw his sister's wince of disgust, and the sting of it made him wilder than their mother's sobbing.

"And do the Episcopalians have a different way of doing it?" he asked.

This was a hit at her milady ways since she'd been maid for the Liggetts on Union Square. The husband was only twenty-eight but already he'd been to Harvard College and was practicing law, had his own brownstone and a wife and two children — not that he'd got it himself; the family had been on the board of Trinity Church since time began and it had all been given to him. They weren't rich like the Vanderbilts and Astors but according to Mary, who picked it up from the cook, they were grander altogether. "They was teaching at Harvard and doctors of divinity when old John Astor was still trapping muskrats," she'd told him last time. New York's great caught it altogether from the Liggetts. The Gardiner's Island girls were "fleshy," Peter Cooper was coarse, Sam Ward immoral, old Vanderbilt a pirate. To hear Mary tell it, nobody in New York would do at all beyond a few people he'd never heard of and some Episcopalian divines.

"You'll be apostasizing next," he said and that fetched her. She flushed.

"And have you become Defender of the Faith now?" she said, trying to put in the knife. But he only grinned. Though he hadn't been to mass since Easter past, it only painted a blacker picture of the brute, dogfighting brother. But he was blood of her blood. She couldn't drain him out of her.

"You can still believe and eat from a plate," she tried again.

"Where'd you hear it?" he said. "Would the Liggetts be telling you so themselves?"

That stung her. She flushed again. She knew as well as he what was said of the Catholic Irish at the Liggetts' kind of parties when they thought the servants weren't in earshot.

"I'd of thought they was more concerned about all them convent gardens full of babies' bones," he said.

His mother stopped sobbing in shock.

"Or Maria Monk."

"What's that you say?" his brother Frank said, so startled he let his razor fall into his water basin. The whole world knew the story of Maria, kidnapped and held prisoner in a convent for the priests' pleasures. It had been exploded years before, though in election years it still came up — the Catholics outraged, the Protestants saying, "Where there's smoke there's fire." Still, the story was indecent and not fit for his mother's ears.

"Yer low," his sister said. "Ye've sunk very low." He noticed with pleasure he'd unhinged her enough so she was losing the new accent.

"We'll hear no more of that name in this house," his brother said, wiping lather from his face and flinging down the cloth.

"I'm not talking of this house. "I'm talking of the Liggetts."

"An' what's the likes of you know of the Liggetts?" his sister flung at him. "Comin' in here bloody from yer street brawls, yellin' at yer mother —" His mother let out another sob; he could have killed Mary. "Swillin' from a pail an' eatin' from the stove like a pig at the trough."

She was finding her range and lobbing in her shells where it hurt now. He felt them burst inside him and spread redly over his brain, though he'd goaded her to it so he could know for sure she was comparing him to the clean, cold, educated Liggetts. He pictured them in file, the boy in a white suit, the girl in corkscrew curls and crinoline, the parents filled with French champagne and strawberries, taking their neat little walk to an opera at the Academy of Music. He had a raging desire to grab them up like china dolls, tear off their fine clothes and break their heads open and leave them there on the cobblestones in the horse dung, broken.

"I didn't take me day off and come here to listen to yer filthy tongue workin' over a clean family like the Liggetts," Mary said, her careful you's and *your's* gone out the window. She got up, suddenly aware she was losing control. "I'll be saying good day."

"Don't leave, Mary dear," his mother cried.

"Let her go if she wants. She's got too fine for the shanty Irish."

"Watch yerself, now, Tom," his father warned.

"And who's shanty here, I'd like to know?" his mother said hotly. "Back in Cork, we had our own little place an' a garden, I'm sure."

"So you're a Liggett yourself now?" he said, barely knowing what he was saying, just going for the throat. "At ten dollars a month and board and a room in the attic."

"It'll do me," she said, not much liking the attic but keeping her head.

"You're a nigger slave," he said. "That's all you are to your Liggetts."

"An' what are you?" she said coldly, looking him up and down from the grease-stained pants to the red shirt caked with blood and mud from the street.

"You'll find that out," he said, not quite knowing, but whatever it was, it would be bad for the Liggetts.

"I'll tell you," she said, pulling her *you's* and *your's* back around her like a cloak. "It's clear to the eye. You're a thief and a brawler and for all I know of it, a murderer already. What you are is scum."

He moved toward her but Frank jumped up, knocking back his chair and stood between them. "Leave her be or, head an' all, I'll let ye have it."

Frank usually gave way before him, though he was older. Something came in Casey's face when he was mad that made Frank uncertain. But this time was different. His rage with Mary being half rage with his mother, and rage with himself, it gave Frank the edge. The razor was in Frank's hand, wet from the basin, and the room grew quiet.

"I'll give it to you, Tom," Frank said.

His father's rocking had stopped. His sister didn't stir. Only his mother said softly: "Holy Mother, save us now," and then fell silent as if she were afraid another word might tip the balance.

Slowly, bitterly, he realized he wasn't going to jump Frank. If he

feinted and seized the razor and got Frank and then went after
Mary, no matter if he killed them both, the Liggetts were still too
far for him to reach. And beyond the Liggetts, there were hundreds
more going their clean cool rounds to operas and church board
meetings, and then off to their summer houses when the heat baked
the tenements and epidemics hit the city.

"Get back, Tom," Frank said and suddenly his head was throb-
bing. He raised his arm and brushed his forehead in confusion.
The whole evening crowded in on him — Pretty Boy's fingers inching up his face, the burnt and dying piled into carts, the dirty alley
and the stinking tenement. They were all barriers hemming him
in while beyond them the Liggetts walked off to pick strawberries
through long green grasses. The room suddenly grew orange as the
kerosene lamp seemed to shed the queer light that comes before a
city thunderstorm in August. He was afraid he was going to pass
out but he refused to give them the satisfaction. Making a last
demand of his will, he turned round and got to the bedroom door.

"Tom!" his mother said as he got the door open.

The room turned from orange to blood-red and he held onto the
doorknob hard. "I'm warning you — keep out of my way."

She made a swift little indrawing sound as if he'd struck her, the
sound he hated. But he didn't turn round. He had only the
strength to get through the door and feel his way down the dark
corridor to the bedroom.

It was dark and smelled sour; there were no windows. He found
the bed he shared with Frank, sank down on the twisted lump of
blanket, and leaned against the wall. For a time, lights seemed to be
revolving like an election-night pinwheel inside his head. But
though he went hot and then cold so his sweat was chilling him, he
didn't pass out. Perhaps the food took a grip.

After a bit, the fireworks went out and he felt the top of the sea
chest beside his bed for the candle and brimstone matches. He
gave himself a light to find the night jar. He was not going to run
the gauntlet through the kitchen and go down five flights to the
privy out back.

Relieving himself, he averted his eyes from the crucifix above the bed. There was a sliver of palm from Palm Sunday stuck through it that protected them from lightning. Finishing, he turned and kicked off his boots, unbuttoned his shirt and examined his bruises. There was an ugly one on his shoulder. He drew his head back to make out if Pretty Boy had bitten him but there was a prickling at the base of his skull as the wound began tearing open and he gave it up. He felt himself to be sure his ribs were all sound, which he thought they were, though there was soreness on one side and another great bruise forming. He smelt like a goat and thought of washing but the bucket was in the kitchen and he gave that up too.

He searched his pockets for the stub of a cigar he'd put away half-smoked at noon and not finding it, took out the knuckles and bit of lead pipe and stuck them under his pillow. Then to show he was asleep if anybody came in wanting to continue the argument, he pinched out the candle and tried to get easy.

He found he couldn't lie on his back nor twist his neck either to lie on his face. He swore some at Pretty Boy. Finally he lay on his side, one arm doubled to raise his head. With no windows to the room, it was black as the pit, so soon his eyes were closed and with that he was fighting with Mary again. He saw Frank gripping the razor with himself backing down and he went hot and his eyes flew open. "The hell with that," he told himself. If he kept it up, he'd be slamming back in the kitchen wrestling Frank for the razor.

He tried to fix on something calming. The picture that came was of himself sitting on a hillock in the summer evening watching through the open shanty door while his mother's lamp went on and the fireflies appeared. He used to catch them in his hands and watch the greenish light the way his mother described the fairy barrows. But tonight, he was perverse. In a flash he'd jumped to the old village, and not in the good times — early, when smoke rose from the chimney and across the summer air came the sound of his father shoeing the horses from up at the castle — but later toward the end, in the dark days. When the potato crop failed two years running and the famine came, the landlords fell in earnest to clearing the land. They evicted by dozens, then hundreds, whole villages, the thatched roofs set afire by paupers brought in from the next county while the sheriff stood about with his uniformed troopers.

Then the wandering began. The starving roamed the roads bearing fever and the bloody flux. The fever sheds were hammered together down the road in Skibbereen. He'd not seen them himself but word went through the village. After that, there was fear in each man for himself. The village was blocked from contagion but the fear seeped through the blockade and neighbors grew suspicious of old neighbors. Still, news came through. Those who could were getting out. And not only those with passage money. Two thousand souls from Sligo, the estates of Lord Palmerston, and three thousand from Kerry, the Marquess of Lansdowne's holdings, were shipped off at their honors' expense. In America they'd be begging in the streets but they'd got out alive. The whole country was fleeing.

One day he found a placard flaming by the chapel gate announcing passage to New York on a ship sailing in a fortnight from Liverpool. The next Sunday there were more — to Boston and Canada from Queenstown and Cork. And then suddenly the nights were restless with midnight knocks and whisperings. One morning the candler down the street was gone. The week after, the tavern was shut up and the family gone with the bailiffs coming round for unpaid bills. But by then the moonlight birds were safely flown.

Next, he was wakened himself, pulled out of the straw, and his mother was dressing him. She was strangely distraught and kept casting doubts before his father who was rushing in and out with shawlsful of clothes and bedding. But there was no stopping him that night; he was bold on poteen as if a great light were guiding him.

All at once his brother and two sisters were pushed out and himself swept up in his father's arms and carried out of the cottage into a night of winds, river mist and the looming shapes of horses.

" 'Tis Sir James' Red Rob," he said in surprise, for every child of six knew the castle's hunters. And then he saw his father lifting his sisters up onto Star, Sir James' gray mare with the blaze on her forehead. They'd been brought down that day for spring shoeing at his father's smithy.

"See, Daniel, even the childer know the beasts," his mother cried.

"Up, woman! Into the saddle behind yer daughters. We'll be saving them this night," his father said in queer, exalted tones.

"Ye'll save yerself into prison an' us cast on the roads to starve in a ditch."

"Ye'll starve for sure if ye stay here. Up, Catharine!" He lifted her up behind Anne and Mary and handed her a bundled shawl to carry. Then he sat Frank and Tom on Red Rob and swung into the saddle.

"We'll be seen!"

"Sure, ye've been heard and seen already. Half the village is crowding round the windows. An' won't they be forgetting it by morning?" And that was true. In the five hundred years since the black Statute of Kilkenny, the Irish remembered nothing when it came to the police.

"Me fire! Is me fire out?" his mother cried anxiously.

He laughed wildly at that, almost to the edge of crying. "I wonder was those Our Lady's words when they was setting off for Egypt."

" 'Tis no time for blasphemy," his mother said and crossed herself.

But his father seemed not to hear. He reached down for Star's bridle and the two hunters went slowly through the safety of darkness. Then they climbed away from the village street. His father held him fast and he felt Frank's arms about his waist. Rob snorted, his breath rising white in the river mist. And the wind and mist felt strange, so County Cork grew confused with Egypt.

Leaving by stealth and by night from the village, they had no priest's blessing nor neighbors wishing them Godspeed and giving them journey-cakes. At Cork the horses vanished but they themselves boarded the Liverpool steamer in a flurry of prosperity, each child holding a licorice whip and his father wild with drink, so that in the excitement they barely felt the rain drenching them on the open deck.

They ran about and hung over the side trying for the sight of the pigs and cattle sheltered below, till his mother lost her head and slapped Anne's cheek. It was a moment he remembered when the rest had blurred, Anne's face like a statue, her black hair hid beneath the sopping shawl, her black lashes spread wide and her gray eyes startled at their mother's blow. The rain slid down her face as if she were crying though she wasn't crying.

"I'll not have ye running wild," his mother said. "Yer thirteen an' too free altogether with a pack of strangers."

"Sure there's no harm in it. Let them run and be seeing to remember this day," his father said.

"I'm surprised that ye'd want it," his mother said bitterly, but his father was too excited for her shaft to strike him. He grabbed Anne to him and then reached out for Tom.

"We're leaving hunger behind us and a ruined land. And our own kind wandering till death overtakes them. An' do ye see what's leavin' with us? The pigs and cattle — Irish pigs an' Irish cattle. An' where are they bound? Fer the tables of England."

"Daniel!" his mother said, shrinking into herself.

But he paid her no mind. "Across the poor country, they're passing the starving. Sure the potatoes has failed, not the cattle nor pigs. But they're off to feed England. And who's selling them? The gentry! Yer fine Irish gentry!"

"Yer mad with drink!"

"I'm a thief, ye've been saying. Then what's them pigs I'd like to know? With the people starving? It's murder!"

"Sh!" his mother said, pinched with rain and fear.

But his father's hands gripped his shoulders. "Tom, remember!" he said in the voice of a prophet. "Ye remember them pigs!"

At Liverpool, they thought they were alive with luck in finding a ship that was leaving that day and would save them from the thieving lodging houses and his father from the tavernkeepers. They just had time to go to the emigrant provision stores along the wharves for the pots they needed for cooking on deck. And while they were there, the storekeeper showed them the hooks and nails they'd need also to drive into the ship's walls for suspending their cheese and salt fish from the rats. The rats gave them pause, and before they left his father bought a special sea chest to withstand the rats' gnawing.

Their ship was a four-hundred-ton freighter carrying tobacco from the States and returning in ballast. They left on a fine day so all were on deck with the fiddlers playing as the tug took the line over their bow and hurried her out of the dock and down the Mersey. Sails were hoisted, the tug cast off, and with the ebb tide behind them, and with much crying and singing, their voyage started. An hour later, they saw a lighter was following. And when they felt the mouth of the Mersey they dropped anchor, and Tom and his father watched in wonder while casks and boxes were passed over the side to the lighter.

" 'Tis strange. Perhaps they put something on her in error," his father said.

"I hope those isn't our biscuits leaving," said the fiddler, a whiskery squint-eyed old spalpeen from Tipperary.

"Our biscuits?" his father said and then fell thoughtful. "The law," he said at last. " 'Tis a crime they're committing." The law ordered a pound of breadstuffs for each passenger daily plus enough men to work her. They'd passed inspection in Liverpool before they started.

"An' are ye planning a lawsuit? Or will ye complain to the captain? I'm sure he don't know nothing about it," the old fiddler grinned.

" 'Tis a crime just the same," his father muttered truculently.

"And them that commits one will commit another. Open yer eyes, man," the fiddler said. "D'ye think crime ended just because ye left Ireland?"

His father sighed.

"Sure, that's better," the fiddler said. "I was fearin' ye'd be ending at the bottom of the sea."

It was clear soon enough that the ship's biscuits had gone into the lighter and what was left was poor. The water ran short and there were only three cabooses set up on the deck for cooking so that the food lines were long and often they waited from morning to late afternoon for a turn to heat their oatmeal. Once they ate it raw but the results were so wracking they didn't do it again.

When the great storm blew up, the hatches were battened and for days altogether they huddled beneath the six-foot ceiling, pressed in their double tiers of berths that were squeezed between the main deck and the hold, four seasick miserable souls to a berth, with no toilets and the air so foul the doctor refused to come down to aid the dying.

The ship's fever was the start of the dying, and soon after came the dysentery. The hold was blazing with fever and the cries of delirium terrified those who were still well. An infant at the breast died, and then the old fiddler, and then the day never passed without the heart-stopping splash of shot-weighted corpses. Tom fell ill first with bloody stool and next he knew Frank was ill, too, and finally his mother, all hot and raving in the one berth together. A seaman began a secret trade in grog and his father, grown desperate, bought some for them all to break the fever, then doctored himself, and soon he was out of his mind and fighting with four Galway men in the berth above.

Tom never knew for sure, for he didn't want to, what happened to Anne in the melee of drunken Irish and grog-selling seamen. Sometimes he surfaced to cries and wild laughter and saw terrifying shadows thrown by the oil lamp that swung from the low ceiling but he turned and grasped his mother to still her mutterings and soon he was struggling with nightmares again. It was days before his fever broke and by then Anne had altered. She was drawn into herself, screwed up in a ball on the inside of their berth. When they tried to pull her out, she screamed and wept, her face contorted, and cried blasphemies to the devil who was beside her berth. And that way she stayed, fouling the berth and only eating from a pan they handed in to her. Even when the good weather came and the hatches were opened so all but the dying tried to crawl out on deck, they couldn't move her.

After five weeks, when they sailed into New York harbor, the boarding health officers found her that way and took her, struggling, from the ship to the hospital on Staten Island. Tom stood watching her go, carried off with the fever victims.

He saw her only once again, long later, when they were already living in Shantytown, and he went with his mother one visitor's day to the lunatic asylum on Blackwell's Island. As they got off the ferry they saw Anne. She was outside the high fence with six other women, all in white straw hats and calico dresses and locked together by a long cable rope fastened to their leather belts. At the end of the rope was an iron cart and in it another woman they were dragging.

He stood staring, not recognizing Anne at first. "What's that?" he asked.

His mother began weeping. She'd been over before. " 'Tis what they call the Lunatic Chariot," she said. "They say it's kind. They get the air. And the way they're locked together, they can't be throwing themselves in the river water."

"Don't they mind? Look, there's our Anne! She's the one from the end."

"I see, I see her," his mother said. "I can't tell does she mind. She don't say. I don't think she knows me at all. Sir James's horses — ah, Jesus, weren't we punished for them enough?"

"Don't cry," he said. "I don't like that cart at all. I'll wait here till yer through."

And he returned to the ferry landing and never went back with her again.

But though he never went back and he tried to put it from his head, whenever he was off his guard it was apt to come back and for a searing moment it was a summer day again filled with sycamore trees and scarlet roses while Anne in calico and a white straw hat strained at her rope to draw the Lunatic Chariot.

It came to him again as he was lying in the dark cradling his broken head and he frowned and changed position. He returned to the hill above the shanty, but now it irritated him and seeking relief, he tried a picture from his earlier, deeper dreaming. He was back in Cork once more, no longer Tom Casey but Sir James himself, jumping Red Rob over stone fences on a morning's hunting. He stopped at a cabin and a woman opened. He bent to enter the cabin, all shadows, and the husband stood up from the peat fire and made him the tenant's tribute of an eggshell full of whiskey.

At that, he suddenly felt better. All his muscles relaxed and before he knew it, he had plunged into sleep.

♣ 3 ♣

He did not go to work next day, nor the day after. His father stopped by the Harlem shop to tell his foreman he'd been hurt in the fire, and while he was there he'd the luck to pick up work as a blacksmith at the Harlem stables. The regular smith was off on a drunk. So the mother was happy with the old man working, and Dan Casey had his few pints in peace of an evening, and there was no one to trouble Tom for staying in bed.

It was not that he'd been so hurt he had to stay there. For twenty-four hours he was weak as a cat and the pain came and went in his skull, but lashings of strong tea and a fried steak or two put him right. Still he lay abed. He stayed in the dark bedroom with not even a candle burning, only turning when his brother Frank came in from the night horsecar run and groped his way to the bed. When his mother ran down to the store, he got up and crept out to the rocking chair. And on Saturday which was visiting day at Blackwell's Island, he had the kitchen to himself. But as soon as he heard her feet on the stairs returning, he was up and back to the bedroom again.

He was not sure who it was that he was avoiding. Partly it was like a creature going to earth till its wounds healed. But partly it was a need to sort out his thoughts, know where he was going and how to go there. He lay waiting for the thoughts but none arrived beyond memories of himself rolling on the street with Pretty Boy, Mary calling him scum, once an uneasy flash of the future if Pretty Boy had gotten to his eyes. He saw himself in a doorway with a begging sign about his neck, or on Blackwell's in the Almshouse near Anne's lunatic asylum.

But he went on waiting dumbly for it all to come together. He slept a lot but as soon as he was awake, he lay still, his eyes closed or staring before him, not seeing. Scanlon came by one evening and gave him a report of the Pacific Engine Company's hearing at police court, Big John Maguire standing by them in their trouble. And he heard Turk was matched against Mutual Engine Company's Duke in Jack Devlin's ratpit.

But Scanlon was only an interruption from the waiting. Tom lay back against the whitewashed wall, the candle guttering on the sea chest, and watched Scanlon chewing his cigar butt but afraid to light it in Mrs. Casey's house. She had it in her head that Tom's ruin was due to low consorting and she'd picked up the rumor that Scanlon's mother drank. Besides, his father worked the docks while Mr. Casey was a veterinary surgeon when he wasn't picking up work as a smith, and there was a sharpness in her eye that didn't let Scanlon forget it. When Dan Casey offered him a beer, she gave her head a quick shake, as if to say the mere sight of drink might send Scanlon raving, it running in the blood, and herself offered tea which Scanlon refused, not wanting to try jiggling the cup on his knee. He sensed the time wasn't right for pouring it in the saucer. Tom himself lay withdrawn through it all, impatient to get back to his waiting for the grand idea, and the only time his interest sharpened was at the mention of Maguire.

At first he hesitated to speak of Maguire, as if the ward's betrayal in last fall's election was some cowardly act he and Scanlon shared between them. But Scanlon seemed to have no shame of the sort. What was done was done and over, he seemed to feel. They'd feared Tammany had sold them out, so they'd voted against Tammany. It was Tammany's lookout not to give such an impression. Cheered by Scanlon's shamelessness, Casey brought himself to say: "Maguire come himself, did he? To the court to get the boys off?"

"That he did, in all his glory. At nine in the morning," Scanlon said.

"That was big-hearted of him. Considering."

Scanlon thought it over and grinned. "Well, if some had been

for him and some against, it might of gone bad for the ones that
was against. But you can't take it out on a whole ward nor a city,
now can you?"

There was truth in that. There'd been so many of them in it,
there was small room for a grudge. The loss of the whole Irish vote
was a natural calamity, like an Act of God. His cheerfulness growing, Casey said: "And he had no trouble about getting the boys
off?"

"Ah, about the trouble, I can't say. Not being in their mighty
councils as to what goes on in arrangin' such matters," Scanlon
said.

"He must have had trouble."

" 'Tis likely. Since the courts is now packed with the Mozart Hall
judges. Still, Tammany must have a man here and there. You don't
get rid of them all as quick as that."

"Perhaps he made some deal. Like they do."

"Well, whatever he did, it was grand," Scanlon said. "Tim and
Bill got off with a warning. However, with Jack, the judge give him
a fight, Jack being a regular visitor lately — that muss in the Bull-
head and last year the Assault. This time the judge says, 'It's thirty
days in the workhouse for you, me fighting Irishman.' "

"And Jack got thirty?"

"Well, at that, Maguire and the judge fell to whisperin'. I guess
another plum Tammany was savin' was shook off the tree."

"Sentence suspended?" Casey smiled.

"Egzactly."

"Good for Maguire. Good for Jack! Did he say anything after?"

" 'Thank God,' as I recall. He said the judge had him going at
first."

"I mean Maguire," Casey said impatiently. "After court, did he
speak?"

"Now let me see. If he did, 'twas nothing earthshaking. Hoped
he'd see us all at his outing at Coney Island — free beefsteaks,
clams and beer."

"He's having the outing?"

"Didn't I just say he invited us?"

"It costs like hell." They both were silent, considering what their betrayal had cost Tammany. Fernando Wood would be collecting only for himself and his Mozart Hall bunch now that he'd bolted Tammany and won by himself. And he was a notorious squeezer. Not only from the sale of police jobs, from the gamblers and saloons that stayed open on Sunday and the whores in the cribs, but they said he collected from the very prisoners in the Tombs. Before, when Wood was the Tammany mayor, though some had stuck to his hands, part trickled down to the poor in food baskets, emergency rent and, of course, the summer outings and winter political balls. But with Wood having no ward setup, they'd be seeing little of it. It was a shock, at this point, Maguire going on with his outing.

"He must have put a bit away," Scanlon said. They fell silent again, feeling mean, till Casey changed the subject.

"What else did he say? Besides the outing?"

"Nothing else," Scanlon said, and went on staring at a rathole in the wall. It had a brick stuck against it but the brick had been worked away like the devils had been heaving it about. Finally, he gave his head a shake. "He was in a rush to see some other judge. About Donahue's widow." Donahue had been killed last year when his ladder went down at a fire with a wall collapsing. "They started dispossess proceedings."

Coals of fire on their heads. It was sure now, Casey thought, Maguire had nothing to do with the Native American movement, nor did Tammany either; it had been what Maguire assured them, just Wood spreading rumors.

"Did he say nothing of the fight?" Casey said as their cheer evaporated.

"What fight?"

"That night," Casey said, and then as Scanlon shook his head, thinking he meant the general fight between Pacific Company and Mutual, he let him think so. Actually, at the back of his mind a hope briefly flickered that Maguire had seen him fighting Pretty Boy and perhaps admired his style. Then the hope was doused. Most of it was only himself astraddle trying to smash Pretty Boy's skull against the cobblestones.

His interest waned then, and what with Mrs. Casey looking in all the time to make sure Scanlon wasn't smuggling whiskey nor telling indecent stories, Scanlon grew uneasy. He chewed on his cigar, looked hard at the rathole, then finally got up, having satisfied duty. Once escaped, he didn't come back, and for the next few days Tom lay still, simply shifting back and forth from his bed to the kitchen.

On Sunday morning there was a queer change in his condition. His mood was still to wait but his body was restless as if he needed to be up and moving. He crawled over Frank's sleeping body and went out to the kitchen, past his mother who was dressed for mass up the street at St. Stephen's. She was standing by the stove having tea and baker's bread.

He opened the window and leaned out.

" 'Twill make the house impossible," she said to him.

She meant the stench from the privies; she always complained when they opened the window and she kept the house reeking of camphor against it, not just during epidemics like everybody else did.

"It isn't bad," he said.

" 'Tis always bad."

He didn't answer, just leaned out farther and twisted his body to look up. It was mild with bright sun and the sky a clear blue. He turned and looked down at the privies, rain barrels and the lean-to shack where the Italian organ grinder was living. The door to the shack was open and he could see the grinder's monkey dodging in and out on a long dirty cord. The monkey wasn't dressed yet in his military uniform with brass buttons and he was looking free and easy like a monkey in the jungle. Casey ducked back from the window, took a chunk of bread that was lying on the table, and tossed it down. The monkey dodged away, then went cautiously to the bread and picked it up. He looked about, turned his head and spotted Casey, and let out a burst of chatter.

"What's that yer doing?" his mother asked. "Throwing away me good bread."

"The Eyetalian's monk," he said. "He's running about."

"Dirty animals," his mother said. "Probably covered with germans."

"What, the monk?" he asked, swinging back from the window and scratching at himself in his long underwear. "And what's germans?"

"These germans may be causin' all manner of horrible diseases. They're little creatures like insects."

"Who says?"

"Yer father was hearing about it at work. 'Twas in the newspaper."

"Believe the papers, you're crazy." He felt the teapot, and it being still warm, took a cup from the shelf, poured tea into it, and added sugar and milk from the pitcher.

"Milk's on the turn," he said.

"I saw that. I wonder is our milkman holding back the fresh."

He didn't answer, not wanting to get into her running battle with the milk vendor. Every Monday she ran downstairs at the first cry of "Milk ho!" and the two of them fell to it before she handed over the jug. There was every reason the milk was fresh. The cows were nearby. She had seen them herself, stabled in the sheds beside the distillery where they could get the cheap mash, and they were milked every day by tramps who worked for their night's lodging in the stables. But she suspected the fresh milk was held back till the old milk was sold.

"Ye coming with me to mass?" his mother said.

"I was to mass Easter."

"An' won't be again till Easter next," she said. But she hadn't the hope of winning that gave her real spark and when he contented himself with blowing on his saucer, she finished her bread, swigged down her tea, and taking her shawl from one of the nails above the water bucket, said: "I'm off then. Tell yer father to fill the bucket. We're out."

"I'll do it."

"Are ye better then? Ye'll be going' to work Monday?"

"I only said I'd fill the bucket." he said, giving her a look across his saucer.

She hadn't time to do battle so she threw the shawl about her and hustled off for mass.

Alone, he finished his tea, cut two slices of bread and ate them sprinkled with sugar, then got the mirror and considered a bit of beard he'd been growing. Finally he got up, found the razor and with water from the kettle and a piece of soap from the bottom of his brother's shaving mug, he shaved it off. He went back to the bedroom for his boots, put on his red shirt and his pants and pulled his boots over them, then grabbed last week's newspaper and the wooden bucket and went down to the back-yard hydrant.

He looked for the monkey but he was already gone out on his rounds with the organ grinder, and while he used the privy he considered the monkey having germans that brought on diseases. He'd seen the monkey scratching but he was sure that was just fleas. What size now, he wondered, were germans — and what kinds of diseases. Into his head flew pockmarked faces and a man with his nose eaten off he'd seen begging near Barnum's Museum. He remembered the hold of the ship, with them burning up with fever. But there were no monkeys on the ship. And no monkeys on Blackwell's where they died in droves of the consumption every year. All in all, he decided, it was unlikely there were germans.

Opening the newspaper and holding it to the light coming in the crescent, he turned past the front page ads, to a story on page two about the Democratic National Convention. They'd refused to draw up a federal slave code to protect slavery in the territories, and eight Southern delegations had walked out. He frowned and then tried the editorial about how the great national Democratic party was being broken up by a bunch of blacks. But he slowed down to spell out the hard words and then gave it up altogether. He read an ad for a runaway slave — there was fifty dollars offered, so he noted his scars. Then he looked for accounts of fires and read a statement from the Common Council that a third of the fires were due to arson. There was nothing else but shipping news and an account of a man impaled on a wrought-iron fence when he fell from a dive on Mulberry Street. So he tore off several pieces of paper, completed his trip to the privy, and leaving the Herald for the next visitor, went back to the hydrant, pumped water and ran his mother's bucket back upstairs for her.

On the street again, his feet turned toward the firehouse. Sunday morning was the time for cleaning the engine. All the members and runners would be gathered taking down axes to grind and polish, scouring the signal lamps and torches and filling them with oil. There'd be great polishing of brass, much oiling and greasing the wheels and straightening and rewinding ropes. It would be a specially fine time with the boys got off by Maguire, but his feet slowed thinking of them all, and he with his head still marked by Pretty Boy. And his grand idea hadn't come yet; all at once, going to the firehouse seemed a diversion from his waiting.

An omnibus appearing, he felt in his pocket for sixpence, then broke into a run and swung himself up before it passed him. He handed his fare through the roof trapdoor to the driver who was yelling down at him for scaring the horses, but not wanting a fight, he went and sat down in the rear of the bus.

He rode all the way to South Ferry in a dream, not noticing who got on or minding the sights of the morning city. Finally, the driver shouted, "End of the line," and he realized everybody else had left. He rose and jumped down to the cobblestones, then stood uncertain which way to go next.

On his right lay the Battery. He could see the fortress curve of Castle Garden. But it was not what it was even when he was a boy with the fine merchant houses looking over the green grass and old trees, past the granite promenade to the sparkling bay, and the paths filled every bright afternoon with ladies of fashion and top-hatted gentlemen strolling to take the breeze. In those days, Castle Garden was a theater; but in the few years since, it had become the immigrant depot. The rich merchants had moved uptown, there were no more fashionable ladies. The grass was ruined and the iron fence broken. The wall promenade near the bay was decayed, and ragged Irish and Germans sat under the trees while drunks lay where the grass had been. In a way, it was progress — the immigrant depot with all its officials protected the greenhorns from what his own family, landing just anywhere, had not been protected from — the immigrant runners from the boardinghouses coming to blows over them and finally carrying them off like prizes to the cheating landlords who overcharged them, gave wrong change for their money, and lied to keep them when they tried to leave. Their own baggage wasn't stolen but often the greenhorns' baggage was, and the landlords in cahoots with the thieves. That part was to the good. But it was galling to see how the touch of his own kind lay on the city like a blight. The old merchants' houses, turned to tenements already, gazed out on the ruin through their broken dirty windows. He felt hot, as if he himself were accused, the way he'd felt in the kitchen when Mary saw him wiping his greasy fingers on his pants. "Dirty Celts," was what the look said. Abruptly, he turned from the Battery and wandered along the South Street docks toward the forest of masts that spread up the East River as far as he could see.

Square-riggers from every port in the world ran their bowsprits over South Street. Clippers, stately Indiamen, packet ships from Liverpool, London and Savannah, schooners from the Southern coastal trade, their bright ensigns and house flags flying in the breeze above the masts and network of rigging. Sunday morning it was quiet. The piers and wharves were swept clean; the sailors were polishing brass, sluicing down, overhauling the running rigging or just sitting with their pipes in the sun in holiday rig.

He passed a floating chapel for seamen, a cross and church bell at its masthead; not too crowded, he saw. A few dram shops were open, their floors clean-sanded for the day, the bartenders in clean shirts. At a woodcarving shop he stopped, and though it was closed, he looked in the leaded window at the ships' figureheads. He studied the bust of a woman with black hair and examined a square block with a profile outline sketched on two sides and ready to be carved. Then he strolled on smelling the spices from the East In-diamen — from the Indies and the South Sea Islands — and passed the foot of Wall Street where the square-rigged clipper ships waited to take the trip to California.

Hands in his pockets, he examined them, and his sense of wait-ing quickened as if California might be the idea he was waiting for. San Francisco and the mines up the Sacramento. He could dig up passage money and gamble his way playing faro. And yet, even as he thought it, he was strolling on.

He passed the Norfolk and New Orleans packets, silent now, their bales of cotton and hogsheads of sugar already unloaded and driven to the warehouses, and he passed Burling Slip where ba-

nanas and oranges came in from the West Indies. He wondered
which schooners were the blackbirding ships, readying for trips to
the west coast of Africa for blacks. The fine phrase ran through his
head: "Blackbirds, Wool, and Ivory in the Hold." There was good
money in it, but danger too; if they were captured by the British
corvettes there was prison, maybe hanging. Besides, the slavers
wanted seasoned seamen in case they had to run from a British
man-of-war. If he went to sea at all, he'd have to start as a green
hand.

At Fulton Market, as he studied the sloops and looked in at the
large covered boxes floating in the East River full of the fish they
were keeping for Monday market, he considered shipping out as a
seaman. There were a hundred and fifty thousand of them belong-
ing to the Port of New York, and all preyed upon by land sharks.
The sharks boarded the homecoming vessel off Sandy Hook,
claimed the debts the seaman had run up the last time he was in
port. Then they took him off to the sailors' boardinghouses on
Water and Cherry Streets, to the dance halls and groggeries and
the low damp cellars filled with bloated women, and robbed him of
what was left of his wages. At last, his drink was drugged and he
was shanghaied again, waking with an aching head to find himself
broke and outward bound for Hong Kong or Papeete. The ship-
owners and merchants were driving in fine hansoms and barouches,
marrying their daughters into old Dutch families, and right now
this Sunday were sitting like saints in red velvet-lined pews in a few
gray, spired churches. But a sailor would never climb out of the
fo'c'sle.

As the knowledge rushed through him, the old rage started rising. There was nowhere he could break through. Everywhere was
the wall. Suddenly the ships sickened him and he turned up Fulton
and headed for the Bowery.

It was after one o'clock when his eye caught on Kitty Donahue.
At first, he didn't know why. She was just another sharp-dressed
shopgirl, and not even a pretty one, being too freckled for his taste
and bony. But still he'd fixed upon her as she stood, her arm linked
through the arm of a girl friend, the Bowery crowds streaming

around them as they examined posters for a Wild West menagerie.

As he watched her, it began to come back to him that she was poor Old Smoke Donahue's daughter. He'd last seen her in September when Donahue died from an ironworks wall collapsing. It had been a momentous funeral with all the boys present in uniform from the Pacific Engine Company. They'd kept the body on ice for five days to make the affair on Sunday when they could put on a show.

He didn't intend to hail her. She meant less than nothing to him, just the daughter of a fellow fireman, but he didn't want to be seen by anyone from the neighborhood with his head still bruised and battered. He dodged back behind a peddler selling violet soap, but by then it was too late. She'd recognized him. As she waved, he made his way reluctantly through a knot of newsboys lined up before the Bowery Theater.

In the confusion of the introductions, he missed the friend's name, only gathering that she worked at a counter in the same shop as Kitty. But before he had time to sort it out, the friend bent to Kitty and whispered, then ran down the block and disappeared.

"What got into her?" he said with the sense he was being trapped.

"She just remembered she had to visit her aunt," Kitty said with a dogged liar's air.

He found they were strolling down the street together past the freak museums. "And what's her aunt? The Tattooed Woman?"

Kitty blushed and laughed. "Ah now, not at all. She lives around the corner. Honest. She does needlework for our store." She laughed again and he felt easier. Her friend had been too quick altogether to leave, but Kitty's nervy, high-pitched laugh was reassuring, and her thin-faced Irish look set him at ease. Really she was too bony a girl to be afraid of. And she hadn't mentioned his head. He appreciated that.

"How's your mother?" he asked as they pushed through a mob of sweeper boys and begging girls pressing into a minstrel show.

"Ah, the poor creature," she said, looking sad, and he remembered with dismay that Scanlon said the Donahues were being dis-

possessed. Maguire was trying to get them an extension. He wondered how they'd had the nerve to go to him, then recalled Donahue had been killed before the election. But the dispossess made it
tricky, talking to her. He cast about, and since she'd mentioned a
store, he said: "How's the job?"

"Ah fine," she said. "It's the dull season now.'

It seemed a safe subject to pursue. He congratulated himself.

"And what's the dull season?"

"Spring to fall," she said. "We only work ten hours. Saving Saturday it's thirteen."

"And is it hard work?" he asked.

"Not hard. Except on the feet. My counter's in the basement
though — all by gaslight. No air and so hot your head feels baked."
She laughed. "Look at me. It's Sunday and here I'm complaining."

"You're not complaining at all," he said, making certain not to
ask what the lively season was. Half of him wanted to get away and
leave her with her dangerous widows and dispossesses and baking
head in hot store basements. But her friend had left her alone. And
she wasn't so bad. He liked that high laugh as if he was so far above
her he made her nervous, being young and strong and with the fire
department. And having Maguire on her mother's case drew him
on. He itched to ask about him, though he didn't see how he'd do
that and still avoid the dispossess.

Then hearing the "Fresh oysters!" cry, he said: "Would you like
a bite to eat?"

"That would be grand. If you have the time," she said, and let
him lead her to an oyster cart.

He stuffed her full of oysters as fast as the man could pry them
open with his knife and sprinkle them with pepper sauce. She had
an amazing capacity for such a small, thin girl. She devoured a
shilling's worth of oysters at a penny apiece in less than three minutes and then was dabbing at her lips with a wisp of handkerchief.
She moved like a mouse, he thought, as he watched her quick, neat
gestures. She was willing and eager. On impulse, he caught her arm
and turned her with him into a beer garden. He sat her down at a
table and ordered beer.

"Well now," he said, looking pleased, for it was a fine place he'd picked. By the look of it, it would hold a thousand people. There was a balcony and at one end of the room an orchestra with a cluster of balloons beside the trombone player. And respectable as you'd want. You had to watch that with a young girl. It was not like some of the dives along the street, but full of clean, washed German families, the children too, sitting over pigs' knuckles and beer.

"Will it do?" he asked, suddenly feeling he owned the place himself.

"It's fine," she said too quickly and he wondered if she was worrying about his spending too much. Then he saw she was secretly plucking at the white tablecloth and guessed she was shy around so much starched linen, orchestras and all the mirrors and gilt. And as he watched, she tipped her head back and examined the globes on the chandelier above them. "Please God it stays up," she said.

He liked her openness himself but he was not so keen about it before the waiter who'd come back with their steins. So he paid him quickly and lifted his.

"Ah, I'm thirsty," she said, and drank half of hers off. "Ah, that's good," she said finally, and he was relieved she did not go at it again but sat back and laced her fingers in her lap.

And then he could not think what to say next. It was like picking his way across a pond not fast frozen; at any time he could crash through to store basements and dispossesses. Moreover, with these good Irish girls you had to be careful. An idle word and you found yourself sitting over a dish of tea with their mothers and next thing it was the priest and a houseful of crying children.

On the other hand, she was getting nervous at the silence. If he didn't begin, she'd have a try at it herself. And God knew where they'd end, if she picked on the engine company. Donahue's death, at the best, at the worst, she'd ask after his head and how he came to get clobbered. With all the choices being alarming, he decided to strike through to the heart of the matter.

"You been seeing Maguire."

She was taken back at that. She went red and nervous tears sprung to her eyes as she saw the whole world knew about her family's troubles. Casey wondered how he'd shut her up if she really started crying. He cursed all nice girls; they were mostly salt water.

Perhaps she felt the chill or perhaps she had more guts than he knew. It might be she recalled that Donahue's old fire company was bound to hear they were being put out. It wasn't the same thing as having it printed in the papers.

She grabbed her beer with one of her queer mouse gestures, drank, stared hard at the foam, and when she lifted her head, the tears had been withdrawn. Her eyes were clear gray again and only her face a bit stiff to show she was on edge.

"He's been helping us," she said. "We fell behind after Dad's death. There was the collection for us but it seemed to go fast. I went to work at the store but it's only two dollars a week, and there's five of us. The three kids and mother."

"I know that," he said quick, to stem the flood. She was explaining like he was some sort of policeman accusing her of running off with the fire company collection.

"That's the five mouths to feed," she said. "Mother thought she could do needlework but she don't own her own machine so she'd have to work for the sweaters."

He knew all about that, too. His own mother had thought of it back when she was harping on his schooling. If you didn't have your own sewing machine so you couldn't work at home, you found a factory that would take you or you worked for the sweaters who had cellars of machines. They took work from the manufacturers and paid by the dozen pieces. It was rotten pay too.

"She'd do best to get embroidery," he said. Embroidery was done home. But it was a worry in a different way. The rich silks and velvets could get spoilt by the kids the moment you looked away. You'd be years paying off for a second's distraction. Still, it was better than the sweaters.

"That's what Mr. Maguire said," she answered. "Still, you have to have pull, some rich woman who wants it. He said he'd help there."

So he was back with relief to Maguire, just when he felt drowning in her misfortunes.

"You seem mighty close to the great man," he said.

She looked at him quickly and he nearly lost his temper for the tears were in her eyes again. But this time, her mouth was soft, her color pink, and altogether he didn't feel his danger as before. She was just grateful, he decided. Or perhaps she was ashamed of going to Maguire at all, knowing how the ward had voted for Wood. For a second, he wondered if it wasn't something more. Maguire was a real hero, all black ringlets and fighter's body tricked out in silk shirts, diamond studs, and smelling of barber's violets. He even went hot to be filling her with beer and oysters if she was blushing for Maguire. But then he knew that couldn't be it. Such a mouse of a girl and Maguire newly married.

He was married just last summer and his wife was a beauty. Once he'd seen her himself, riding out on Sunday with Maguire beside her in their steel-wheeled buggy behind a matched pair of trotters on their way to Harlem Lane. Her name was Lily. She had masses of light-brown curls and a face to knock your breath out. No heiress, of course, but cuts above Maguire, the Tipperary cottier's boy. Her father was captain of one of Vanderbilt's steamboats.

"What's he like?" he asked, and as she looked surprised, he was afraid she'd think him ignorant. Lots of the Pacific Company boys knew Maguire. He hurried to add: "I know myself what he's like. But what's your judgment of the man?"

"Why he's grand," she said, still surprised, and he felt like reaching across and rapping her. The word had no meaning at all. An oyster feed was grand, the beer garden was grand, the spring air, a German band, everything was grand to her. But before he made a fool of himself by roaring at her, he stopped and tried to think what he was driving at.

Did he want to know if she thought Maguire had sold them out to the Native Americans? He knew Maguire hadn't. It was Wood's rumors alone that had panicked them all. And what would a poor shopgirl know about it anyway? It was something else was pushing him forward. He felt maddened — he could not spot it and yet he needed to know — something. It was a kind of hunger he had toward Maguire. But what the hunger was for, he had no idea. Feeling he'd been hit on the nose with a plank, he backed off but kept on circling.

"How'd you come to meet him?"

"Well there's nothing strange about that," she said, picking up after all the silence and dark looks. She lifted the stein and made wet rings on the tablecloth. " 'Twas my mother. She was sick with fever and they was trying to lock us out. She was so hot and making no sense and the babies tumbling about. I was afraid they'd be falling sick too. And there I was at the store. If I left off my job, they're quick to fire and where would we be then? Mrs. Scanlon came down but she's not altogether —" She paused delicately.

"She drinks," he said, pressing on. He'd forgot that the Donahues lived in Scanlon's tenement. It came back to him now. He'd been there to the wake. Mobs of firemen and ward captains jamming the poor dark rooms with the paid criers called in and Mrs. Donahue shredding her dress and keening about her brave Donahue, the sun of her soul. You didn't often hear the keening on this side. It was too wild and old-fashioned and embarrassed the young folks. Maguire had been by to sit at the casket. But he'd missed Maguire at the wake too.

"So I was out of my wits with Mother's sickness and the babies," she was saying. "I got home around midnight from the store to find Mother raving and Mrs. Scanlon in a heap overtaken by the drink. I just sat down and cried, I was that scared and not knowing where to turn. And then comes a knock at the door." She paused.

He said softly: "Maguire."

"Himself," she said. "Our little Jimmy had been down to the Comet and told him."

The Comet was Maguire's saloon. Not the famous Comet on Mott Street where the prizefighters went and big Tammany men like Tweed and Honest John Kelly, but Maguire's own Comet on Second Avenue. It was a fine big saloon with a white-painted stove in the middle, the sawdust on the floor, and a great long bar with a mirror behind it reflecting the glasses and colored bottles and decanters. Maguire held court in the back room while all the woes of the ward trailed past him.

"How old is Jimmy?" he asked and she blushed.

"Jimmy's eight."

"And he'd got ahold of the idea himself?"

"Well not entirely. I'd been kind of talking to myself that morning. He might of overheard. About how if the ward hadn't all turned against him — not that Dad did. He was a great Tammany man."

"And he was killed in September."

She gave him a look but she knew better than to argue. They'd all been great Tammany men till just before the election.

He saw they'd stall right there as long as she felt she had to defend her position. "Ah, Jimmy did the right thing. It was a lot of muck about Tammany. Didn't they just make Conners Grand Sachem?"

"Did they now?" she said, surprised. "And is he one of ours?"

"He is."

"Well, that shows you," she said, very red in the face to find herself carrying the point in such an unexpected way. Without a man in the house, she hadn't heard it before.

"So what happened when Maguire appeared?" he asked. "Did he come by himself?"

"No, with Mr. Hanley. He's one of his captains, a big man with a red face."

"I seen him about," Casey said. He'd been at Donahue's wake; Hanley was a great man to visit funerals with Maguire. He'd gone to the California gold rush back in '50 with Maguire, and he still wore a nugget for a stud in his shirtfront. But they didn't make their fortunes in California. They did that in New York with Maguire's fighting later.

"And behind them comes an old man with a bag."

"Who's this?" he said.

"Hush, ye'll hear. Ah, a lovely old man, such kind eyes and white hair billowing. Quite stout and short he was."

"My God, it's Dr. Francis. He's a terrible great nob."

"Himself."

He lives in a fine house in Greenwich Village and runs Bellevue. You hear about him in the papers."

" 'Twas like the visit of angels. At first they don't know which is

the patient. Mrs. Scanlon's out cold. But Dr. Francis looks at
Mother and right away sees it's pneumonia," she said. "Maguire
nods to Hanley who lifts her like a feather and she's down the
stairs with Dr. Francis. I went down with them and saw her into
his barouche."

"So then what?" he asked impatiently. "Where's Maguire by
now?"

"Back upstairs wrestling Mrs. Scanlon. She's come to ugly and
she's a big woman. But Maguire's handling her fine. Does he drink,
do you know?"

"I think once. He don't now."

"Well, he handled her splendid. Kind of joking and laughing.
Soon she's trying to kiss his cheek and get him to dance with her.
Then old Scanlon comes by and lures her upstairs."

"And what did he do then?"

She stared into her beer. By now the foam was off it. "Let's see
now. There was money. He gave me money for the week to feed
the children. And told me to stay home till I found a neighbor
who'd watch them."

"What about your job?"

"He said he'd fix it," she said. When she looked up, her face was
lit like in church. "And he did. God knows how."

"Ah, they do that through Tammany," he said to be knowing
after all the gossoon questions. "Your store don't want trouble with
the big guns. They don't like their assessment raised for a start. All
a man like Maguire does, he sends word and it's done."

"But won't he have trouble doing that now?" she asked, and
then paused, not liking to speak of the election directly.

"Ah no. They do it through deals, one party swapping with the
other. 'I take care of you when I'm in. You take care of me when
you're in.'" He wasn't sure it was that easy, not with Wood so
recently driven out of Tammany and probably slavering for blood.
Still, he said it with force and she seemed satisfied. She must have
figured that he being a fireman, he knew the inside of politics.

"Well, Mother's back now," she said. "If she can just get the
embroidery, and young Jim can be apprenticed. And of course
there's the dispossess."

"Don't give it a thought. Maguire's sure to be talking to the landlord."

"But the landlord's gone to Europe. Before he left, he started court action."

"Court action," Casey laughed. "And ain't that Maguire's stomping ground?"

"You think so?"

"I do. Forget the court action. That's where the landlord played into your hands, throwing out a fireman's widow. It's a joke."

She smiled weakly and for a few moments he looked across at her pleased, as if he'd done it for her himself. Then slowly, the old discontent stirred within him.

"You just saw him the once?" he asked, disappointed. He'd heard the same fairy tale about Maguire half a dozen times, the details altered, but really the same story. It wasn't what he wanted.

"Just the once. At midnight and all, it seemed like I was only dreaming," she said, continuing to smile until she sensed his mood had changed. She stirred uneasily and picked through her memory.

"Our Jimmy almost saw him again," she said, talking faster. "Mother baked bread and sent Jimmy with it to the Comet last Saturday night. 'From Donahue's widow. God bless you,' the card said. We got a phrenologist lives in the building to write it. He has a lovely hand, just like copperplating."

He was finishing his beer. "What did he say to Jimmy?"

"He was gone. Jimmy'd missed him by a minute. He was off to a dogfight."

He nodded, barely hearing. The afternoon's well-being was seeping away. He hadn't known what he was after, chasing Maguire, but whatever it was, he wasn't going to get it. He'd go back to the Harlem shop and the rows with his mother and brother, nothing different, only now he'd been licked fighting Pretty Boy, everything was darker.

"He's wild about dogfights, the bartender told Jimmy," she was saying. "It's a new craze of his. Every Saturday at Jack Devlin's ratpit."

Something was rattling in the back of his head. He stayed still and let her chatter on about dogfights and ratpits but he paid no mind. He dove deep within himself and listened till he matched it up with Scanlon. Scanlon's visit to him, sitting on his bed and refusing a teacup, afraid to smoke for fear Mrs. Casey wouldn't like it. There was news about Turk. A dogfight at Devlin's ratpit. Matched against Mutual Company's dog, Duke, would make it uncommon. But he didn't know when. He hadn't bothered to pay attention.

"I got to leave," he said suddenly. "I want to find Scanlon."

"Oh yes," she said, sitting straight and eager and pretending it was the usual way to end an engagement. He was in such a hurry, she left her beer on the table.

He rushed her out to the sunshine so quickly he nearly burst into a German band. Two omnibuses were passing and he hailed the one headed uptown. He handed her up without asking did she want to go home but she didn't protest, just sat watching the city pass as he forgot her.

He had a thought to ask her to the Bowery next Saturday night when he swung her down at Twenty-eighth Street. He had a sense he was treating her shabby. Still, there was Scanlon on his mind, and finding out about Turk's ratpit fight.

"Thanks," she was saying. "I've enjoyed myself I'm sure." The look on her face was hopeful and anxious. She was waiting to see if he'd fix another meeting.

But he didn't have time with his mind on finding Scanlon. At this hour on Sunday, he was at the gang's clubhouse.

"I'll see you," he said and headed down the street. But there, it was still daylight. She could make her way home safely.

❧ 4 ❧

THE street gangs met in tenements with escape runways over roofs and fences, or under waterfront piers and on the dumps. But the Arsenal Gang had their own clubhouse. Fourth Avenue was too rocky to grade so that though the side streets were built up as far as Forty-second Street, there were squatters along Fourth still. Droves of pigs and herds of goats wandered among the rocks, and here and there was a tenement, a resort like Hell's Roost, or the rundown Reunion Hotel before the country opened up to the north in desolate crags and sunken lots broken by lonely-looking brownstone houses built on speculation. There was still plenty of room.

The gang had taken over a vacant lot and among the goats and squatters' shacks had built its headquarters from wood picked up about the neighborhood. It had a stovepipe for a chimney and a lone tree gave it a rural air, though beneath its dirt floors the cars of three lines were dragged through the tunnel by horse team from the locomotive sheds at Forty-second to their terminals in the east twenties.

In a midnight raid two years ago, the Gas Works Gang from Twenty-second Street had burned down the clubhouse, and when it was rebuilt the rule against sleeping there at night was changed. The rule was made in the first place after Horse Masterson burned it down one January night when he'd been thrown out of his stable hayloft for drinking and stumbled into the clubhouse to get warm. There being a big supply of coal on hand, picked up beside the tracks where the locomotives dumped their ashes, Horse got over-generous with himself, setting fire to the roof. But between fires set by members and fires set by other gangs, there was no choice. From the time the clubhouse was rebuilt, it was constantly manned and armed. Pistols were stockpiled, ammunition and the minor weapons — paving stones, axes, and knives — so that lately in the neighborhood it was called the Arsenal.

This Sunday afternoon being warm and fair, the Arsenal's door was open and an easy spirit moved the members. A collection had been taken and Paddy Sullivan made the run to the tavern to bring back the growler. Mose Barry and he were sitting on boxes under the lone tree drinking cold beer. As Casey came up, they nodded. Carroll and Hap Martin were pitching pennies against the far wall of the shanty and just glanced at him without speaking.

Casey went to the open clubhouse door and leaned in looking for Scanlon but he only saw Horse Masterson sitting in a shaft of daylight going through his box of burglar's tools. They weren't first-class tools, only bits and pieces he'd managed to scrape from a fence who was setting him up, but they were his first real possessions and he fussed over them like a mother.

Horse had drifted into the neighborhood when he was twelve, a runaway from Troy, New York, come downriver working a canalboat that discharged on the North River docks. But there were thousands of children homeless about the city, stealing where they could to eat and bunking in doorways and hay barges on the river. Every day they were swept into the city jails for crimes from theft to murder. An Aid Society had started packing them off to work for farmers in the West, but as fast as one load of kids was off the streets, another was dumped on them. Sometimes it was the smallpox killing off their mothers, and fathers if they had them, or the immigration with no parent surviving the trip across. But oftener it was the drink that broke up families and sent them scattering like new-hatched cockroaches.

For a while Horse slept in the breweries — haylofts in winter, coal boxes in summer. The stablemen threw him bread. The rest he got helping the brewery laborers or by hitting the grocers, pinch potatoes and run, cooking out in the open. By the time the gang formed, they were calling him Horse for his smell from sleeping in stables, and they made him a member. Like Paddy Sullivan, who'd been sent out begging at ten downtown in Slaughter Alley and with his first profits had kept going, Horse was a street rat, never to school or in church, and the Arsenal was home.

"Where's Scanlon?" Casey asked as Horse looked up.

Horse shifted his wad of tobacco and cast an eye toward the spittoon. But he wasn't quite ready and shifted the wad back. "Gone walking."

"Where to?"

Horse shrugged. He was so used to not giving out information, he had trouble recalling that with the gang he was supposed to talk. But prodded by the silence, he managed to remember. "River."

"By himself?" That wasn't like Scanlon.

"No."

"Who?"

Horse sighed and gave a rub to his nippers. They were the thin pliers he had for reaching into a lock to turn the key. "That Maggie."

Casey grunted. The Pig Girl was what she was called in the ward. Pie-faced and pockmarked, she came from the swill-gatherers' shanties by the river at Dutch Hill above Forty-second Street. Every morning she set out trailing the streets with her father, filling their swill cans and setting them on their broken-down cart. At dark they returned with the swill for their pigs. Last year she was pregnant. By her father, some said, though that was hard to tell. Whenever she ran away, she slept with the men in the hay barges on the river. She got big as a cow and then one day turned up with the swill cans and no sign of baby. So it probably turned up on a dump or a doorway. Nobody asked. If they had, they'd only have been told it was dead. And dead it was by now, that was sure. Even if it made it as far as a doorway. The foundling death rate was nine out of ten at the Blackwell's Island Almshouse where the abandoned babies were sent.

Still, pockmarks and all, she was some sort of a female.

"She come in?" Casey asked, shooting a look toward the heap of dirty straw that served Paddy and Horse as a bed. It didn't look disturbed.

"She wasn't in the mood," Horse said.

Casey nodded. She was a big girl and strong from lifting swill cans. She'd have to be in the mood, by daylight anyway, with a tenement down the way and all the old women hanging out the windows. But it seemed Scanlon felt it was worth giving a try by himself. He'd probably walked her to the bushes and old sheds by the river. Casey hoped her father didn't find them; he kept an ax in the swill cart.

Seeing Horse return to his polishing, Casey went back outside. Carroll and Hap Martin tried to hook him for the penny pitching but he was broke from meeting Kitty. They kidded him some. He had the name for being tight. But he worked for his money at the Harlem shop, while they just knocked over drunks they found in the alleys, so with them it was easy come, easy go. He'd rolled a few drunks himself to show he wasn't yellow, though of course they knew he wasn't from the gang fights. Besides, only he and Scanlon of them all were with the firemen. His stock was high in spite of being closefisted. After Mencken was found with his legs off in the tunnel, he and Scanlon were joint leaders. So the name-calling had no real edge to it. He took a draft from the growler and put his back against the tree next to Paddy and Mose Barry.

They looked up to see what he had on his mind but since he wanted to hear about the dogfight so much, a wary perversity stopped him from coming out with it. Instead, he fished in his pocket for a cigar butt and lit it.

"Maggie come by," Mose told him and he nodded.

"She got them big big lice today. Don't know where she picked up lice like them. We'll have to throw Scanlon in a kerosene barrel if he gets to her," Paddy said.

For a while, he and Mose swapped lice stories — lice they'd seen in the Tombs prison, lice in the Boy's House of Refuge on Randall's Island, a strange type of white louse Paddy knew that bred at Five Points. From lice they wandered to rats — brown tenement rats, the savage black rats from the Greenwich Village livery stables, the great gray wharf rats with six-inch whiskers. From wharf rats, they jumped to the public hanging of the river pirate Hicks, which was coming off July thirteenth on Bedloe's Island in the harbor. Ads were already appearing for excursion boats taking picnickers to the scene, the picnics to come after. The question was whether they could collect excursion money from the tavernkeepers. It was a delicate point and Casey followed it with more interest than he had the lice. The gangs down at Five Points and the waterfront were already collecting. The tavern and storekeepers had already either chipped in for the gangs' annual Thieves Ball and summer moonlight sail, or their premises were wrecked. But the Five Points and waterfront gangs had political support. The Arsenal Gang was newer and while they'd fought the Gas Works Gang's invasions and sometimes joined in with the Pacific Company in driving off alien fire engines, neither Maguire nor Mozart Hall might stand for a shakedown of the local merchants by an independent outfit. With no pull to use on the police, they'd just be scooped up and sent to Sing Sing or the Blackwell's Island penitentiary like common criminals. It was too big a risk. Casey said so and Paddy moaned with desire to watch Hicks kicking.

"Maybe next year," Casey said.

"He ain't gonna be here next year," Paddy said.

But it was no good. They'd thrown Tammany out of office and Mozart Hall had no machinery in the ward. Maybe if Tammany came back, they could do Maguire a few favors.

"Let me just go sound 'em out, nothing rough," Paddy said.

"I got something better," Casey said.

"And what's that? We swim to Bedloe's and hide back of the gallows?"

"For God's sake, forget Hicks." It was time to see what Turk could do for them. He threw away his cigar and Mose and Paddy moved closer.

On weekdays, Devlin's was an ordinary livery stable on Second Avenue. The horses were kept in the basement, the hired carriages on the ground floor, and the three higher stories were let out to tenants. The smell of horse dung rose through the building but that was really a benefit since, as was well known, the smell of horse dung cured consumption. The drawback to living over Devlin's wasn't the horses; it was Saturday nights when the stables turned into Devlin's ratpit.

In the early evening an enclosure three feet high and thirteen by sixteen was knocked together. Rough wooden benches were lined up outside it. And by nine o' clock the men were packing in.

It was mostly a rough crowd — butchers from the slaughterhouses, shipyard and gas house workers from the Eighteenth Ward. But here and there were top-hatted swells from Fifth Avenue, a few sportsmen, and politicians.

The usual card was ratbaiting first. A dozen or so rats, big vicious grays from the wharves, were dropped in the enclosure with a terrier in their midst and the betting was how many rats were killed in half an hour. After that was a dogfight, then a cockfight or a billygoat battle, and a bare-knuckle prize fight. In the fast downtown ratpits like Kit Burns's on the waterfront or Tommy Norris's in the Village, there were boxing matches between women wearing just trunks, and more florid exhibitions for the later evening. But Devlin's ratpit had no whorehouse upstairs and kept its program to sports alone. On the Saturday night Turk was set to fight Mutual Company's Duke, the slated events were ratbaiting, dogfighting, and a neighborhood free 'n easy.

Casey and Scanlon arrived about nine with Turk in a hack barouche which Pacific Company had hired to dignify the occasion. Mutual Company's Duke was already waiting near the hayloft by the scales. Like Turk, he was part bullterrier with cropped tail and ears. His handler was Bob Miller, one of Mutual's pipemen, and in spite of the strain between the companies everybody was behaving like sportsmen and the weighing-in went well. Duke was twenty-six pounds; Turk a shade over twenty-five.

About then, however, there was a stir at the door as Pacific's men started in and the Mutual men saw them. But nothing ugly happened. There was just a tightening of tension as Pacific Company took the benches across the pit from the Mutual men. Jack

Devlin carried it off by announcing the ratbaiting. The lanterns were hung above the pit, the rats let loose, and then Devlin's own dog Frisco dropped in among the rats and the evening started.

Between the squealing of the rats and the shouts of the men leaning over the pit, Casey didn't hear Pretty Boy coming up to the scales in the stable corner. One minute he was nowhere and the next he was there, duded up, his hair pomaded, kneeling down in the straw, one arm about Mutual's Duke. It gave Casey a shock to see him. Last he'd heard Pretty Boy was being carted off in the wagon on the night of the fire. Casey hoped he'd got thirty days in the workhouse on Blackwell's. But he couldn't actually ask without bringing up their fight and have people remembering again he'd been licked. And now it looked like somebody had got off the Mutual boys just as Maguire had got off the Pacific Company. All the while Casey had pictured Pretty Boy dragging rocks to build the Blackwell's seawall, Pretty Boy had been lounging in his dive, the Eagle.

It was galling to think of himself working on a locomotive, covered with grease and sweat in the Harlem shop, while Pretty Boy was cool and dandified. They were both of an age and both from poor families. What really made the difference was Pretty Boy's girls.

He'd started out with a regular sweetheart when he was sixteen, and then, running short of money, he'd fixed her up with a swell. By seventeen he had another, from a shop, he'd promised to marry. There was talk that for the next year he'd even worked as a cadet for Jane the Grabber, swinging up into New England passing for a drummer and sweet-talking girls into eloping to a preacher. They ended in New York, of course, working in Jane's houses. But some cadet made off with the daughter of a lieutenant governor and the system exploded. Whatever it was he'd been doing, Pretty Boy reappeared on the streets of New York and, cool as you please, bought into the Eagle. He didn't own it outright, he had two partners. But the girls upstairs were his. And with the way he looked and dressed, there were those who took him for the owner. Just the way he was holding onto Duke now, you wouldn't think it was Miller trained him.

Anger making Casey suspicous, he looked down at Pretty Boy just as he was holding Duke so tight he must have hurt him and the Duke growled so Pretty Boy drew back, not wanting to get bitten.

"Keep your hands off the dog," Miller said.

Pretty Boy smiled at him blandly, still crouched down in the straw, and the brilliant eyes were so guileless, Casey was all at once certain.

"I'll need to taste him," Casey said.

Miller flared. "Taste your own dog. Go to hell."

"What is it?" Scanlon said. "You see him peppering Mutual's dog?"

He hadn't seen anything but the look in Pretty Boy's eyes. Still, that was enough. He signaled to Devlin who came trotting back across the stable.

"Taste or wash," he said stolidly.

They couldn't talk him out of it and as the commotion grew and the Pacific boys began looking from their benches, Devlin surrendered.

"Ye'll wash," he announced. "Ye'll both wash. I'll have no red pepper on dogs in this pit." He yelled to his nigger stablehand to heat water and bring it in buckets.

By the time the washing had started, the pit had run out of rats and to keep the boys quiet Devlin threw in a pickup dogfight. It wasn't much, just two rat terriers Devlin kept out in back, and they didn't feel much like fighting, so the boys' interest wandered and they would have drifted over but it was too risky having rival fire companies crowding each other round the dogs. So Devlin glowered at anybody who looked like he was curious until Maguire's captain, Hanley, arrived. Tammany in or out, Hanley was a force for order, and Devlin scurried over and parleyed with him. When he came back he seemed relieved.

"Mr. Hanley's a fine man. Did ye see that nugget he wears for a stud? It's from the California gold mines," he informed them, trying to take their minds off the way Casey and Miller were glaring at each other.

"Where's Maguire?" Casey asked him.

"He'll be along," Devlin said. "He's been coming here regular."

"Is he coming sure tonight?" Casey said.

"He'll be along," Devlin repeated. "What's more to the point, Mr. Hanley's just agreed to referee yer dogs."

"Get him here then to go over these towels," Casey said. And as Devlin looked martyred: "Towels and blankets both. And there'll be a search in the pit to see what the dogs' handlers is got in their pockets. I trained this dog myself. I'm not having him blinded. Or poisoned with strychnine."

"Holy God," Devlin muttered but he looked sharper at Miller and Pretty Boy than he had earlier. With both fire companies present, he didn't want it ending with the sack of Devlin's. It was best to play safe. He went off again and brought back Hanley.

Hanley was a big red-faced man, growing a tub now since the lean California days with Maguire. Still, nugget and all, there was nothing fancy to him, and the way he acted, you could tell he knew dogs. He made no jokes either, which some might, seeing they weren't real bullterriers but only mutts with a strain of bull in them. He examined the towels and the dogs were dried and put in the horseblankets after Hanley had been over them.

"Is Mr. Maguire coming?" Casey asked him as they saw the rat terriers removed from the pit and brought Turk and Duke forward toward the lights. He was trying not to be impressed by Hanley, but at the last minute it seemed only respectful to add the Mister to Maguire's name.

"Not tonight," Hanley told him. "He's back at the Comet going over his receipts."

With a pang, Casey handed Turk down to the pit and climbed in after. Duke came in near them and then Miller climbed over. As Hanley searched them for the last time, Casey barely noticed through his disappointment. At the last, as the blankets came off the dogs, he cast a look toward the front as if Maguire might be looming in the doorway but the lanterns dimmed his vision. Then the blankets were out of the pit and Hanley was ordering them to set the dogs free.

For a moment, both dogs crouched in the center of the pit, growling. Then suddenly, Duke sprang and caught Turk by the leg.

Turk shook him off and got Duke by the throat, hurling him down, but Duke caught Turk's ear and gradually loosening his hold, got Turk's front leg in his teeth and pressed till they heard the bones cracking.

At that, Turk was galvanized. He threw Duke twice in succession with a neckhold. And then the tables were turned as Duke caught Turk's leg again and began chewing it.

Turk broke away twice, only to be caught both times. Then both dogs took to throwing one another by the ears. But Turk had started to fight on three legs.

By the end of an hour, Duke threw Turk with a hind-leg hold and Turk got from under. Casey saw with a sinking heart that Turk had been hurt too much by the leg-chewing. On three legs, his lameness was cutting away at his courage.

Suddenly, Turk swerved to the side of the pit and was leaping out when Duke grabbed him from behind and dragged him back in again. Turk turned to the side of the pit and with a terrific lunge, managed to escape. But Duke followed and catching him by the under jaw, clung on, refusing to loose his hold.

There was no chance left. Casey threw down the towel. But when he picked up the water bucket to separate the dogs, Miller seized his arm.

"You've won," Casey said. "I'm just saving my dog."

"Throw them back in the pit," Miller said.

"It's not to the finish."

"It is now," Miller said. "Ye've talked of pepper and poison. Now let it go to the finish."

From the corner of his eye, Casey saw Pretty Boy move to heave the dogs back in the pit. For a moment, with Duke attached to Turk's jaw, Casey thought it was over already and no good done by protesting. But then Turk's leg twitched and he knew there was still life in him. Suddenly, Pretty Boy's move to fling him back to his death became another murderous assault upon himself. He hurled half the water bucket at Miller and dove in to save Turk.

He knocked Pretty Boy into the first row of benches, caught up the water bucket again, doused both dogs with what was left in it, and as Duke let go, he dragged Turk out from under. Pretty Boy caught his arm and he turned and butted him in the stomach. But as Pretty Boy went down, he made the old saloon roll and came up with his knife out.

At that, the whole Pacific Company rose like one man and jumped him. Next second, Mutual Company was swarming over the Pacific.

Hanley was shouting from the pit and Devlin was pleading for order to save his stable, but the noise was too great to hear them. In another minute the wood benches would have come into action and the knives and pistols come out, and after that nothing but a police platoon could have sorted them out.

But it was just then that Maguire, having finished his receipts and feeling wide awake, decided on a dogfight.

He came riding up in a hack and from his pier fighting days, recognized the roar at once. He got out to watch the fray, but there was no heat in him till, as he was paying off his driver, a break in the noise let Hanley's shout come through. Maguire raised his head and listened. It was Hanley all right. His body stiffened at one of his captains letting a crowd get in that condition. Waving the driver to keep the change, and with his gold-headed stick raised, he came sweeping through the stable door like an ancient Irish chieftain.

"Hanley!" he bellowed, and at the sound of his voice vibrating the rafters, a shock went through the bodies piled up around the dogpit. Perhaps their guilt about him added to his normal power. They did not actually stop fighting but they began to move more slowly like men fighting under water.

For an instant, Maguire stood glaring at the tangle of red firemen's shirts and boots with here and there a sportsman or a ward lieutenant's stovepipe hat. Then, carried on an inner whirlwind, he rushed past the benches, vaulted into the pit, and hammered the top of the enclosure with the heavy head of his stick.

"Goddammit!" he cried in the same terrible tones he had used to call Hanley. "Stop your brawling!" This time, the fighting slackened still more. Nobody was actually letting go a hold he might have, but nobody was pressing either.

"Pacific Company! Attention!" Bang with the stick again. "Mutual Company!" Another bang. And then as silence fell, he jerked his head at Hanley.

"Get over there and straighten them out."

And Hanley, at two hundred and eighty pounds of easy living, nipped out of the pit as if he was twenty again and began pulling two fire companies and assorted spectators apart.

At the bottom of the pile, clawed and bloody, he uncovered Casey and Pretty Boy.

It was a peculiar moment. Once the force of his reflex outrage was over, he was facing men who had slipped out from his authority, let him down, and handed the city to Fernando Wood. Tammany was broken without them and they knew it. And yet, they'd stopped fighting at the sound of his voice. They'd betrayed him and still they came back like prodigal sons as soon as the law picked them up or the landlord locked them out. They were his and they were not his either. He had to go carefully. Controlling his temper, he slipped the gold handle of his stock back in his hand again. "Now what's going on here?" he asked.

"Fighting over the dogs," Hanley told him.

"He pulled a knife," Casey said.

"He tried to quit," Pretty Boy said.

They'd all spoken at once. Maguire turned and gazed down at Duke who was panting in the pit where he'd leaped to be out of the way. He was bleeding and seemed confused by the excitement. Maguire leveled the stick at him.

"Whose dog?" he asked.

"Ours," Pretty Boy said. "Mutual Company."

Maguire regarded his satin vest and pomaded hair. "And are you claimin' to be a fireman?" he asked. His voice was mild but the sting was there. It was clear enough what Pretty Boy was. His whole manner proclaimed it. But he wasn't groveling over it; he was proud enough of what he was.

"I run with the Mutual. I'm a saloonkeeper. The Eagle on Twenty-first Street."

And that's not all he was neither, Maguire's look seemed to say, running over him. There were grades in saloons. Maguire kept no girls in the rooms above his Comet. Still, saloonkeepers, nor pimps neither, didn't operate long without protection. Fernando Wood had been giving them plenty when he was the Tammany mayor, and now that he'd walked out he was giving them plenty still. In its own small way the Eagle was a force, since the fighting gang from the New York Gas Works hung around it. The gang were Native Americans, tough native butchers and slaughterhouse boys who liked nothing better than cracking Irish heads. He'd fought the like himself in his pier-brawling days. They were all Wood men now, though Wood denied it. Where else would they go? Not to the rich Republican party, all Abolitionists. So protection was there, Wood protection, and out of his ward, too. He couldn't crack down, the way the elections had swung.

Pretty Boy was bleeding from a cut beneath one eye but he managed to look sardonic and faintly challenging. He showed guts enough, and Maguire gave him that. So he swung to Casey who, turncoat or not, was part of his own ward. He looked at the fireman's shirt and the crack in his lip.

"Pacific Company?" he said. "And is it true you tried to quit?"

"There was no talk of a fight to the finish," Casey said. His voice was low but he'd set his jaw as he did when he was worried. "My dog lost. I threw the towel. There's no need to kill him."

Maguire frowned. Pacific Company had been his so long, he forgot for the moment that they'd deserted him and he flared up in a proprietor's way at the talk of quitting. "An' where's this losing dog that caused so much trouble?"

Casey turned and the crowd moved unsurely, looking back in the shadows for Turk.

"He's there," Devlin said, pointing.

Maguire stepped over the enclosure and with Hanley carrying the lantern and Casey trailing behind, they proceeded to the corner where Scanlon had dragged Turk.

There wasn't much dog left. He was lying on his side with his breath coming shallow and bleeding all over. His right front leg looked like it had been through a grinder and when Hanley held up the lantern so the light shone on him, his eyelid twitched and they saw the white showing.

Maguire grunted and signaled to Hanley to lower the lantern. "I don't see you gained much for your quitting," he told Casey. "You'll not get him home alive."

"I'll get him home," Casey said, and at his tone, Maguire turned his head. He saw the odd eyes, flat and hard, and set in the head in a veiled way that Maguire had met once or twice in dangerous fighters. Before, he'd only been looking at a Pacific Company fireman. Now he was looking at Casey himself and he was puzzled.

"Is he your dog?" he asked.

"He is."

"You train him?"

"I found him myself on the streets and I trained him."

Maguire was curious. The eyes did not match the sentimental dog-lover. "Is it for that you'd be willing to start all these men fighting?" he asked finally.

"It wasn't agreed in advance there'd be a fight to the finish," Casey said. "They tried to run that in."

"Is it true?" Maguire asked Hanley and his ward captain nodded.

So it was a matter of honor, a man not wanting to be crowded. Too bad they could not stay like that, true to honor and loyal to a leader when election time came, instead of scattering like sheep at the first blast of rumor. This one had scattered too, for all his fighter's look. And then for no planned reason, but out of a spring of bitterness that came welling up in him, Maguire heard himself say wryly: "What might you be now? One of these new Mozart Hall Democrats?"

Casey glanced at him quickly. Maguire was near six foot and he himself two inches shorter so he had to look up, which put him at a disadvantage. But he stared up blandly, trying to master his expression, while inside him conflicting feelings warred. He must have been lunatic to desert Maguire, the great hero, with his black locks and yellow diamonds, matched horses, Maguire the chieftain, who could draw men on to acts that by themselves would be beyond them. Could Fernando Wood do that — the slick millionaire shipowner who would use any step in his scramble to be President, who'd go up on Irish backs if need be. And for that he'd deserted Maguire, the cottier's boy, who was one of his own. Regret twisted in him. He wanted to cry out, to say he was sorry and ask Maguire to forgive and take him back. And yet, something stopped him, some cold, careful other part of him. It might be the wrong move to say he was sorry. It brought back all the starveling, bowing tenants scraping before the Cork landlords. Before passion could betray him, he hesitated.

Then as he paused, a secret compartment within him seemed to open. It was not so much remembering that Maguire himself came from peasant stock and might burn with the same shame of the years of submission and slave's groveling as he did. He really did not think. There was no time for it. But he slid into Maguire and around and found a hurt, stung man who yearned for sure ground where there had been bog and Irish mist, yes or no instead of the answering question, and men who admitted a wrong when they were caught instead of weeping like wild children.

"Are you Mozart Hall?" Maguire repeated.

Casey decided. He would throw on all or nothing. "I left you for Wood. They said you'd sold us out."

Silence fell like a blow on the stable.

"Ah, did you now?" Maguire said, surprised, for no one had dared to say the words, though knowing it was scalding him. His free hand clenched and Casey stood firm. It was touch and go if Maguire would strike. But instead Maguire said: "And you believed it?"

"Enough to wonder. I saw your diamonds and your horses and I thought a man might."

Maguire stared at him hard, trying to make out what was behind it. He didn't hear truth often and he didn't much like it either. But at least this one wasn't crawling, asking favors.

"I was wrong," Casey said finally. There was no point driving the man daft. "Any fool could see that now. But there it is. You asked and I tell you the truth."

"Ah, here's an honest man," Maguire said, letting his breath out with a long sigh as the tension broke between them. His eyes lit for an instant and Casey saw he'd guessed right.

Still, though Maguire might be satisfied, the men weren't. Some were Wood men still, and some unsure what they were. They'd been stopped from their brawl before it was finished. Their blood wasn't cool yet and the evening unsettled. There was also the matter of Pacific Company's good name. The word quitter had been thrown out. Even if they'd run out on him, Maguire didn't like to chance its sticking.

"An' would you be willing to fight now yourself?" Maguire asked. "Instead of your dog, if we found you a match?"

Casey looked at him with rising hope. The thing he'd wondered lying in his bed in the dark bedroom, that maybe Maguire had seen him fight Pretty Boy the night of the fire, suddenly fell into place. But this time it was better than banging somebody's head against the street in the shadows, better than Maguire seeing Turk fight. It wasn't just showing off, but a chance to play Maguire's champion. His face lit with the idea and he looked through the stable gloom toward Pretty Boy.

Maguire followed his gaze. They were the right height and weight, and they'd been at the bottom of the pile when Hanley uncovered them. It was Mutual Company against Pacific, and Native American against Irish. But best of all, an erring Tammany boy had returned to the party and in full public gaze would battle a Wood man. He'd already sighted Horse Masterson who'd been in the pileup and was edging close to Casey. As he'd known about Pretty Boy, he knew also what Horse was. And old Scanlon's son nearby — the Arsenal Gang was what they both were. Which meant Casey ran with a gang, and was not just a fireman. He wouldn't be outmatched with a man too knowing for him.

"And are you a hero too?" Maguire called across to Pretty Boy. "Will you fight Pacific's man here?"

"Why not?" Pretty Boy said in his languid whoremaster's way. His lovely face was insultingly cool. His eyes glittered with artifice. "Just say when and where."

But Casey didn't want that. He wanted here and now before Maguire forgot him. To force it, he was peeling down to his undershirt.

As Pacific Company let out a shout, Maguire hesitated. He'd intended a fight in a week when there'd be time for the men to line up back of Casey and follow him back to the Tammany fold, perhaps in Jones's Wood by the river north of Seventieth Street. Still, with the Pacific Company's cry in his ears, he did not like to check the men again. They'd take only so much stopping before they turned ugly. And he'd already found out how they could run away wild. Control didn't lie in checking but in knowing how to ride them. So he raised his arm to Pretty Boy, ignoring the sardonic tilt Pretty Boy gave his head. With matters so advanced, there was no chance for argument. As Pretty Boy took off his coat and unbuttoned his satin vest, an answering roar went up from Mutual Company.

Maguire led them back to the enclosure and they climbed into the ratpit. He gave no instructions. There'd be no rounds or fancy English rules, just a good, honest pier fight, the kind that made his own name famous.

They were each about five feet ten, Casey heavier, being built stocky. But Pretty Boy was lithe and hard and he carried himself more gracefully.

They began a light sparring, Casey holding himself wary and flat-footed as Pretty Boy circled, looking for a chance to jump. The dancing lasted five or ten minutes. Once Pretty Boy smashed Casey's jaw but Casey pulled his head in closer and didn't let it rock him. At last, finding no opening, Pretty Boy grew impatient and made a rush for it. But Casey was too fast. As Pretty Boy lunged, Casey ducked quick as lightning, and grabbed him by the ankles.

In a flash, he threw Pretty Boy over his head and as Pretty Boy went down, he only had time to roll on his back before Casey was on him.

Clawing wildly, they butted and pounded each other against the dirt of the pit. Pretty Boy tore Casey's face with his teeth. Casey went for his eyes, gouging in with his nails.

In a minute, they were both punished severely and showing it. There was a gash in Casey's cheek where the flesh had been torn open. Blood was streaming from both of Pretty Boy's eyes. They didn't change positions, for the moment they were down, both Mutual and Pacific companies vaulted into the enclosure and Maguire could not get them to quit the pit, so the two struggling bodies were pressing against the feet of the crowd. But neither man was favored. There was no interference. And for ten minutes more the struggle lasted. But Pretty Boy was beneath, and with Casey's weight against him he was a sure loser. And shortly his voice came, rough and suffocated as if he was drowning in his blood. "I'm done," he said. "Let me up, goddammit."

A cheer went up from Pacific Company and before a general fight could start, Maguire climbed into the pit and began the announcement.

He didn't know Casey's name and leaned over to Hanley. But Hanley didn't know it either. He ended by asking Casey.

"Casey. Tom Casey," Tom said. So he wouldn't seem to stagger, he leaned against the enclosure. Scanlon passed him a rag and he pressed it to the gash in his cheek. But his eyes didn't change. They were cold still and level, and he kept them on Maguire.

Maguire liked him. Or rather, he liked his qualities; the way he wouldn't back down on the dog, his refusal to let Pretty Boy rush him. He had a hotter head than that himself, but he admired the good sense. And then there was the way Casey had admitted he'd bolted at election, even spoken of Maguire's diamonds and his suspicion Maguire had sold them out. Truth under stress was a hallmark of loyalty. He wavered at that, his instinct cautious about the veiled greenish eyes. Still, his need to believe it carried him partway while Casey's courage and the heat of the hour carried him the rest.

"Come see me at the Comet," he told him. And as Casey's face lit, with one eye puffed and the blood streaming from the rag he held to his cheek, in that instant of real emotion as he saw how much the words meant, Maguire truly loved him. On impulse, he sealed his part of the bargain. "I could use a fighting man," he said.

♣ 5 ♣

ON the morning of the great Hicks hanging, Tom Casey found himself at Collins Dock aboard the steamer *Red Jacket*. The Arsenal Gang was amazed by his rise in the world. Riddled with envy and awe, they had trouble even talking to him. By a flurry of drunk-rolling and a second-story job on a warehouse pulled off by Horse Masterson, they had managed to scrape up the fare for an excursion on the steamboat *Chicopee*, which after the hanging was to run up the Hudson River as far as West Point, refreshments provided. But the *Red Jacket* was the official ship. Hicks himself was going over on her, along with the United States marshal and the sheriff, thirteen attending doctors, a large body of reporters, celebrated sports, gamblers and pugilists, and a grand crowd altogether from City Hall.

But what seemed a triumph at the gang's clubhouse had lost much of its shine by the *Red Jacket*. Standing at the rail between Maguire and Hanley, Casey was in a vise of self-consciousness. The black frock coat that had seemed such a buy at the secondhand Jewstore on Chatham Street and which had wrung tears of joyful admiration from his mother when he strolled into her kitchen, now seemed greenish and seedy. His trousers were too narrow as if he could never sit down in them. He regretted not having gone for a brocade vest. Maguire was wearing one, and it might have made a difference, diverting the eye from the coat, so to speak. As far as the stovepipe hat went, he'd fancied himself having one but now it was his, it made his life miserable. On his head it bound him; while off, you could neither stuff it in a pocket nor do anything but carry it. He kept trying to slide his hands in his pockets, but they wouldn't fit since the trousers were made different from his old work pants. And though he'd scrubbed at his nails with kerosene since he'd quit the railroad shop and gone to help Maguire, it was only a week, and the grease was still there like the veins inside shrimp. He was near crazy with suspicion that every burst of laughter was meant for him so that a kind of theater scene kept going through his head — some tailored swell went too far and he picked him up, whirled him and pitched him in the river. But he couldn't do that; it would be the end of him with Maguire. So instead he stood sullen at Maguire's side, his fingers crawling up and down from his pockets, and the whole first part of his success was ruined. Then suddenly the dockside crowd gave a roar and he saw Hicks was arriving from the Tombs in a curtained carriage.

With everybody watching Hicks, he came out of himself cautiously. Careful not to split the shoulders of his frock coat, he leaned on the railing. And there was Hicks coming out on the dock. The crowd below gave a sigh and Casey stared at Hicks hard.

He seemed a pleasant sort, wearing a suit of blue cloth. With his hands fastened in front of him, he looked mild. Actually, they said he had scattered victims from Panama to California, though what he was being hung for was piracy aboard an oyster sloop. He'd got drunk on Water Street, and waking to find he'd been shanghaied on the *E. A. Johnson,* had murdered the two crew members and the captain with an ax, then cast off in the dinghy with the loose valuables. The *Johnson* was found drifting, her decks bloodstained. And soon after, Hicks was picked up with Captain Burr's watch. It was a clear-cut case. Hicks was guilty, there was no doubt of that. And yet, seeing him so quiet in his cheap blue suit, being led on board by Marshal Rynders and Sheriff Kelly, he didn't seem the hound of hell that the newspapers had made him. He seemed just a man like any man, smoother than Horse Masterson, slighter built than Casey himself. He was bearing himself well, not too much bravado nor yet was he cringing, for all he knew he'd be dead in two hours. His confessor was with him, so he looked to have made his peace with the church, and perhaps some queer kind of grace had descended on him like the dove in the stained-glass windows.

Still, it was rare tough luck going out that way. Lots of men committed murder. Take U. S. Marshal Rynders, ex-Mississippi riverboat man, Native American gang leader, rioter, knuckle-duster and dirk man. There must have been men in his time that Rynders had put under. And it might be more than Hicks had. And yet there was Rynders with his past forgotten, the darling of Tammany, taking Hicks to the gallows, when it might have been the other way around.

As Hicks came on board, Casey turned from the rail and watched Hicks being led through the after-saloon toward a cabin below. At close range, he saw Hicks had little anchors embroidered in white on his collar. It was an odd piece of vanity. Unless it was Barnum got the suit for him. There'd been something in the papers about Barnum dickering for a plaster cast of his head to display in the American Museum with the mermaids and cannibal clubs. It might have been Barnum because Hicks didn't seem that sort. Close to, he was calm as he'd been from a distance. On impulse, Casey gave him a wink as he passed, and then Maguire turning, he made his face a blank.

It came to him then there were stories about Maguire too. On the trip to California when he'd been a faro gambler, there'd been an assault with intent to kill that had been settled by complaint or dropped *nolle pros*. Later, there was a pistol murder of a Native American thug that had never come to trial, the witnesses having vanished. That had been in the days Maguire was drinking, and it was probably the reason he'd given up the drink. But then Hicks had been drinking the night he'd been shanghaied. It was a strange world and no use trying to claim it was a fair one.

The recollection of Maguire's past relaxed him. He wasn't such a god, no matter if his coat fit and he smelled of barber's violets. He was a man like Hicks or Rynders — hang or be marshal, it all depended on where the ball lodged when the wheel quit spinning. The big thing was guts, and keep doubling your bets.

Seeing Hicks had helped him, too. With a man so near hanging, tight pants and an old frock coat seemed less worth worrying

about. By the time Maguire led the way into the saloon and he
bellied up to the sandwiches, Casey felt better, and after two drinks
of bad bar whiskey, he was leaning back on his elbows and the
hell with it if the shoulders split.

For pride's sake, he couldn't ask who the men were that came
buzzing about Maguire. He thought he recognized the famous
prizefighters Dick Lynch and Tom Hyer from their pictures that
hung in the saloons next to Washington and Queen Victoria. And
others were big men down at City Hall, he couldn't be sure which,
though you could tell what they were by the rich, cheerful way they
moved. One he saw he couldn't miss — nearly six feet and stout,
with large ruddy features, growing bald, with a short red beard and
a merry look in his eyes. He seemed alive with fun. Wherever he
moved, he left men laughing, so the jokes must be dirty. He was
wondering was it "Brains" Sweeny, till he heard him called Bill.

"Is that Big Bill Tweed now?" he asked Hanley quick before his
pride could prevent him from asking.

Hanley glanced across the saloon, and then regarded Casey
dourly. There was no missing Hanley didn't like him. It was jeal-
ousy, he thought, since Maguire had taken him up. And yet fear
kept touching him that the night of the dogfight, Hanley had felt
his stand with Maguire had been calculation. It was honesty, he
told himself. And yet part of him knew it was part conniving,
though Hanley's thinking so he didn't like. Still, it wasn't smart to
show it. He was forever seesawing like that with Hanley between
rage and caution.

Finally, Hanley deigned to answer. "It's the Boss," he said.

So he was jerked up short and he flushed to be caught so. The
insiders weren't saying Bill Tweed anymore. There must be truth to
the rumors that it was Tweed led the fight that drove Wood out of
Tammany. Now they were grouping around Tweed and it was Boss
instead of Big Bill. Deep matters and subtle, the way a man might
sink in quicksand entirely if he used the wrong word. He'd keep to
himself, then, and bad luck to Hanley.

He looked around for Wood, but he didn't see him. Perhaps he
thought a hanging was beneath a mayor's dignity. It was too bad;

he'd have liked to see him eye to eye with Tweed. Though perhaps that's why the two of them weren't on board together. The thought he'd hit upon it sent joy shooting through him. There were interlocking parts, like on a locomotive — shafts, bearings and sockets; if you just knew enough, you could put it all together and who knew where it could take you.

Feeling deep, he turned to the bar, and then just as he was about to signal the bartender to set down the bottle, he saw in the bar mirror that Maguire was watching him. He's worried I'll be drinking too much and disgrace him, he thought, and at that he felt like smiling. It might be Maguire's weakness but it wasn't his. And to make his point, he didn't signal after all, but turned and strolled to the sandwich table. After a minute he let himself catch Maguire's eye, and Maguire was raising his hand to come over. So when he waded through the men in the saloon, he had his reward. Maguire introduced him to Sheriff Kelly.

But Honest John Kelly was another kind altogether from a genial man like Tweed. He was keen and cold and on his dignity, which of course he was entitled to be, having been alderman and then sent to sit in the Congress in Washington. Still, Tweed had been alderman and to Congress too, yet he'd kept his easy manner and his loose and lively tongue that kept the crowd around him laughing. After a few minutes of Kelly, Casey felt himself stiffening inside the frock coat.

But Maguire was still trying to break the ice for him. "He's a real hero," Maguire was telling Kelly. "You should have seen him in that ratpit waiting his chance, and then on his man like a tiger."

"Ah," Sheriff Kelly said, and his gaze lightened a bit.

"The Sheriff was a great fighter himself," Maguire said. "The killer of the Ivy Green saloon, we called him. 'Twas a place on Elm Street."

To his surprise, Kelly laughed. For a moment, he was different from the cold man Casey had been introduced to. In a hurry, Casey said: "Ah, I've heard it. And the musses that went on with the Volunteers too."

Kelly looked at him severe. He wasn't sure he liked a new man, fighter or no, talking up so free, even if it was referring to his own fame with the Volunteers. But Maguire said: "Casey's with Pacific Company."

"Is that so now?" Kelly said, softening slightly again. And with a strange glance, almost shy: "An' do ye care much, tell me, for the new steam engine?"

Casey looked at him quick. Actually, he was not opposed to steam like the older men were. There was talk of the Pacific getting one themselves, and he'd been among the loudest that supported it. But Kelly's day had been with hand-pumps.

"I'd hate to see the hand-pumps go, and that's the truth," he said.

Kelly regarded him keenly.

"There's great history to them, and great men who worked them," Casey continued. "But I've seen the new steam beat us, on a great fire, high up. A man can only work so long. Steam's got no heart to wear out."

Kelly's eye held him a moment longer, then he sighed and nodded. Casey felt Kelly was sad but in a sentimental way that wasn't really painful. And he'd had his tribute, too. His eyes had lighted though he'd tried to hide the greedy way he'd snatched at the bit about the great men who'd worked the hand-pumps. He was proud of his fire fighting, and he liked a man who catered to his pride.

Just then, the tide turned favorable to a landing at Bedloe's Island and the *Red Jacket* cast off with a great shout from her passengers. They slipped out of the dock and, turning away from Bedloe's, headed up river to view the *Great Eastern* paddle-wheeler on exhibit in her dock before they settled down to the hanging.

Next, Hicks came up from his cabin, and when he stepped into the saloon, the sporting crowd crushed about to shake his hand. In all the push, Kelly wandered off and next Casey saw him talking stiffly to Tweed. Nor could all Tweed's joking make his face show the life that Casey got from it with fire engines.

His spirits soaring, Casey shoved the stovepipe far back on his head and declared himself the success that the Arsenal believed. Not seeing Maguire about, he celebrated with a drink, then strolled out on deck and hung over the rail to fix in his mind his exchange with the great Kelly.

The rest of the morning slipped by like he was dreaming. He seemed lifted above the hat and the frockcoat like saints rising from the ground and floating in midair.

After viewing the *Great Eastern*, the *Red Jacket's* head was turned and she sailed directly for Bedloe's, making her way through the hundreds of craft that had come for the hanging. Casey kept an eye out for the *Chicopee*, and when he saw her, he tried to spot Horse Masterson or some of the gang. But the *Chicopee* was jammed and they were probably in the saloon lapping up the free refreshments, so he didn't get the satisfaction of having them see him land. It was a grand moment, too, passing all the gaily-flagged boats and tying up to the official berth on the wharf. Once moored, Marshal Rynders asked them all to leave except the physicians, reporters and officials. Casey found Maguire again and they left the boat together with Hanley, marching abreast up the hill to the rear of the gallows with a squad of city police going before them.

Atop the hill they had a fine view of the bay, alive with watercraft. There were several barges in tow, excursion steamers, hundreds of rowboats, all crowded and beflagged. Two white-winged yachts glided by and Tom wondered whose they were but Hanley was listening and he refused to ask. Even the sloop *E. A. Johnson* was there, bright with flags and filled with friends of the murdered Captain Burr.

They watched while the procession disembarked: a platoon of soldiers, then the prisoner walking between Rynders and Kelly on the one side, his confessor on the other, next the physicians, the press and another group of soldiers bringing up the rear. Instead of the hat Hicks wore when he first came aboard, he had on the black gallows cap but from its top fluttered colored ribbons, while a black silk cape hung from his shoulders. He looked the jaunty pirate then. Casey stirred with admiration for the way he chose to go.

At the gallows on the water's edge, the troops formed a hollow square and with the police, doctors, and press looking on, Hicks and his confessor knelt down on the greensward. When Hicks rose from prayer and stood beneath the rope, the spectators in the boats, thinking the officials were hiding the view, began to shout and yell for them to stand aside.

But from then on, it went like clockwork. Hicks just had time to look out on the sunlit bay dotted brightly with his executioners. He must have seen the *Johnson*, too. Then the gallows cap came down over his face, the check on the weight was cut, and he was run into the air.

Casey held his breath. He'd been afraid he might go green or make a fool of himself, it being his first execution. But he didn't have to fear. Hicks seemed to go quickly. There was nothing to call a struggle. After twelve minutes, they lowered his body and the doctors examined it. Then they ran him up again for another quarter of an hour. Finally, they took him down, placed him in a coffin, and Maguire told them it would be sent by towboat to the undertaker and after released to friends who were taking it.

For a while longer, they lingered on the hill. The flotilla of boats broke up. One excursion steamer that had advertised combining the Hicks hanging with meeting the ship that was bringing John C. Heenan back from his English championship fight, fired two guns in farewell to Hicks, then turned to greet Heenan. Casey and Maguire trooped back down the hill and the *Red Jacket* cast off for another pleasure excursion up the Hudson.

Only toward the end did the glory of the day cloud. A red-faced man gave a drunken speech in the saloon, thanking Rynders for the splendid way he'd handled the execution. Rynders, looking stern, said a painful duty had been performed. And then Casey joined in when they gave him three cheers. Rynders stopped them at once, and as the cheering trailed off, Casey had a sense he'd been caught in a wrong. He flushed, feeling angry with Rynders for his cant. With insiders all together, it went against him to pretend. Still, when he saw Maguire wasn't in the saloon and hadn't seen him cheering, his anger faded. Nor was Kelly near either. He began to feel no harm was done and perhaps he'd had a political lesson of value.

His spirits lifting again, he put the cheering from his mind as if he hadn't joined in. It came to him then how strong the fumes of the whiskey were, and all at once he wondered if the drinking had driven Maguire away. A warmth toward Maguire came over him at that. The weakness of the man made him feel protective, and he strode out on deck in case Maguire was feeling low.

With Wood's Mozart Hall Democracy hogging the old Tammany positions, it was more than a month before Maguire found Casey a place on the city payroll. He hung around the Comet as a bouncer and kept order at Maguire's Coney Island clambake when the constituents, driven wild by so much free ears of corn, beefsteaks and beer, began to get out of hand around the carousel and chuck-a-luck games. He was using a blackjack, finally, on the steamer back to town. He took bail money down to the police station for bartenders arrested for violating excise laws and collected the rent from the tenants who lived above the Comet. But Casey himself squeezed by with small sums Maguire irregularly remembered to dole out to him.

By the end of July, his mother was starting to grumble about politicians' promises, and even he was wondering did he quit the locomotive shop too soon. One night he went out with the Arsenal Gang drunk-rolling and came back with a few dollars. But now it seemed a risky business, considering he was starting a meteoric rise in politics.

In August the appointment came through. Tammany in or out, Maguire was still sitting with the City Council, and Wood needed votes to put his measures through. Casey was made attendant in the Jefferson Market Court. The salary was twelve hundred a year, not so much as some were making, but still not too bad, and it was a jump up from mechanic, being connected with the law in a manner of speaking. In a burst of civic pride, Casey went down to the court to see where he was supposed to be working. But no one knew what to do with him there and he was just in the way, besides being missing when Maguire needed him. So he contented himself with collecting his paycheck and took out his elation by buying a brocade vest at the Chatham Street Jew-store, and putting down payment on a diamond stickpin. For the rest, he gave himself to his duties for Maguire.

In the morning, while Maguire and Hanley visited the police

courts to help constituents who'd drunk too deeply the previous
night, and later while they did the rounds of municipal district
courts to aid others in more serious trouble, Casey leaned against
the wall of the Pacific Company firehouse where he helped answer
calls that came in on the telegraph, and generally cemented the
company's Tammany connections that had come unstuck in the
last fall's election. At noon, he reported to the Comet. For a long
time it remained a grand moment, that promenade past the casks
and barrels piled up on the sidewalk and the great blocks of ice
coming in from the ice wagons, and then the crossing of the
threshold for the day. The saloon was spacious and cool in the
bright blaze of August. The sawdust was clean and soft to the feet.
The long bar ran the length of the wall and the great mirror behind it gave back the shining rows of glasses and the grand array of
varicolored bottles and decanters. Not many customers were lined
up at the bar at that hour, a few workmen from the Hunter's Point
ferry, a watchman from Bellevue Hospital and the block's policeman sitting cozy in the special chair they kept for him. But those
that were there saw his entrance and they knew by his manner he
was on the inside of politics.

If Maguire wasn't leaning at the end of the bar Casey said to the
bartender: "Boss in?" And when the bartender jerked his head toward the back room, he walked easy toward the door and strolled
in to get his orders for the day.

There were near a dozen like himself in and out of that back
room. All were older, tough canny men in shiny top hats and
clothes flashier than his, who were also on the city payroll. But they
were election district captains and did subtler work than he, report-
ing who was in need and who in trouble and the best way to help
while Maguire took notes in a little book he carried. He'd taught
himself to write in the last few years.

The district captains were busier at election time than in the
summer, attending primaries and conventions. For the rest, they
played pinochle or forty-five at the Comet's back-room tables, and
on pleasant afternoons they lounged at Broadway and Fifth Avenue or in the corridors of City Hall, smoking good cigars and discussing fine points of municipal affairs.

But Casey ran bail to the courts, at night was Comet bouncer, and in between Maguire sent him off to visit at the gang's Arsenal. Though nothing had been said definite, Casey gathered the gang had a future as repeaters. In the past when the ward needed them, they'd been ordered from the older downtown wards. But after last fall's disaster, Maguire saw the need of installing a local guard.

Once Maguire took Casey to a funeral and once to a wedding. And at the St. Stephen's Church Fair, Casey went along while Maguire passed him money to take chances on everything. But Hanley was always present, and there was no denying Hanley was trying to freeze him out. It was "D'you remember the way we worked our way to Frisco playing faro on the boat?" or "That was the night ye fought George Thompson at Mare Island. Ye bled like a pig. Remember I kept sucking that blood bruise above yer eye?" Anything to bind Maguire to him and cut Casey out as a treacherous climber. He was like a jealous woman with a new young rival.

And lunatic as it sounded, there was a kind of truth to Hanley's fear. For what drew Maguire was Casey's youth and muscle. The night in the ratpit — Maguire was always retelling it. And he liked to hear all the old fights with Pretty Boy — the free 'n easy at the Eagle and the big gang battle they'd had last year in the Fourth Avenue tunnel. Maguire went round with him to the Arsenal one day and Casey and Horse put on a match, Horse having the good sense to let Casey beat him before too much blood was flowing. Maguire seemed to be trying to cross a bridge into the new generation, while Hanley, all red-face and bloat, was pulling Maguire back toward the past when the men were cast iron and the times were grander.

It was true enough Hanley had been a good man. Born in Tipperary like Maguire, he'd met Maguire on the New York docks and they'd fought together, drunk together, challenged all comers once in Rynders' sporting saloon and were beat unconscious together. For two years they had met the immigrant ships and fought other runners for the prize of greenhorns and their baggage to carry off to the boardinghouses. And then they had left for California to get rich in the great gold rush. They took a private cruise to Queen Charlotte's Island on the track of a rumor that the Sitka Indians had found gold. There was drink and bloodshed and three lives lost before they got back, not finding gold, and then Maguire settled down to fighting in San Francisco with Hanley as his second. After that they came back to New York and Maguire fought them into Tammany support and eventually the Comet.

Maguire was still built like a champion but Hanley was one of those men whose body gives out early. Fifty pounds overweight, he groaned when he heaved his bulk from the back-room chair and set out with Maguire on the ward's activities. His feet swelled in hot weather clear up past his ankles. But still he flogged himself to show up at all the wakes and funerals and dawn calls to fires, the weddings, trips to police courts, clambakes, target shoots, political processions. And past midnight he was gasping as he tagged Maguire to dogfights, the way if he stayed home for a day, a thief would spirit Maguire away. And it had all got worse with the coming of Casey. What was fresh and new to him was the martyrdom of Hanley. At two in the morning Casey was leaning over the rat-pits, yelling on the dogs, his eye cold and hard for any thug who might get out of line, while Maguire sat back pleased as a boy and Hanley, red in the face, was glowering, stealing away to pull on his flask. For where Maguire had had to quit the drink after all the trouble he got into, Hanley never showed it and so he kept swigging, chewing mouthfuls of cloves so Maguire wouldn't tumble to him. But the worst of all for Hanley was watching Casey at the fires.

At fires, Casey shone. Whether it was clearing the sidewalks for the engine to run smoothly rather than bumping along the street cobblestones — for years, the Council had threatened to dissolve any company that ran on the sidewalk, but the companies still did it — or fighting the street gangs that sprang to attack for the honor of rival companies; whether it was defending the engine against sidewalk committees that tried to jump her and take over, or the race to rush past another engine, Casey was the image of the risen Irish heroes. He labored at the brakes till the stroke was nearly one hundred and twenty and the crowd was yelling "Stave her sides in!" They washed other companies to wild cheering: "She's up to the rabbits!" till "She's over!" and the licked company withdrew from the pumping line to let the water out the tail screw. When he was relieved at the brakes, instead of resting as he used to, or vanishing inside to make off with handy valuables, he now grabbed an ax and let go at smoldering partitions, rescued children, or ran into belches of smoke with the bed key from the Pacific's toolbox so some family's precious bed could be unbolted and carried through the flames to safety.

There was no way to hint such a man was calculating. And neither could Hanley avoid the fires. At the sound of the engines, every captain in the district was out of bed tugging on his pants, as the fires were great vote-catchers. Each burned-out tenant set up in a hotel, given clothes or fed might mean half a dozen votes for the next twenty years. Hanley had to appear, and once there, he had to watch while Casey pumped and hacked, saving property and lives in a red, volcanic glare. Perhaps Hanley hoped he'd be smothered in the smoke or hit by the hot beam of a falling floor — Casey didn't know. But he supposed Hanley hoped it. He'd have been praying for it himself if he'd been in Hanley's shoes. He did his own best to prevent it. And he'd been around fires long enough to have a shrewd eye for the difference between a gamble and suicide.

The last week in August, there was a midnight fire in the lumberyard that ran along First Avenue across from Scanlon's tenement. It was the real dog days, hot and humid with the refuse stinking in the streets and the backyard privies almost lethal, with the diphtheria and measles and baby diarrhea deaths soaring and every family jammed on the rooftops to sleep, so that at the first glow, the alarm was given.

But even though they got to it early, and being so near the river that they didn't need hydrants, just dropped hose at the foot of Thirty-fifth Street, the lumber was dry and it caught on like tinder. Next, an east wind came up and the flames looked to jump the avenue to Scanlon's tenement. There was no fighting with other companies, there being water for all from the river.

Still, with everybody tending strictly to business, besides the tenants in Scanlon's tenement passing buckets up from their hydrant to wet down their roof, it was touch and go till dawn with three firemen from Hose Company Eleven overcome and a heart attack victim.

At dawn a thunderstorm broke. The city lit up in flashes of greenish light and the crashes of thunder hit one after the other while the sky opened and Niagara came down. The fire hissed like a jungleful of snakes with the thunder rattling windows and the lightning flaring. In ten minutes the lumberyard was flooded and by the time the storm went traveling east across the river toward Brooklyn, they found themselves standing foolish and drenched, with Scanlon's building saved.

Maguire clapped Casey's shoulder and put a dripping Hanley in his buggy. The heart attack victim and overcome firemen were loaded in a cart and two men of Hose Eleven wheeled them off toward Bellevue. The sopping wet Father Cummings from St. Stephen's was trying to calm an old woman in a screaming fit — whether from fear of thunder or a case of the trimmins it was hard to say. It was too wet for a pickup dogfight and too hot for a bonfire, which the fire companies sometimes put on when a big fire was over, and the hose companies were rewinding while the hook and ladders rolled off.

Then Kitty Donahue appeared with two towels and a bottle. She must have been helping wet down the roof and got caught in the downpour. She was wet to the skin with her fine hair plastered to her face.

"Well now, that's kind," Casey said, drawing back from a towel which looked new white smuggled home from Kitty's store, and he like a chimney sweep with ash and char.

"Ah, take it, 'tis little enough and you saving us all from being burnt to a crisp," Kitty said, pushing on the towel again and waving another at Scanlon. Scanlon was grinning like one of Barnum's apes. He took the towel which at once turned to grime but he was eyeing Kitty too hard to notice. When Casey shook his head, she pressed the bottle on to Scanlon who threw his head back like a good child and half the bottle disappeared. To save it, Casey grabbed it.

" 'Tis a bit we keep on hand for medicine," Kitty said to Casey, making clear they were respectable though there was no man about the house since Donahue was killed. "It was a cruel downpour and you're wet through. Drink up. It may save you a bout of pneumonia."

"Well I will then," Casey said, seeing if he didn't Scanlon would finish it all.

"That was grand," Scanlon said. "It's what I needed. I can feel it doing me good." He kept kneading the towel, which now was the size of a wet handkerchief, until Casey looked at him to see was he hit on the head in the fire. But it seemed it was only Kitty. Something about her was drawing him. So then Casey looked at Kitty. She was wet with her clothes sticking to her and her bony face gleaming with sweat and rain. You could see the shape of her clear, though what there was of her was scanty. Still, her eyes were shining and there was her eagerness with her bottle and dabs of toweling that made him smile. He remembered their afternoon on the Bowery and the way he'd fed her up made him feel like a benefactor. The hour in the beer garden had been the start of his good luck too, with her knowing Maguire was mad about dogfights. Between that and the bottle, and seeing her reflected in Scanlon's moonstruck look, he found himself kindled.

"You still eating oysters?" he asked her, grinning.

She shot him a glance full of hope, and then looked vaguely over his ear as if she wasn't sure of his meaning. She smiled though, so he'd know that whatever it was, she wasn't taking offense.

"Last I saw you, you was eating up an oyster cart," he said and Scanlon looked smashed by the news that Casey had an inside track.

She laughed at that, ending in a ladylike shriek she must have picked up from a customer. "I was a disgrace," she said and he figured she'd heard that somewhere too.

Still, he felt like he was tickling her. Her half-pleasure, half-pain drew him on to tickle her more. "Let's see if you can disgrace yourself more tomorrow night. I'll take you to Al's Oyster House. It's two blocks from the beer garden."

"Ah, I'd love it," she said, and then looked stricken, her hand flying to her mouth. "Tomorrow's Saturday," she said.

"What's wrong with that?"

"It's our late night at the store. We're open till ten. And after, I have to write up my book."

Out of the corner of his eye, Casey could see Scanlon watching. It increased his sense he'd missed something about Kitty.

"Tell me your shop's name," he asked, moving in to wrap her up. "I'll be there at ten-thirty."

"It's not too late?' she asked.

"It's the shank of the evening," he told her easily. "After we're back, I'll just run by and catch Maguire."

"That's fine then," she said, her voice weak and impressed.

Scanlon sighed and looked down. Then his hands jerked in dismay as he saw what he'd done to her towel. "Ah, I've ruint you."

"It's no trouble, it'll wash," she told him kindly. There was no giggling or shrieking with Scanlon, Casey noticed. Of course, they'd been neighbors in the same tenement for years. She knew the Scanlons lived like pigs, Mrs. Scanlon with the drink, and the old man on the docks fighting niggers for his chance to unload the banana boats. Still, she was easy and nice with him, the same as she'd behave with little Jimmy Donahue. Not that Scanlon wanted that, the way he was ready to hurl himself in the river over dirtying her towel. Yet it was how she was with Scanlon that made her seem a real girl. Her thin face and small bones with no flesh on them didn't seem drawbacks then so much, but just the way Kitty Donahue was, hard-working, with her own troubles but keeping her end up, and sometimes her face lit so she was nearly pretty.

It was Scanlon's bad luck if he couldn't speak out. No man could be doing it for him. And it might teach him she was no Holy Queen of Heaven, but just a girl like any other. She wanted her bit of fun at the end of a hard week, an oyster house, a blackface minstrel show, or a steamboat trip to Coney Island. He wouldn't do all that himself because a man could get trapped showing too much interest. But there was no denying he liked showing off to Scanlon how easy it was. He got her shop name and address, and then handing back her towel and bottle, turned, leaving her there, and dragged Scanlon off to drain the Pacific's tail screw.

The trip to Al's Oyster House went so well that almost without thinking of it, he found himself hiring a buggy the next Sunday and going by Kitty's place on his way to the Harlem Road. He yelled and word was passed along by the old women hanging out the windows till she came down, looking fussed, but her hair freshly combed, and without running back to tell her mother, she got in and he geed the horse and they were off toward Fifth Avenue.

It was a lovely day with the heat wave broken and he had a sense of success, trotting between the two fine rows of ailanthus trees, eyeing the rich houses of brownstone, brick and marble. With her listening, he got telling stories about the swells, the stuff his sister Mary had picked up working for the Liggetts. How old Vanderbilt come from nothing, dirt-farming, and then running a skiff ferry from Staten Island. About the great William Astor's looney brother, locked in with his keeper in a walled house at Fourteenth Street and Ninth Avenue. By the time they were passing Vanderbilt's marble French chateau at Fifty-second, he almost had the sense himself they might drop in for tea.

Then a butcher boy from the Bowery came by racing in a cart and he settled seriously to driving till he got bottled behind a lady's victoria as they entered Central Park. After that, there were carriages by the hundreds, gigs, phaetons, victorias and large-wheeled tilburies, with grooms and Negro coachmen in livery. And there was one *grande daumont* with two footmen on the step behind. Everybody was out, the poor in hired gigs and buggies, and the rich with horses so fine he forgot Kitty entirely.

From then on, he saw her often. All through September, they made the Bowery on Saturday nights, and on Sundays went trotting or they wandered up Twenty-third Street, window-shopping, and going into the Eden Musée waxworks, playing checkers with Ajilb, the automatic player. In October the Prince of Wales came to town and, though so much fuss for the English outraged them, they walked to Madison Square Park and stood outside the Fifth Avenue Hotel with the crowd, glowering at the start of the royal procession.

Then, in five minutes, it was suddenly all over.

They'd been rowing on the East River past Kip's Bay and the Hunter's Point ferry in a lazy way, just taking in the sights, Blackwell's Island with its gold and rust trees and last scarlet roses of October, made sinister by knowing that what seemed fine palaces were really the Asylum, the Almshouse, and Penitentiary; watching the fast-sailing, flat-bottomed scows and the sloops and a sidewheeler that went by them. They passed the old Shot Tower, and just north of Jones' Wood, Casey rowed to shore and tied up to the bank. Kitty sat very straight and uncertain and when she moved to get out, he reached over and grabbed her to him.

She seemed to like it at first. He kissed her a few times and she said "No" but he knew she had to say that. He just kept on kissing and mussing her up to get her off her balance. Then she began about his being rough and said, "Ye'll upset the boat." So to keep her quiet, he pushed her against the seat and shut her mouth with his while he let his hands go over her. She started wriggling at that and pushing at his hands. It was the struggle that undid him. She was so small and weak, her fighting struck him as fake. And from one second to the next, he was suddenly in earnest, holding her down and hitching up her dress.

"Tom!" she yelled at that, and raked his face.

He paused in surprise, one hand caught in the snare of her petticoat and drawers. She clawed him again.

"Yer crazy!" she shouted. "Let me go!"

She'd drawn blood. He could feel it. But before he could hit her, she rippled sideways like an eel and the boat nearly tipped over. By the time they'd got it righted, he was cooled off but mad. He dabbed his hand in the river to wipe the blood from his face. It was only a bit but he felt foolish and disfigured.

"My God!" she said. "Do ye think I'm one of yer fancy women?"

He didn't answer. In fact, it was still touch and go with him if he would hit her. Moving in a rage, he untied the rowboat, poled out with an oar, and got them headed home.

She straightened her clothes and after awhile, said: "I'm Donahue's daughter. From your own Company."

"I thought you was the Queen of Sheba," he said sourly.

They went past Jones' Wood in silence. They could see the last of the season's picnickers in the October woods, building fires on the shore.

"I'm a respectable girl," she said, passing the Shot Tower.

"I can tell that," he said, with his cuts stinging.

"Well, what else could I do?" she asked, going by the Ferry.

But by then he was worrying what Maguire would say about his face and he didn't bother answering. At the landing she stepped ashore without his help, and waited while he pulled in the boat.

"Go on home," he said.

"Ye've got to pay off the boatman," she said. "An' when will I see you next?"

Caught between exasperation and the knowledge he'd behaved badly, he set his jaw. She lingered, and then as the boatman approached, he said again: "Go on home."

She whirled about at that, and the last he saw her, she was walking fast across a vacant lot, stepping over broken bottles and barrel staves, as she headed for her tenement.

The next few days, he wore her marks on his face. The gang at the Arsenal thought they were funny, but Maguire was straitlaced about women and he had to make up a story he'd been visiting his sister and she'd flown into a lunatic rage. Maguire looked at him doubtfully, but he knew one of the Casey girls was in the Asylum and it seemed a thing could happen. So Maguire backed off, not liking to pry into family troubles, while if Hanley was suspicious, he kept it to himself.

But once he was easy about Maguire, Casey grew uneasy about Kitty. He knew he'd been wrong jumping at her like that. She had no choice but defending herself. If she hadn't, it could have ended in calamity, her pregnant and the priest coming round having talks with his mother and threats to have more at the Comet with Maguire. Before he knew what hit him, he'd be married with a family coming and the sweet bud of his youth blighted. So he didn't blame her for fighting, though he wished she had shorter nails. What he minded was the scene itself, him lunging and getting his face raked and then nearly upsetting the boat. It made him out a fool. And damned if he'd be that and apologize too. He supposed he'd see her again but he put it off a day or so till he could do it natural. Then suddenly he was swamped by the Lincoln-Douglas elections.

The biggest part of the furor was national and dealt with great issues he only knew from the papers, the South wanting to reopen the slave trade with the African Coast that now was illegal, though there were slavers leaving every week from New York harbor, and no great secret about it. The South wanted a Slave Code extended for the new territories, and if they didn't get it, they were threatening disunion, while the great merchants and bankers and ship owners who traded in cotton were wild, claiming secession would bankrupt them all and turn New York into a fishing village. There were rumors the Abolitionists were smuggling arsenic and strychnine to slaves in the South to poison their masters, and with the South having four million Negroes from all accounts crazy to rise and kill, you could see how the stories got worse every day.

Casey didn't know about that. What he did know was the Democrats opposed abolition. And Tammany being Democratic, they were opposing it too. The thing that was clear was Casey'd be for Stephen Douglas. That settled, he could fill in the rest as he went along.

He already knew about Stephen Douglas. Douglas had been the hero of the Irish ever since Casey was a boy. He'd got his start as a schoolmaster in Vermont and rose to fame as Illinois senator when he'd tried to push through a bill in '49 to give a hundred and sixty acres of public land to any family who'd cultivate them. His stock had come down some since '54 when he'd backed the bill to make Kansas and Nebraska territories. Some said he was doing it for the northern route railway money. And it was true he'd made his fortune, though it was from buying tracts outside Chicago. Four years ago he'd married a Southern belle, and their place was the social hub of Washington. But it seemed a poor thing to fault a man for getting ahead when they'd all do it if they could. Besides, a lot of the talk about demagoguery was just from Abolitionists because Douglas had supported the fugitive-slave law.

The Abolitionists, now, were a cat of another color. Wild-eyed reformers crying over the blacks all the time they were talking up the Catholic menace and how the Irish were low drunkards enslaved by the Pope of Rome. The new Republican party was honeycombed with Abolitionists as well as Native Americans and the remains of the old-time Whigs. So you could scarcely expect to find any Irish supporting them. Their candidate, Lincoln, was well known to be a crazy man. The *New York Herald* came right out and called him that, an illiterate Western boor, an Abolitionist of the reddest dye, who'd carry them all to disaster if he gained control.

The trouble was, on the ninth of October, Pennsylvania's state election had gone Republican, while everybody agreed Pennsylvania was the pivotal state. The big Wall Street bankers had sunk money to save it, as well as Tammany sending out their crack repeaters. Casey had hoped he'd go but he hadn't been sent.

And then Pennsylvania had gone down the Republican drain. Now all was gloom; it looked like Lincoln would take the country. Stocks were falling as the wise money pulled out of the market fearing trouble if Lincoln got in. The cotton brokers were crying they were ruined along with bankers with loans out to the South, and the merchants with Southern credits on their books.

Still, the fight wasn't lost till the sixth of November. The orders from Tammany were to lick Lincoln in New York. Already fake names were on the books and election day the gangs of repeaters would go out with Casey leading the Arsenal Gang to hold the polls.

Till then, they were keeping busy. They'd broken up an Abolitionist meeting in Brooklyn and another in Jersey. Every night they protected their own speakers who were out on the streets on platforms made of boards and whiskey barrels, explaining the Fusion movement. They were calling it Fusion in New York this time instead of Democratic, combining the Union Party that backed Bell with the Squatter Sovereignty Democrats — Douglas — as well as the fire-eating Southern Democrats for Breckenridge. And then, October 23rd, was the grandest procession New York had ever seen, the Anti-Lincoln Fusion Torchlight Parade, with Casey marching in it.

They began on Park Row outside Tammany, carrying Chinese lanterns and blue lights and poles with iron pots on the top burning oil and kerosene. Casey had expected to be wearing his stovepipe and frock coat like Maguire and Hanley, with the new diamond pin blazing in his shirt front. But Tammany had wanted a show of loyal firemen and at the last, he found himself in his red fireman's shirt, marching with the Pacific Company. A fireman was a popular thing to be and the crowds jamming Broadway cheered them louder than the politicians as they passed. But it was strange thinking how he'd scrambled to make something of himself and then when he'd made it, they put him back as a fireman.

Nobody on the curb could have told he was more than that, marching beside Scanlon, both of them in red shirts. Nor did the crowd know that the gang spruced up behind Pacific and letting off Roman candles and rockets as they went, was his own band of repeaters.

At Park Row when they'd started, he'd felt glum, seeing Hanley and Maguire before him in shiny hats and himself just another fireman. But as they swung across Fourteenth Street past the fine brownstones on Union Square, he looked for his sister Mary at the Liggetts. And instead of the servants, he saw a young nob at the open door with a lady beside him. It was the Liggetts themselves. God knows what they were thinking, watching that great torchlight army, the power of Tammany, go streaming by their doorway. But all at once it pleased him to be hidden in his fireman's outfit, with them unaware his own strong-arm men were setting off the rockets that were dazzling their eyes. It fed his sense of power, their not knowing it. And long after he'd swung round the corner and was marching up Fifth Avenue, he was feeling like a tiger creeping up on a pair of lambs.

So the night got better as it went along. Going up Fifth, just as the band struck up "Dixie Land" for the hundredth time, Hanley began to waver like his feet was giving him trouble. He figured Hanley wanted a drink, but with Maguire at his side, he couldn't step out of line. He glanced sideways at Scanlon to see if Scanlon noticed. But Scanlon was busy wig-wagging his torch in time to the beat of the drums and didn't look to right or left. He remembered there was a coolness between them since he'd turned up with his face scratched. There were no actual words between them and Scanlon was careful not to mention Kitty, but Scanlon had withdrawn as though if he spoke they'd both of them end on the pavement. At that, it came back to him about Kitty and his good feeling went. It seemed to him suddenly he'd acted crazy, and all he wanted was for it to be as it had been before the fatal rowboat trip. Never had she seemed so desirable as she did as he went marching up Fifth Avenue in step with the band with the line of lights flowing before him. They turned at Twenty-sixth Street, and as they circled back down Fourth Avenue, he was craning his neck hoping to see her in the crowds pouring out on the sidewalks before the tenements. Everything seemed possible, the priest and church, Kitty Casey in a stylish dress, wheeling his son in a baby carriage. He could hardly wait for the parade to end so he could to make it up with her. Her didn't notice when Hanley stumbled and flung his arms out. And when Hanley went down, he nearly fell over him.

At first they thought it was only a faint. Hanley had been having the dyspepsia lately so that once he'd gone white in the Comet's back room. They pulled him onto the curb and sent the parade along. But when Scanlon held his torch for them, they saw Hanley's face was dull red and his mouth twisted funny so spit dribbled down his cheek and was wetting the wood pavement.

Maguire looked up from where he was loosening Hanley's collar. "Get me a hack!" he told Casey. Luckily, they were at Twenty-fourth which was a stable street, and Casey was back in a few minutes with a commandeered barouche.

They loaded Hanley into it, Casey and Scanlon stuffing him through the hack door with Maguire roaring and cursing their carelessness. But Hanley was a stout man and it wasn't easy getting all of him in without banging parts of him. Finally, they had him loaded on the floor with Maguire cradling his head against his knee and Casey leaped into the double seat opposite, holding Hanley's plug hat.

"Can I come?" Scanlon yelled. But he'd picked up his torch which he'd laid down to help with Hanley and it had caught again and was flaming.

Maguire just yelled through the roof to the driver.

"One Bond Street! Goddammit, get started or I'll take the damn thing meself!" And the driver cracked the reins and they were off, nearly knocking Scanlon down.

As they careened through Twenty-fourth Street and turned into Broadway to avoid the parade, Maguire held Hanley against his leg and kept stroking his hair, saying "There now, ye'll be fine, there now," in a distracted way till Casey feared he was losing his mind.

"You're not taking him to Bellevue?" Casey said, though that was evident with them careening south. When Maguire didn't answer, nor for that matter, seem to hear him, he bent to see Hanley's face. But the passing gas lights were too dim and he could tell nothing beyond hearing a nasty rasp like a dog's snarl coming out of Hanley's throat.

As they came to Greenwich Village, Hanley seemed to quiver all over and Maguire roared to the driver. The hack leaped over the street cobblestones while Casey hung onto the sides as lights went flashing by and he heard the shouts of other drivers. Then they plunged around a corner and pulled up with much cursing and neighing.

"Say we're comin'!" Maguire ordered, and as the driver hurried up the steps of a fashionable little Federal house, Casey jumped out and Maguire lowered Hanley down. Then with his arms about their shoulders, they carried him up the walk, with his feet dragging.

It was a white house, three stories high with dormer windows sticking out of the roof and a wooden door with eagles carved on it and a fine brass knocker, highly polished. All a man could want, Casey thought, and peeked a look along the street as the driver hammered away at the knocker. Trees and gas lamps, more fine houses. Just the place a man should live if he could afford it. He began to wish he'd worn his frock coat.

Then the carved door flew open and a little Negro maid stuck her head at them. She looked scared, as if they were too big altogether, and one of them drunk, so she'd like to slam the door. But Maguire put a ham-hand out and brushed the door back so it banged the foyer wall.

"Get the doctor!" he said.

"He's not here," she said.

"Bring him this way," Maguire said to Casey, leading the way into the study, and they dragged Hanley along. His head had fallen to his chest and the snarling noises had stopped. The little maid danced along after them, not knowing what to do with them.

"Where is he?' Maguire said as they piled Hanley down on a bombazine-covered lounge with grapes and leaves carved on its mahogany back.

The maid was clasping her hands together. She must have been new and none of the other servants around to help her either. They were probably all to the parade.

"We've got a man dyin' here," Maguire said. "Now tell me where the doctor is and we'll get him."

"He's gone up Fourth Avenue watching the fireworks."

"Hurry," Maguire told Casey. "White hair, short man, red face —"

But as soon as Casey realized it was Doctor Francis he wanted, he was racing back through the house and out the door past the barouche driver who was still waiting in the foyer.

He found him standing on a stoop watching the Paterson, New Jersey, delegation march past—a stout, ruddy man with white neckcloth and a crown of snowy hair. He must have been used to rough sorts rushing up for his help, for in spite of the Paterson drum and bugle corps and a burst of rockets that went up so he couldn't make out what Casey was yelling, he came right away and they tore down the street together.

As soon as they got to the study, Dr. Francis grabbed his stethoscope from his desk and went directly to Hanley. He opened his shirt, listened for his heart, then pulled at his lower lids and inspected his eyes. He tipped Hanley's head back so the mouth opened, took a pin from his lapel, and stuck it to Hanley's tongue. There was no movement from Hanley, though, and at last Dr. Francis moved his head forward so his mouth shut and with a curious light movement of his hands, closed Hanley's eyes.

"Oh my God," Maguire said.

Dr. Francis put his hands on his thighs and pushed himself to his feet.

"Tell me what happened," he said to Maguire.

Maguire moved helplessly. "I don't know. We was just walking along, marching in the parade. He was the same as always. Maybe a bit tired. I guess he stumbled once."

"I saw that," Casey said, but neither man seemed to hear him.

"But to go out so fast," Maguire said.

"Not so fast," Dr. Francis said. "He was a big man. He was overweight. He'd had little spells before. I told him to slow down."

"He never told me that," Maguire said.

Dr. Francis sighed. "Well, at least it took him quickly. It was apoplexy, you know, not his heart. He wouldn't have liked being crippled."

"But he should have told me," Maguire said softly. He looked around the room, first at Casey, who felt a chill go through him. There was something about the look that would make a dog howl. Then he stared at Dr. Francis. Suddenly, he slammed his fist on the doctor's desk. "Why didn't he tell me he was supposed to slow down?" he cried. "This way I've murdered him!"

"Now, John," Dr. Francis said.

"Hanley!" Maguire yelled, not to the body but raising his head as if to reach Hanley's soul floating somewhere above them. Casey felt his skin crawl.

Dr. Francis jumped forward just as Maguire fell to pounding his great fists on the desk screaming "Hanley!" He caught Maguire's shoulders and sat him in the desk chair and jerked his white mane at Casey.

"Bring the whiskey. It's there. Quick now!"

While Dr. Francis held Maguire in his chair, soothing him and calling his name to break through the pounding, Casey leaped to the tray set out near the bookshelves, grabbed up the decanter and poured a big slug into a glass standing beside it. When he got to the desk, the doctor had been thrown off and Maguire had pitched the papers and inkwell off the desk. He looked about to wreck the room. So Casey slammed down the glass and tackled him. He was a great powerful man, not yet forty, and built like a bull. Casey had to put a knee in his stomach before he could pin him back in the chair. But with the wind knocked out, he began to come around. As he sat gasping, Dr. Francis held the glass to him.

"Get that down, John," he said.

Maguire looked dazedly at the whiskey. Dr. Francis set it in his hand.

"Go on, John," Dr. Francis said. "It's all right. I'm your doctor."

Slowly, Maguire moved. He belted down the whiskey and Dr. Francis handed the glass to Casey and signaled him to pour another.

♣ 6 ♣

Hᴀɴʟᴇʏ's wake began next day in the house he'd bought his sisters down on Bank Street. Actually, he'd been living at the Fifth Avenue Hotel, a grand place facing the park with fireplaces in all the rooms and a dining room where all the famous came — Daniel Drew, Gould and Vanderbilt, Larry Jerome, Edwin Booth, Sam Tilden, and Tweed. If he ever got the money, Casey planned he'd live there. He could do it for $2.50 a day with four meals, too. He'd walked in one day and asked at the desk. But for a wake, you needed family. They took Hanley to his sisters.

They were three Irishwomen, older than Hanley who had been the baby. One was widowed with her children scattered, and still with old-country ways since she'd not got out in the world much. They'd got her into a corset but the way she was pulling at it, it was clear she'd never been into a harness before. But the other two had been in service and they were polished up a bit. They sat by the coffin, crying and reminiscing how they'd saved from their wages to bring Hanley out of Tipperary, and not knowing who all the people were. Mobs kept arriving and viewing the body laid out puttylike, with the candles burning. To keep Hanley for a Sunday funeral when everyone could go, they had him packed in ice. There was no disguising the sound of it, dripping into the hidden dishpans. It made Casey uneasy, so as soon as he'd paid his respects to the sisters and knelt awhile at the coffin, he wandered back into the kitchen to see was Maguire there.

He wasn't, which surprised him, only some of the Comet's back-room crowd and the Comet bartender handing out liquor and slicing up ham and a great cheese for sandwiches. He strolled to the window and looked out at the garden to see had Maguire gone out for air. But Maguire wasn't under the grape arbor or by the canna beds.

"Has the Boss been by?" he asked the bartender, trying for an easy note. But the moment he asked it he was sorry, because all the district captains fell silent over their drinks and their jaws stopped chewing.

"Not yet," the bartender said. "And haven't you seen him yourself?"

"Not for a couple of hours," Casey said, lying fast, and pouring himself a drink while he thought things over.

He'd last seen Maguire at two that morning, sitting with O'Connor, the undertaker, who also owned the stables where Maguire kept his horses. Before that, there'd been breaking the news to Hanley's sisters, and then when they reached O'Connor's, he'd sent two stablehands to Dr. Francis for the body. While they were waiting, they worked out the coffin and hearse arrangements and O'Connor said he'd speak with Father Cummings at St. Stephen's about the cemetery lot. Maguire was calmer but he was stowing away O'Connor's whiskey at an alarming rate. Casey tried to slow him down, but Maguire brushed him away and next minute he'd sent him packing off home. Casey didn't like to leave, but Maguire wasn't showing his drink and O'Connor was an old friend who'd get him safe home if he fell on his face. So the truth was O'Connor's was the last place he had seen him.

Next day, he'd gone by the Comet but found it closed with a scrap of crepe on the door out of respect to Hanley and a sign it would be shut all week. He walked over to Madison and prowled past Maguire's house, a fine three-story brick with lace curtains in the windows and a horse's head hitching post at the curb. But he'd never been asked in and the idea that the beautiful Mrs. Maguire might be home made him shy from bothering them. With no sign of a carriage, he'd decided they might even have left for the wake. So he'd jumped on an omnibus and come direct to Bank Street.

But now there was no Maguire and with the district captains and hangers-on all pricking up their ears, he tossed off his drink and cleared out of the kitchen to prevent further questions.

Back in the parlor, a shawly woman with a basket on her arm was coming through the door. She looked familiar but at first he couldn't place her in that sharp company with all the district captain's wives sitting around in their best black with their hoop skirts and lace handkerchieves. She took a frightened look around and then set her chin and said defiantly: "Mrs. Donahue." So he knew it was Kitty's mother come to pay her debt for Hanley's help the night she'd gone to Bellevue with pneumonia. She'd brought boiled eggs in the basket for the crowd at the wake. There'd be a lot of Mrs. Donahues in that room before the day was through. For a moment his heart pounded, thinking Kitty would be coming in behind her. But then he remembered it was Wednesday and Kitty would be at the store. She'd likely come by that night. And suddenly he made up his mind to come back then, too. They'd make it up and it would all be as it was. They'd go sailing on the ferry to Staten Island. When January came, they'd ice-skate by torchlight in Central Park. And if it happened he had to marry, well, it had to happen sometime.

Mrs. Donahue looked over the room and spotted Hanley's sister, the widowed country woman. In two shakes, they were talking by the coffin, crying and rattling their rosary beads, and the sister was telling the way Hanley had been as a boy.

By God, where's Maguire? he thought. It was close to a scandal the way he wasn't there. Maybe he was sick from all the drink. Or his wife was angry and wouldn't come with him. She was pregnant, Casey'd heard, and sometimes they got skittery with the first child coming. But sick or not, angry wife or not, he'd have to get himself together, and Mrs. Maguire too, for his best friend's wake.

If Maguire was still drinking, of course, she might be having trouble whipping him into shape. She was young and when they married, she'd probably never seen Maguire drunk. Maguire knew where to get hold of him but with the Comet closed, it occurred to Casey that Mrs. Maguire would have no idea where he lived. She might be praying he'd show up this minute.

Suddenly he knew he must go back to Madison Avenue, walk

boldly up to the fine brick house, bang the knocker and find out what was happening. With Hanley gone, Maguire had no other man close to take care of him.

Before he changed his mind again, he told one of Hanley's sisters he'd be back and went striding out the front door. He went down the steps and up the tree-lined street, looking for a free driver. But it was a quiet neighborhood and the hackneys didn't come through much. He'd nearly turned the corner when the porter from the Comet came limping down the street and waved his arms at him.

He was an old man with bad feet who rarely shaved and often was far gone in drink. Maguire let him sweep up the sawdust and mop down the floors in return for his meals. They tried to keep him off the whiskey though that was sometimes hard to do. But today he was sober. Casey couldn't be sure at first. He looked like some kind of queer bird with his hair wild and his Adam's apple bobbing in his scrawny neck. But when he got close enough to smell him, he could tell he was sober. He was whispering, though, from the extreme of his excitement.

"Oh my God, Mr. Casey, I was that scared I'd miss ye," he said, clutching at Casey's frock coat so that Casey stepped back, Old Jack's hand not being a thing that was ever too clean. "I tried yer place but they said ye'd gone out an' all I could think was ye might have come to see poor Mr. Hanley, God rest him."

Old Jack had no teeth and it took Casey a second to unscramble the sense of it.

"I didn't know who to go to. Herself, ye know, I couldn't do that. An' the fine captains, though they're friends of his I know, still it didn't seem right. If Mr. Hanley'd still been with us, Heaven rest his soul —"

"What is it?" Casey said, seeing there was trouble. For all Jack's blather, he could tell that much. "Is it Maguire?" he asked, grabbing the old man's bony shoulders as if to pluck it out of him.

Old Jack's mouth worked. He'd trouble talking for a moment, but he nodded.

"Is he hurt?" Casey said.

"Worse than that. I haven't told a soul. Wild horses couldn't drag it out of me."

"Oh my Jaysus," Casey said, in a fury of impatience. "What is it, man?"

"'Tis a girl. A young girl, not more than a child. He's got her locked in there and him like a ravin' beast. God knows what he's been doin' to her."

"My God," Casey said, stunned. It was the last thing he'd have thought of with a straitlaced man like Maguire. "Where is he? Goddammit, tell me."

"I let meself in the saloon to mop up," Old Jack whispered. "It's closed, ye know, fer Mr. Hanley, God have mercy on him. An' I hear kind of cryings — 'twas the poor child in her distress —"

"In the Comet? The back room?" Casey asked and Old Jack bobbed his head. "I'll take care of it. Stay away for awhile. And don't say a word, not to anybody."

"They can cut out me tongue first," Old Jack said, pocketing the change that Casey slipped to him. "But it's terrible, terrible. Who'd have thought a man like Mr. Maguire, and poor Mr. Hanley not yet laid in his grave —"

But Casey didn't stay to hear. He was racing up the street toward the first hackney he could find.

At the Comet he paid his driver, then started for the door before he remembered he'd forgot to ask Old Jack for the key. He might have hammered but not knowing what he'd find, he felt he'd better ease in carefully. So he went on around the alley and found Maguire's buggy, the horse browsing on the grass that grew between the paving stones. He swore. If he'd tried the back this morning, he might have saved Maguire from whatever he was doing when Old Jack arrived. Still, if it was just a tart, no great harm was done. And maybe Jack was mistaken. He didn't know if Jack had guessed her age from her voice or knelt down and copped a look through the keyhole to be sure.

He didn't hear a thing himself, though he stood still and listened, only the chink of the bit in the mare's mouth as she went on chewing. He went softly to the back door, felt above the doorframe for a key, and then found the door open. The kitchen was quiet. The range was out, and nothing stirring, with the black and white cat sleeping in the sun beside the windowsill. The kitchen let out on the bar and that was silent, too. He stood looking over the great empty room with the dirty sawdust on the floor still and the rows of glasses catching at the dim light. It was chilly in October without a fire in the white pot-bellied stove. He wondered if Jack could have been mistaken. Perhaps by getting sober he'd brought on a case of trimmins.

And then, in the back room, he heard a female wailing. It was an unnerving sound, soft and hopeless as if she'd been crying and then tired, and now was starting up again. He whistled to himself and felt his hip for his blackjack. Maguire at thirty-seven was still a wicked match; and drunk, he mightn't see Casey as a rescue party.

He went to the back-room door, bent down and put his eye to the keyhole, but he saw nothing except an overturned table and part of a smashed whiskey bottle. He tried his hand on the knob and turned gently. The crying stopped, and he had the sense she was holding her breath, listening.

"Jaysus," he said, and shook the door. "Maguire," he called softly, and then louder: "Maguire! Let me in. It's Casey."

But no sound. His eye caught a key in the kitchen door, and he went over and got it. He knocked again and called. There was nothing else to do. He slipped the key in the lock and swung the door inward.

It was bad, he saw at once. And got worse the more he took in. The air reeked of spilled whiskey, furniture was turned over, a disheveled Maguire was passed out in the big chair in the corner. And the girl, that made a chill go up his spine. She was not fourteen, or if that, just barely, her hair still in braids, and sweet Christ, a lady. His gaze flicked across the room seeing the little bonnet ripped off her, her gloves crumpled on the floor, the torn dress beneath the blue cape she was cowering behind, her face smeared with crying.

"Maguire!" he shouted. And then, fearing with the door open she'd go rushing into the street in that condition, he closed the door, locked it, and dropped the key back in his pocket. She drew her breath in at that and he saw what she was thinking.

"No," he said. "I just want to find out what's going on here."

But she didn't look like she believed him. There was a bruise on one bare shoulder and she was holding her middle the way Maguire had hurt her.

Goddammit, he thought, the man's a dangerous lunatic. He strode to the corner, took hold, and shook him hard till he raised his head and the blue eyes opened cloudily.

"Hello, Casey," he said, his face growing dark.

Casey backed out of range and kept tense in case he jumped him, to be sure he'd reach his blackjack.

But Maguire had collapsed again in his chair. "Drink," he said.

"By God, you've had enough of that to last you," Casey said, and as Maguire frowned: "Where'd you get the girl?" he asked.

Maguire's head came up fast. He turned and saw her on the floor, and something came back. "Ah God," he said, and spread his legs and put his elbows on them to hold his head between his hands so his face was hidden. Casey stared at the black curls wet with sweat. Maguire's shirt was undone, and he must have seen his bare chest with the holy medal gleaming in the hair. He got up, swayed, then steadied and turned his back to fasten himself up. Christ, he's crazier sober than drunk, Casey thought. But he wasn't going to turn ugly. It was only keeping him from dying when he remembered all he'd done. The blackjack not needed, he sat on a table, swinging one leg, and when Maguire turned, he asked: "What happened?"

Maguire stared at him helplessly, then down at the girl, and extended a hand to help her up. She cried out at that, and covered herself with her hands to ward him off.

"Please," she said. "Please don't," and fell forward, sobbing.

So they sat there not meeting each other's gaze and listening to her. But when she saw they weren't going to touch her, she quieted some, and Casey said: "She looks damn young."

Pain flickered across Maguire's face.

"Who is she?" Casey asked and Maguire shook his head.

"Where'd you meet her?"

"Downtown, I think. I took the buggy from O'Connor's and closed up the Comet. Then I headed downtown. I remember I was thinking I'd go to the waterfront."

"When?"

"I don't know. It was dark still."

"It wasn't," the girl said suddenly. "It was morning, quite early. This morning at eight."

"Ah," Casey said, relieved she wasn't gone out of her mind with whatever had happened. Anne's landing in Blackwell's made him nervous about that, with the young ones, anyway. But she still seemed sane enough. Young, God knows, and wiry built, thin arms and legs and her bust just swelling. Her face was pretty, or had been before the crying. She had hazel eyes and pale skin with delicate bones framed by dark red braids, the shade that put him in mind of a good Irish setter. The thought of full breeding made him anxious. Whoever she was, in her bonnet and cape, she'd be missed. Even now, with six hours lapsed, the police in Murray Hill or Washington Square, or even their own precinct that covered part of Fifth Avenue, might be looking for her.

"How did you come to meet Mr. Maguire here?" he asked her. He thought he did well talking in her own language, but she just shot a look toward Maguire, and when he shook his head, she stared back at Casey, not understanding Maguire's silence.

"He don't remember," Casey told her. "He was drinking. You'd better tell me how it was."

"Well," she said, putting her thin hands together and locking them. He had a flash of admiration for her, the way, still trembling, she was holding herself together. They bred spirit and guts into the Episcopalians. An Irish girl would be a dismal heap howling in the corner.

"I'd just come off the steamer. From Utica. I was trying to find my sister's. I'm — I was to stay with her," she said, and then memory of what had happened fell between her and her sister's, and she drew in her breath.

"Go on," he said quickly to stop her thinking too much.

She nodded obediently. By God, they trained their kids well. Even in her predicament, she was behaving like a captive queen.

"This gentleman drove up. I thought for a moment he might be a hackney —." She trembled to a halt in apology. "But he seemed very kind. And when I said where I was going —"

"Where was that?" Casey said.

"The Astor House."

His heart sank. A lot of good families lived at the Astor House to avoid troubles with servants or preparing meals. "Go on," he said.

"He told me he'd take me there. He took my bag and I got in." She paused. "He did seem odd after we started —"

Casey looked at Maguire, but Maguire just dropped his head in his hands again and stared hard at his shoe tips.

"That was the drink," Casey said.

"Oh?" she said, as if she didn't understand. He supposed her family was teetotalers, too. "I felt he might be ill. Well, we rode for a long time. I'd thought the Astor House was nearer my boat landing."

"It is," Casey said. "Broadway and Vesey."

The child's eyes rested on him, large and pure, as if she were asking why Maguire had lied to her. It made him uncomfortable, so God only knew what Maguire was suffering.

"Then we drove into an alley and he stopped. It was so small, with tenements around. It didn't seem like a hotel. But he said it was the back entrance. I wasn't sure. He took me by the arm and pushed me in the door to a kitchen —"

Maguire groaned. It was a terrible sound to hear from a man and Casey saw that the sweat was starting on Maguire's forehead.

"What happened then?" he asked. But at that, Maguire pushed himself out of his chair so it tipped over and went crashing behind him.

"Stop! That's enough now! We won't hear the rest!" Maguire said. And the girl, too, she'd clamped her lips shut and was sitting straight and white, avoiding meeting his gaze. But in a queer sort of way, she and Maguire seemed joined in silent agony.

"Take her home," Maguire said to him.

"Wait now," he said. "You can't just pack the girl home like—" He'd almost said "like a hooker" but stopped in time. Maguire'd given him a look like he'd knock him through the wall. And that made him mad. You'd think he'd had the girl himself the way Maguire was twisting it around.

"If she tells her sister," he began.

"I'd never!" she said.

Casey looked at her with sudden hope.

"But do you think I could go home?" she asked timidly. "I mean, after —" She stopped in confusion and blood mounted to her face.

"Ah, of course you can," Casey said with as much gentleness as he could put in his voice. "And who's to know? If you keep it to yourself. No one would guess."

"But my dress and my — clothes." She'd been about to say "underclothes" and Casey guessed they'd been torn, too. If that was all. The way she moved when she tried to stand up, he guessed Maguire had near ripped her apart. She'd dropped her little handkerchief, and he saw blood on it. Maguire whitened and his features fined, so he guessed Maguire had seen it too.

"Here, let me — to buy new clothes with," he said, trying to get back to a subject that didn't pass the bounds of decency.

"I couldn't!" the girl cried and Maguire went whiter yet, seeing she thought he was trying to pay her.

"Well, then," he paused and with a convulsive movement of his lips as if it killed him to say it, though his conscience made him: "Maybe if ye'd see a doctor."

"Oh no," she said softly. That had been the worst, you could tell. She'd die before she'd let a doctor examine her abused body. Jaysus God, the kind of trouble Maguire ran to, he'd be needing a platoon to keep him out of prison.

"Perhaps, if I just tried —" the girl said, tugging at her dress. Casey had never thought he was chaste-minded, but he found himself like Maguire looking away while she tried to put herself in order. She must have tucked things in here and there, and then with her blue cape over it all, she looked almost right. He stooped and handed her her bonnet and she put it over her hair and then he gave her the crumpled gloves.

"I'll ride you to the hotel," Casey said, and then to Maguire: "If you'll loan me the buggy."

"Take it, take it," Maguire said quickly.

"The trouble with a hackney —"

Maguire threw up his hands to stop explanations. He didn't want to hear what a hack driver might think of a young girl and a man coming out of a closed saloon.

"If ye need," he tried to say, then stopped and made himself go on to her: "If ye run into any trouble —"

"That's all right. She'll be all right," Casey interrupted. Bad enough if she did, either her sister finding out, or, God prevent it, if she was pregnant. In either case, she'd know where to come. No use anticipating and bringing on hysterics.

"All right," Maguire said. "But if you do, just send a note. I'll do anything, anything in the world."

"Ah, she knows that," Casey said. Before Maguire could break out with any more, he unlocked the door and motioned her through. He didn't like leaving Maguire. The way he was feeling, he might put a bullet through his head, if only to finish the creature that came crawling out of him when he was drunk.

"You'll go home now?" he asked and Maguire nodded absently. "She'll be wondering where you are," he said, and Maguire gave him a terrible look. The other one, the fine captain's daughter, was walking up and down in their home wondering what had become of him. Casey didn't envy him that homecoming. If she wept, it would be worse than if she met him hot-eyed. But home he had to go, with the monster still inside him.

"I'll be meeting you later at Hanley's," Casey said. There was the wake to be gone to, too. Maguire had forgotten about that. He ran his hands through his hair and looked around for his top hat. There was a half bottle on a table but at least he didn't cast a look at that.

"Wait, ye may need dough," Maguire said and felt in his pockets. But wherever he'd been before picking up the girl, they'd cleaned him out.

"I have enough," Casey said.

Though the man was a lunatic, he found his heart twisted to leave him standing there, the liquor souring his stomach and with that fearsome afternoon stretching before him. But Maguire had done it to himself. And the girl had to be got home. There was nothing to do but turn his back.

He headed the mare to Broadway and they went a mile or so in silence. Females were strange creatures, Casey was thinking. After all she'd been through, she was already drawing into herself like the model of propriety, her legs close together beneath her skirts with her cloth shoe tips peeping out. Her hands in her lap clutched her little reticule as she watched out the buggy at the sights, the gaudy signboards, the red brick houses with green area railings, taking in the omnibuses, the jostling hackney cabs and coaches, the gigs and tilburies with their coachmen in livery.

On one corner, a Republican speaker was mounted on a crate haranguing a crowd. He carried a sign reading LINCOLN AND HAMLIN. Here and there, they passed burned-out old barrels from rally bonfires. She was sitting so straight and proper, no one would guess what had just happened to her, as if at any moment, she might turn and ask him in a sweet child's voice what he thought of election prospects. He wondered was her family Abolitionists. With her ignorance of liquor, they were probably Drys and Abolitionists.

Still, she was so good and uncomplaining, and her courage so grand, he wanted to say something, just to show he sympathized.

"What's your name?" he asked.

She looked at him, wondering, and he felt she might not want him to know her name. But before he could tell her he understood that, she answered: "Victoria Livingston."

He felt she'd jabbed him in the stomach, till he realized if she came from Utica, it coudn't be the social Livingstons, though maybe a cadet branch.

"How old are you?" he said, just to get his mind off the Livingstons.

"Thirteen."

"Ah God," came out of him before he knew he had spoken.

She studied the strings of her reticule closely as if to keep herself from crying. They were just passing the little park and drawing up before the Astor House, and he didn't want her crying. Luckily, just then a barrel organ started up and she saw the dancing monkey. She nearly smiled and relief flooded him. Next second, the doorman helped her down, and she ran across the pavement and vanished inside while he found himself tipping his plug hat after her.

He was already whipping up the horse before it came to him she'd forgotten her luggage. He reined in the horse and began look-for it frantically, pulling up the lap rug, but is wasn't there any-where. Yet she'd had to have it, traveling from Utica. He even thought she'd mentioned it, probably an ordinary carpetbag with her nameplate on it, too large to get lost right beside them in the buggy. Of course, someone might have pinched it while she was inside the Comet. Yet it wasn't likely. The neighborhood thieves knew Maguire's buggy. He wondered had she grabbed it up as she left but he didn't think she had. He brought back the image of her running across the pavement into the Astor House.

Then something about the memory caught him, her litheness, the quick movement, when only a short time before she'd moved with such difficulty as if Maguire had done her damage. He frowned, not thinking really. It was just a queer thing, together with the missing carpetbag. On impulse, he shouted at a stableboy loitering by the barrel organ, threw him the reins to hold, jumped down from the buggy, and ran into the Astor House to ask did she lose her bag.

The lobby was a fine place with deep carpets and shining glass globes clustered in the chandeliers, with carved mahogany chairs, and grand ladies and gentlemen sitting in them. He felt too rough to be in a place like that so his hand flew to his hat and he took it off quickly. And perhaps he did look out of place for all his frock coat and narrow pants, since next instant a smooth-looking assist-ant manager was at his side saying could he help.

"Ah no, I just wanted —" Casey said. And then, fearing the man would think he had no business there at all, he added: "Did Miss Livingston go up already? I wanted to ask about her bag."

"Miss Livingston?" the man said, looking so bland and distant that Casey yearned to muss him up.

"Miss Victoria Livingston. She's come to stay with her sister. But I don't know the sister's name. She might be married." At that, the manager looked as if he were making it all up and he blurted: "The young girl who just came in, bonnet and blue cape. I think she's lost her bag."

"Oh yes," the manager said. "I saw her. But she's not staying here."

"Her sister," Casey started.

"She asked for no one. She didn't come to the desk. I offered to help but she said she'd made a mistake."

"A mistake?" Casey said in surprise. "What did she say then?"

"Why, nothing," the man said. "Nothing at all. She just turned and went out."

"Out? With me there all the time?"

"Not the front. Out the side way."

Casey stared through him, not seeing him, his thoughts like the wake of a paddlewheeler dragging in the river water and churning it up. Maguire came drifting to him, and the young girl Maguire had forced when he couldn't remember, her lady ways, Maguire's conscience, and then the missing bag and the quick, active way she'd run across the sidewalk.

"By God!" he said. It might be a mistake about the hotel or it might not. She'd surely accepted no money. But if she came back to Maguire after her sister threw her out, or maybe finding herself pregnant, there was nothing Maguire wouldn't give her to make it right. "Is that the door?" he asked. And before the man could answer, he threw himself across the lobby and sprinted through it.

He ran halfway up Vesey Street before he realized she was gone and proceeding on foot, he'd no chance to catch her. So he rushed back to the front of the Astor House, took the buggy from the stable boy, and whipping up the mare, tore up Vesey again, narrowly missing upsetting a lady's light phaeton.

At Church Street, he pulled in hard, and with a dray wagon driver behind him cursing, looked up and down the street without sighting her blue cape. He drove a block, stopped, examined a stream of hackney cabs, ladies with parasols and rich cloaks with gaudy hoods, shopgirls. A factory girl sent out on an errand passed by, her shawl drawn around her thin body, and then a rich merchant. Behind him, the traffic was piling up and a cart filled with pineapples just off a West Indiaman jostled his horse, making it shy.

Then, way down Barclay, he saw a blue cape like hers getting into a hackney barouche. He wasn't sure it was hers, but the shade was very like. He whipped up, passed the pineapple cart, and fell in two cabs behind.

They cut across Broadway and dashed up Park Row leaving the brick houses and trees and bright doorplates behind them. He had to make his mare step to keep up with them. Once he nearly ran down a street urchin selling newspapers and with the boy running beside him yelling obscenely, he nearly lost them altogether.

As the neighborhood got poorer he frowned. Sharp she might be, and up to some kind of games, but young she was, too, and a lady, nicely brought up. She'd not venture into the fourth ward waterfront. Yet the tenements got worse as the network of streets tightened. Women screaming from the windows, barefoot children on the pavement, an old sow pig chewing on a cabbage stalk held him up, and he almost turned back in discouragement, for the blue cape in the cab before him was only that, a blue cape. Some light woman could be getting out if the barouche ever stopped.

Suddenly it did stop, pulled up before a junkman's shop, and he drew up hard and watched the barouche door open. And, by God, it was Victoria got out. She looked a bit different. Her bonnet was off, swinging on her arm, and her hair was out of braids hanging down her shoulders, but the right red setter color. Except for the bonnet, she was the same, a frail child, maybe thirteen as she claimed, all thin arms and legs and delicate, fine bones.

She paid off the driver, digging in the reticule with her narrow child's fingers. Then, getting up on the curb, she nearly slipped on a fish head that was lying in the street. She bent over in a flash, her skirts went flying up, and in a second her cloth shoes were off, her stockings peeled too, and stuffing them into the reticule, she went swinging barefoot up Water Street.

"Sweet Jaysus," he whispered. There was no hope for it — if the horse was stolen on them, Maguire could maybe get it back. He wound the reins about his buggy whip holder and lowered himself to the street after her.

For two more blocks she led him past pawnbrokers and ragpickers' cellars, saloons and bucket shops with men lurching out carry-

ing stale beer by the bucketful. His own shoes were slippery with
fish and cabbage leaves and offal thrown out of the windows. They
went by the cockpits and ratpits where what went on made Devlin's
look like Sunday school, past tumbler dives where the stale beer
was mixed with whiskey so potent the drinker grew drunk the instant he swallowed it. In front of one tenement, two men were
fighting on the pavement and a gang of children were watching
with hard, experienced eyes. But she simply went into the street
and circled around them without looking, then came back to the
sidewalk before a row of sailors' boardinghouses.

She passed stale beer dives in the basements that once were the
low gable-roofed houses of Dutch burghers and Revolutionary aris-
tocrats, but now beer-soaked women were hanging out calling at
him. Already, by late afternoon, the accordions were starting up inside the saloons. He heard a cracked piano and a screeching like a
parrot behind a swinging door. He craned his neck to see in. And
when he looked around, she'd vanished.

He stood and gazed around him cautiously. It was still light. At
night, dressed the way he was, he'd last about five minutes. But he
was a powerfully built man and he looked rough, even in the plug
hat with the diamond on his front. He'd been uneasy about it in
the Astor House, but now he moved his thick shoulders inside his
coat to free his arms, touched his hip for his blackjack, and settled
into the wary swagger that warned he was a gang fighter.

The last place he'd seen her was outside a counter restaurant that
wasn't over five feet wide, so it wasn't there she went. Next door
was an oyster saloon and that was where he entered.

He stood in the swinging doors with the daylight behind him
and took it all in, the bar with sailors standing, a marmoset on one
man's shoulder, the big mirror and plug ugly behind the stick, a
few tables toward the rear, dirty sawdust on the floor, pictures of
Tom Hyer and Yankee Heenan on the walls, and a big colored
picture of Stephen Douglas decorated with red, white and blue
crepe paper, and stuck in one corner a small American flag. But if
she'd come in at all, she'd gone up like smoke.

They weren't liking the look of him either. Hard faces turned to him. He glanced over the bartender, saw the bouncer in back, and at one table, a group of beggars, the blind man with his patch off, staring at him boldly, the cripple's fingers crawling toward his crutch in case he'd need a weapon. There was no sense asking about the girl. If he went in at all, he'd be hit on the head and wake up shanghaied.

Then, just as he moved to back out, a man turned from a table to see what was causing the stillness and let out a cry. "Casey!"

It was Horse Masterson with a crooked-nosed stranger. They both seemed to be regulars, for as he went over and joined them, the hard looks slid away and the bartender went back to drawing beer. Even the bouncer in the back relaxed.

He shook hands with Horse and sat down. The stranger coughed and smiled. Casey guessed it was Horse's fence and they'd been cooking a job. Maybe more burglar tools had changed hands for Horse was looking pleased.

"Did a girl come in just now? Blue cape and red hair?" he asked, not beating around the bush with an old Arsenal member.

"Sure," Horse said. "That's Claire."

"My God, how old is she?"

Horse looked embarrassed. "Well now, I never asked. Course a lot of these hoors is young these days. They got an oyster house full of them over at Chatham and William, run from nine years to the oldest is about fifteen."

"But the way she talks. She sounds real."

Horse considered. "Maybe not to some swell she wouldn't."

Casey's face darkened and Horse said quickly: "She can put it on good, though. She was rescued by the Five Points Mission fer a year. I guess she learned it there, watchin' the ministerin' angels. But she couldn't take all that psalm-singin', so she come back to the waterfront."

"I got to see her," Casey said.

"Why not?" Horse said, getting up. "I'll tell the bouncer you're straight and get him to take you in."

"But if she cuts up, I don't want to get kilt here."

"How's that?" Horse said, grinning.

Casey considered. There was no way around it. And Horse was part of Maguire's machine now as an election repeater. He told him fast, and Horse nodded.

"She's got her nerve. But that's past being funny, playing games on a man like Maguire. The saloon here had no part of it."

"I'm not saying that," Casey said.

"They don't want trouble. They been contributing regular."

"If you say so," Casey said. "But I still don't like the look of that bouncer."

"Ah, if that's all. Come along," Horse said. "Name's Mike Farrell. He's been Tammany for years, was sent to Philadelphia repeating in the October elections." Horse rose. "I'll introduce you. And then just go on through. The last room on the right."

"Pleased to meet you," Casey said, shaking hands again with Horse's fence. He pushed back his chair and followed Horse to meet Mike Farrell.

She had her dress halfway over her head when he flung open the door. An old blonde slut was on the bed in the corner and when she jumped up with a shriek, Claire whirled and poked her head out the neck of her dress again. She froze, then started yelling for the bouncer and tugging her dress down. The blonde grabbed a bottle but before she could break it and go for him, Casey jumped her, broke her hold on the bottle and kicked it under her bed. Then he kicked open the door, shoved her out in the hall, and slamming the door shut, he leaned his back against it.

Claire stopped yelling at that and they both stood listening as the blonde rushed up the hall still screaming murder. Next moment, there was silence as Mike Farrell stopped her. Claire's gaze flickered. She waited but Mike didn't come charging in. There was more silence as she thought it over.

"Hello, Victoria," Casey said, still not moving.

She looked at him steadily, the great hazel eyes pure, and for a moment he thought she was making up a story of how she got waylaid again on her trip from Utica. Then, with no warning, she was on him like a cat, trying to scratch his eyes and get past him out the door.

She took him by surprise and had him going trying to scrape her off him. Then he grabbed her thin wrists, pulled them down, and belted her across her cheek. She screamed and he picked her up and threw her over his shoulder like a sack of coffee and before she'd time to start clawing his back, he pitched her on the blonde's bed. The words that came streaming out of her were nothing like Victoria. She twisted sideways and scrambled under his arm, but he caught her with his other hand and slammed her back on the mattress. Then he pinned her down by her shoulders and when she tried to knee him, he lay flat on top of her. She was finished then, and knew it. She went limp and stared at his face above her.

"That was wicked, the trick you played on Maguire," he got out, still breathing hard.

She returned his gaze, unwinking, like an animal in a trap waiting its chance to slip out.

"He's having a bad time right now, figuring he ruined a nice little girl."

Her eyes changed at that as thought slipped through them. "I'm only thirteen," she whispered. She couldn't talk much louder; he was pressing the air out of her. Somehow their position was beginning to have its effect on him. He felt himself harden, pushing up against her stomach. She felt it, too, and didn't like it. She tried again to twist away but he held her down with one hand and began to unbutton her dress.

"Is that so?" he said. "Let's have a look and see." A button resisted him and he pulled the rest of the dress down by ripping it. As he pulled away from her to peel the dress off, she got the air to cry out and her face blazed with rage. She tried again to call for Mike and he said: "Ah stop that. He's not coming."

Then as she sprang off the bed, he put one arm about her waist, and stripped the drawers off her.

"Now let's talk it over," he said, tossing her back on the bed, rolling on top of her as he freed himself from his pants. He kicked her legs apart and holding her down, thrust himself right into her.

She yelled. She'd had no chance to move about and protect herself and it was true she was young and built small. Once in, he settled down, just holding still in her while he looked her over naked. Her breasts were small, barely swelling, with no brown rings about them yet like the older whores he'd had. He rolled a nipple between his fingers and made it stand up, then crossed his hand over and pulled at the other.

"Hurry up and get it over," she whispered. "You're too heavy."

"Am I now?" he said cheerfully. "First I think I'll ask some questions."

"Later," she said, but he just went on playing with her. When she twisted to make him lose his head, he dug in deeper so she lost her breath again, and put her head back helplessly. He took hold of a handful of the red setter hair and examined it. It was in truth a lovely color. He played it over her breasts and then felt them through the screen of it.

"Where'd you pick Maguire up?" he asked.

"Stop that," she said. "Ah, please now, hurry and get off. We can talk then." But he shifted his weight so he was heavier and waited, and at last she saw the quicker she answered, the sooner he'd be through.

"Right here on Water Street," she said. "He was driving along looking which place he'd go into. I hailed him and he stopped. It was a straight deal at first. But he didn't want to come in. He didn't like the look of the saloon."

"Or you saw he was drunk and saw his diamonds and figured it might be a bit of blackmail."

"No! At first —" He moved again and she hissed, "All right, it's what you say."

"You asked did he have a place. And swung right into the buggy and on to the Comet." She nodded. "What time was this?"

"Three o'clock."

"Not eight in the morning with you fresh off the boat."

"No. Three. Now are you done?"

"You pull these jobs much?"

"No, I never —" He put his hands beneath her and pulled hei tight to him and she gasped and cried: "Yes, I do! If I can. I have to live."

"You live here."

"On sailors and thugs. What do you think they pay? Do you

want me to die here? A worn-out old tramp like that blonde you
threw out?"

He looked at her thoughtfully, seeing the fine, light bones and
the clear skin, and the anger about Maguire started to fade. "How
long have you been doing this?" he asked.

"Not a year. Look, I told you what you wanted. I told the truth.
Leave my life till after. I swear to God you're killing me. Just give
me room, let me breathe, and I'll show you a good time."

"I'll bet you will, too," he said. "Tell me first — how much did
you roll Maguire for?"

"Not a penny!" she said and then as he moved she went on
quickly: "It's under the mattress on the other bed. Two hundred
dollars. Take it! Ah my God!" And she turned her head on the
counterpane and started to cry.

"I'll take it when I go," he said, and let her lie back. It crossed
his mind he'd like to take the dough and leave it at that with her.
But he'd gone too far to be able to stop. He wasn't mad any more,
though, nor had the wish to hurt her. He drew the long red hair
over her while he rode her easy but still not quick like she'd
wanted. He hoped for more from her than just her tight, cold face.
And after a bit, she saw that and turned to him. He wasn't sure if
she was putting on, but she moved with him and talked to him. At
the last, she was coaxing and tossing herself at him till he did lose
his head. It seemed to him he felt a shudder deep inside her and he
held her thin body tight, but he was too far gone himself to take an
oath on it.

He put his head on her heart and while he lay panting and the
sweat sprang over her, he heard her pulse going fast, but that could
be just the exercise. He liked her, though. Even if she'd been putting on a whore's show. Perhaps it was the chase she'd led him, and
the relief about Maguire, but it was the best he'd ever had. When
she pushed his chest with her palms, he rolled over and lay studying her.

It was amazing the child she looked — sweet, clear eyes and the
moist bloom of her flesh, with the little collarbone showing above
the blue cape she'd pulled over her when he moved. There was a
bruise on one shoulder. He wondered had Maguire given it to her,

or was it one of her other customers. Now it was over, she had such a chaste look it was hard to believe she hustled in a cheap oyster saloon. He recollected how he'd touched his hat to her as she'd run in the Astor House. It was a tribute pulled from him by gentle blood and breeding. He grinned, remembering it, and she looked curious but wouldn't give him the satisfaction of asking. Still, she had all the signs that his mother said went with the gentry — narrow hands, bird-boned wrists, thin fine nose. He reached down and picked up her foot and inspected it. Beneath the grime, he saw it was narrow with a high arch. His mother was mad over high arches.

"Where'd you come from?" he asked.

"My mother wasn't married," she said, frowning. "Her father threw her out when I was to be born. He was a judge in Kingston, Jamaica. The West Indies. My father was a married plantation owner. He sent my mother to New York and for years we lived in a house in Greenwich Village. With two Negro servants, a victoria, and two bay horses. I went to convent school. Then suddenly, my father died. He was thrown from a horse. Without making a will. And the income stopped —"

"When was this?" Casey asked.

"A year ago," she said. "We moved to a small hotel. The servants stayed with us but we were starving. My mother fell ill and the doctor came one night, and right there, in the sitting room, and my mother dying in the bedroom, he —" She paused and turned her head, her voice thickening with the memory of it.

"And when was it the Mission picked you up off the streets?" he asked.

She turned her head sharply. "Mission?" she asked.

"The Five Points Mission. You was a rescued girl there. Scooped up from the streets dirty with no shoes. Two or three years back," he said. He wasn't sure about being dirty and shoeless, but it was a good guess. The Mission grabbed up the worst as a matter of pride. "Then you run away from there on account of the psalm-singing."

"Ah," she said, with the same convent girl gaze he was getting to know. She smiled. And next, she threw her head back, flinging her arms above her hair and laughing wildly. He watched the curve of her throat, long and so fair-skinned he could see the blue veins in it. He was afraid she'd go into hysterics and laid his palm on her the way he'd quiet a high-strung horse.

"Was they Irish, your parents?" he said.

"Scofield." She stopped laughing. "English. My name's Claire Scofield."

"That can be Irish," he said.

"Can it?" she said, frowning. She hadn't known that, and he wondered had she picked out the name, too, like she'd picked out Livingston, both names that made him think of silverware, cut glass, and great gilt mirrors.

The chances were there was drink at the back of it, a father run away and a mother that drank, having five or six children and renting one corner of a cellar room. She might have done tobacco stripping at six, sitting on the damp floor while the older boys brined and sweetened the tobacco before they stemmed it. And another kept the knives of the cutting machines clean with sponges dipped in rum. He'd seen the children like that, with the tobacco lying in piles on the floor and under the table at one end where the cigars were rolled. They worked ten hours a day. The chances were she came from that, or a twine factory, or sewing on buttons, matchmaking, feather-cutting. They could do all that by six.

Why not run away, live on the hay barges or curl up in coal boxes with boys like Horse Masterson. And then the Mission and the quick eyes watching how the visiting ladies looked, the ears hearing how they spoke, the swift brain wanting all they had, but the mission life too dull after the years of wild street freedom. He could see all that. He'd done the wanting part himself, though he'd not started so low with his father a veterinary.

He was lying on his side dreaming, so he didn't hear her at first and she had to repeat it: "Would you set me up in a room so you'd have me to yourself?"

It surprised him so, he laughed. She was a child still.

"Ah, I'd like that," he said. "But I'm a poor man, not Maguire." Mentioning Maguire reminded him he was due back at the wake and he rolled over, got up, and fastened his pants again.

"It wouldn't cost you much," she said, rolling over on her stomach and watching him comb his hair with his fingers and grab up his stovepipe from the floor.

"I'll be back, though, to see you," he said. He went over to the other bed, pulled back the mattress, and stuffed Maguire's roll in his pocket. She must have fumed to see the money go that she'd spent the whole night earning. Relenting, he pulled it out again and peeled off two tens and let them flutter down on her.

She got up then, ignoring them, and pulled the blue cape tight around her. "You won't see me here if you do," she said coldly.

"Where will you be?" he asked. He thought and pulled out another ten. Maguire was lucky seeing any of his money at all. But she ignored that ten too.

"Back to the Mission," she said, and as he looked at her in surprise, she said: "Isn't it better than here? Take a good look around."

He turned and took a look at the room. Even by the dim light of the gas jet, he saw the dirty counterpane, the broken window pasted up with old newspaper, the pitcher with a crack in it sitting on the battered bureau beside a Stephen Douglas button. With bugs in the bed probably. Thinking about it, he itched. And drunk sailors were no bargain. Not to mention Horse Masterson.

"Or I might go to Mr. Brace and get sent to the West."

Charles Loring Brace was the head of a society to ship homeless children West to help out farm families. "And is some farmer's wife going to like it, you waggling your tail around her kitchen? While her husband's wondering how he'll get you to the barn?" he grinned.

"I don't look like that," she said.

That was so. Maguire knew it to his cost. She could probably go West. Though the life was hard, he'd heard, and she'd likely be back after a year or two, as she'd come back from the Mission. Still, he didn't like the thought of never seeing her again. Or if he did, then years later, painted up, with her clean jaw-line blurring.

In the instant that she seemed disappearing in the distance, fading from sight on some Western farm, he pushed his hat back from his forehead.

"Are you going now?" she asked impatiently, still cool about the money he'd grabbed from the mattess.

Maguire was suffering, sitting beside Hanley's coffin and waiting to hear he'd got his little victim home safely. He had to go and he knew it. There were no two ways about that. Yet, he put his hands on her shoulders and rolled the fabric of the cape between his thumbs.

"Ah no," she said. "I've been up the whole night."

"Don't I know that?" he asked, and pulled the blue cape open. It was amazing how so little that was woman yet made his blood run hot. Partly it was her stories. Lies they were, and yet he pictured the doctor in the hotel sitting room, forcing the plantation owner's daughter.

"If you want, get me rooms. I'll be easy to support," she said.

"We'll see about that part of it," he said.

"Promise now."

The wake could wait, he realized, and tossed his hat on the bureau. She was still murmuring, he noticed, as he lifted her from the floor and laid her back against the soiled counterpane with the American eagle embroidered on it.

PART TWO

1863

♣

THE REPEATER

7

I<small>N</small> the morning it showered but then the sky grew blue and white clouds trailed across it. By late afternoon, Central Park had filled with carriages, matched pairs, coachmen, footmen, ladies with parasols and gentlemen in bowlers. There was no sign of war.

But the young Catholic chaplain who came walking south past the reservoir was not seeing the carriages. He had just left the military hospital at the north end of the park and his eyes were still vague with memory of pallid young faces moist with pain and young bodies panting with the nearness of death. He heard the sounds of the sick and wounded breaking the ward silence, saw the whitewashed walls, the rows of narrow iron bedsteads with the white bonneted Sisters of Charity gliding in with pans, sponging sweating faces, spooning out brandy, administering morphine. Instead of the park lilacs, he smelled diarrhea and gangrene. Lately his lungs were full of it.

As he went about the wards hearing confession from the men confined to their beds, he absorbed the death smells. As he wrote letters for illiterate Western farm boys and blond Rebel soldiers fading far from the red clay of their Georgia fields, pain and weakness seeped into his black chaplain's frock coat. He performed the last rites over boys who still had the rugged frames and tanned faces of health and youth, wrote condolence letters to their homefolk, wrapped up their small effects, the tobacco pouches, daguerreotypes, the dented watches. Last week, when the first shiploads arrived in New York harbor from Chancellorsville, a basketful of amputated limbs had stood outside the surgery. Most had been operated on already in kerosene-lit tents hastily set up behind the lines, but by the time they reached New York, the stumps were infected and they went to surgery again. Aides held them down while the surgeons took their scalpels from plush cases, wiped them on pus-stained coats, and bent to work. And then half the operations were ending in blood poisoning. The very air of the hospital seemed to cause putrefaction.

Some died peacefully. Yesterday, he'd stopped by the cot of a farmer's son from Massachusetts, brought in with a wound in the abdomen. The boy lay quietly in a half doze, his eyes shut. Then suddenly, he opened his eyes and looked around.

"What is it, my son?" Dr. McGlynn said. Even though he was only twenty-six himself, the boy was much younger. "Would you like anything?"

"Oh no. I just wondered who was with me," the boy smiled. And in another minute, with no struggle, and still with the same kind of peacefulness, he sighed and was gone.

But that morning there had been a hard death, a sergeant from a Maryland regiment. He'd been doing well till during the night he'd hemorrhaged suddenly and at morning he was hemorrhaging still. The water pail by the side of his cot was almost full with blood and pieces of bloody muslin. He was struggling for breath, his blue eyes glazing over and Dr. McGlynn could hear the faint choking in his throat. A Sister was beside him but there was nothing to be done. Across the ward, a checkers game was going on. A Wisconsin lieutenant was reading Darwin's *Origin of Species*. Through the windows the breeze brought the scent of cut grass and lilacs. Dr. McGlynn lingered by the cot while three doctors and two other patients came up in their stockinged feet. And then with a last spasm and wrenching cataract of blood, he was dead. The group moved away. A Sister bound a white bandage around and under the jaw, took away the propping pillows, and as the head fell back, she placed his arms gently by his side and threw the white sheet over him.

As Dr. McGlynn walked past the reservoir, the Maryland sergeant was in the forefront of his mind. But behind was a great crowd, as if his parishioners spilled over from the hospital across the battlefields. He saw them clad in blue or gray, marching in summer heat, covered with dust and staggering under their loads, and in the rain singing along the muddy roads. In the rain, he'd heard, they always sang. Though sometimes the cheerful song stopped and after a pause, the cry went up: "I want to go home," till it passed down the whole column.

For a year he'd been gathering their memories. He knew how they smoked dried tea leaves and crushed coffee grounds when the tobacco ran out, collected rainwater that settled in the white oak stumps for their diarrhea. He knew how they felt in the wearing, frequent halts when the artillery moved down the same roads and the column separated, the men taking to the woods till the road was clear again; and how it felt after living on salt pork and hard-tack for weeks to take noon rest beside a cornfield, scrambling to pull the ripe ears from the stalks and roasting them above a wood fire. They brought their marches and the battles with them to the hospital and they'd become his memories too, so he felt sometimes he'd lived them. But other times he was only himself, looking at them, all the young faces and hurt, sickened bodies, with a tenderness they didn't feel for themselves. He saw them abandoned by their officers at Bull Run, the rich men and politicians who had mustered the regiments at the start of the war and marched them down Broadway under flags and banners to the blaring of bands. He saw them lying wounded on the field, untended, while the ambulances ran important personages about. And often at night, he came up from his room in the chaplain's cottage and sat in the ward watching the curtains billow and the moonlight filter in, listening to their soft breathing. They were only farm boys, mechanics from the towns, mill workers, carpenters. And yet, in their suffering, they were so gentle and brave and oddly decorous. They did not rail or complain. They lay quiet in their pain, and when they died, they usually went in silence. Their patience seemed to him a kind of holy mystery.

Still thinking of the Maryland sergeant, he stepped from the walk, heard a shout, caught a glimpse of a driver's black face, the hooves of rearing horses. As he leaped back, his blood seemed to fill with a lighter, wilder fluid. And as the horses righted themselves and the smart victoria went past, he felt suddenly weak. There was a bench nearby but he refused to give in and instead leaned against its back.

"Yer all right, Father?" a voice said and he turned to see a park workman was kneeling, weeding shrubs. He was an old Irishman, his hands brown with dirt.

"I'm fine, thank you," he said.

"Yer white as a sheet. I thought maybe 'twas yer heart."

"Nothing like that. My heart's fine," he said quickly, embarrassed the old workman should see a young man like himself turning pale from surprise. He thought of saying he'd been ill, but the illness was long over. He'd had no hemorrhaging for a year. It was only nerves now and he found them shameful.

"Well then, 'twas the shock," the workman said more cheerfully. " 'Twould startle any man bein' run down by a crazy nigger."

"It wasn't his fault," Dr. McGlynn said, his spirit sinking with an old weariness.

"Ah Father, beggin' yer pardon, it was. An' don't I see it every day? They're dangers to life and limb. Give them a coachman's livery, they go stark mad with the pride of it."

He felt he should stay and grasp the chance to talk about the blacks. He might make a dent in the deep, easy hatred. Though like as not, the man's priest would undo it next Sunday. At that, it swept over him he was late and had miles yet he'd planned to walk.

"They'll be coming north by thousands now they're freed, takin' over the city," the workman said.

"No, no," Dr. McGlynn said, but the man had begun orating, the dark, prophetic spirit moving him.

As Dr. McGlynn leaned against the bench, trying to shut off his hearing, he stared at the carriages going by in steady procession. Victorias, barouches, hansom carriages with matching livery and harness, filled with silk and satin women and men who buttoned their waistcoats with diamonds — the war profiteers were taking the air. He was not sure where all the money had come from. Where had it been six years before when the people were starving in the Panic of '57? Suddenly now all this money, so the city had taken on an air of carnival, women arriving at the theater in silver- and gold-powdered wigs, crowding into Tiffany's, and hundreds of new carriages jockeying each afternoon to get into Central Park. It was stocks, he supposed. He knew that, for his own mother had some. And fortunes were made in soldiers' uniforms, in carbines and cartridges. It seemed a dark way to bring on prosperity. The women driving by began to strike him as jeweled beetles feasting on the swollen bodies sprawled across the fields of Bull Run and Chancellorsville. As he watched the gay carriages, they sickened him.

"They're swarming all over the docks now," the old workman was saying, his voice high with hatred. "Waitin' tables and in serv- ice too, the way a white man can't get a job."

"You've got a job," Dr. McGlynn said.

The workman stopped at his tone. It was cold even to his own ears, and he felt his face stiffen. For a moment, they stood staring at each other, the man startled by the priest, the priest struggling to control himself.

"Ah Father, 'tis easy fer you. Ye don't have to feed a family," the old man said, wheedling. "Me own boy's a longshoreman on the North River docks, I know what I'm saying —"

He knew he should stay but tears were stinging his eyes and he didn't dare. "Watch your nerves," he heard his doctor's voice say. "Don't get too tired or too hungry. Be careful not to overwork." He who'd never had a nerve, had sailed through his life, six foot tall and all muscle, and now a few carriages and an old workman had set him crying.

"I didn't mean to set yer back up," the workman was saying.

He wanted to explain. But the explanation would be more upset- ting than his anger. A priest wasn't allowed to have nervous break- downs. Abandoning the field, he turned and fled. He pictured the old workman staring after him, and humiliation flooded him. At Fifth Avenue, he changed his plan to walk and flagged a hack. Giving his mother's address, he settled into the carriage and began the familiar struggle to compose himself. He hadn't said his daily office yet, so he began with that.

When the barouche stopped on Third Avenue, he got down, paid the driver, and then lingered, gazing at his mother's house. It was not grand like the brownstone and marble palaces on Madison or Fifth, but it was quite different from the teeming, dismal red brick tenements only a block away on Second. Two stories of white frame with a sloping attic and trumpet vines already in May starting their climb up the verandah posts, with a grass patch before it and Persian lilacs at the foot of the verandah steps, it was a clean, solid, self-respecting house, even a proud house, with its freshly laundered lace curtains at the windows and the knocker polished brightly on the white front door. There had been another house once, far downtown, but he remembered this one better since they'd moved here on his father's death and that had happened when he was nine. This one had always been a widow's house, full of growing children but a widow's house for all that, a snugly-off, well-ordered, fresh-pie-smelling, rugs-airing-on-the-back-line, priests-visiting-in-the-parlor widow's house. As the older children grew up and went out in the world, it became ever more shining, floors waxed, tables oil-polished, back hedge trimmed. The glass bells over the dried flowers never showed a finger mark. And the life of the house grew yearly more entwined with St. Stephen's down the street. The last three boys all had served at the altar. At Christmas and Easter, the parlor was laid out with their surplices as the washerwoman washed and ironed them. They played Old Cat and chased the fire engines. At election time they collected barrels for bonfires. In summer they stole off to swim in the East River. But the lines were short and tightly drawn. Before they knew it, they were back, their shirts clean, necks inspected, bedding thrown back to air every morning, with homemade bread cooling after school, ready for them to slice and spread with applesauce as they settled down to study. Well-ordered, safe, guided, it was a greeting card childhood. If there had been a lack at all, it was not having a father. And yet, it was easy to imagine him not too far away, in waistcoat and gold watch chain, smiling down upon them from a background of stars sparkling like the studded dome in St. Stephen's, the big, great-hearted Irishman who'd emigrated to New York and fought his way up till he became a famous contractor.

He'd built the white marble Stewart's Department Store and the fine French's Hotel, and provided for them all before being called to heaven.

Standing on the sidewalk, his eyes following the Maytime tracery of the green trumpet vines up the verandah posts, he tried to recall some childhood break in the comfort that might have warned him the world wasn't made of clean white houses and the incensed air of St. Stephen's. He'd seen the tenements, of course, with drunken women leaning out the windows screaming at their men as they staggered from the corner groggery. But that was drink, that was sin. He'd seen the dirty children huddled, sharp-eyed, in doorways. But either his mother or his older brothers had hurried him by in a way that signaled danger, and their threat to him was sin too. He'd seen the Pig Girl with her father gathering swill and heard the boys sniggering, but that was lust. There were baskets for the poor at Thanksgiving and Christmas, but that was comfortably sad and sent from heaven to chasten. Had there never been a sight so shocking, he wondered, that the pretty scenery had torn for him. There must have been. As he stood searching his memory, the surface of his mind caught the movement of a starched lace curtain in a front window, but he brushed it away. All his childhood in his mother's house, he'd been in a state of enchanted blindness. It wasn't till he'd got to Rome that he'd begun to separate poverty from wickedness. *Blessed are the poor,* he thought. He'd always known the words, and he tried to recall what they had meant to him. Vaguely, pastel pictures began to float back of the meek and the grateful, wistful peaked faces accepting Christmas baskets. It was all false and sentimental; the real poor weren't like that. The real poor were bloated faces in tenement windows, young eyes peeking from coal grates looking for a chance to rob, the cheery, hating voice of an old Irish workman saying, "They'll be comin' north by thousands, tryin' to take over the city." The real poor were deformed, their future crippled in them.

Gradually he was aware of some difference in atmosphere and he surfaced to find the front door was thrown open and his mother was standing watching him.

He had the old quick sense of her good looks, her waved, white hair, the widow's black crinoline with crisp lace at the throat, as she stood straight and slender, her hands clasped before her skirt. Eleven children and she looked like she had never married at all. And then as their gaze touched across the golden May air, he felt the warning tap of the foil, the old antagonist's salute. With a ripple of nerves, he walked toward the verandah.

"You're late," she said. "I was worried." Her voice was calm.

"I'm sorry. I walked part way." Struck by a disinclination to let her see his face closely, he delayed by the steps to examine the lilacs. "They're fine this year," he said, but she didn't answer, merely waiting.

At last he sighed, let the spray spring free into the air, and climbed the steps and kissed her cheek. Her eyes were wide and quick, reading his mood, checking his mouth and the telltale muscles beneath the eyes. She did not hide her concern, even made it quite open, so he knew how irritating his being late had been to her. Usually she behaved as if his illness hadn't happened.

"The way you were standing, I thought you didn't recognize the house," she said with a half-smile.

It could have meant anything, a joke, or something with more edge to it. He could not be sure. Perhaps she wasn't sure herself. Perhaps she was simply raw from all his nonsense. For it was nonsense she felt had caused his trouble, boyish nonsense to the point of mischief, a headstrong young priest having wild ideas, baiting his parishioners in his first appointment. By the time it grew more serious, with his nerves gone and the hemorrhaging from the stomach, the way she saw it was so set that his near dying was only a grotesque extension of the rest. She'd nursed him to health herself, sitting day after day by his bed in the St. Ann's rectory, spooning out the doctor's laudanum and ordering custards from the cook while she rolled bandages for the Union wounded. She was tireless in her care. But as soon as he was out of danger, he saw the look return to her face, the exasperated bewilderment of a proud, impatient mother who sees a brilliant son tossing away his future.

And it had happened as she'd feared. As soon as he'd recovered, he was relieved of St. Ann's parish. And all for foolishness, she saw, for pressing abolition in a church of scandalized rich Catholics.

And not his parishioners only, that was bad enough, but with his archbishop against him, the man who'd arranged his education in Rome. He'd argued the pronouncements of Archbishop Hughes himself.

So her last bright hope, the gold-medal scholar from the College of Propaganda who'd received a rich pastorate at the age of twenty-five, was hurled down to army chaplain. He might have climbed far — a bishopric, or farther. She might have mothered a great cardinal. Even yet, if he recovered his sense and remembered his vow of obedience, there might be hope. But he arrived late to tea from wandering moonstruck through Central Park. It was all in her half-smile. Or he supposed it was there. It was hard to be sure. She was a restrained and subtle woman. A half-smile, he knew, was sometimes her way of screaming, her raging — a mild: "I thought you didn't recognize the house."

But he couldn't afford to show her he knew, fresh as he was from his rout by the old Irish workman. Brushing her cheek with his lips, he straightened, hung his black hat on the mirrored hall hat rack, and started toward the kitchen.

"Where are you going?" she asked, and he turned.

"Aren't we having tea?"

She was waiting by the parlor. His heart sank as he saw it was to be a formal visit. She'd decided to remind him he was after all a priest. He could yet fall back on a son's rights. He could laugh, showing off his youth and height, demand the kitchen, and carry her before him by the force of sheer animal spirits. A part of her would be relieved by the return of malechild arrogance. But it would be false, a resumption of a role that had once been natural. It was bad enough for them to be at odds. If he started play acting, too, their troubles might never be untangled. And he still had hopes of that, of one grace-struck hour when they'd see calmly into one another's hearts. So he turned and followed her into the parlor.

Ah, old parlor! he thought, my mortal enemy. It was the same. Dark, perpetually cold, and arranged for the pride of the soul. A woman's confessor should see her parlor. The piano, never played, cruel horsehair sofa covered with black bombazine, rococo carving of vine leaves writhing above its back, belled dried flowers, the dead, cold grate, the cherry rocking chair slatted behind like an instrument of torture. And lace curtains, the badge one is respectable though Irish. He smiled at it but it still brought a chill to his heart. *Not the parlor! I'm your son!* he felt like crying. Instead, he asked: "Where's Cecelia?" Younger than he, red-cheeked and fond, his sister Cecelia was his last hope.

"Her Sodality meets today."

Of course it did. He should have known. She'd been away the last time he'd been invited on a Thursday.

"And Annie?" Annie was the cook, an old widow with a wart between her eyes. When angry she threatened to go West, cooking for the wagon trains. "Won't she expect me to say hello?"

"She's gone to market."

You've sent her out at this hour? he nearly asked. But instead, he stretched his feet before him and accepted her way of placing him. Isolated in the formal parlor, he was not to be a son, nor a brother, nor yet the little master of the house, former consumer of applesauce and oatmeal bread, former champion eater of rhubarb pies. He was the priest, link in a sacred chain and sworn to obedience within a holy army.

"May I help you fix the tea then?" he asked her mildly.

Further irked by his tone, for like most women, he suspected, she despised her men when they were humble, she said: "No need. It's ready a long time." And with that reminder he'd been late, she turned and he listened to her footsteps tapping cleanly along the hardwood hall.

He sat staring at his shoe tips, made a steeple of his fingers, watched the dust motes along a shaft of late afternoon sun that invaded the verandah and the vines. Then he got up and wandered about the room inspecting the debris thrown up by immigration, a marriage and eleven childhoods.

Dried shamrocks in the glass bell, brought over on their wedding trip, the long voyage from Donegal; a small portrait of his father done in one night by an itinerant painter who'd come to the door just a year before his death. It was that picture, prosperous and benign, with white cravat and watch chain, that had been the model of Peter McGlynn in heaven, looking down on his brood from a background of stars. From all accounts he was an expansive, good-humored man, fighting the bustling city, buying contracts, entertaining, and yet straitlaced in the ways that counted with a hard-handed, dour-faced Irishman like A. T. Stewart. Otherwise he never would have been the contractor on Stewart's white marble emporium. Standing before the picture now, he wondered what his father would have thought of the St. Ann's failure. It was a good-humored face. But it was the good humor of action, of high spirits and love of dog-eat-dog competition; the face of a man who drops dead at forty-five. What would that face make of a rash young priest lecturing his Astor Place parishioners? Of conscience-searching over selling a black man's children into perpetual bondage? He was afraid he knew, and sighing, he moved on past a paperweight model of the Crystal Palace, a shell brought back from Cape May, a nugget sent from California by one of his brothers, was it Peter or Daniel? Or maybe David, Frank or John. They'd all gone to the gold fields, and all stayed to resettle in the new land. He wondered was it Sarah McGlynn they'd left. Surely so many children had not fled one family since the Famine. Only Cecelia remained, and himself, a girl and a broken priest, weak ending to a line of gold-rush adventurers.

Hearing her footsteps returning, he got up, took the tray from her and held it while she cleared the piecrust table. He said grace, then the cozy came off the teapot, cups rattled in their saucers. She poured milk and tea and passed the muffin basket. At last no more evasion was possible. They faced each other in the dimming parlor air.

"How is the hospital?" she asked.

"Full," he said. "They're bringing them in still from Chancellorsville."

"I feel for their mothers," she said. "This wicked war." But she was for war just the same. Not on account of slavery, but because secession was the flouting of legitimate government, God being the giver of all authority. Following Archbishop Hughes as always, she saw secession only as the carrying out of private judgment. "I had Annie make up two dozen jars of raspberry syrup."

"Thank you," he said. "They like that best. It's cooling for the fevers. I'll take the jars when I go."

Her head lifted quickly. "Annie can drop them off in the morning," she said. "You won't want to be carrying a basket if you stop by St. Stephen's."

Ah, he thought, Dr. Cummings and St. Stephen's. They were her great new hope to recoup the St. Ann's disaster. Dr. Cummings was their own pastor. It was he who'd politicked for Archbishop Hughes' sending Sarah McGlynn's boy to Rome. He was an old man now, worn out and failing, and his assistant when the end came might take over the pastorate. She'd hinted at it before, but today in her impatience she was flinging him at Dr. Cumming's head. Rebuke sprang to his lips. "And am I stopping by St. Stephen's?"

She considered him. In a mood of more patience, she'd have smiled and withdrawn, then returned by a more circuitous way. But by being late, he'd let her deepen her arguments. Her blue eyes severe, she spoke straight across the table.

"Surely you planned to see him? And he ill?"

"Is it something new? Is he in bed?"

"No, but he's old and ill. The work's too much for his strength. Surely you know that," she said, bright tears springing to her eyes at the shame of his pretending not to understand. "Don't go if you wish. Though why you shouldn't — a fine old man who's always loved you. Who fought for your great chance and followed each step of the way. Why, I used to carry over each letter of yours to the rectory. He'd take out his glasses and read so proudly, as I'd read it myself —" She broke off, shocked to find herself near crying. He was shocked, too. It was bitter, he saw, what he'd done to her. How great her pleasure in him must have been that she wept to recall it now, as married women wept at weddings, remembering the hope of happiness. Confused, he reached out to touch her hand, but she pulled it back. She did not like crying women. And should she be rebuked for her strength, he wondered. Raising a big family, seeing they were sheltered and fed, kept busy and out of trouble, took a tremendous strength. Without it, they might have come to harm at his father's death. But she had risen to their need and it had shaped her into what she was, a stiff-backboned woman with pride her natural weakness.

"I'll go," he said, pierced by the knowledge of what St. Ann's loss had meant to her. She was old now, or growing old. Any day some chill or accident might end her life before she saw it hadn't been recklessness that made him fight, but a vision of God's law that men must be brothers.

But there was no time for it now, when he had upset her. "I'll go, of course I'll go," he said. "It's just that they're busy at the hospital. Every hand is some use."

"This war," she said, relieved to change her private grief for something large. "And now this draft. Trampling our liberties."

He looked at her in surprise. "Archbishop Hughes is supporting the draft."

"I know," she said softly. "I know he is. I was surprised at that. The Irish have been hoodwinked. If they'd known it would end this way, fought over abolition, not a one would have enlisted. We'll all be taxed the rest of our lives to take care of the Negroes."

"Taxed," he repeated, appalled at the turn her thoughts had taken.

"Who else do you think's to support them when they're freed? Those ruined plantations can't support them."

He sat staring at her, words failing. It was bad enough, the fear for money in the midst of the country's catastrophe, though her few widow's stocks were what was keeping the roof of her house over her. But he knew by the line of argument she'd been reading the Catholic *Record*. That astonished him because the archbishop had withdrawn support from it in March when the *Record* had come out for armed resistance to the draft. It was one thing that he should defy the archbishop on the point of slavery. But that an old Irish lady should grow truculent in the other direction, opposing the draft, astonished him nearly to laughter. It was not really funny, of course; the Archbishop was ill as Dr. Cummings, too sick to change the *Record*'s policy, though for years it had been his mouthpiece. And that was the harm. The Irish kept reading it, armed rebellion and all, and many not knowing it no longer reflected Hughes. It might work real mischief.

And yet he could not think of that now but returned to his mother's outlawry. Her stand on taxes and the Negroes and slavery was deplorable, but to see the spokeswoman for obedience sitting mutinously across the tea table —. It isn't funny, he told himself, it's hysteria, too much strain and then relief at finding she was rebelling too. But he felt his lips twitch.

She gave him a sharp look and lifted the teapot. "More tea?" she asked.

First tears from her and then laughter from him. It was out of the question. He lifted his cup and saucer and together they pulled to draw the visit back on the track of propriety.

When he came down the verandah steps, he stood watching the white cat from the St. Stephen's rectory chasing gnats in the late afternoon sunshine. She bounded on the patch of grass, twisting high in the air.

"Come here, Maeve," he said.

But she only glanced at him and then crouched in the grass again. He knew Dr. Cummings didn't want her to be out. The last rectory cat was run down by a dray wagon. He scooped her up and started around the corner with a complaining white cat shedding hairs on his frock coat.

At the corner, she wriggled nearly free, and to catch her before she fell, he lunged forward and ended by upsetting a child. He had the sense of too many things happening at once. The child, who was barely two, a toddler in booties clinging to its mother's skirts, smacked down hard on its behind, and as he knelt to it, Maeve flew off like the wind, a white streak in the evening air, while the child caught its breath, its skin reddened, and it fell to screaming.

"Great heavens, I'm sorry," he blurted, looking up along the expanse of shabby brown skirt to its mother. She was carrying another infant and dragging a market bag so full the potatoes threatened to fall out. And as she set down the bag, it did slide over on its side and indeed the potatoes went rolling.

"Oh my, let me do that," he said. The clerical ejaculations always struck him as ridiculous, though he'd trained himself to say them instead of something stronger. But the bowdlerized, castrated oaths made him feel more foolish. First the cat, then the child, and now relinquishing the child to the arms of its mother, he hurried to the curb and began rescuing potatoes.

"Ah, your reverence," she said, looking helplessly over her shoulder. "You'll be dirtying your hands." But of course she couldn't move, kneeling down as she was to the howling child, and now the infant started too. He saw the two of them with savage clarity — a young priest fresh from tea with his mother and carrying a white cat, upsetting a hard-pressed woman coming home with her poor potatoes to feed her family. When her first thought was of his hands, he felt his face burn with shame.

Juggling potatoes, he came back and stuck them in her market bag, then hovered wondering how to help her with the children.

"Now there, yer all right," she was telling the crying boy. She set him on his feet, took his hand and rose, heaving the infant to a more secure position. But now both her hands were engaged. There was no way for her to take the market bag. She gave him a look half annoyed with herself, but he knew she was close to tears. "It's been one of those days, Father."

"So I see," he said. "And I wasn't much comfort." He picked up the market bag. "Which way do you go?"

"Ah no!" she said, scandalized. "I can't have you doin' that!" But the screaming of the babies drowned her out. He began walking instead of arguing, and she fell in after him.

"Where do you live?" he asked.

"Down on First. I hate to put you out. I shouldn't have tried it with both babies, but nobody was home an' you know how they are. Somehow they find the matches or the lye." She broke off. "Ye'll be young Father McGlynn. Or is it Doctor, now I've heard?"

He looked down in surprise, and for the first time really looked at her. She was his own age, thin and dark-haired, but drawn-looking with one front tooth already darkening as the root of it deadened. He didn't recognize her and yet he might know her all the same. It was his old neighborhood. Trying not to hurt her feelings, he smiled, hoping to draw her out. But she saw through the device and gave a hoot of laughter.

"Ah, ye'll not remember me." And then she stopped. "Though you might now, at that, if you used to chase the engines. Or knew my father. He was a pipeman with Pacific Company."

He cast his mind back. He'd been a great runner for the Pacific. It was his mother's big trial, that as soon as the fire bell sounded, he went dashing after the Pacific. She was afraid he might take up with toughs or flash-men, or be set on by the street gangs. But he was an openfaced boy surrounded by his brothers and usually with a dog, too, so clearly excited and admiring of the shining hand-pumps that he'd come to no harm. The firemen all knew him and kept an eye out for him. And now he tried to conjure back the Pacific pipemen. He'd seen them at a hundred fires, working close to the flames like heroes in a melodrama.

"Donahue, he was," she said. "Frank Donahue."

"Of course," he said. He did think he remembered. "And you're —"

"Kitty Donahue." She glanced down at the children. "That is to say I'm Kitty Scanlon now. I was married three years ago. We cross the street here." And as they wound together past the produce carts and the streetcar working up Second Avenue, her voice brightened as she put her own troubles behind her with native good manners. "I remember you when we was children."

"School?" he said, and then as she shook her head, he regretted it. He'd gone to public schools himself but poor girls rarely went to school. They were needed to work or help mind the family.

But she wasn't dampened. "Ye were an altar boy. An' yer brothers were too. I can still see how you looked in yer red cassocks at Christmas, bobbing up an' down the altar about Dr. Cummings."

He shifted the market bag to his other hand and struggled with a vague guilt. It had to do with the warm incensed church, himself in his red cassock, his white surplice thrown over it, ironed and fresh-starched by his mother's launderwoman, while all the while a bony-faced girl had been watching him, not begrudging him school or his future or his white house.

"Then we heard you was off to Rome. To a fine college with Greek and Latin. Was it true you was made a doctor, just the same as Dr. Cummings?"

He felt like groaning, but instead he nodded.

She steered him round the corner of First and headed toward a row of scrummy red-brick tenements. "An' now I hear ye've yer own church. St. Joseph's is it? In Greenwich Village?"

"That was several years back. I was assistant pastor there. Before I went to St. Ann's."

"Ah now I remember. It was St. Ann's I'd heard." Suddenly, she looked uneasy. "I've not been round to mass lately. It's hard with the babies. An' Scanlon's not much for church."

"You must go for yourself," he heard himself say automatically. If she didn't know about the St. Ann's trouble, clearly she wasn't a member of the St. Stephen's altar society. They kept wondrously informed on the clerical gossip. He wondered did honesty insist he tell her he'd become a chaplain. She'd have known if she'd looked at the insignia on his hat. Though in the first years of the war, so many chaplains rigged themselves up in personal fancy dress, with epaulets and even swords, a woman might miss seeing a small thing like a silver pin. And it really didn't concern her. Then he looked down at her, startled. She'd stopped dead and whirled around.

"Well we're here, Father. I do thank you. I'll just take that now," she said, letting loose the toddler's hand and reaching for her market bag.

"Can I help you in?" he asked and she gave a high, nervous laugh.

"Ah, God help us, it's five flights up. I can't let you do that. An' I've not tidied the place either."

He nearly insisted. The bag was heavy even for him, and with two babies, she'd never make it in one trip. And then he suddenly understood she really didn't want him to come in. Perhaps it was only foolishness about her sticks of furniture, but he had to honor it. He handed over the market bag.

"Thank you, Father. I'm much obliged," she said, and he had the sense she was willing him away frantically. She swung round and began shoving at the front door. But it was heavy and gave her trouble.

"Here, I'll do that," he said, and reached over her shoulder to push at it.

"Let it be!" she said almost rudely. But the door was still stuck. She glanced back and as her face changed to false surprise, he knew what she'd been avoiding was upon her. "Ah, hello, Scanlon," she said brightly. "Yer home early."

Dr. McGlynn turned to see the man who had come up behind him. She must have sighted him down the block and tried to stop them meeting. For a moment, he wondered why. Scanlon seemed an ordinary young Irishman, dark-haired and earnest, the sort who worked on the docks or cut beef in a packinghouse. He was roughly dressed with a sweater beneath his coat. Then his eye caught Scanlon's ring, the large kind that was good in a fight. And the hands far too clean for a workingman's hands. He smelled mildly of whiskey, too, as he'd had the long, uneventful day of the night predator.

"Ye've been to church I see," he said to his wife, bantering. "An' did ye light a candle fer me?" You couldn't tell he minded until she answered swiftly.

"That's where yer wrong, Scanlon. Yer entirely too quick." She cast a look at Dr. McGlynn and he saw she was hoping to pull it off in a way Scanlon wouldn't mind and yet the priest wouldn't know she was choosing her words carefully. "If ye'd look close you'd see. 'Tis young Dr. McGlynn that comes from the white house near the rectory. Ye'll recall him serving at the altar —"

"I wouldn't know about that," Scanlon said shortly.

"The more shame for you then," she said, firing up now she'd decided on what line to take. " 'Tis a fact he'd been sent off to Rome and after years of studying, he'd come back a doctor. He has a fine church of his own now down near Astor Place."

"Ah," Scanlon said, eyeing him. But the mention of St. Ann's had made Dr. McGlynn as uneasy as Scanlon. Yet he didn't see himself explaining his misfortunes to a strange flash-man, or whatever he was — something illicit by the looks of the hands and the ring, a footpad or a burglar.

He compromised by offering: "I ran into Kitty here. Actually, I did — I knocked the baby down, in fact —"

"And picked him right up," Kitty said quickly. "An' got my potatoes from the street. An' then wouldn't hear but he'd see me safely home."

Scanlon shifted uncomfortably. Priests and church might be one thing. But this one had been protecting his family in his absence. There was only one reaction his code permitted.

"Well, Father, we got to thank you." Uncomfortable as it was for him, he tried to change around, even half raised a hand toward his cap in a half-forgotten gesture. And then it didn't seem enough. The old-country generosities were there beneath the New World surface. "Won't you come in now you're here? It's not so grand but you're welcome."

"I'd like to but I can't. I was on my way to the St. Stephen's rectory," Dr. McGlynn said.

"Ah well, now. That's too bad," Scanlon said, relieved. And yet he'd softened, responding perhaps to the young priest's own diffidence. His eyes sparked for the first time with a light close to mischief. "You do come back to me now. Not from the altar, but the fires. Wasn't it you had the big dog? A St. Bernard was it?"

"Only half," Dr. McGlynn said. "The other half was mongrel."

"I once thought to steal him off you. He would have made a grand big dog for fighting. But I couldn't see how I was to get away with it."

Dr. McGlynn hesitated. Then he smiled. Footpad or not, there was something about Scanlon. "He was a big dog," he said finally.

"That he was," Scanlon said. And for a moment they stood silent, thinking back to the fires and the boys chasing after them. It all came back, the fire bell, the envied lead boy with the lamp, the strong men dragging the ropes attached to the musical snuffbox of an engine, racing to beat the other companies. The new steam engines were so heavy they needed horses and the horses were too sensible to race. It wasn't the same; the great days were passing.

They were so deep in remembering, they didn't see the stranger till Kitty started. He wasn't so tall as Dr. McGlynn, but he was burly, with a curiously Irish look, his head held tilted to the side in a way that seemed challenging. He was a ward man, Dr. McGlynn guessed from the hat worn back from his forehead, the diamond

pin in his vest, and the sharp cut of the pants below the natty frock
coat. Nothing first-rate like Big John Maguire. He was too showily
tough to be anything first-rate. He was the strong arm somewhere,
bouncing perhaps in a Tammany saloon or roughing the opposition
at the polls election day — all he hated and disliked, the sort who
made him ashamed for the rest of the Irish.

"Hello, Casey," Scanlon said.

Casey nodded and the odd eyes slid across the little party. "I'm
not keeping you from something?"

Kitty shouted, "Ah now, Casey!" She pushed the toddler before
her. "Say hello to yer Uncle Casey." Her voice was high and merry
but underneath it there was tension. McGlynn supposed he caused
it himself by being present. Sometimes the Tammany toughs liked
the church; sometimes they didn't. This one didn't. The child
pushed against his leg and Casey ruffled its hair but his eyes kept
sliding back to the priest.

" 'Tis Dr. McGlynn, Casey. You'll remember him," Kitty said
placatingly. "He's one of Mrs. McGlynn's boys from the white
house next to the rectory. He's been to Rome to be a doctor an'
now he's got his own big church."

"I did have. I don't now," Dr. McGlynn said. He'd not felt the
need to clear up the Scanlons' misunderstanding but with this man
he felt a danger in not defining himself clearly. "I'm a chaplain."

Casey nodded, his gaze picking out the silver pin on the priest's
hat. He wasn't muscle only, Dr. McGlynn saw; he was quick.

"I know the house. I didn't know you was a friend of Scanlons',"
Casey said.

Kitty let out a self-deprecating shriek. "Friend!" she said and
rushed into her story. There was getting to be a certain glibness to
it, but Dr. McGlynn found himself disliking the man for getting
her off balance.

"As for that," he said, damming the flow of explanations, "we're
old friends." It was foolish on the face of it. Already Casey knew
they'd barely met, and what he didn't know yet, he'd find out in a
shake once the Scanlons were alone with him. But that was only on
the face of it. Really, he was answering the tone. He didn't like
Casey's, and man of peace or not, he was letting him know it.

Casey caught that too. The head tilted sharply, though the hazel eyes were cool enough.

"And when do you go rushing back to the wars, Father?" he asked.

As the bracing shot of anger went through him, Christian love was forgotten. There were no guilts to hold him back, no church obedience he was flouting, not even the sadness he'd felt for the old workman. There was only a man before him like a lion with its paw claiming right to its prey. It was a fine, wild feeling, free from shame and simple.

"I'm stationed here," he said. "I haven't been to the wars." And then on impulse: "Have you?"

Casey stepped back at that and looked him over carefully. It was a strange sensation, perhaps a missionary priest felt it when he was examined by a savage. At last, he said: "No, I'm like you, Father. Stationed here."

"And in a good cause, Mr. Casey?" he asked.

Humor glimmered in Casey's eyes. He glanced down at his waistcoat and the diamond pin buttoning it. "The best of all."

"Are you really sure of that?"

Casey answered by opening the tenement door with one tug of his big hand. With a nervous air, Kitty pushed the toddler ahead and scooted in. Scanlon took longer. If he'd thought of a friendly phrase, he might have said it. But nothing came out and he vanished. Dr. McGlynn was left outside and at the last, Casey turned.

"I can see and feel and touch it. Have you anything as good, Father?"

Before Dr. McGlynn could answer, he'd stepped into the tenement and pulled shut the peeling door.

8

It was after six when Casey left the Scanlons' but the May days were long so the sunlight had only richened and the shadows of the rain barrels and lampposts loomed behind him as he hurried toward Maguire's.

At Third Avenue he was stopped by a horsecar and leaned to see if it was his brother Frank driving, but it wasn't. As he passed the firehouse, they yelled for him to come in but he saw one of the glorious Fire Zouaves was visiting, newly returned from war and still in his fez and blue uniform, no doubt drunk and telling lies about the acres of Rebs he'd shot, so he quickened his step. But then he recollected he was headed for Maguire's where he'd find the same thing. Between a Zouave and a returning Colonel Maguire, he'd almost choose the Zouave. At least the Zouave wasn't throwing himself a welcome-home political ball.

It had been bad enough when Maguire marched off. The crowds cheering outside the Tompkins Square armory were holding up the Third and Fourth Avenue horsecars. The officers' baggage was arriving on an Adams Express eight-horse wagon, the horses all decorated with American flags and the driver with a banner: *Remember Lexington and Concord*. Then a carriage drew up with the new Colonel John Maguire and the crowd went wild at the sight of the hero. He was one of the first politicians who'd mustered his own regiment and got the governor to commission him, bought uniforms and carbines and was off to save the Union. When he'd sighted Casey, he shouldered through the crowd and collared him.

"You're sure you won't change your mind and come?" he said, his forehead gleaming sweat with the excitement of the hour. "It'll be a grand outing."

Signed on for two years, Casey thought, and it would be a grand outing. Perhaps if he'd volunteered for ninety days as some of the men were doing, Casey might have gone. But two years — there was nothing small about Maguire.

"It's too rich for me," Casey said, and Maguire paused and nodded. To do him justice, he'd been poor himself and understood that a poor man with one leg on the ladder would be a fool to jump down and go chasing off to war. Casey hadn't had to claim his old mother was ill nor that his father couldn't keep her. And maybe Maguire's better judgment told him it was wise to leave a man behind who'd see the ward machinery didn't fall apart. He'd be uneasy off warring if he had to wonder were the Republicans or Wood's Mozart Hall boring in. So it was Maguire's last try for him, with the crowds surging about them and flags waving in the air, while next to them two Zouaves were examining each other's revolvers. He'd simply clapped him on the back, then the drum major wheeled his band into line and they were off in a long blue line of Union overcoats, carrying knapsacks and blanket rolls, their bayonets glancing in the sun as they marched down Broadway with a dozen Negro servants bringing up the rear.

Fire engines at the street corners jangled their bells at them. The houses were bright with Union flags and banners were hung from the stores: TRUST IN GOD AND KEEP YOUR POWDER DRY. The ferry building was jammed. The wharves and the ships lying at the docks were plastered with flags and crowded with onlookers, so they had to push their way into the depot. The last Casey saw of Maguire, the boat was steaming across river to the cheering from the wharves, with ringing bells and whistles from every craft afloat while Maguire's band answered with "The Girl I Left Behind Me."

The next few months were the hardest on Casey, for Maguire came back twice on leave, and to hear him tell it there was never anything on earth like Washington that May and June. Dress parades, band concerts and promenading under the lilacs and horse chestnut trees. The streets were gay with different uniforms, for every company had its own. Their unit was quartered in the Senate while others were under the Capitol dome and still more in the House. They marched for their meals to the hotels, hooting and chaffing one another and scuffing with the waiters for their food. The town was one wild political clambake.

Casey nearly changed his mind and went — till Ball's Bluff the next October when the Union troops fell back under fire in the dusk, fleeing down the steep hillside to the water and were clubbed and bayoneted trying to get in the few boats. And by then, the ninety-day men were coming home. A few reenlisted but not many. Most had had their fill of sparse provisions, army red tape, drunken politician-colonels who fled, deserting them in battle.

Not that Maguire was one of those. He was no coward nor did he touch a drop of whiskey in the whole two years. In fact, to Casey's eye, he took to it so well he seemed to have lost his senses. At Bull Run, he had held his ground, calling out to his men who, seeing the West Point Battery send its caissons plunging back through the lines for more ammunition, thought all was lost and broke into headlong rout. That night with the Centreville highway between Manassas and Alexandria filled with fugitives, mounted officers outstripping the privates afoot, and the fields covered with blankets and cartridge boxes thrown out of the wagons to lighten them, Maguire was wandering the battlefield in the leaden rain caring for his wounded till the ambulances came.

At Antietam, he'd been caught up in victory, though the corn and trees were red with blood and the dead lay in rows where they'd stood before the action started. At Fredericksburg, it was worse. He was part of Sumner's center thrown against the heights above. The troops charged six times, and six times melted away under murderous artillery fire, losing nearly half the men and the rest so scattered the river bank was covered with stragglers.

He was wounded at Fredericksburg, a ball grazing his arm, nothing too bad, though he nearly died of measles that swept the army hospital. After that, he came back on leave, saw his wife and infant son and visited round the ward.

There was nothing he actually said or did that set Casey's teeth on edge. He didn't talk much of the war, only groused about Lincoln and complained of the troubles they'd had getting provisions. He'd made a great killing one payday when they'd set up a gambling saloon in the woods, with a thousand men gathered round the tables before the piles of banknotes. He took a childish pride in that winning.

And yet something in Maguire's manner made Casey uneasy, some look in his eyes, as if he'd seen deeper or farther in war than a man could see in peace, which was nonsense. Or maybe there was the hint that while Maguire risked his life, Casey stayed home and took care of his hide. Though it couldn't be that either. Maguire had seen Casey plunge into too many burning buildings with the Pacific Volunteers to think him a coward. But still, it was like a slur on Casey's canniness, risking only where it showed and there was a chance to gain. It seemed to Casey that Maguire implied there was pettiness to being shrewd. But Maguire never put it into words and half the time Casey thought he was imagining it. So they never had it out. The leave was up and Maguire departed, getting back in time for Chancellorsville.

There in the woods by the river road before the brick Chancellorsville House, the ground was strewn with overcoats that the men threw off as the river mist rose and the sun came out hot. The Union right was caught playing cards and sleeping beneath the trees. Attacking with a rush, Stonewall Jackson sent ten thousand Union men flying through the woods before he went down with a mortal wound, while Hooker, in a dream, lay paralyzed against a windowsill, unable to give orders. The woods caught fire that day, so hundreds of Union wounded were burned in the dry leaves. In the fog that fell next night, Maguire blundered into Sedgwick's troops and was carried with them back across the Rappahannock.

Maguire's war ended. His regiment's hitch was up, and they returned in glory leaving the war to the new draftees. Before a turnout of two militia regiments and untold fire engines, their procession was reviewed by the mayor in front of City Hall. They passed through the eastern gate of City Hall Park up Broadway and marched down Fourth Avenue to be dismissed at the same armory where they'd started two years before.

It was over, thank God, Casey thought, as he hurried to Maguire's house. Or it would be over once they got him out of uniform. As he stood before the brick house and struck politely on the knocker, he wondered would Maguire be wearing it that night. As the maid led him into the crimson and mahogany drawing room, he found Maguire staring at the embroidered fire screen and sure enough, he was dressed for battle.

Hearing Casey, he turned and stared at him vaguely as if his mind was a great way off and he was having his troubles drawing it back to peacetime trifles. Being such a giant, and broad to match, with his black hair springing up where his hands had raked through it and his uniform unbuttoned like an officer in a play, his movements carried a charge of importance. Bringing Casey into focus, he struck the mantel with his hand as if to force himself into the present, and Casey hooked his thumbs in his pockets and was damned if he'd speak first.

"Well, sit down," Maguire said finally. "You want tea?"

"No I don't," Casey said. Since Maguire didn't drink, or at least not very often and then he was likely to end in the police station, he took a dark view of drink and never offered it, except to voters. Usually Casey didn't mind but today tea struck a righteous note. He didn't sit down either but flipped his frock coattails and locked his hands beneath them.

Maguire shot a sharp look at him and then sighed and decided not to press it. He sank into the crimson armchair beside the fireplace and lifted his feet to rest on the scuttle.

"You get that bartender?" he asked. It was an extra bartender he was after for the ball that night.

"I got Scanlon."

"He don't drink?" Maguire said suspiciously.

"Sure he drinks. Like an honest man," Casey said in a sudden blaze. There was silence from the crimson chair. Its back was to him, so he couldn't see Maguire's face, and his anger fading, he felt suddenly he was being reckless. Maguire hadn't really crossed him but he wondered now had he stirred him up. He strolled round to the mantel and saw the dark face was troubled. "He takes a drink now and then. But it's sure he won't get drunk on you."

"That's all right then," Maguire said. He was back staring at the fire screen as if he hadn't heard.

Casey took a quick look at the wall clock with the old Crystal Palace on it. It was past six-thirty and he was late for Claire. If it hadn't been for running into the priest, he'd not have gone upstairs with the Scanlons and that had set him back. But business first. He stared round at the room hoping Maguire would come out of it. He examined the red stuffed furniture, the bouquet of wax flowers under glass, the gilt mirror with the frame of grapes and leaves, and at last he fell to studying the picture on the near wall. It was called "Rescuing the Child," a fire scene with a hand-drawn machine and a fireman in red shirt and black fire hat going up a ladder to a smoking window. But he knew it so well that Claire kept floating to his mind and finally he felt like yelling at Maguire to hurry.

"We got Scanlon. And Carroll and Paddy Sullivan, in case of trouble. They'll be bringing girls but they'll be on the lookout too," he said, summing it up for him. "I stopped by the Comet. It's all set. And the last invitation was delivered this morning."

Maguire shifted in his chair, put a hand in his breast pocket and took out his cigar case. He offered one to Casey but thinking he might get away quicker if he kept it brisk, Casey shook his head and waited while Maguire took the devil's time lighting up. But the cigar seemed to help. Maguire squinted at the glowing end and began to check.

"Paddy and Carroll — the girls they bring now. They'll be good girls?" He stopped, embarrassed. "It's not that I care for myself but Mrs. Maguire'll be there with her lot of lady friends."

Casey stared at him, exasperated. Political balls weren't church picnics. Everybody showed up who helped in the district from pimps to aldermen. "As for that, I can't be sure. I can't guarantee their morals," Casey began and seeing he'd stepped into a bad spot, Maguire threw up his hand.

"All right. I know," he said.

"But there'll be no real professionals," Casey compromised.

"Fine, that's all I was after," Maguire said and skipped on to another subject. "The champagne's in?" And as Casey nodded, "The cigars? And the spread?"

"It's a grand spread. All you ordered. The pheasant and the hams and smoked oysters. Everything is in."

"You're sure Tweed got his invitation?"

"I delivered it myself. Not into his own hand —" and as Maguire frowned: "But the next best thing. I came by his office as Connolly was going in. So Connolly was our messenger."

"Good," Maguire said. "That's as good as we could want. Not that he'll come, you know. But I'd like him to feel we thought of him."

"Yet maybe he'll come," Casey said. "After all, you've been away saving the Union for him."

Maguire gave him an uneasy look. He didn't care for irony. And certain things he didn't like put in words. If Casey was tempted to touch on Tweed's war millions, all made in the past two years buying at forced auction and selling to the city at prices ten times higher, or worse yet, the suspicion he was behind the Bounty Ring, Maguire was as good as telling him he didn't care to hear it. He might be a hero, Casey thought, but he had a woman's way of blurring facts. Still, maybe it was as well if it made Maguire tell him to go.

"If that's the lot, I'll be off," Casey tried.

"What's your hurry?" Maguire said. "It's a sad time of day, not yet dark and the light dying. Sit for a bit till the lamps are lighted."

God, he was going Irish, Casey thought, wilder than ever to get away to Claire. With some men he'd have come right out with it, but Maguire was straitlaced except on his binges, and there hadn't been one of those in years, not since Claire herself got him into a swindle.

But while he cast about for an excuse, there was the sound of feet on the hall staircase. Maguire started and threw an arm across the back of the crimson chair.

"Busy in here!" he shouted but the drawing room door opened and Mrs. Maguire was peeping in.

"Sorry," she said. "I didn't know you had company." And then, seeing Casey, she smiled: "Mr. Casey. How's your mother?"

"Fine, Ma'am," he said automatically. She was a lovely figure of a woman and always friendly but he'd never got the hang of her. Her upbringing lay between them, he supposed, the piano lessons and convent school. Her small talk spun round him like spider webs. "How's your mother?" and "What do you make of this weather?" and "What's this new speech of President Lincoln?" They usually began with his mother. Mrs. Maguire had never met her but she seemed to have a great craving for news of Mrs. Casey's health. "She's fine, considering her age." She should just once see his mother, he thought, flinging on her black shawl and flying downstairs to row with the milkman.

"Be sure she takes care in this weather," she said.

"Yes I will," Casey said, feeling clumsier each second. My God, he thought, a man like Maguire must get to feeling like an ape.

But it seemed he wasn't slated for the whole program today. Mrs. Maguire removed her gaze and said to her husband: "I just looked in to say we'd be out in the garden."

Maguire made a quick movement of his hand as if to sweep her from the room. "Wrap up warm," he said. "Run along. I'll be out in a minute."

And then the door opened wider and a baby came staggering in. He was so swaddled in outdoor clothes with a tam-o'-shanter, coat and muffler too, it was hard to get a look at him. Then Casey saw the great head and huge blue eyes. The child fell forward on his knees and Maguire cursed, jumped out of his chair, and ran to pick him up.

Casey knew then that the whispers were true. They'd thought at first he was a normal child, even handsomer than most. But as the months passed and he didn't walk right nor learn anything he should, the servants grew uneasy, with Maguire away at war.

"Ah no, dear, let Mr. Casey see your son," Mrs. Maguire was saying.

But Maguire shouted in to him: "I'll just see them to the garden."

So Mrs. Maguire wasn't admitting it. Casey had heard of women like that who went their whole lives through pretending. Ah God, he thought, that was what Maguire had been staring in the grate about, not playing the hero. If he'd had his time of that, he was properly paid back.

"I'll be running along," Casey shouted.

"There's no need! I'll be right with you!" Maguire's voice echoed through the house in his progress toward the garden.

But Casey thought ahead to when Maguire would come back and have to look him in the face, unsure whether to speak out. A proud man could hate for life for what he might say at such a time.

It was best to go. Maguire'd think he hadn't heard. Moving quick as a cat for all his muscle, Casey turned from the fireplace, sped down the hall and out the door.

He was nearly to Claire's flat in Greenwich Village when he realized at this hour she'd be demanding to be taken out to supper. So he stopped in a saloon for broiled oysters and pale ale. Coming out, he spotted a vending woman carrying a tray of wild strawberries on her head. Claire was mad about strawberries so he bought two splint basketsful, and feeling pleased with himself, went juggling his packages past the red brick storefronts still open, though the lamps were lit inside and the lamplighter was already starting down Bleecker Street. His own ward had fish vendors and the milkman, but never wild strawberries.

Bleecker itself was known as the Street of the Mistresses. Tucked away over umbrella shops and knife grinders were actresses and journalists, poets and old revolutionists from the German troubles back in '48. No one cared to bother about girls like Claire, so the street was filling up with them. It gave him such a bouyant feeling to be strolling through the long May twilight in a free and easy place that before he got to her door, he'd bought white lilacs too, though that got him in a row, the flower man insisting on the new postal currency. Sorting through his pockets, Casey found three different kinds of state charter banknotes and they'd not do, but when he handed back the lilacs, the man settled for two ferry tickets. There were constant barters since the start of the war.

And then, climbing two flights of stairs above the cabinetmaker's, he found Claire wasn't home.

"What do you mean, she's not in? She knew I'd be down tonight," he said to Ruby in a rage.

"Now don't that just beat all," Ruby said in an innocent way that neither of them took seriously. Casey struggled through the door into the kitchen and flung his parcels on the table.

"Mm, oysters," Ruby said, poking at them. "And strawberries. She'll sure like those," she cooed falsely.

He tossed the lilacs in the tin tub that Claire used to bathe in beside the stove. The sight recalled her naked and suddenly he was furious with disappointment. That would get him nowhere, though, so instead of shouting he fell silent and considered Ruby.

She was a handsome high-yellow girl, not so young as Claire but young enough. He'd had her once himself when Claire was out and he'd found she knew considerable from her teens in the black and tan rookeries. In fact, she knew altogether too much to suit him. Claire's charm was that she forgot. Every time was the first. Her hypocrisy was complete; it made him want to laugh. And though this minute he felt like strangling her, he knew he'd not be feeling that way long. He leaned against the drainboard and watched Ruby for an opening.

"Where'd she go?" he asked for a start.

"Now I don't know that," Ruby said, bending down and sniffing at the lilacs. "I better put these in water less they wilt."

"Do you think I ought to wait?" he said, reaching into his pocket and taking out his new cigar case. Ruby peered up from the washtub and he held out the case. She liked cigars.

"Well now that's nice," she said, took one and lighted up. "Thank you kindly. But don't you got something on for tonight? Some big ball?"

"I do," he said.

"Mm," Ruby said. "She might be late."

Realizing he was hungry, he leaned across to the table, hooked an oyster and threw it down while he considered. So it was the ball, he understood. She'd been at him to take her with him and he'd refused, so she'd gone out. He should have figured that she might —these balls were a running fight with them. Though, all the same, it was annoying. It wasn't even as if he hurt her feelings. She knew it wasn't her morals. She'd be a queen at the balls among the sweatshop girls the cadets were always bringing to soften up. It was only that Maguire might drop dead if he saw her. And she'd brought it on herself by playing tricks on him. So that was out; he'd not weaken on it. Still, if he knew where she was, he'd go get her, not to waste the evening.

"Where'd she go?" he asked, still chewing.

"I don't remember."

So she knew. And would tell, if he approached it right. In fact, he began to guess Claire had given her instructions.

Deep inside, he relaxed. Since the start, he'd been afraid she'd find someone richer or with airs more to her taste. The first he'd know, she'd not be in, and next she'd vanish from him for good. Even after three years he remembered her threat to disappear out West. But Ruby had told him it wasn't that. Anything else, he was a match for. With cheaters, you cheated. "Too bad," he lied. "I'd fixed it up for a surprise — I was going to take her with me."

"Well now, that's a shame," Ruby said and raised her head so her cigar was tilted toward the ceiling. "Maybe if I rack my mind."

"Try," he said, with an edge of sarcasm. She was wearing a yellow dress he'd bought for Claire last year. Let out at the seams to fit, but there was no sign of wear. It made him sore how Claire flung his money away. He supposed Ruby had been telling her fortune in the tarot cards again and had come up with something grand. Ruby claimed to be part gypsy, and he supposed it might be true. Her mother was a runaway mulatto slave working the black and tan cribs. They were rough as the waterfront and got a wide trade from Indian harpooners to Lascars and Chinese sailors.

"I do believe," she said slowly, drawing the thought down from the ceiling, "I do believe she might of let drop she was off to Chambers Street."

"Chambers Street," he echoed, not liking it.

"Yes, I think she might of dropped it," Ruby said. "She went to tea with Madame Restell."

He grunted. Claire knew where to hit. There were reasons he backed off from Restell. She was rich, for one thing, and that gave her great influence. Besides, she was the city's big abortionist. And, religious though he wasn't, he'd seen the woodcuts in the pamphlets they'd circulated when she was up on murder charges, as a blood-dripping bat perched on a mound of babies' skulls, so she gave him a creepy feeling. There were other reasons as well, too humiliating to want to think about, so he shoved them from his mind. His eye fell on the tin tub again and the vision of Claire returning, he had a sudden longing to drag her out of Restell's, bring her home, and give her a good hiding.

"You got some ice?" he asked Ruby and as she nodded, he added: "Put the ale on it. Then clear out."

She grinned and tipped out her cigar to save. He hesitated, then pulled a bank bill from his pocket and threw it on the table. "Put the flowers in water, too," he said.

She hadn't earned the note. She'd only fed him what Claire had given her to say. And she always left at night; the little flat was too small for her to stay. But then the bill was one of the wildcats that had been flooding the city since the war gobbled up the metal coins. That morning a bank clerk had thumbed through *Kemper's Bank Note Detector* and finally refused it. The chances were it was counterfeit.

His spirits fell as the Negro butler led him past the marble busts of Washington and Franklin draped in silk Stars and Stripes that stood in the entranceway and they walked over Persian carpets and took the step down to the tasseled and beaded drawing room. Madame Restell blossomed above the silver teapot in scarlet tea gown and diamonds. And seated on the wine-colored sofa beside Claire was Madame's husband, Old Doc Mauriceau.

The greetings went badly. Claire flashed a look at him and he guessed by her glint he was right — she'd told Ruby to hold out till he'd promised about the ball. Well, she'd discover she was wrong once back inside her flat. A clout on the jaw was what she had coming to her. But the pleasure of the thought threw him off and before he knew what he was doing, he found he'd returned Madame's bow and was shaking hands with Mauriceau. That unnerved him. He'd detested the man since he'd had to visit him after his first go-round with Claire. "Men's Intimate Complaints" was the way the *Herald* ad put it, but the shame of the actual visit rankled. And not a month later he'd had to pack Claire off for Madame's Corrective Powders, and when that didn't work, she'd stayed overnight in the hospital upstairs. Considering it all, he'd have thought she'd hate to set eyes on them again. But he supposed so much silver and mahogany had dazzled her. She'd pulled her pretty airs, got taken up, and now here they were all cozy together. It made him want to shout and lay about, but taking a hold on his temper, he told himself to bide his time, and sat down carefully in a little velvet chair.

"Well, Mr. Casey, it's a long time, isn't it?" Mauriceau said heartily. He had a ruddy face and French moustaches. French me eye, Casey thought. It was a known fact his name was Charley Lohman and he'd been a *Herald* compositor till he'd hooked up with Madame and become a fancy clap doctor. Casey rested a cold eye on him and Mauriceau ducked behind a teacup.

"Tea?" Restell asked in her low, cooing dove's voice. Ah, but she was another bird altogether. Bold black eyes and black hair, though that might be dye — she must be over fifty. The treacle in her voice didn't fool him. Serving maid she'd started out and millionairess she'd ended, riding out each fine day in an open carriage with a giant mulatto footman clinging on behind. Murderess she was, and made of nails, for all her sweet voice. She'd been tried twice for manslaughter and had spent a year on Blackwell's Island, though even there she'd a feather bed, her own clothes, and her meals were sent in; she'd rented the warden's own quarters. But that was years ago. Now she'd learned to send out Christmas presents, usually bags of new gold pieces.

"Tea, Mr. Casey?" she repeated and he shook his head.

"Thank you, ma'am. I just et oysters." But she had a fine bold look to her and he admired her stable. If he had her money, it was what he'd do with it himself — sink it in good horses, Cuban thoroughbreds, mahogany stalls and silver trappings. If she'd just made her money another way, or if she didn't know all that she did of his private affairs, it might be they'd get on. Lots of bigger men than he made out with her like blazes — Chief of Police Matsell, railroad tycoons, judges and senators, all drank her champagne and gobbled up her pheasant. And little Claire was already on the inside track. Suddenly, it came to him there was no telling who the Madame might put her up to meeting if she ever got the knife in him. Moving in the little chair, he sweetened his refusing tea by taking half a turkey sandwich.

But it was too late to court favor. They'd gone on from him and like two matrons of fashion were discussing the great palace Madame was building just across from St. Patrick's Cathedral. They'd been building for a year now and it would take another year yet. As Madame fell to talking of Parian marble and the virtues of mahogany, Claire drank it all in as if she might do the same herself.

Ah God, he thought, running his gaze over the delicate lines of her. How slender she was with her skin pale against the dark red hair coiled round her ears. Once more it came to him she looked too frail to live, as if the least breath of wind might carry her off. Perhaps he was too hard on her. He gave her points for the life she'd lived, surviving the waterfront like a starving stray cat that crawled up his leg still scratching and clawing. For all her lies and conniving, he liked a tricky brawler and she was that for sure. And sixteen was very young; she was only that last month.

"Casey," he heard and he came back to the company to find she was addressing him. "Was it tonight you have Mr. Maguire's ball?"

"Yes, that's right," he said, resting his hands on his knees should she want to be up and off.

"I don't want you to be late for it," she said and he glared. The hellcat wasn't leaving till he'd come out with it in front of witnesses. Well, they'd settle that later, not in front of Madame and Mauriceau.

"I wondered now would you want to come too?" he said sweetly.

"Well," she said, looking down at her thin fingers and taking her time so Restell didn't see her jump for it. "Perhaps I might at that." He nearly smiled at her casualness; Mrs. Astor was no match for her. Torn between laughing and wanting to clout her for her airs, instead he got up and said they'd better be running.

"Run along, my dears," Madame Restell said, beaming with kindliness and wiping her strong fingers sparkling with diamonds. Through all the folderol, she managed to shoot a wise look at Claire. "Good girl" the look said, "that's the way to play your cards." So they'd been discussing him. He'd give Claire another one for that once he got her safe home from Murderer's Roost.

But his troubles weren't over yet. He had to nod to Madame and though he tried to get away with forgetting Doc Mauriceau, Claire managed to drop her fan and while he was avoiding picking it up, Mauriceau stuck a hand in his stomach and there was nothing to do but give it a crushing he'd not forget in a hurry. Then Restell tugged the velvet bell cord and the black butler glided in and led them toward the door.

When he thought it was safely over and they were standing by the curb trying to flag a hack, a high-wheeled gig flew up with a fine bay in a froth. By God, I'd not do that to her if she was mine, Casey thought. He was so taken with the horse, he didn't see the driver till he was down tying the bay to the hitching post, and even so he first saw the sporty porkpie hat and checked vest fastened with a diamond. To his shock, he saw it was Pretty Boy.

They eyed each other. They hadn't met in two years, since Pretty Boy had left the neighborhood and opened a new Eagle saloon on the Bowery. And yet Casey felt a word would do it. In an instant, they'd be rolling in the street going for each other's eyes. But the word didn't come. Pretty Boy looked from Casey to Claire and his blue eyes flashed in the way he had. He smiled his artificial smile so showily insincere it was an insult in itself. Then he nodded formally and went up the brownstone steps.

Casey's mind was a blur from the shame of having to flag a hired cab right before Pretty Boy's expensive gig. He'd known he was doing well but he'd not counted on having his nose rubbed in it. Though he didn't turn around, he felt Pretty Boy's gaze boring into his shoulders and he went hot as he wondered was Claire look-

ing back at him. He felt she was and flung himself before the first
cab he saw to drag her off at once from the scene of misfortune. As
he held the door open, relief washed over him for having the wits
to lie about Maguire's ball. If he hadn't, she'd be having tea with
Pretty Boy and he knew how he'd feel if his last sight of the house
had been Pretty Boy arriving.

And then the thought struck him — she might have intended
that. The suspicion struck his heart so he didn't dare to move, only
glanced sideways at her in the light of the streetlamp. But he saw
only the fragile little profile, gazing at the yellow fan in her lap.

Did you plan this? Do you know him? he felt like grabbing her
and shouting.

He ran back over Pretty Boy's manner. But that false widening
of the flower eyes and triangle of a smile could mean a hundred
things or nothing. It was possible they'd met — in Pretty Boy's
profession, he'd have known Restell for years. And with Claire always there — the knowledge made him feel like groaning. He sat
still, though, and waited to see if she'd ask who was the man who'd
bowed.

But the barouche bounced along the Belgian bricks toward the
Village and the gas lamps flickered past and she didn't ask a thing,
simply gathered her shawl about her, snapped the fan shut and fell
to nibbling at its edges.

"What the hell's on your mind?" he asked, unable to stand the
silence.

She went on nibbling a second and then she sighed with pleasure. "I was thinking that, after all, I might just wear my old black
velvet."

He sat up on the canopied bed, swung his feet over the side, and
after brooding for a minute, got up and padded across the room to
the satin wing chair where his clothes were piled. He knew the
time had come to tell her she'd been tricked and wasn't going to
Maguire's ball, and he waited for the pleasure he'd expected, but it
didn't come. He pulled his drawers on and then his shirt and bent
toward her vanity mirror to get his tie done casually. While he

was there, he stole a peek at her through the gauzy bed curtains, lit by the bedstand candles. She'd turned over in the bedclothes and was lying on her stomach stuffing herself with oysters.

"Want an ale?" he said, relenting. Let her eat before he told her; she'd not be eating much after.

She nodded, her red hair coming uncoiled and flooding down her naked back. Then she made a scissors movement with her legs to underline it. He grinned. You could see the street girl plain when she was hungry. He sailed out to the kitchen and came back with two pale ales. He handed one inside the gauze, then set his glass on the vanity, combed his hair, and stole a look. The glass was drained, on the bedstand table, and she was back to wolfing oysters.

"Have you known Pretty Boy long?" he asked.

She made an incoherent noise and he said: "What?"

She threw her head up and shook her hair from her face. "Never heard of him," she said.

He watched her closely but she was busy choosing the best strawberries from the dish.

"The pimp that runs the Bowery Eagle. We saw him going into Restell's."

"Mm," she said disapprovingly. "I wish you wouldn't use that language. I don't know all your friends."

"He's no friend of mine," he said.

"Then why ask me?" she said, looking around in the sheets till she found her napkin and wiped her fingers carefully. As she sat on one elbow, the candlelight flickered across her till she drew the sheets up decorously. He sighed, seeing himself defeated in trying to surprise it out of her.

"He looked like you did. You might of met him at Restell's," he said, as vague and bored as herself, bending back to the mirror to give his hair another swipe. In any case, he'd have to come to the point about Maguire's ball. There was no use delaying. She'd give Maguire a heart attack.

"Listen, Claire," he began, and stopped dead, his eye caught by the fanned corners of a bunch of pawn tickets stuck beneath her powder bowl. "What in hell's this?" he asked.

She sat up and craned her head through the gauze. He raised the tickets and waved them at her.

"Oh," she said. "Those are pawn tickets."

"I figured that," he said dryly. "What in Christ have you been hocking? The clothes I buy you? I give you money. You don't get a quarter what they're worth."

"They're not mine," she said, sitting back against the pillows.

"Oh no?" he said, raising the cover on her jewel box to poke through it. That was a mistake, he realized; she'd never be able to pawn the junk he gave her. Before she pointed it out, he went over to the oak wardrobe and turned the key to swing it open. But that was a bad thought, too. All her clothes seemed to be there, though he wasn't much for identifying female clothes.

She'd locked her fingers about her knees raised beneath the sheet, and in the smug silence, he began to feel foolish, so he raised his voice. "What are you doing with them?"

"Nothing yet," she said. "I only just found them."

He stared down. "You found them."

"On the street. In an envelope."

"Where's the envelope?"

She shrugged. "I threw it out. Don't be silly. What have I got to hock?" And it was true. He wasn't a rich man and he kept her on short rations, good enough for an ex-oyster girl, but she wasn't satisfied with that. They'd had some fierce rows about it.

But standing before the silly bed she'd decked out in gauze from a play she'd seen on the Southern aristocracy, he had an awful thought. Pretty Boy was doing well. And while he'd started by living off women, he had the whoremaster's fancy for them. What he'd got from them he might end by giving.

He stood clutching the pawn tickets trying to think how to force truth from her. Fury at Maguire's penury whirled him one way while fear of Pretty Boy's talents whirled him that. He'd heard rumors of Pretty Boy's skills that struck him hard in the pit of his stomach. She was a cool one but who knew — a sudden vision assailed him of her stripping down in a secret lair above the Eagle, and he sank on the bed while the sweat broke over him.

"Don't be silly," she said, patting his knee. Dismissing the tickets, she took her hair in her two hands, swept it up on her head, pinned it and hung over the bed and tugged out a box. While he stared at her thin shoulders, she flipped the cover from the box and drew out a gold wig. Still hanging upside down, she fitted it on her head.

She sat up straight then, rising naked from the swirl of sheets, looking strange as a mermaid. "A man Ruby knows got it for me. It only cost me ten dollars."

"Pinched," he said automatically.

"As for that, how would I know?" she said gaily. She struck her palms together in delight. "Don't you see? He'll never know me."

"Who?" he said. And then he realized she meant Maguire. Vaguely, through a mist of jealous terror, he gazed at a cool little face and the wig powdered with gold. There was no trace left at all of the ruined little redhead he'd found sobbing at the Comet.

He'd never beat the truth from her. He began to think she didn't know it herself. But there'd be no peace either if he went to the ball leaving her. If Pretty Boy was involved, her revenge could be terrible. At that, the visions of the Eagle came back so vividly, he jumped up to hide his face from her and began pulling on his trousers.

"What are you doing?" she asked.

Not trusting his voice, he grabbed the ale from the vanity and cleared his throat with it. "Come on," he said. "If we're going let's get to it."

She jumped naked to the rug so the candle flames quivered. "You'll have to lace me up!" she cried.

He stared at her with love and hatred. *I'll lace you good, one of these days,* but he didn't dare to say it.

It was after eleven before their hack drew up before the Comet and, even from outside, Casey saw the ball was already approaching the pitch of carnival. A butcher he knew from a Twenty-third Street slaughterhouse was being thrown out by Paddy Sullivan and as he came tumbling across the pavement, the band struck up again and the shadows leaped across the leaded windowpanes.

Since Maguire would be sore he was late, Casey threw Claire's wrap in the checkroom and turned her over to Paddy, gold wig and all, though she didn't fancy that a bit. You'd have thought she'd never met scum like Paddy before, much less hustling it in water-front saloons. But Paddy's face stiffened beneath the pomaded hair and he looked struck on the skull to be talking with a lady. At that, Claire loosened up and began patronizing him a bit. So leaving Paddy to his torment, Casey pushed through the dancers to report in to Maguire.

He found him in the back with Mrs. Maguire and a bunch of her lady friends sitting around on rented chairs and looking strained as missionaries watching the natives' ceremonies.

"Sorry, Boss, I got held up," Casey said.

"Goddammit, now you're here, start pitching this scum out," Maguire said. He was raging mad, Casey saw, standing under the big red, white and blue paper bell with the WELCOME HOME, BIG JOHN streamer across it. In another second he'd be jumping in himself, and after all, he was supposed to be the generous, easygoing hero. So Casey took a look around to see what had disturbed the ladies.

At first sight it didn't look different from most ward balls. They usually started quiet enough but by midnight they livened up. Union flags were everywhere and a long trestle table against the far wall was filled with ham, turkey and oysters. It looked like a Firemen's Ball except the painted engines weren't in the center of the room. The bar was frantic. Scanlon was working like a demon beside two other bartenders to keep the beer and whiskey flowing. For all Maguire's worries about Scanlon drinking, he had no cause to be upset at that. For the rest, there were the ordinary sights — the shiny hat brigade, election district captains dancing with their wives and daughters or standing about the sidelines swapping Tammany gossip — no harm in that. A few factory girls — he could tell them by their teeth, which were brown from taking snuff. Standing above the whirling spools twelve hours a day to reknit broken strands, the air was white with cotton so they breathed it in except for the snuff helping them to spit it out about them on the floor. Let Mrs. Maguire try it, if she was upset by brown-toothed girls. There were shipyard workers and butchers, and domestics and shopgirls, all glad of a free ball. And, of course, the Arsenal repeaters were whirling them around, making time if they could and passing themselves off as rising young politicians.

There was the trouble, Casey saw, his own Arsenal Gang. They'd got too big for their britches since the start of the war had set them to bounty-jumping. They'd begun in the city, enlisting a dozen times apiece and bribing the Governor's Island depot sergeants to let them desert. But now they'd got grander — wandering the country like a strolling company, enlisting and escaping in a circuit from Poughkeepsie to Albany to Troy, Utica, Buffalo, Rochester, Elmira and back to New York. In their last month's swing, with Horse Masterson as their leader-broker, they'd made close to thirty thousand dollars. God knows, everyone was doing it — either that or selling forged enlistment papers — city judges, army surgeons, clerks and officers, so only one in four enlisted men ever reached the Union front. Tweed himself was taking his rake-off and there were some said so was the governor. But it wasn't easy to keep control of men making that kind of money. Last November, he'd had all he could do to hold the gang in the city till after election so he could repeat them at the polls. His mind was half made up he'd have to go with them on their next swing to keep it in their minds he was still their leader. But right now he was going to have to pitch in bodily.

Horse Masterson, drunk as an owl, had swaggered in with the Pig Girl, dressed in her swill-gathering clothes, and Mose Barry had spotted them and was howling jovially as he shouldered through the dancers. He didn't blame Maguire for reddening. Flexing to free his shoulders in his coat, Casey cruised across the floor and threw an arm around Horse.

"Come outside and have a drink," he said. "Bring your girlfriend too."

"Hello, Casey," Horse grinned. He was showing his affluence, Casey saw; he'd had his front teeth filled with gold. Times had changed since he'd slept in the Arsenal and worked with second-hand burglar's tools. But he was the same easygoing Horse. Dragging the Pig Woman by her arm, he let himself be led toward the door. And then as they were nearly to the street, Horse spotted Claire with Paddy Sullivan.

He'd known her too long around the oyster saloon to be fooled by a wig and a black velvet ball gown. "Claire, hey Claire!" he shouted.

There was nothing for it. Casey swung him about, dug a knee in his stomach and took out more insurance by clipping him on the jaw.

As Horse sagged, Paddy Sullivan caught him beneath the armpits and started dragging him out. He moved from old habit but it didn't stop him from complaining. "What'd ye do that fer?" he asked. "He was comin' wit ye quietly."

Whatever else he did, he wasn't explaining himself to Paddy. With all the touring to Poughkeepsie, the man was getting above himself. Instead, he grabbed the Pig Woman and propelled her out the door. She mumbled and he set her going on her way back to her Dutch Hill shanty. Then when Paddy seated Horse against the building, they watched him slip sidewise to rest on the pavement. Afterwards, they stood taking drafts of the spring night and watching the midnight moon.

"The Boss is sore," Casey said finally. "You shouldn't of let her in."

"Ach! I know. 'Twas a slip. I was talkin' to yer lady," Paddy said in contrition.

"If he tries to come back —"

"He'll not come back. Not that I don't think you was hasty." But when Casey didn't answer, Paddy sighed, renouncing hard feelings. "Did ye see them new gold teeth on him now? I hope ye didn't knock them out, he's that proud. Let's take a look."

"Don't wake him."

"I'll be tender as a mother," Paddy said, and straddling Horse, was bending down to see his mouth when there was a flurry inside and Mrs. Maguire came sailing out with her ladies and Maguire glowering in the rear of the procession.

There was insincere talk of its being late and "See the moon!" while Paddy and Casey ran down the street to wake their drivers. But despite all the kissing and thanking, when the ladies drove off, there was no denying Maguire felt his ball wasn't going well.

"Now you listen to me, boys," he said grimly. But before he

went on, there was a roar from inside. "Ah, Christ, what's that?" he cried. "Casey, Paddy! Every man who starts a muss, take him out and break his head!"

So they flew back inside and just in time, for an ironworks man had wandered to the kitchen and found Petey, the nigger cook Casey'd borrowed from the firehouse.

"By Jaysus, he's poisoning us!" the ironworks man was shouting, getting Petey against the wall. "We fight their war and now they're trying to poison us!"

Half the dancers had piled into the kitchen and Casey started grabbing coats to pitch them out but by the time he got in, he found Petey half strangled and the ironworks man in the trimmins claiming whole black regiments were climbing through the kitchen windows. Casey knocked him out with a bottle and then jumped to put the damper on another fight. When he got the chance, he pushed Petey out the back and sent him dashing for the firehouse. The way the city was going, he should have known it wasn't smart to have a black in sight once the liquor started flowing.

He got the kitchen cleared and the band back to playing, but by then the evening sagged and though Maguire still stood bravely under his crepe paper bell with the Welcome Home sign, it was plain his night was ruined. With another man, Casey might have given him a few drinks and cheered him up, but he'd as soon feed whiskey to Comanches. He stood beside him for awhile but Maguire just kept shifting his cigar in his face and staring in despair at the clock, so seeing his sacrifice wasn't doing any good, Casey slid out to dance with Claire.

But if Maguire's mood was black, Claire was no ray of sunshine. It had been beneath her to dance with Paddy and since the shiny hat brigade were all with their wives, they didn't dare to cast an eye on a gold-wigged mystery. So all through the fighting, she'd been standing, waiting, and now it seemed she'd got dressed just to be stepped on by Casey. He did his best but quick as he was in a fight, he was heavy-footed at dancing. He pushed her once around the floor and then she claimed she had a headache.

"I'll catch a hack and go home," she said.

At once, Pretty Boy sprang to his mind wearing a velvet lounge coat and smelling of musk. He was sure she was going to the Eagle to finish the night and he felt if she tried to leave, he'd lose his head and knock her down.

"Come, let's try again. I'll get the hang of it," he said. But she was getting her stubborn look and he felt a wild rage rising. They'd have been at each other's throats, but as she looked past him, her eyes opened wide and if he didn't know her, he'd have thought she was having a religious vision.

He frowned as all about him, he felt the saloon change. The dancers stopped whirling, there was a muting of laughter, and then the band missed a beat and started up again, madly playing "Hail to the Chief." He turned as Tweed sauntered from the cloakroom escorted by his retinue.

He was enough to put the life's blood back into any faltering party. Six foot, corpulent with ruddy skin, a proud intelligent nose, and a reddish short beard and moustache tickling his smiling mouth. With the ribald stories going round about him, it was like having a visit from King Carnival himself.

Maguire came striding over and pumped his hand like he'd saved his life. And indeed it seemed he had, the way the blood had come back in Maguire's face and he'd grown a foot taller till he looked like himself again, the great Irish champion. As they stood clasping hands and clapping shoulders, it was a glorious sight, the meeting of great chieftains, so the crowd gave a roar and ended up with a tiger. Even the brown-toothed spooling girls knew he was someone secret and exciting, more than the mayor or governor, the one who made the game go round. He was with two other men that Casey recognized from carrying messages to the Amen table at the Fifth Avenue Hotel where the giant winds of war were fanned to power and unleashed. They were new war millionaires. One made soldiers' uniforms that were apt to come apart when they got wet — they were made from the sweepings of wool factories stuck together with glue. The other he wasn't sure about — it was either broken-down army mules or cannons that exploded. But they were grand just the same, near as good as Astors in their evening dress, tall black hats and huge diamonds. Maguire marched them to the bar and the champagne started flowing.

Claire wanted to dance then. And for once, Casey did himself. The whole evening had changed and Maguire was on top of the world. He'd not dreamed Tweed would appear. It was a sign his star was rising.

Pretty Boy receded like bad dreams on sunlit waking and Casey took her twice round the floor and her face didn't lose its joy no matter that he forgot and swung her rougher than she liked.

Then came the bolt from the blue. Paddy Sullivan waded through the dancers and tapped him on the shoulder. At first, he thought Paddy wanted a dance himself and looked sharp to see was he drunk to have got his nerve up. Chances were Claire would say no and Paddy'd not like the insult. But not at all, it was a message. Mr. Tweed begged for the honor.

"Jaysus," Casey said, and Maguire's orders came back about not letting hustlers in. For an instant he saw her clearly, tearful and screaming as she'd been on the dirty counterpane in the back room of a cheap saloon. A man shrewd as Tweed would peg her in a second.

But even as he flinched, Claire dug her small fingers in his arm, and smiling innocently, told him to walk her to the bar. There was nothing for it; she'd not miss Tweed. It'd be like pulling a fish from a cat and that cat mean and hungry. It was the first time in years he'd prayed. He sent his petition straight to the Queen of Heaven that the wig would fool Maguire. And then with his ears ringing, he marched her over and leaned back weak against the bar as Tweed laughed and circled away with her.

Till the end of his life, he thought he'd recall those first fearful moments while the Boss of New York waltzed about with his oyster girl. Dimly Casey saw that despite his height and girth, Tweed was light as a butterfly; laughing all the while, just pausing to tell a story and then the two of them were laughing again and spinning round like two June bugs. They were a sight, the great red-bearded man, growing stout but powerful still from his days as foreman of Americus Six Engine, and the frail gold-haired sixteen-year-old who could walk beneath his outstretched arm. Gradually the other dancers stopped and watched, till at the end they were the only two still waltzing. The band wasn't sure when to stop and made a try at going on but then Tweed gave them a sign and walked Claire back to the bar.

"Champagne, my dear?" he said and without waiting for her reply, signaled Scanlon, who smacked another glass on the bar and splashed it full. Tweed handed it to her gently as if it was mother's milk. "I was telling Miss Scofield that blondes are perfidious. I hear the city detectives are baffled now by one young lady. You don't mind if I repeat?"

"Oh my no," said Claire so sweetly Casey gave her a look to let her know she was laying on the innocence beyond all human belief. She stared at him round-eyed over her champagne glass.

"It seems the young blonde, very much the lady, speaks well, gently bred, takes a room in a boardinghouse. She's come to town from upstate," Tweed said.

"Oh God," Casey thought, giving Maguire a look. But Maguire was basking in Tweed's showing up so he wasn't even hearing.

"While the other boarders are out to work, she goes through their rooms, picks up the best clothes, valuables, rings and watches, don't you know, packs them in her own bags and out the door and vanishes."

"Goodness!" Claire said.

"To a fence?" Casey asked.

Tweed glanced at him lazily. Casey felt that, without seeming to do so, Tweed was sizing him up, measuring his chest and shoulders, seeing a fighter half his age who'd been dancing with the blonde. Then he looked in Casey's face as if to ask: "But how bright?" And when Casey put a glint in his eyes, Tweed's gaze touched his as if to say: "Too bright for that," and slid away good-humoredly.

"To the pawnshop," he said. "She'd better find herself a fence. Because the superintendent tells me his men already have the pawnshop staked."

"Her description?" Claire asked.

Tweed raised his glass. "All too good. I feel I'd know her myself. And I've never seen her. Well, here's to crime." They touched glasses. Then Tweed drained his off and said to Maguire: "You've put on a fine party. But it's been a long night."

"Of course," Maguire said. "It's been grand having you."

"You know I wouldn't miss your homecoming. Still," Tweed said thoughtfully, "you could do me a favor."

"Anything," Maguire said. Certainly Tweed had made a success of his ball and he was prepared to give away the ward in a surge of generosity. But Casey tensed to get the bill.

"Then let me carry off a lady. As a party favor."

Maguire's face froze. It wasn't his sort of a joke. And with Tweed's reputation, he might well think the worst. Casey held his breath lest Maguire would counter by mentioning Mrs. Tweed. But he didn't have to worry.

Tweed went on: "And her escort, of course. Just for a late supper. Afterwards, I'll drop them home."

"If you wish — I see no harm," Maguire muttered in relief he wasn't being pressed into pandering at his point of age and honor.

"You will, sir?" Tweed asked Casey. "I hope you'll accept."

Casey was as relieved as Maguire. Pretty Boy had disappeared entirely from his worry about the pawn tickets. And it was a great chance, being noticed by the Boss, altogether different from their meeting aboard the *Red Jacket*, or the messages he'd run to Tweed when he was just another ward heeler, no more to be remembered than the man who serves the supper. But before he answered, Claire fluted: "How nice of you!"

So the two of them, wrapped round snug and warm as war millionaires, were being wafted out the door on their way to Delmonico's. Casey knew it would be Delmonico's; Tweed ended his routs there nearly every night.

♣ 9 ♣

Early on a July Monday, Casey left Claire's flat in Greenwich Village and made his way uptown to his firehouse.

At Twenty-eighth Street he dropped off the omnibus foggily, for they'd spent the whole of Sunday at Coney Island and not caught the homebound ferry till midnight. He'd left Claire still sleeping, her head beneath the pillow. When he'd put a hand on her bare shoulder, she'd whimpered "It's too hot," and burrowed in still farther.

It was hot for a fact, close and muggy with a dull, lifeless sky. As he walked up the street he unbuttoned his collar. A stray newsboy ran up but though he held the paper folded, Casey got a squint at it. They were still trickling in stories of the Vicksburg surrender nine days before. So he didn't buy though the kid spit with rage for losing the three cents; they had a good racket going, fobbing off the old stories by dashing round crying "Extra."

He was crossing Fourth Avenue when he saw the crowd, maybe a dozen men, rough-dressed in work clothes. One was carrying a copper pan he was beating like a gong and they were roughhousing and calling to the windows as they passed. At that hour, they should be going to work but they didn't look it and he nearly yelled to find what was up but then it struck him they looked drunk and he was too sleepy to bother. He continued down the street and turned into the station.

There was no one in front but the lead boy and he was dozing so

Casey walked past the engine to the kitchen. He found black Petey making tea and frying steak.

"'Lo, Mr. Casey," Petey said. "Had your breakfast?" When Casey shook his head, he reached down and threw on another beefsteak and a mound of fried potatoes. "Newspaper on the table," Petey said.

Casey sat beside the open window and stared out at old Turk who was lying in the shade of a big hydrangea bush. Seeing Casey, he half rose but he'd been lame since the fight in Devlin's ratpit and it was too hot to drag himself inside. He lay down again and Casey shifted his gaze to the new mascot, a billy goat tethered to a stake near the privy. He was a good enough goat but half the companies had them; he wondered should they buy some wild animal from a menagerie to drag along in processions the way the Eagle Hook and Ladder had a wild eagle chained to their ladder.

He was still revolving it as Petey gave him his cup and saucer and poured his tea.

"Steak ready in a minute, Mr. Casey," Petey said.

Casey grunted.

Next to the goat was a cauldron not washed yet from the company's chowder party Saturday night. Since he'd met Claire he'd been missing the parties. He was listed as a sleep-in bunker to avoid his mother's tears and dark predictions for his soul when he was gone all night but the boys were making jokes about his being away so much and he supposed he'd get more today over skipping the chowder party. He wasn't in the mood for it and half made up his mind to leave as quick as he'd had his steak. He'd steal a nap down at the riverbank till time to stop by the Comet and see had Maguire come back from taking his family to Saratoga.

That decided, he poured his tea in the saucer, blowing on it to cool it, and as soon as Petey fixed his steak, he wolfed it and stood up.

"I'll be around," he said to Petey. "If there's a call, I'll hear the bell."

Petey almost spoke but then he seemed to resign himself, picked up the dirty dishes, and dropped them in the wooden bucket to wash. Casey wondered mildly what was bothering him but he wanted to get out, so it was easier not to notice. He slipped the newspaper beneath his arm — his brother firemen would be sore, but they could get along without it — and started from the kitchen. But then he saw he was too late. Scanlon came in with a face like thunder.

He'd been drinking, Casey saw, and that was odd; he'd never seen Scanlon drinking in the morning before.

In any case, he was raging. He knocked into a chair and cursed it, then slammed to the window.

"And what's got into you?" Casey said but Scanlon didn't answer and Casey glanced at Petey but Petey shook his head. Casey wondered had he and Kitty fought or was it just another child coming. They'd had two in three years and were just scraping by with Scanlon stealing here and there and the ward jobs Casey threw his way. Scanlon hadn't gone for the bounty-jumping. Kitty was afraid with their luck he'd be picked up for deserting. And that brought him to the draft. There'd been the first drawing Saturday.

"You're not drafted?" he asked Scanlon.

Scanlon whirled. "An' how the divil should I be drafted when they've not drawn our district yet?" The question seemed to have driven him mad, that Casey should be caring so little he'd not known it.

"Ah well," said Casey, making allowances. It was sure the man was worried half to death at the chance of being drafted and leaving a young wife to feed their two babies on the air. "I didn't get a chance to read the papers."

And that was the wrong thing to say, too. It brought the thought of Casey lolling in iniquity while Scanlon was cooped in a hot tenement with a wife and two babies crawling over him. No doubt he saw Casey and a lewd gold-wigged vision promenading Tweed's steam yacht hobnobbing with the Belmonts. God knows it wasn't true, still Casey had been to no pains to dispel the general illusion that started the night they whisked off to Delmonico's.

Choked with fury, Scanlon yelled: "Well, when you do you'll see it's today they're drawing. Not that it'll bother you. If yer picked, ye'll have no trouble. Maguire'll put up yer exemption money."

And that was true too. On payment of three hundred dollars, a man could buy off. It was what was making the people furious.

"Never mind, they may not draw you," Casey said. "And if they do, we'll see can Maguire help you out."

"Will he buy off the whole ward?" Scanlon muttered. There was sense to that. The quotas had to be met for each district and pull only extended so far. It was doubtful Maguire would help if Scanlon was drawn. Still, it was Scanlon's only chance for he'd not raise three hundred by himself. Realizing he'd best not quarrel, he crammed his rage back.

Mistaking silence for the end of trouble, Petey said: "Had your breakfast, Mr. Scanlon?"

All the fury Scanlon leashed then came springing out at Petey.

"Givin' charity is it? Think I can't buy me own breakfast? While you sit on yer fat behind swilling down the company steaks? Yer all alike, lazy scum, an' we're hauled off to save yer hides an' die — Ye'll be eatin' yer thick steaks while me own children are starvin' —"

"Easy, Scanlon," Casey said but it was too late. Scanlon lunged at Petey and he had to jump him from behind, pulling his coat down his arms to hold him fast. While Scanlon struggled, he tried to talk sense but Scanlon wasn't listening, only saying what he'd do to Petey, and finally Casey had to threaten he'd not try to help him with his exemption.

That cooled him down, the thought of marching off and leaving Kitty with the babies. While he still had his ear, Casey sweetened it a bit. "Come, I'll buy a drink while we think what you ought to do."

When he felt Scanlon go slack, he hurried him out before he changed his mind. He might decide after all to pay the blacks for the war by murdering poor Petey.

But they never got to the saloon. Once on the street, they saw crowds and a great milling of men and horses on Third Avenue.

"What's that now?" Casey said.

Scanlon squinted. "An accident with the cars?"

It was the street railway cars surely. There was a line of them piling up along the street. "Come, let's see," Casey said and they trotted to the Avenue. But as they drew closer, they saw it wasn't any kind of accident at all. One of the drivers was just then throwing down the reins and jumping to join the crowd.

"By Jaysus, it's Frank," Casey said. "Now we'll find out what's up." He and Scanlon pushed through and Casey grabbed his brother's arm.

"What's going on?" Casey yelled.

"I don't know," Frank shouted back. "Unless they're sore about the draft. They was standing on the tracks so as not to let us pass."

"But you jumped down by yourself," Casey said. "I saw you do it."

"An' how much further would I get if I had a call to join the martyrs?" Frank said.

He had a point. Before him three cars were stopped southward bound and two more going north. They were empty of passengers, the horses cropping grass along the tracks.

"Take a look around you, man," Frank said and Casey turned and took a look.

At first they seemed the same crowd as at fires — factory men and butchers, cart drivers, day laborers, a few women now too, rough drabs who'd been leaning out the windows and had come down to join the fun. Poking up at a distance, he saw a crudely lettered placard reading NO DRAFT, so Frank was right. That was what it was about. But they didn't seem dangerous, except perhaps the sheer weight of them. There were several hundred now where earlier there'd been a dozen. And they'd been gathering a few weapons — paving bricks, but here and there a man had a bowie knife in his belt. He saw one rusty musket. The rest had sticks and stones. And all were drinking. He wondered where they'd got the money, till across the street he saw they'd pushed into a saloon and got a keg. The keeper wasn't chancing a refusal and the wrecking of his place.

But saloonkeepers didn't stand for that. He'd be sending a boy running out the back to get the cops. Then Casey realized that was

strange, too — with a mob stopping cars and pushing into the saloons, he'd have expected cops already. He turned back to Scanlon
and then he stopped.

A couple of the men were laying axes to a telegraph pole. Hyp-
notized, the crowd watched till the pole plunged into a tangle of
wires and a great cheer went soaring to the dull, hot sky. He knew
then what was different. The crowds at fires were half good-humored and half angry, and so was this one; but at the fires the fun
and fury was scattered. This one was stopping cars and cutting
wires; it had an enemy and purpose.

"The draft," he said, and Scanlon clapped his shoulder.

"The goddamn draft," Scanlon said as if he was talking to himself, working out the possibilities.

Casey felt a thrill go through him. It felt like whiskey did, the
people rising. Five hundred years of oppression was in his blood as
in the others, and now it struck back at a cruel law.

"On to Headquarters!" a man was bawling.

Draft headquarters, of course, Casey thought; it was all leading
up to strike at headquarters. But there were two drawings today,
one on Broadway, one on Third. The crowd hesitated and argued.

"What's it matter?" Scanlon yelled.

And that was true. The essential was momentum, so the crowd
didn't die but kept in motion, engulfing new recruits till it grew
into a mob. In another moment, the crowd felt the need to move
itself. Without decision being made, it began to surge ahead.
Dragging telegraph wires and rolling the beer keg, the men headed
north toward the drawing at the provost marshal's office.

They went slowly, stopping to raid grogshops and shinny up
poles to hack down more wires. There were no cars running now.
And over on Second Casey saw they were stopped, too. Looking
through a cross street, he saw one of the cars with two drunks
jigging on its roof.

And then at Forty-fourth, the forerunners stopped, backing up
the men behind as a kind of sigh ran through them. Casey felt
gooseflesh creep up his arms when he saw what it was — a mob,
not in hundreds but in thousands, was waiting there already.

"Holy God," Scanlon breathed and Casey felt Frank lose his balance and brush against him. Next they moved like a brook rushing down to join the sea.

The police were at last in evidence, some sixty of them. But with that kind of mob they could only bar the doors. They'd not tried to stop the sacking of the saloon beside the draft office. The windows were out and the shuttered door ripped down. Beer kegs were set on the street. Men knelt beside them, wetting themselves in the beer.

What was odd was the sense of waiting. The blinds of the draft office were still drawn.

"What time is it?" Scanlon asked and Casey tried to guess. What with the telegraph wire cutting and the detour they'd made to a piano factory to demand the men be let out to join them or they'd burn it down, they must have taken two hours to move twenty-five blocks.

"After ten," he said.

"The drawing was to start at nine," Scanlon said. "They must have called it off."

It was likely, Casey thought. He wondered should he head back to the Comet to find Maguire. The great insurrection was turning into a drunken holiday. Already a man beside them had shaped some telegraph wire into a cane and was doing a minstrel dance around it.

Then the window blinds shot up inside, and the mob came quivering to life. It roared defiance and a stone went sailing through the draft window. Sweeping the police aside, a dozen men brought a pole and battered down the front door. In the back of the crowd Casey looked for Scanlon and saw him wriggling his way toward the front. In a second he was gone through the door and up the stairs. A big woman in a shawl came elbowing her way in on Casey and while he shoved her from his way, Frank disappeared on him too. The crowd was surging forward and it took all his strength to keep on his feet. He lost track of what was happening then, only struggled and pushed back and felt himself dragged forward by the rip. A woman screamed and he knew she'd gone down but there was no hope for her at all.

Suddenly he was at the entrance, and in the instant caution touched him, for all his gooseflesh and the pull within him. Catching hold of the wall, he held to it and let those after him go by. He began pushing sideways, keeping close to the wall, until the mob's tug lessened and, finding himself in an eddy, he dragged clear and came out before the ruined saloon.

For a moment, he looked up at the sky and sucked in air. Across the way he saw the women hanging out the tenement windows above a carriage factory and stables. From overhead came a shower of glass. He ducked inside the saloon as the sound of wrecking started — a chair was pitched from the draft office, and the leg of a desk as the axes went to work. In a few moments more came a great yell of triumph — the draft wheel, he supposed, or maybe not, for the yell had changed to screaming. Wondering had the cops put up a fight, he ducked outside to see, but they were most of them still there, looking nervous, their locust clubs at the ready.

The mob rushed out faster than it had gone dashing in. Looking up, Casey saw the windows were all knocked out but he had to make a run across the street before he saw the first spurt of flame licking up a wall and leaping toward the air. My God, he thought, the wires are down. From old training, he nearly ran to let his engine company know. But there was another pull inside him that resisted the draft as much as Scanlon; let the office burn, they'd only got what they'd deserved.

The cops felt different. At the first sight of fire, they started striking back with their locust sticks, battering at the heads and shoulders as they struggled through the door. The women inside went on screaming. Outside a man went down. Soon Casey heard a shot and then another. He took cover again, this time inside the stables where the horses were rearing in their stalls.

There were some good horses there. One gray mare in particular, lunging and neighing. He liked a horse like that. Cuban maybe by the looks of her. She looked like Restell's Cuban thoroughbreds. So he slammed the front doors shut and bolted them, then coaxed the horses from their stalls and out the back alley and two blocks over to another stable.

When he came back, the street was changed. The carriage factory and the tenement apartments above it had gone up. The women who'd been hanging out the windows were pushing through the mob holding their children.

By then the fire companies had sighted the smoke and were dragging their hose carts and engines through. Hearing a roar go up, he found an empty keg and climbed atop it to see if Pacific Engine was arriving but it was only men struggling. They'd got somebody down, he figured. When the underman wriggled free, Casey saw a well-dressed man about sixty. They caught him again and bore him down. Then the crowd moved in.

"Jaysus," he said, crawling down from the keg. It was the police superintendent. He must have been touring the draft offices and blundered in without a guard.

By two o'clock Casey was covered with ash and hauling the Pacific engine rope through the crowd that stretched down Third Avenue. He was so tired he kept slipping on the cobbles and he felt like half the things he'd seen were from his dreams. There had been Decker, the chief fire engineer, who'd arrived with the Pacific. He'd mounted a broken table and gave a speech to great cheering. The mob had turned friendly for Decker. It was sweet to watch, the way he softened that great beast so they let the hand-pumps move in.

They let Casey and the other firemen fall to work. It didn't take long because there was so little left to save, but the search for victims in the char took longer. They found a dozen, dead and injured, and the crowd carried off the living.

When Scanlon showed up, he was drunk and God only knew where he'd been since he'd rushed in the draft office, but his pockets were stuffed with enrollment slips. So he wouldn't be picked up and shot, Casey grabbed them and scattered them on the bloody street. He seized Scanlon by the arm and led him back to the Pacific where he set him to winding hose. At the familiar feel of the leather, Scanlon went on with it by himself. They packed up the Pacific and started hauling her home.

But they'd not gone a block before they heard shots to the south and next moment, to the west, a plume of smoke was rising.

"It's not far, let's take her boys," his foreman shouted. "Step out lively!"

With a groan, Casey put a hand back to the tongue and guided her around the corner.

It was the old Bull's Head Market Hotel. When they arrived the door was off its hinges, its windows out, and it was blazing like a pine torch while the cattle from its stockade stampeded across the market barriers. Frightened steers were rushing off while the mob trailed away with the bar stock and every portable — chairs and vases, the guests' clothing. One old crone went by him with a cage of canaries. He supposed they were from the lobby.

He saw Horse and Paddy Sullivan staggering off with an iron safe. The aproned bartender came running after them but Horse only turned and struck him once and he went down.

"Holy Christ, it's Horse and Paddy," Casey said, turning to Scanlon. But Scanlon had already dropped the rope and was staggering off to lend a hand with the safe.

Mose Barry came jumping from the blazing stoop and dashed off with a gold-framed picture. Casey looked around. The whole Arsenal Gang was there looting, and perhaps it had done the firing too. Staggering through the smoke was the Pig Girl carrying an armload of hoop-skirt dresses. As he watched, disbelieving the vision, she jumped down the stoop, fending off a steer that turned the corner sharp. She took out down the street and caught up with Horse and Scanlon. Heaving the dresses about her neck like a boa, she reached down to help with the safe and they turned a corner out of sight.

They gave up trying to make the firehouse. The crowd south was too thick and besides smoke was rising every way they looked. Turning north, they bucked a mob that was chasing a pickpocket. They were after him by hundreds. A dozen were knocked down and trampled. Casey hauled a woman to her feet. Her arm was hanging limp and blood was streaming down her cheek but she was laughing.

"Yer the boy, my chicken!" she kept screaming in his face till he let her go and she dropped.

The fire bells had been ringing in his ears so long he was floating on the sound and gone lunatic like the rest. He dragged the rope, unwound the hose, manned the brakes, and dragged out bodies. Part time he had the sense he was jumping surf at Coney Island but he was just rising and falling with the fire bell.

Passing the Colored Orphan Asylum, he came abruptly to his senses and saw it sharp and clear: the big white frame house with green shutters, surrounded by lawn and shade trees, the graveled carriage path invaded by the mob that had swarmed over the picket fence. They'd trampled the vegetable garden and ruined the flowers as they howled for the nigger brats and rows of dark, childish faces peered down at them from the windows.

Already two files of children were marching out and the faces at the windows were vanishing. But before the last child was gone, the men were at the door. Beds, chairs and tables began flying out the windows to the mob waiting below. Then a pack of screaming drunks took out across the grass to get the children.

"Take them!" Casey's foreman shouted and the company grabbed up spanners and hose nozzles just as Chief Decker's special company came trotting into sight hauling hose carts and pumpers. Together they waded in, and when the drunks were driven back, Decker threw his company round the children, standing guard with poles and axes. When the parlor curtains began blazing, they couldn't move without deserting the children, so they watched as the house went up, sending sparks flying into the trees.

The mob was brawling over children's toys when Maguire drove by in his buggy. He jumped to the gravel and looked sickly at the fighting that was going on over the lawn. A young whore lay bleeding with the knife wound in her breast and Maguire stooped to look but she was dead. He rose and came to the firemen's circle about the small, dark children.

"All safe?" Maguire asked.

"So far," Decker said.

"Better get them to the station house," and Decker nodded. "I'll take the buggy on around and meet you there."

As the companies began to move with Decker in the lead and the children filing hand in hand, the firemen in the rear dragging their hose carts and pumpers, Casey fell out of line and walked Maguire to his buggy. He was still dressed in his Saratoga outfit, the cream sporting top hat and light trousers giving off the expensive air of fast horses, French cuisine and mint juleps beneath the trees. But his face was gray like a man who's been hit in the stomach.

"My God," he said.

Casey nodded. He was still seeing frightened rows of eyes along the windows. He said: "They'll be bringing in the troops?"

"They're going to have to. Pull them out of Gettysburg," Maguire said. He turned again to the young whore. They were tying a rope to her foot and two men were dragging her off. One of her belled red boots was left behind on the grass.

"They've got the armory at Twenty-first," Maguire said. "I don't know they'll keep it long, but long enough to get rifles and cartridges. The Harlem tracks are torn up. There's hell to pay in Greenwich Village."

That brought Casey up. "What's going on in the Village?"

Maguire nodded at the smoldering Asylum. "What do you think? The niggers."

Casey nodded. There was a big Negro section near Claire. And he'd seen Scanlon himself blaming Petey for the draft.

"They've started hanging," Maguire said. "Dragging them out of the houses, man or woman don't make no difference. Might hang you too, if you've got one hid."

Casey ran an arm across his sweaty forehead. He hadn't worried about Claire. She'd know enough to lie low. But he'd forgotten that she had Ruby.

"Jump in the buggy. I'll drive you over," Maguire said, meaning the station house.

"I can't now," Casey said. He turned and started off.

"Casey!" Maguire yelled. He must have thought the day had turned his head.

There was no use telling Maguire; it would offend his sense of morals. He started running down the gravel path with Maguire's shouts echoing in his ears.

There were no cabs or omnibuses, and no buggies left unprotected. At Twenty-third, he sat on the curb to catch his breath. The iron shutters were closed on the Fifth Avenue Hotel but the front doors were open. He turned to get a peek inside but his clothes were torn and ashy and the doorman clapped his pistol. Casey grinned at the thought of the swells clustered in the bar waiting for the revolution.

Rich carriages were rolling past escaping north to Westchester. The black drivers were lashing the horses; the trappings caught the waning light. He watched a crowd chase a cop into a brownstone but as they started stoning windows, he got up and loped along.

The lamplighters hadn't come and when he reached Bleecker Street, he found it dark. The stores were closed, their shutters drawn, except for the saloon on Claire's corner. It had been sacked. Its whiskey bottles were gone and the great bar mirror was cracked. He followed the trail of glass along the sidewalk. The cabinetmaker's sign was gone and he listened on Claire's stairs, then hearing nothing, took the steps two at a time and burst around her landing to find her door was smashed.

His hands were shaking as he struck a match, went through the kitchen, and lit the parlor gas jet. It was ransacked, chairs overturned, her dresses torn and strewn on the floor. He hurried through and hardening himself to what he'd find, struck another match to see the bedroom. But there was nothing, just the vanity on its side, drawers open, and the ripped gauze bed curtains trailing idly.

"Claire," he called. There was no answer. He dropped the match and ground it out on the carpet.

In the dark, he tried to think. The mob had come, maybe following Ruby home, but the two women were tricky as vixens. Perhaps they'd doubled back, hiding in another flat, or out the window on the bedsheets, maybe up to the roof and over, skinning

down a drainpipe. There was no blood; they'd got away. He just
didn't know where they'd run next. Ruby would probably go to
earth in Thompson Street, but he wasn't certain about Claire.

The thought of Restell's came to him. He turned and ran back
down the stairs.

The darkened Village streets weren't crowded like the upper
wards, but there were pistol shots and restless fire bells, and puffs
of flame two streets over. As he passed the Negro section, a dozen
men went rushing by the cross street chasing someone. He heard
the screaming when they caught him, but he didn't go to see. He
just kept jogging downtown toward the glare and red smoke billowing.

At Chambers Street, he stopped unsurely. Restell's house was
dark. He climbed the steps and rang the bell but no one answered
and he stood staring up at the shuttered windows. She might have
joined the flight to Westchester, though he hadn't seen her carriage in the wild procession swaying up Fifth Avenue.

Then he remembered Restell ran a hospital. Claire herself had
lain in one of the beds in the upper stories. There was a baby farm
for some, while others had the operation. She'd not be throwing
them out — there were rich women among them, and the mistresses of big politicians.

Running down to the Belgian bricks, he found a loose chunk
and heaved it hard at an iron shutter. It rang out in the night and
he shouted: "Claire! It's Casey!"

It was like disturbing a nest of copperheads. There was a rush
from behind and he was pinioned. He stared around startled in
the dark and saw they were cops from some doorway. Restell had
an armed guard ready, pieced off from the station house. She'd had
it before, back in '46 when the mob gathered at her house in
Greenwich Street. She'd learned then about mobs.

"It's all right," he said quick, before they started using their
clubs. "I'm Casey from John Maguire's ward."

"Are you now?" one said dourly, looking like they'd beat him
anyway. He might like the dough but not the assignment.

Still, they'd been listening in the house. The shutter he'd struck with the paving stone opened and Restell took a peep. She was carrying a candle and he caught a glimpse of lace and diamonds.

"Hello, dear," floated down.

"You got Claire?" he yelled. The two cops loosed his arms.

"Claire?" she said, surprised. She must have thought he was bringing a message from one of her big friends downtown, perhaps that they were sending a platoon of troops to swell the guard. "I haven't seen her." Her voice was still sweet but the welcome was gone from it.

He pressed on just the same. "Where is she?"

"How would I know?" A plump arm reached for the shutter. "Now go on home, there's a boy. Quit throwing stones at my windows."

"I got to find her!" he yelled, in a rage at the woman with her police guard better than the mayor had, closing the shutters on him. "Restell!" he shouted.

There was a pause. The cops didn't like to strike him down if he was Maguire's man, and Restell didn't want him shouting out her name, reminding the whole neighborhood she was there, with maybe a stray mob overhearing. The shutter cracked again and her shadowed face looked down coldly.

"Try the Eagle," she said. "On the Bowery."

He felt like the blood was draining out of him. The iron shutter slammed shut.

"Get off," a cop said and shoved him. He staggered and righted himself, then stood gazing at the cobbles, his head blurred with shock. But when the cop started after him, he stumbled on. He headed east, his legs carrying him toward Pretty Boy's place.

Printing House Square was jammed when he got there, with a mob of thousands stretching far up Broadway. Torches were lit and he saw the snub-nosed howitzers and bayonet ranks of infantry protecting City Hall. But in the Square there were only the quick-raiding parties of police. One had been by just before Casey came. The injured were crawling about.

There had been trouble at Greeley's *Tribune*. Half the windows were stoned out and it looked partly burned. Lanterns hung from the upper windows, and the staff were posted in them as sentries, holding pistols and carbines at the ready while they searched the Square below for another attempt to storm them.

He was nearly across the Square when he was swept up by a crowd that was moving together. A sailor handed him a whiskey bottle; he needed it, he realized, and took a swig.

"We're hunting niggers," the sailor chuckled, throwing an arm about his shoulders.

"Are you now?" Casey said, using their impetus to move him through. He was one hell of a cheery sailor.

"Had a good one already," the sailor said. "Set him afire."

"Well that's fine," Casey said, draining the bottle. Finding a clear place, he stepped out but the sailor hung on his shoulder, so he turned and brought the bottle up. As the sailor sagged, Casey ducked and came up free of the arm. Before the sailor's pals figured it out, he was running up Park Row. Behind him, he heard the *Tribune*'s carbines start to crack as they stood off another raiding party.

The Bowery was dark. The theaters were closed, the concert saloons and beer gardens shuttered. There were no hot-corn girls, peanut vendors, no organ grinders. The bowling alleys were silent and the oyster signs hung idly. He passed a shooting gallery that had been broken into but it was the only casualty on the block.

The next block was livelier. A saloon had been sacked. The windows were knocked out and upstairs where the girls were there had been some rock-throwing. He frowned, wondering now they had started on the blacks would the whores be getting it next. If they did, Pretty Boy would be in for trouble.

He got to the Eagle to find a mob. The men were already dragging girls down the stairs when he shouldered his way in. The saloon was wrecked, kegs gushing on the floor, bottles smashed, and the fighting was still brisk as Pretty Boy's bouncers fought their way to the rear alley. He used a table as a shield and edged across to join them.

"Where's Pretty Boy?" he shouted.

They thought they knew him. He was their sort.

"In the back," someone said and he ducked out to the alley.

The stable door across the way was aslant and he kicked it open. He found Pretty Boy backing his horse into the shaft of the sporty gig by the light of a lantern hung on the wall.

He didn't go for his gun, though the thought crossed his mind — Casey saw it in the blue eyes. But if Casey was armed, he already had the draw. Bravado froze him and he went on backing up the horse. By God, Casey thought, he was clean — white linen shirt still half unbuttoned, with the fair throat rising to the shock of curling hair. He'd not had time to put on his coat, though he'd saved his cream hat. It was sitting on a stall post.

"You'll not get far in that gig," Casey said, trying to manage it coolly. "The crowds are thick as herring."

Pretty Boy thought it over. He thought a lot in that instant about how to save his hide. Then he turned his lovely face and smiled.

"Thanks for the tip," he said. He pulled the mare from the shaft, considered saddling her, then decided his time might run out before he did. He got astride her instead.

Casey stood blocking the door. He wasn't thinking but images flashed across his mind. The fair face rising above the unbuttoned shirt reminded him of the Eagle's upper rooms and if he'd had a gun he would have started firing. No one would pin it on him in the midst of this Mardi Gras. But he had no gun. Maguire's men rarely carried them. If they shot it looked bad, while no one minded a fist fight.

"Where's Claire?" he blurted.

It was dawning on Pretty Boy now that he was unarmed. And with his own men in the alley, he knew the mob would soon be coming. He had little time, yet Casey's dumb rage appealed to him. Casey saw it and yet he couldn't move.

"You'll find her at the Ivy Green," he said. "She's on her way there."

"Expecting you?" Casey said.

"If she is you can give her my regards." The blue eyes lighted up. "She's no society girl, is she? I knew that pretty quick. A girl like that wants special handling."

Casey made a sound that surprised him; it was like a baited animal. His hands clenched and Pretty Boy pulled in his reins.

"Not with your fists. Any hod carrier can do that. You don't handle them with your fists."

He'd timed it right. As Casey sprang, Pretty Boy dug his heels in the mare and she went straight through the stable door, scraping Casey against the frame. He went down and rolled over in the straw and dung. He lay up against a post, staring at the lantern flame. He ached with weariness. Still, after a bit, he got up and ran down the alley with the mob still pouring from the Eagle.

He found her as Pretty Boy said, huddled in her black cape in the doorway of the Ivy Green. Her face went tight with fear when she saw him.

"He said to give you his regards," Casey said. He didn't know what he'd do next. He wanted to howl and grab her by the throat.

But she saw that in a flash. She said nothing, only lowered her lashes and waited. A fire bell sounded near. She went on waiting while he searched for what he wanted to do to her. Then a great fatigue hit him. She saw the weakness and her lids flickered.

"Slut," he said and then he stopped, realizing if he killed her, she'd be gone just as sure as if she'd lit out West. It was maddening but he knew he'd not kill her.

"If I'd known where you were, I'd have come to you," she said.

He regarded her bleakly. Perhaps she would, perhaps she wouldn't. And yet the words made a bridge to get them across the present. He grabbed her wrist and started walking.

"Casey," she said. "I'm so tired. Can we find a hotel?"

He wished she'd shut up so he didn't keep wanting to turn and knock her down. Sensing it, she fell in meekly behind.

♣ 10 ♣

Dʀ. MᴄGʟʏɴɴ woke suddenly, not knowing where he was. It seemed to him he was back in his room at the St. Ann's rectory with the light of dusk or dawn dimming the room and himself vague from hemorrhaging. Then he saw the battered stove and the dirt floor. He was in the watchman's shack in the deserted lumber-yard by the river. He looked quickly to the cavalry officer lying beside him, with the fear he might have died.

It didn't look as if he had — there was faint breathing but the hands were cold and the boy didn't stir when Dr. McGlynn chafed them. There was no water in the shack so he'd not been able to wash away the blood to see the ax wound clearly. He'd only bound the blond head with his undershirt and now the face showing beneath the bloody turban was brown-caked and swollen.

He wished he had water, or brandy. But he had nothing, only the dirt floor and the safety of the shack so long as the mob didn't discover them. Moving carefully, he got up and peered from the filthy window. First Avenue was still crowded. He saw no streetcars and he guessed they'd stopped again after the one try to run them. The soldier had been axed when his dismounted platoon tried to rescue a burning horsecar. While the mob chased the soldiers flee-ing south, the priest had found the young lieutenant sitting in a doorway blinded by the blood pouring from a forehead wound. He'd still been conscious so Dr. McGlynn half-led, half-carried him toward Bellevue Hospital. But at the river, he'd collapsed. Dr. Mc-Glynn had seen the shack and dragged him into it for safety.

And then, waiting for darkness to come on, three nights without sleep had been too much for him. He'd slept suddenly without warning, like falling down a well.

Was it afternoon still, he wondered. Time had grown strange; dawn and dusk were interchangeable with the passing of the days of riot. Was it four days, he wondered, or only three. He stood rubbing the scrub on his jaw and tried to pin it down but it wasn't measured time came back to him but only pictures: the mobs chasing Negroes, the station house by the river burning through the night, the stores closed like a week of Sundays, steers and horses galloping through the crowds. He'd seen the streets near the armory covered with clubbed rioters, the living crawling across the dead. He'd seen so much he'd not thought was possible.

At first he'd tried standing on an abandoned wagon, calling out to the crowd that were after a soldier who'd taken refuge in a brownstone. He'd thought they'd listen to a priest. But priests were nothing now; the mob was drunk and wanted blood. They'd flung him aside, battered down the door, and had their victim.

After that, he'd wandered in a daze. He'd bought newspapers as if the papers might explain it. But the papers only charted the fact of the rising fever — the crowds bayoneted by soldiers, women grabbing the bayonets and plunging them into the wounded; whole blocks burned out in the Negro sections. Riker's Island was full of Negroes, all the station houses packed; the rest had fled to Brooklyn and New Jersey.

Troops poured in, infantry, cavalry, with the horses dragging the artillery, back from Gettysburg. New York's Seventh returned, and at last the Irish Sixty-ninth marched through the streets, its green banners flying, bagpipes skirling the Irish tunes. Archbishop Hughes called for a mass gathering on Friday. But it was not Friday yet and the battle was still raging.

At some point that he'd forgotten, he quit looking for explanations and started rescuing where he could. At first he brought them, mainly Negroes, to the station house on Twenty-second till the station house was burned, and then he hid them in empty basements. This morning, he'd got two children aboard the Thirty-fifth Street boat that was taking the Colored Orphanage children to

Blackwell's Island. After that there was a Brooklyn private he'd led as far as the Bellevue gate. Then there'd been the streetcar burning and the young cavalryman.

But the blond cavalryman was worse wounded than the private. He wondered could he drag him the two blocks south to Bellevue, even under cover of night. And could he do it without killing him. Standing by the window, he wondered could he find a body of passing troops. If they came to the shack, they might take him by litter.

He took another look at the man, who was still and cold with shock. He was doing nothing for him here, just letting life ease away. He decided he had to try. In case he was a Catholic, he'd already given him absolution. So now, commending his soul to God, he eased from the shack and walked with careful innocence across the lumberyard into the street.

He went up First without seeing more than shuttered stores and a child capering with a stolen soldier's cap. But thinking he heard drumtaps on Second, he hurried toward them till the sound was swallowed up by fire bells. He stood stranded. The crowd was still boiling about the charred cars on Second; the horses moved restlessly about the streets. In the distance he saw the white blur of a naked body, a soldier probably. He'd seen the women stripping them. He looked about for a covering, perhaps burlap in a basement. And while he was turning through a garbage barrel, a hoarse voice whispered: "Father! Help me!"

He squinted down the filthy steps but all he saw was an iron door, its lock hanging. He was gazing up at a shuttered varnish factory when the voice came again, and looking down, he saw the door gape open like an oyster shell.

It was dark in the basement. He edged down the steps and looked in before he saw the frightened Negro.

"Who are you?" Dr. McGlynn said.

"Petey Jones. Cook for Pacific Engine."

"You'd be safer in the firehouse."

"Nossir. Pardon, Father," Petey said. "But the men is gone. Some drunks come in after me. I jumped over the back fence and hid out. Yesterday I busted this here lock off."

He'd forgotten the fire companies were busy night and day and the enginehouses were unprotected.

"Hide till dark. I'll come and get you," Dr. McGlynn said.

"I'm scared alone."

"We'll get to the station house on Thirty-fifth. The near one's been burned."

Petey paused, disappointed. Then he said: "Have you got a bite to eat? I ain't had nothing for three days. And I been fighting the rats." He held his hand out and showed a gash. "I must of fell asleep and a devil took this piece."

Dr. McGlynn felt in his frock coat. He'd had a chunk of bread but it was gone. "I'll bring food back with me tonight." He looked over his shoulder and saw three boys coming up the street. "Shut the door!" he said to Petey.

But it was too late. They'd seen him talking at the bottom of the steps.

"Nigger!" the cry went up. "We got a nigger!" The sound echoed along the street and from nowhere, out of doorways and around corners, a crowd appeared and began lurching toward him.

Dr. McGlynn stood frozen. If the basement had no back exit, Petey was finished. They'd surge in and beat him to death like cornering an animal. He thought quickly. They were close by St. Stephen's. Priests they might disregard, but the church and altar must be safe. He burst in the door and yelled: "Come with me!" At the urgency in his voice, Petey came running out the door and bounded up the steps.

"St. Stephen's!" Dr. McGlynn said. "Run for St. Stephen's!"

With the mob at their heels, they flew along Twenty-eighth Street. The tenements were just a blur going by. They leaped out in the street to avoid a steer's carcass and dodged across Third Avenue. The three boys were just behind them but the rest of the mob was trailing slower. Four days of rout and drink were taking effect.

It was on the corner of Third that Petey tripped and went down. He picked himself up but by then the three boys were on him like terriers. Dr. McGlynn tore the smallest one away and sent him flying. Then he waded in and grabbed the others by their collars.

"Let go!" he shouted, shaking them. "In the name of Christ, you let him go!"

They were only boys and weren't drunk either. It was enough to loose their holds and he was a great, strong man for all his priest's dress. He hurled them into the gutter. But Petey still lay dazed on the ground. They'd not make it to the church. There was only his mother's house. He reached down, hauled Petey up and not even feeling the strain of it, carried him up the walk and bounced him up the verandah steps.

The trumpet vines still wound peacefully about the posts, the white door was spotless with its brass knocker polished bright. It was like a dream from childhood's idyll. He pounded with both fists and shouted: "Let me in!"

She was there behind the lace curtains. He saw them tremble. He looked desperately over his shoulder and saw the mob was coming and redoubled his beating on the door, crying to her, and at last she weakened and came running. He heard the bolt slide and the door cracked open. But she'd put herself in the opening and he hesitated to hurl her back.

"Let us in!" he shouted. "I've a man here in danger!"

"Go to the church!"

"I can't. There's no time! Let us in!"

"My God, they'll kill us!" she cried agony. "They'll burn the house, it's all I have —"

At that, he slid an arm through the door and swept her against the far wall. He grabbed Petey and pushed him in just as the mob surged up the steps. Then he put his back to the door and slammed his weight hard against it.

"Go through the back!" he ordered Petey.

But before Petey moved, the blows were coming against the door. Dr. McGlynn tried to slip the bolt but as his weight shifted, they got their purchase and the door came open.

"Run, Petey!" he yelled.

And Petey ran, with the mob after him. He ran down the hall, upsetting the mirrored hat rack behind him but they jumped over it as he sped around the corner to the kitchen. He passed old Annie who screamed and went on screaming while the kitchen table crashed and the chair overturned and the pots went flying. Then the kitchen door was locked. They caught him as he tried to fumble his way out.

Dr. McGlynn ran to the kitchen but Petey was beaten to the ground already and the shining hardwood floor was running with his blood.

"I'm the priest of your God!" Dr. McGlynn yelled. But they were laughing and shouting in a drunken dream. They didn't hear him, only flung him out of the way when he tried to wrench them back.

"Get some clothesline!" someone said.

"It's in the yard."

They pulled the bolt on the door and dragged Petey to the yard, leaving blood on the grass as they went through the cabbage roses. They stripped him of his pants and boots, leaving only his undershirt, cut the clothesline down so the white sheets dotted the lawn.

They flung one end over the limb of the apple tree covered now with hard green apples. Petey screamed as they drew him up. Dr. McGlynn rushed out but they knocked him back. And then as he lay against the stoop in a bed of marigolds, they set Petey's shirt on fire. He could not watch. He rolled over and started praying as long as Petey's screaming lasted.

He didn't know how long it was before he heard the sound of drums. After that, the soldiers were thundering through the house and leaping down on the bloody grass. There was a burst of gunfire. A man fell wounded in the chest. Dr. McGlynn saw the blood welling before he was pulled over the back fence as the mob went fleeing.

A lieutenant cut Petey down. He lay curled in the grass and Dr. McGlynn said the last rites. Annie came creeping from the stoop, skirting the ruined roses, and stood with her old hands held under her apron.

"Poor soul," she said. She stood, her head bowed, and at last she raised it. "But what'll we do with him?" she said.

Dr. McGlynn looked around. "We'll lay him out in the parlor.

Till they come from the fire company. Pacific Engine. He was their cook."

He picked Petey up and, with the lieutenant, carried him back through the kitchen and the hall. Mrs. McGlynn was by the front door. Her eyes widened as she saw the blood and nakedness. Then, slowly, she looked at her son's face.

"I couldn't," she said and she meant she couldn't have opened the door sooner, that her house was all she had, that she was a widow, that the world was hard for a lone woman.

He didn't answer, didn't nod, simply stared, and in a minute, she said: "Horrible." And she meant the mob was vile. She'd not expected excesses when she'd been against the draft. A small clean riot, she'd have countenanced, maybe firing a draft office, but this was different. It was blood on her kitchen floor and Petey hanging in flames from her own tree in her backyard.

He stared at her till with a shiver she whirled and put her hands up so she couldn't see.

He pushed open the parlor door and looked around at the unplayed piano, the belled dried flowers, the cherry rocking chair like an instrument of torture. They placed Petey on the sofa with the vine leaf carving on its back. The heat wave was broken, he realized; a breeze was blowing in from the verandah. It drifted along the floor and set the lace curtains to stirring. He took a knitted afghan from a chair and tucked it about the burned black body.

There was no floor space left in Bellevue. The injured long ago had filled the bunks and the mattresses on the floor and now even the bare boards were crowded. Faster than corpses were dragged off by the watchmen and stacked in the dead house, their places were filled by more recent wounded. They came in carts and wheelbarrows, carried by friends, and some crawled there by themselves, reeking of whiskey, urine and vomit. In the stifling room beside the amphitheater where he sat with the blond cavalryman, Dr. McGlynn felt himself half-fainting from heat and stench.

A wave of weakness swept over him and he dug his nails in his palms to hold to consciousness. When it passed, he got up and hurried over bodies to a window and flung it open. Outside it was still storming. Lightning cracked the sky and as the thunder shook the building, the gas jets quivered and nearly blew out from the rush of rain and wind. He took a breath and pulled the shutter.

The room around him was like hell. And it was the same all the way down the building to the doors, children sobbing, women moaning and begging for help from the dirty nurses and the watchmen stepping over him. As he watched, another surgeon came in carrying his mahogany amputation case, stepped into the doctor's room to take off his frock coat and wind his bloody butcher's apron around him. He'd enter the amphitheater still smoking his cigar. He'd be putting it down when his assistant lifted the lantern and three men held the patient and it was time to operate. They were telegraphing the police stations to find more surgeons. Every hour brought more cartridge wounds and broken heads and stab wounds from bayonets. Half would die from blood poisoning, Dr. McGlynn knew from his own army hospital. The unclaimed would be buried on Hart's Island. But that was only half the dead — the rest were carried off and buried in the dirt cellars of the slum wards, or rowed across the river after nightfall and thrown in holes dug in the open country.

Stepping back over a gasping laborer, he sat down on the floor beside the cavalryman who was moving now in delirium. "Charge! Take the ridge!" he was yelling but his voice came out soft and hoarse.

"It's all right, it's all right," Father McGlynn said and took his hand and the cavalryman lay still.

The riots were ending. They had to end with fresh regiments coming into the city. And Archbishop Hughes' mass meeting was tomorrow. He'd tell the Irish to go home. Why hadn't he spoken sooner, Dr. McGlynn thought; he felt bitterly that Hughes had been too busy writing letters to the *Herald* to defend himself against the *Tribune*'s charges that his stand against abolition had started it all. But the riots would end.

Why had they taken the turn they had, he wondered. The cavalryman sighed and Dr. McGlynn gripped his hand harder. The Irish had turned on the blacks but not the war profiteers whose guns exploded in their hands, whose uniforms of shoddy came apart in the first rain; not the slumlords and plunderers, the Tammany leaders who grew rich. They took their charity baskets and poor relief and stood on the sidewalks and cheered their exploiters. Tammany's stock stayed high through all four days of riot. Judge Barnard, Tweed's tool, had been cheered when he'd swaggered out to save the Republican mayor's house. And Tweed himself was applauded when he came riding by in the governor's carriage.

He looked about at the groaning women, partly drunk still, wakening to pain, the men stained with blood, their own now as well as others. And as he looked at them, he saw Petey sway flaming from the apple tree. He was sickened as he gazed at them. Their faces seemed coarse, their minds dull and brutal. They were Christ's tares, irredeemable.

He recognized the train of thought as quick as he had taken it. It was what the slave owners said about their slaves. First, the slumlords and politicians stunt them: no schools, no training, a filthy room with cockroaches swarming over the walls, the children running like wild dogs or set to working dipping chocolates, sweeping factory floors, sent on errands by the whores. With abhorrence, the genteel turned away, giving the degradation of their victims as the reason they should never escape from it.

In the fetid Bellevue hour, as he left his cavalryman to say the words of absolution over the dying, stumbling from hunger and fatigue, new strength flowed into him. He felt he'd been lost in a mist where love and anger were at war, old loyalty with guilt, where he struggled against what he loved — Archbishop Hughes, St. Ann's, his mother's desire for his welfare. The fight had broken his health and nearly dissolved his will. Now, in the midst of death, with the pesthouse quivering under the thunderclaps and the rain seething on the windowsill, his shattered self stirred and fused. There must be a way to change the stunting social mold. He felt lifted with the force of a whirlwind.

"Dominus noster Jesus Christus vos absolvat et ego . . . vos absolvo . . ." The words came out above the dying as his mind soared free of the stench and his spirit felt light as silk and shot with radiance. He'd find help and they'd move the mountain if they must; he had the faith. "God's will on earth," came to him and his soul echoed to the phrase. The words seemed to have come from nowhere, to be sent.

"Ah, God, Father," the voice was saying. A hand caught his sleeve. "Father, help me."

He came back from the heights where he was flying. It was a young woman, battered and dirty. Her cheek was bruised and her hair escaped its pins and was straying down her sweating face.

"Thank God you're here," she said, and he got up uncertainly. She seemed familiar. He tried to place her. She had a toddler by her skirt.

"I'm Kitty Scanlon. Donahue's daughter," she said, but the names meant nothing. "Pacific Engine," she said, and then he saw Donahue, the pipeman, magnificent in his red shirt directing water on the flames of a big smoking building.

"Of course," he said. "I'm sorry, Kitty."

But she was beyond having her feelings hurt over his forgetting her. She fell to sobbing and he saw she was half wild with fear and shock.

"The baby's shot," she cried. "They shot my baby!"

He looked down, puzzled. The child was dirty and drugged with fatigue but he seemed whole enough.

She clutched at him as if words failing, she'd shake the truth into him. "Not him! Praise be to God. We was burned out — our building's gone. Scanlon wasn't there. We got caught up in the crowd. My God, the things I've seen, straight out of hell!"

"It's all right," he said soothingly and put a hand on her shoulder to steady her.

"But my baby!" she screamed. "They shot him!"

"Who did? The soldiers?" he said. He supposed she'd been caught in some mob storming someplace, the arsenal or steam works, and been caught by the troops firing. Perhaps it had turned her head; the child looked fine.

"No!" she cried. "It was one of ours. He wasn't looking, only shooting, at horses, pigs, at everything that was alive. He hit my baby in the face. I brought him here and now the doctors say they're busy. Can you make them see him, Father?"

"I'll try," he said unsurely and then looking behind her, he saw the baby, shrouded in a piece of burlap sacking, carried in Scanlon's arms.

Scanlon's face was puffed with days of drink and riot. His hands were black with ash and he was wearing a Zouave cap with a bullet hole in it, and a silk cravat wound about his throat he'd torn from some shop window. Only the suffering in his slumped shoulders made him look human.

"Hello, Scanlon," Dr. McGlynn said.

He was avoiding the priest's gaze. But at last he raised his eyes and pain was reflected in them. The priest held out his arms and Scanlon gave him the burlap bundle. He tried to speak but no sound came through his cracked lips.

Dr. McGlynn stood holding the baby which was silent, not moving or crying. This is the monster, he thought looking at Scanlon, and he is terrible. He may be irredeemable, his children after him the same, generations unknown, dragging murder through the cities. And yet, he has a soul. If the mold that stunted him were broken —

Scanlon groaned. The thoughtful, abstract look had pierced through him, unearthly as the day of judgment. In his pain, inspiration came to him. He reached up and unwound the silk cravat, slipped the Zouave cap from his head, and flung them from him.

THE ALDERMAN

✧ 11 ✧

The windows were open in the aldermanic chambers and Casey stared past the red drapes at the bright May treetops in City Hall Park. By leaning against the alderman from the Sixteenth District, he could catch a glimpse of sky; by turning completely around, he could see the benches behind the green curved rail where the visitors and newspapermen were waiting. Once the annual appropriations had been made and the issuance of city bonds and stocks affirmed, the reporters grew bored and noisy; he suspected they had a bottle and he didn't blame them. He'd been cooped up himself since two o'clock and now it was five with aldermen still proposing resolutions to place gas lamps and curb and gutter stones, to flag sidewalks and pave streets with Belgian blocks. Like responses at the mass, the board passed resolutions or laid over till next meeting.

He fell back on lighting a panatela, shifting in his red chair and drawing another horse's head on his notepaper. He'd put down a row of figures earlier and he toted it up again and found his $1200 total was correct. That was for a crosswalk he'd got laid, a gas lamp out front of a saloon, and three men fitted on the lists of commissioners of deeds. It had all gone through before the appropriations started. It wasn't what Tweed's inner circle were making with their contracts for city buildings and public works and their great railroad connections, but for three hours' work, it was more than he'd made in a year repairing locomotives. A wave of good feeling flowed through him and he leaned back in his chair to view the gas

globes hanging from the gilt ceiling. Once this year was over and
he'd filled out Maguire's term left empty when Maguire went up
to the State Senate, he'd run for alderman on his own. There'd be
more money as he went along, railroad franchises men wanted, cor-
porations needing bills passed, and all good and clean, no need to
sink to the dirty graft, blackmailing whores and gamblers. He'd
have a racing gig by summer with a Cuban thoroughbred, and
maybe change his hotel room for a suite.

"We got to remember there's the Fourth of July coming,"
Thunderbolt Norton was saying, and Casey looked up hopefully.
Once the money for the Fourth was voted, they'd be sure to adjourn. Thunderbolt, he thought, was worth thinking about. Thunderbolt had a row of shacks and an old hotel at Coney Island. Now
the boys were packing them for political clambakes and in winter
they were used as houses of assignation. Casey wondered should he
let the gig go and sink his money in real estate. He considered it,
retracing his horse's heads, while thirty thousand was voted for the
Fourth of July celebration and five council members were named
to make the arrangements. They'd do well on that, buying fireworks for ten times what they were worth and the companies kicking back — though with that kind of dough at stake, there'd be a
big split to Tweed.

"We have a motion to adjourn," the president was saying. Casey
took out his cigar and said "Aye."

But Thunderbolt and four others objected. There were still pick-
ings to be wrung from the session. They went back to general
orders: free drinking hydrants, more streets paved with Belgian
blocks, a vacant lot fenced in, a new sewer in Thunderbolt's ward.
At last adjournment was affirmed.

"This Board stands adjourned till Monday next, whatever the
date is. Two o'clock," the president said and rapped his gavel. The
men all pushed back from the aldermanic table.

On his way through the lobby, the *Tribune* reporter got him.
"What's the hundred thousand dollars for city printing?" he asked.

He was one of Horace Greeley's bright boys, picking on Casey
because Casey was green. Tweed owned the New York Printing
Company. But Casey smiled. "Ain't my committee," he said, put

his hands on the reporter's shoulders, and still smiling, moved him
out of the way.

"And forty thousand more for removing dead animals from the
streets?" he cried.

"Ain't mine neither," Casey called back and kept on going.

Outside City Hall, he flagged a hack and gave the driver the
address of the Comet. Rattling uptown over the cobbles, he wondered should he have hung around after the meeting and waited to
be asked to the Blossom Club with the boys. He was a member but
it was different going in with a mob. Still, he decided not to push.
He'd only been filling the chair for two months; they knew his
record as Maguire's man. His credentials were the best; he could
afford to wait till they came to him. When he'd finished his ward
business and stopped off and seen his mother, he'd drop into the
club for a drink. It was better on his own and asking no favors.

At the Comet, he paid off the driver, threaded his way through
the beer barrels piled on the pavement, and made his entrance
through the swinging doors. It was all so new that he expanded at
playing the alderman, and with Maguire up in Albany he was boss
of the ward, too. He held his arm up to the bartender, saw the beat
cop talking to him, and went over to say he'd got the cop's brother
on the force. Then he opened the back office and no sooner took
his coat off when the line came filing in.

First the saloonkeeper who'd got his gas lamp voted, then two
Cork boys come to see were they made commissioners of deeds,
followed by a father of four who was just laid off for the drink.
Casey promised to get him back digging city sewer pipes before his
family starved. A district captain stopped by for free drinks then
cleared out when two Sisters of Mercy came in for a donation.
Casey made it a good one and wound up business for the day.

Being a Monday, there were no wakes since the burials were
Sunday when the men were off work, and he strolled peacefully
through the May twilight on his way to his mother's house. It was
just a rented frame house but she had a piece of garden out in
back. He'd moved her in when his father died three years before in
the cholera epidemic, and found it cheaper after all than the old
weekly tenement rent. His brother Frank lived with her and

helped out from his streetcar pay though there was no doubt who was the main provider. And when he'd become alderman, his stock rose still higher. It was good just to visit and let her bring his tea while Frank sat in his father's old chair rocking and glowering.

He was enjoying the prospect so much he nearly overshot the firehouse but he caught himself in time. Enough of the old volunteers had got huffy when the new fire department was formed. To make it worse, it was the end of the hand-drawn engines. Now it was all steamers and horses with the boys on a salary and no racing to the fires or fighting over hydrants. The old vamps sneered and Casey secretly agreed but the department jobs were all ward appointments and went for a proper penny. No need to poison the well. He felt in his pockets for sugar cubes and went in to feed the horses.

By the time he came out, it was after his mother's supper and he quickened his step. But as he neared St. Stephen's church, he saw her coming in her black shawl and by her side was his sister Mary.

He waved and went up to them grinning for he didn't often get a chance at Mary. She kept out of his way since his prosperity.

"Mother," he said and bent to peck her cheek. "And Mary, too, this is grand."

Mary looked vaguely past his ear avoiding the diamond in his waistcoat. If it had been envy moving her, he would have basked in it, but he knew from her air its vulgarity offended her and he felt himself bristle.

"What are you doing off on Monday?" he asked. The Liggetts might be genteel but they weren't famous for giving holidays.

"They're making the Grand Tour," she said, not liking to soil the Liggetts' name by mentioning it before him.

She'd been bad enough before the riots with her Liggetts this, Liggetts that, but now she'd not profane the name in front of the mob. He was that, he knew, she'd made it plain, and all of Tammany with him. She could sleep in an attic and could empty slops, yet instead of hating her tormentors, she loved them more. She was no democrat at all; it was a waste of space on the boat that brought her over from Ireland.

Her perversity made him wild and forgetting caution, he said:

"They're sweating you too hard. You're looking pale. You ought to quit and come live home with your mother."

"I'd rather do honest labor for my bread," she said with the old glint lighting her eye.

She had him where it hurt, the alderman's sister feeling City Hall was so dirty she'd rather work as the Liggetts' maid. Ah, that was Irish, he thought, only the Irish had such cold revengeful pleasures. But the idea ravished her; he could see it in her smile. He never should have led with that. And yet, unable to resist another jab, he said: "You're getting peaked and bony — you'll end up an old maid."

Her smile widened, her eyes sparkling like chilly pools. She made him think of an Irish battle goddess. "An' do you have a list of prospects for me — fine city men like yourself?"

No alley fight ever made him lose his head like Mary. He felt the heat rush to his face but seeing they'd be brawling outside the church, his mother leaped into it, and having her own ways of diversion, she began by peppering him.

"You were late," she cried. "I waited supper for an hour till the potatoes were all burnt."

"I was busy," he roared. "I was held up in the council meeting and after that there was more work, a district captain and two nuns." That was one in the eye for Mary; they weren't too proud to take Tammany rakings. Just singing out the list made him feel better and he increased his satisfaction by pulling out a roll of money. "Here's the rent and some extra," he said, peeling off two bills.

His mother held them stretched out at arm's length to read the denominations. "Ah, it's too much," she cried, gratified, and popped them in her skirt pocket. "We was hurryin' to the foundlings meeting," she said, tucking her hand beneath his arm and he found he was walking along by her. "How long's it been since you was to church?"

With his rise to alderman, she'd stopped lashing out about his soul and right now she was downright roguish, but just the same he'd no desire to be dragged into St. Stephen's.

"It's getting late. I'd best be off. I've got to stop in my club," he said. If the Blossom Club wasn't the Union League, it was just the same a club of the men that ran the city. He threw it out at his sister.

"If that's all ye've to do, drinkin' at clubs, ye can spare a minute," his mother said.

He was trying to loose his arm but she clung to him fast, laughing like she was playing, while she dragged him up the walk. Suddenly, the church door opened. They both froze at the sight of the priest.

"Ah, there you are. We were just about to start," Dr. McGlynn said as he saw her, and then his gaze went on to Casey and he stopped.

It was the same every time they met, the same quick silence and sense of danger like two men jumping at each other from an alley. At old Dan Casey's death it was the same, the two of them meeting at his hospital bed; and at the wake they'd met again. They'd run into each other often since Dr. Cummings died and Dr. McGlynn had taken over the parish. Yet there always was this mortal shock before they both recovered and put a decent surface on it.

There was no getting out of the church tour, though; Casey's mother was determined since he hadn't been inside since St. Stephen's had been extended through to the next street. He ambled along viewing the blue vaulted ceiling, looked at the pillars and the stained-glass windows, clasped his hands behind his back as they paused beneath the painting of the Crucifixion, and made admiring noises at the angels on each side of the white marble altar. Actually, he told himself, it was the part of running a ward that he'd been slighting, sliding by with wedding and christening presents and showing up at the wakes but Maguire had always attended the church side of the weddings and funerals and so far he hadn't started. He'd have to begin and perhaps it was lucky he'd run into McGlynn this way. From all he'd heard from his mother, McGlynn was hard working and not too high and mighty. He lived in the confessional, kept open house for priests in trouble over booze and fights with their superiors and was forever giving away his clothes to men who often turned up dead in Bellevue with McGlynn's name sewn inside their collars, so that the rumors were already starting McGlynn himself was a boozer. That warmed him toward the man. And then there was the new foundling home in the city, instead of just shipping them off to Blackwell's to be taken care of by the paupers. That was the first move McGlynn had made when he became pastor, the St. Stephen's Home for Destitute Children, and eight Sisters of Charity came down from Mount St. Vincent to run it for him.

The rest of the man's virtues Casey knew for himself. When he walked into the hospital to visit his father in August at the height of the '66 cholera epidemic with the dying crowding the beds crying for water, their faces dark and wizened, their skin covered with sweat, and the odor of death and excrement so strong in the hot rooms, he felt weak. But it was McGlynn and the white-robed Sisters of Charity he'd seen moving round the beds. By the time he'd left his father, they'd been out on the lawn helping spread bedding and pillows to be burned. He'd not have gone himself, had there been a decent way out of it. And he didn't tell Claire; she'd not have let him in. But McGlynn had been there, scarcely sleeping from the start of the trouble in May when the ship *Virginia* came into harbor with a thousand steerage passengers and thirty-seven dead of the cholera, until late August when all the lime and coal tar and burned bedding finally stamped it out.

The man seemed to flourish on it. He'd filled out with the years and seemed calmer and surer for all the work and his bed full of strange priests fleeing trouble with their bishops over drink and disobedience. If you had to have a priest, surely that was the sort to have, Casey thought, feeling friendlier each minute as the tour concluded and he saw he was going to take his leave.

"Be sure to ask, Father, if I can be any help to you," he said heartily. "Sometimes with a church assessment, the city council covers with a donation."

"So I hear," Dr. McGlynn said and there was a wryness to his eye that chilled Casey's new warmth. Yet McGlynn had really said nothing.

Casey was still feeling uneasy when the Scanlons turned up. They came clattering in, late he supposed, for the foundlings meeting, Kitty wearing a plain shawl like his mother, and Scanlon —

but he'd never have known Scanlon. He'd left off his cap and jacket for a poor, clean suit he must have picked up secondhand as suitable for church. His own father used to wear an outfit like it when Mrs. Casey got him to Easter mass.

To do Scanlon justice, he seemed uncomfortable and when he saw Casey, he looked caught out in something past explaining. He cast his eyes at the ceiling, then down at his shoes and then he shot a look at Casey who was watching him closely.

But Casey couldn't go on doing that. It lowered his dignity to let McGlynn know his feelings at Scanlon's desertion. Moving carefully, he said good-bye, shook hands with McGlynn, and as he left with measured tread he was asking himself, after all, why shouldn't Scanlon go to church, and even join in the St. Vincent de Paul Society. They were all good Catholics surely.

He hailed a hackney, got in, and told the driver: "Blossom Club."

"Yessir!" the driver said and Casey's spirits rose at the snap of recognition in his voice. But after a bit, he sighed, crossed one knee on the other, and looked out at the city passing. He wondered what it was about McGlynn that bothered him and why, catching Scanlon with him, he felt betrayed.

He was still brooding about Scanlon as he walked into the Blossom Club. He raised a finger to the bartender and looked around, but he was late, the supper hour had started, and there was no one left that mattered, so when the bartender set down the bottle, he only took one drink, then wandered upstairs to the billiard room. But he found just the two Murphy brothers who hung around saloons selling sealed and ready naturalization papers. They'd talk his ear off, so he ducked out again quick. The ballroom was dark and the library empty. Sometimes he liked to stand just looking at the leather binding on the bookshelves, feeling his feet sink in the carpets as he strolled to the heavy drapes and looked down contentedly upon the city street. But tonight Scanlon kept getting in between.

What bothered him, he thought, was that he hadn't known that Scanlon was getting religious. On the surface, Scanlon seemed the same. Casey'd got him on the list of Judge Barnard's Supreme Court officers. There wasn't any work to it, not even showing up, the only payback being at elections. And at the last election, Scanlon seemed like always.

They'd spent the month of October together, dragging Irish from the saloons to Judge Barnard's Supreme Court to be naturalized in time to elect Hoffman governor in the face of upstate opposition. It had been a strange month; a smile crossed his face at the memory of Barnard on the bench from dark till midnight every night scrawling on the piles of naturalization certificates printed up by Tweed's New York Printing Company. Barnard alone naturalized ten thousand. Casey and Scanlon brought the application blanks in with their approval marked, then Barnard scribbled on the certificates and the new citizens were herded in by hundreds to have the oath administered. It was a curious feeling, marching the men through the night in squads, up the courthouse steps and down the gaslit corridors while the city played and slept around them. There'd been no time in October for St. Vincent de Paul meetings.

At the end of October they'd taken gangs registering all over the city. That was a grand feeling too, with the registering clerks all knowing him and giving him a wink as he marched a new gang through. They all registered a dozen times, with him taking them around to the saloons to leave the fake names and addresses with the bartenders for each ward's book.

Election day, Scanlon broke all records. He must have voted thirty times, and the men with him, changing their coats and caps and passing round the bottle till they didn't care how often they voted; half the time they forgot the names that Scanlon gave them and Scanlon had to whisper. Nobody cared; it was like the stupid fun that happened at a party. None of the cops would stop them: Tammany owned the cops. And how could the Republicans challenge, for they were doing the same anytime that they could.

In the end, it hadn't mattered. Tweed decided not to take a chance with upstate strong against Hoffman. They'd got early possession of the telegraph wires and kept them busy till the upstate vote count came through. Then, knowing what the Democrats needed from the city to elect Hoffman, the inspectors of election lumped the votes and declared them without counting. It had been a wild torchlit night in City Hall Park, Scanlon drunk, even Casey a bit drunk, hugging each other and yelling. They'd pushed their way to Tammany's new Hall and found the whiskey flowing, men reeling around the rooms, fireworks exploding. Hoffman was governor, Oakey Hall was mayor. Not the city only but the state was theirs, lock, stock, and barrel.

And all the time, he thought, Scanlon was falling into religious mania. It wasn't the going to church, he told himself, but the meetings in the evenings with the women and the priest that had him worried. Any man could go to church. He might himself. But the evening meetings were the danger, and the hanging around after mass. There was the secrecy of it, too. Scanlon hadn't showed by the flicker of an eyelash what was going on. It was unsettling that could happen. He was so disturbed he stood not moving for half an hour at the library door, staring at the empty grate. Then the mantel clock chimed. He saw the time and the thought of Claire waiting made him whirl, fly out the door and down the stairs.

It was the theater hour and he had trouble catching a free driver. When he got to Florence's oyster saloon he found Claire sitting just inside the door in a straight-backed chair the cashier had put out for her, and one look at her face got him ready for trouble. It was cool as a cameo. Her black lace scarf was drawn tight and her chin was lifted so her plumed hat sat on the dark red hair in a menacing ladylike way.

As he came up, she rose and fell to adjusting the fall of her skirt so as not to annoy herself further by having to look at him.

"Sorry," he said. "I got caught at the club."

She gave him a sideways look. But the mention of the club softened her. She liked him having a club.

"It's not that I mind waiting when it's business," she said. "But waiting *here*."

Surprised, he looked round the front partition to see what it was made her object. The prices were fierce, the sawdust clean, and the long bar on the left was a glittering exhibit of the sporting world.

Even now from where he stood he could see the featherweight Dick Hollywood talking to the owner of a Saratoga gaming house.

"What's wrong with it?" he asked. "By God, if you don't like it, we'll not spend the dough."

"I'm hungry. We'll have to eat," she said quickly, not wanting him stomping out.

Then the waiter came up and as he led them past the bar, Casey nodded to Hollywood and the little man waved. He'd a face like a nutcracker and hands on him like rock from soaking them in brine. Feeling better at being known, Casey revolved Claire's grudge against Florence's as they went toward a table near the rear oyster stand. It seemed odd. She'd been mad about Florence's all spring.

"What's wrong with it?" he pursued when they were seated and their waiter gone for ale and oysters.

She stopped from stripping off her long black gloves. "With what?" she asked and the surprise on her face made her look like a child. He nearly grinned at how she stayed the same for all the changing lady gestures. And yet, the masses of red hair in the elegant chignon, fresh out of studying *Godey's Lady's Book*, the pendant earrings, the erect posture, all spelled class. He'd never have taken her for what she was. To say nothing of where she'd come from.

"What's wrong with Florence's?" he said.

"Nothing, I suppose." She laid the gloves in her lap. "Considering. It's just Florence's."

He paused, bewildered. And then suddenly it came to him. Delmonico's, he thought. "Ah ha," he said, seeing how the wind was blowing.

They had been through this the week before, her hankering after Delmonico's. But he couldn't take her there. Even Tweed didn't take his women to Delmonico's. The night of Maguire's homecoming had been special, a large party after midnight, and she so grand Tweed had smuggled her in. But it had given her fancy ideas with no bearing on the real situation. The only women who went were real ladies dining with their husbands or in groups after a charity concert. He wasn't sure, if it came to that, that he'd get in alone; perhaps at the downtown branch on Chambers but maybe not at

the classy new one on Fifth Avenue. And naturally that was what
Claire wanted.

The thought of the maître d'hôtel blandly saying he'd no room
when he could see the empty tables made his blood freeze. He
pictured the snub in front of all the swells, maybe his sister's Liggetts even, it was their sort went there. He'd not try it, alderman or
not.

But he hadn't been able to tell her that; it made him edgy just
thinking it. He'd put it all on her. And then she'd floored him.
She'd said she'd be respectable enough if he only married her.

Even now the thought astonished him. Her nerve took his
breath away so he couldn't answer. She thought his silence was
consideration and she had them halfway to the church before he
broke into a grin. That did it. She tore into the low Irish, first in a
general way, then growing more specific, fell to mimicking his table
manners, his way of walking, his style of dress, till feeling stabbed,
he roared he'd not be marrying a saloon hustler.

That's when it became a brawl. Knickknacks hurtled through
the air and when one struck him, he started for her, shouting, but
she bit his hand, then flew to her bedroom for the laudanum to
take an overdose. He had to seize the bottle, smash it, and shake
her to stop her screaming. The neighbors battered on the door till
he had to yell at them to fetch a doctor.

They calmed her with a morphine pill and he spent the rest of
the night lying beside her as she slept, wondering was she going
mad. Next dawn she woke fresh-eyed, with not a word about the
evening. He was relieved as he dressed and went back to his hotel
but it left him feeling cautious. And now she was turning up her
nose at Florence's and he had a chilling hunch it was Delmonico's
returning. He'd no wish for a new performance and when the
waiter came with their oysters, he only asked: "Will you have
steak?" Florence's had a famous beef steak broiled over a wood fire
and served on homemade bread slices.

She nodded and he said "Two" to the waiter, then drank his ale
in wary silence.

It was hard to tell how he knew her mood was changing, but
after nine years he'd learned a thing or two. Her brow smoothed

and she lifted her ale glass, sipped it thoughtfully, and when she set it down, she had changed altogether.

"Eh, what's up?" he said suspiciously.

She laughed. "What would be up?" she said, but her face was glowing. She took an oyster, swallowed it, then set her elbows on the table and made a steeple of her fingers.

At that he felt his spine prickling. The steepled fingers were a sure sign. She did that always at the races when she began to pull in winners. His back was to the door and he wondered who'd come in behind him but he didn't move till he saw the waiters rushing. Even the oyster stand man looked like he'd like to be throwing down his shell knife and getting in on the bonanza. He couldn't stand it then and swung around, his napkin still tucked in his vest.

"Friends of yours," she said, delighted, and he saw it was a slumming party from the Fifth Avenue Hotel. Perhaps that was harsh —Florence's wasn't low, only flashy. Anyway, it was Tweed and his new friend the Erie king.

"It's Fisk," he said, turning back, and she gave him an ironic look. Of course, she'd know that from the newspapers; Fisk favored his cartoons: stout and merry, his hair parted in the center and his moustache waxed to points. He was even wearing his famous diamond blazing away like a railroad light.

He'd come up from nowhere, a carnival roustabout selling mildewed blankets to the government during the war. Then last year he'd burst on New York fighting Vanderbilt for the Erie Railway. The papers were full of the struggle. When Vanderbilt got a restraining injunction, Fisk and his partners, Drew and Gould, fled across the river on the ferry carrying Erie's money and records. They holed up at a hotel near the Erie terminal in Jersey City and throughout March the fight raged with the papers headlining every move of the absconded corporation. Vanderbilt thugs arrived in Jersey to spirit them back to New York jurisdiction but Fisk drafted a defense force from the Jersey saloons and set armed Erie clerks to patrolling the Jersey shore in rowboats. In case of a night attack, Fisk planned to fire rockets out the hotel windows, and he'd alerted the state militia.

But then the battle switched to Albany. Fisk and Gould put up a bill forbidding Erie to be controlled by the same financiers as controlled the New York Central Railroad, which ruled out Vanderbilt. The legislature suddenly swarmed with lobbyists, Tweed spearheading the drive for Vanderbilt, Gould showing up with half a million in his carpetbag. Rumors flew that Erie'd pay two million to pass the bill while Vanderbilt might go higher to defeat it. The bidding rose as the legislators shuttled back and forth from Tweed to Gould. At the height of the excitement, an Erie train jumped its track, caught on fire, and its passengers were roasted, forty dead and twice that injured. There was an outcry about the rusted tracks and Vanderbilt pointed at Drew and Fisk while Fisk claimed it was Vanderbilt sabotage. But while the dead were being buried, it was over; Gould had bought the legislature.

There were a few dying rumbles from Vanderbilt over watered Erie stock, then Drew retired with his profits and Fisk and Gould got their money back selling Erie short, bought it up again sharply, and made millions. That fall in the board elections, Tweed showed up as an Erie director. It was clear to all he wasn't the man to hold a grudge when there was profit in new friendship.

Friendship it was. Like two kings they were seen everywhere together, the fine hotels, the opera, Fisk on Tweed's yacht, Tweed on Fisk's new toy, the Narragansett Steamship Line, where Fisk dressed as an admiral greeted his passengers at the gangway every afternoon. He was full of fun, the Erie king, and he was generous. Casey'd seen him at the Fifth Avenue Hotel passing money to the waiters, buying drinks all around, pressing cigars on everyone. The sight of Fisk meant prosperity.

Casey was smiling as he turned and said, "It's Fisk." He felt suddenly grand to be in Florence's drinking ale with beefsteak coming, himself an alderman with world champion featherweights waving to him, and knowing Tweed.

"They're sitting down," Claire told him.

"That's fine," he said.

"Waiters flocking. You'd think they'd smother."

"Ah, they'll do that to them," he said wisely.

She paused and he drank off his ale and signaled for another.

She'd be in fine humor now with the great men coming to Florence's.

"They've given their order," she reported. "They're alone. Why don't you go over?"

He wiped his mouth with his napkin and half laughing at her cheek, he said: "I can't do that."

"Why not? You know Tweed."

"Well sure I do. But just to pass the time of day." As he regarded her tense face, drawn with yearning, he realized she was serious. His smile fading, he explained: "And I wouldn't be knowing him long if I started crashing in on his supper. Not to mention Fisk. He wouldn't know me from a barrel of eels."

"Tweed liked me."

She was starting to exasperate him. The good feeling was ebbing as he felt himself dwindle. An alderman didn't seem so much. The grandeur of the woman was enraging. He tried to bring her to her senses.

"Sure he liked you and why not? A pretty skirt in the middle of the war. He never asked for you again." That wasn't true. Tweed had asked the next time Casey'd met him in the City Hall corridor but Casey wasn't playing. And Tweed had his pick of women. It wasn't worth taking on a boss repeater who was young and might still be foolish.

She gave him a scornful look. She knew all about that, her look said.

The steaks arrived with his second ale. He drank his glass but she didn't speak. Still, he'd not crash in on Tweed, as he wouldn't marry her. It meant his future and he wasn't gambling.

He cut his meat and though it was red and bloody to his taste, his appetite began to fail.

"As we leave, I'll speak a word," he threw to her.

She sighed.

"But that's all. Just a word in passing as we go," he said, so she didn't start building on it.

"Don't bother. It's no matter," she said.

His fork stopped moving in surprise.

"What good would it do?" she said. "You'll never amount to anything anyway. Or if you ever do, I'll be too old to care."

There was no anger in her voice, only the terrible calm ring of truth. He felt she'd smashed him in the stomach and left him bleeding inside. He grunted once, then damned if he'd let her see it, he speared another chunk of beefsteak.

"I'm twenty-two," she said.

"That's as may be," he said.

"What about my future? If you don't get someplace in a hurry?"

"I don't know," he said callously. "Not being a crystal gazer."

"But what's going to happen to me?" Her voice was rising.

"I've got no idea about that," he said flatly. "But if I was you now I'd tear into that steak."

♣ 12 ♣

EARLY in June, Claire looked up from the *Herald* and announced the Narragansett racing meet was starting soon in Providence. Casey was lying on her sofa, his eye caught by a headline about a wrestling match at Harry Hill's saloon.

"I'd like to go," she said.

"We'll see." The conditions of the match were a fair collar and elbow struggle, best two in three falls. Giving the paper a preparatory rattle, he began on the story.

"We could take the night boat up," she said. "A water trip would do us good."

He frowned. The only night boat that went near Providence was Fisk's. He wondered briefly was she plotting something.

"There'll be a band and fireworks," she said. "You'd like that. Wouldn't you?"

"Mm," he said, meaning no. Gathering his concentration, he plunged into the wrestling bout.

But once she'd started, she didn't stop. The Fashion Course wouldn't do, nor the Prospect Park Fair Grounds, nor Jerome Park, but only Providence. By mid-June, he'd agreed but only found he'd set off a sewing frenzy. Every time he came by he found Ruby at her feet with a mouthful of pins and Claire swathed in silks or taffeta. Hatboxes were on all the chairs but when he complained about the cost he was relieved to find they sent them back as soon as they'd copied them. It was uncomfortable just the same, pins stuck in panels and insets so the sofa was a porcupine, and the little flat overcharged like the air before a storm. When he finally exploded and threatened they'd not go, he found it was suddenly done, all bags packed, and Claire waiting demurely for the start of their excursion.

They rode in silence to the pier until he glanced sideways at her sitting in her pale green summer mantle with her high-crowned hat with the ostrich plume. A moonlit cruise overnight with her began to warm his blood, and after that there were the races and he wasn't a bad judge of horses. All in all, his temper sweetened. He tipped the driver more than usual and sent him running ahead with the luggage.

At the gangplank, there was Fisk. Knowing she'd counted on it, since Fisk rushed over from the Erie offices most days to see his passengers aboard, Casey was amused with a bit of malice mixed in, knowing she was expecting heaven to fall at the head-spinning gorgeous sight of her. Fisk was the real sight to see, in his naval uniform with gold buttons, bands and stars, like a regulation admiral except for the Narragansett monograms and, of course, the shirt-front diamond blazing. His moustaches were waxed to points and his ruddy face glowed as if he was ready to burst laughing beneath the heroic pose. He saw Claire coming though; his eyes twinkled. And he didn't try to hide it; Fisk was shameless. He'd not be hard to get, though keeping him two seconds was another matter.

Well, let her have her moment, Casey thought, it'd be over the instant she'd passed. Even now Fisk had forgotten he'd ever seen her before at Florence's. He beamed and bowed.

"Madame, it's good to see you. Come aboard. We'll be right off," he said, a kind of ripple going through him as if he wanted to pinch her cheek the way he might a piece of fruit. There was something infectious about Fisk; with another man, Casey'd feel like smashing him but with Fisk he really didn't. He was less a man than a shocking child.

Ah, but Claire wasn't through yet. He wondered did she act like that with him when she wanted something. If she did, it came off different when he watched. She smiled and swept her lashes till Fisk was glowing and putting his hands together to keep from patting her.

"I believe we met at Florence's," she said.

"Did we?" Fisk said, enchanted but hardly listening. It was as if he was surprised to find she could talk at all. He shot Casey a look as if to say, *Isn't she delightful?* There was more to the look, too. Deeper it was mischievous and said, *How's this man taking this?* And still deeper: *We're men together and women are all like this, the darlings.* Sharing a glance like that with the king of Erie got Casey off his balance. In a dreamlike way, he saw passengers were piling up behind; Fisk waved them to go around.

"You were with Mr. Tweed," Claire said.

"Of course. Marvelous fellow," Fisk said, and raising his hand to placate the jammed-up passengers: "Splendid, splendid!" he cried as if inviting them to join him in admiring the pretty creature he had found.

But if she thought she was going to stand there forever, she was mistaken. Coming to himself with a woman trying to push past him, Casey grabbed hold of Claire's elbow and gave her a shove.

Fisk saw that, too, and laughed with pleasure. The whole situation amused him. "Have a good trip. There'll be a moon. I wish I was coming with you," he said to Casey.

Claire was still smiling but he felt her arm stiffen to resist him. She half turned in a graceful gesture and he thought she might be going to glare. But she never got that far. There was a blow in his back, a kind of scuffling down low, and then Claire was screaming.

"What in hell," he began, looking down at her to see was she hurt but they were in such close quarters on the gangplank, he had trouble seeing. Fisk bent to her and he bent from the other side. It took a moment before she gasped to them: "Purse snatchers. They got my string bag."

At that, he looked and saw a band of ragged boys dashing down the gangplank. He shouted and one looked back but when a man on the pier reached out to collar him, he darted to one side and then they were all racing off like hares. There wasn't much chance, but he had to try. Pushing past the passengers, he struggled down the gangplank and seeing a boy linger, lit out after him.

He was halfway down an alley when a noise like cavalry made

him turn and he saw it was Fisk clattering over the cobblestones to the rescue.

He was already winded so he scarcely got the words out. "Keep going. I'll slow you down," he gasped but Casey came back for him.

"I sent the rest on board," Fisk said. "We'll handle this together." Then the eyes lit with mischief. "I guess we will. She seemed to think so."

"I'll be damned if I know how," Casey started and then he shouted as he saw a boy peeking back around a corner. Together, they bounded after him and then they found the street was full of ragged boys, all screeching and dancing about mocking them.

Casey marked the one with the yellow string bag and bellowing with rage, started for him, when seeing Fisk come pounding round the corner, they all took fright and fled another block and round the corner toward the alley. Fisk dashed on gamely, his face flaming and his moustaches like spears, but at the corner, Casey caught him up.

"What is it?" Fisk whispered. He was sweating but his eyes were lit with mirth like a stout boy playing hide-and-seek. Casey made a sign of quiet and another to double back and Fisk nodded and together they crept back down the street close to the wall and rounded the corner. They stole another short block, then Casey motioned Fisk back and they stood listening till they heard the stealthy sound of bare feet dislodging grit and stones. Casey slowly raised his hand, and then with a savage gesture, signaled Fisk on, and the two of them tore around the corner, both men so broad they blocked the exit. The boys were close. Casey plunged into their midst like a dog flushing birds, caught the yellow string bag as it fell, and then went for the boys, but they were off, whirling and dodging till his head spun. They were young and skinny, some jet black and some mulatto, and so lively they weren't like human boys at all. They fled like shadows so he never touched them, till with a last eerie screeching they vanished and Fisk and he were left alone in the darkening alley.

"Got the purse?" Fisk said and as Casey held it up, Fisk grinned and pulled his handkerchief from his pocket and wiped his face. "That was a romp."

"Funny romp," Casey said. There was something about it strange that made his skin creep like they'd dealt with changelings mocking and luring them on. He had the vague thought they'd been led into ambush, felt his pocket for his knuckles, and kept his eyes sharp to protect Fisk but nothing happened. They walked on and came out safely and saw the pier again with the *Bristol* tied up to it.

"You're a good man. That was cute, doubling back. Been a fighter?" Fisk asked and Casey nodded.

"I fought a bit. Rough and tumble. Just pier brawling."

Fisk felt for his wax and began working on his moustache. "Friend of Tweed's?" he asked, and his eyes were sharp and bright so Casey saw behind the bubbling manner he wasn't missing much. He'd caught her mention of Florence's and probably checked back till he recollected them.

Casey chose his words, not too grand and not too small. "I'm not so close as that. I'm a new alderman. The name's Casey."

They shook hands. "I'll not forget it," Fisk chuckled. "Casey, the fighting alderman." He tucked the wax back in his pocket. "Well, now we're brothers-in-arms, let's join the lady and present our trophy."

Parading back to the ship, they found Claire surrounded by sympathetic travelers and Casey held up the yellow bag to the admiration of the throng. The moonlit trip attracted a sporting crowd so nobody was worried about their marriage lines. In honor of the chase, Fisk swept them all with him to the saloon and ordered champagne. The red plush upholstery and bronze statues with canaries singing in gilt cages made reflected riches run like seltzer through Casey's blood. He rowed his breast pocket with Fisk cigars, scuffed the deep carpet with his feet and eyed the brilliant spittoons with satisfaction. Fisk had just been a New England peddler so it didn't freeze him like the Astor House; it all was possible, was what the canaries were singing.

On the crest of the wave, the boat's whistle split their eardrums,

"Ah my, it's that time," Fisk announced when the noise died. "How very sad. I was having such fun."

"So was I," Claire said. "So were we all."

He looked again like he'd like to pinch but pulled back with a sigh. "Duty calls," he said, shrugging his arms in his admiral's jacket and straightening his face again to vigilance. But his glance wandered back.

"Come along," Claire said like the thought had just occurred to her, carrying her away so she touched her little fingers to the stripes and stars on his sleeve.

"My darling, I'd love it," Fisk beamed. "But cares of state, the heavy toils, I'm weighed down with railroads and steamboats — besides," he added, darting her a look. "I don't have a pretty girl with me the way my lucky friend does."

"Mr. Fisk!" Claire said but she was smiling.

"Honesty is worth two in the bush," Fisk said with abandon.

Then Claire raised her arm and waved across the crowded saloon. "Why, there's Peggy Reed!" she cried to Casey, and as Fisk bowed to leave, she caught his sleeve again. "Wait, you'll love Peggy," she said.

Love Peggy he did, Casey saw through his shock as Fisk's face sparkled with delight. She was blonde and all dimples with a little violet bonnet, bobbing through the crowd and dragging her carpetbag.

"Ah, my dear. Give me that," Fisk cried, grabbing the bag as if its weight would kill her and snapping his fingers in a frenzy for a porter. Three flew up and Peggy dimpled at Fisk in pleasure.

"What are you doing on the *Bristol?*" Claire asked as the introductions went round. Casey hadn't met Peggy himself but he knew her from passing on the stairs at Claire's. She lived on the third floor and was kept by a leather merchant.

"It's my brother, he's stood me up," Peggy said.

"He wouldn't!" Fisk cried, his eyes dancing.

"You don't know my brother," Peggy said. "He's unreliable. We were going to the races and he was to meet me here. I should have known better."

"But you'll come along with us!" Claire said with charity.

"I couldn't," Peggy said. And while each girl was vying to be the more generous, Casey had the same sense of fairyland he'd had with the alley boys. Was it Fisk himself, he wondered, charging the day so everything that happened seemed to be on the stage, or were the boys really darting and screeching like birds, not like gangfighting boys at all. They were real enough themselves, he'd bet on that, honest scum from the black and tan district, but the way they'd danced about, coming back and circling. It was odd he and Fisk had got the purse, too. His mind returned to black and tan, and at that, he thought of Ruby, Claire's maid from the cribs. Ah ha, he thought, and Peggy showing up, ah ha again. *Brother, me eye, she has no more brother than a pigeon.* It was little Claire at her tricks. His mouth opened to start shouting but then he looked at Fisk gathering rosebuds without suspicion.

"Rip my royal halyards, you'll be my guests. And we'll have us a trip you'll never forget!" Fisk was laughing.

My God, she's done it, he thought, flabbergasted. He shot her a look for complicity but she slid her gaze past with a general air of pleasure. He looked at Fisk and thought did he know. He'd not have beat old Vanderbilt out of Erie if he hadn't been shrewd. But it was all fun to Fisk, the circus life, selling mildewed blankets, driving the market up or down, playing a titan battling over Erie. Between the ladies and the laughter, the whole world was a game to Fisk.

He whisked them up to the bridge and, his captain looking nervous, appeared about to run the ship. He gave orders with magnificence, half of them conflicting so they weren't carried out, Casey noticed, and then with much blowing of the whistle, he stood back to let his captain bound into action and put the vessel under weigh.

With the band loudly playing, they moved from the pier and headed down river, circled Manhattan, and steamed out into the Sound. As darkness fell, supper started, and after that, there was the Grand Promenade Concert. Fisk wasn't still for a moment. He bounded to the bandstand to request Peggy's favorite numbers, danced with Claire, sent dispatches to the bridge, identified the lights on shore as they were passing, and finally led them on a tour of the staterooms to admire his canaries. He was a great canary fancier and had them in gilt cages in all the rooms.

Cruising past the shore of Greenwich, Claire leaned on the ship's rail and said: "What's that?"

"Let's see," Fisk said, staring acutely overhead as though fixing the stars. "I calculate that's Greenwich."

"You ought to know it, too," Casey said. "I showed it to you last month when we took the trip around the Sound." It was Tweed's Americus Club he'd pointed out, and the new clubhouse they were building. She'd stood dreaming at it all like it was the gates of heaven.

But tonight she seemed impatient. "No, I mean those lights. See how they're bobbing — I'm sure they're moving."

"Let me see," Fisk said and looked out with the stern air of an admiral protecting his waters. "It's true, they're moving."

"Night fishing," Casey said. The Americus Club did lots of that. In winter they met in town at Tammany or the Blossom Club, but the first of June they moved near Greenwich and opened their summer season.

They leaned on the rail watching and so they didn't miss it when, from out a dark cove, the white yacht came slowly gliding, sails catching the moon, lanterns shining in her spars.

"Ah," they said all together; it was a lovely sight on the dark and gentle Sound.

"She's beautiful," Claire said.

"She's that for sure," said Casey.

They hung there smiling till Claire turned to Fisk. "Let's salute her," she said.

"That's Tweed probably," he chuckled.

"Do you think so?" she said and her voice fell in a hush. "Then maybe we shouldn't."

"Mm," Fisk said. "He knows my ship. But he don't know I'm on it." He gave her a piercing look — Casey had never seen such a look for quickness, before it was lost like a light on water, and Fisk broke into joyful laughter. "Let's see how quick he guesses."

Running down the deck, an animated little stout man, he cried

for deckhands, his band, and fireworks, and sent word speeding to
the captain to slow the ship. In no time at all he had a circus going.
The band filed out on deck with all the brass and strings playing
and the dancers pouring out to see the excitement. On signal, three
deckhands let off fireworks. Rockets burst and the Roman candles
sent fireballs arcing across the Sound sky.

"Louder!" Fisk cried and the band launched into "Dixie" and
then into a mazurka. There was another round of fireworks.

The yacht couldn't help but see them. It hung on the water for a
bit, then picked up wind and approached. As it neared, they saw its
sailors holding lanterns for a giant dressed in summer whites. Casey
saw the shadow of beard and the lights catching his big diamond.
In the darkness was a blonde; a light picked out her hair.

"Hello, Fisk!" the big man called and even in the dark across the
water, there was no mistaking his voice. "Is that you?"

"How's your old tin oven?" Fisk cried, motioning for his band to
stop. It was his own pet phrase and identified him.

"Fair enough. Why are you on the *Bristol?*"

"Entertaining friends of yours," Fisk called.

"Ah now, that's not quite true," Casey started, afraid Tweed
would think he was claiming too close a friendship, but Claire
caught his arm and anyway, the damage was done. Tweed leaned
forward with interest and Fisk told the deckhands to hold up their
lanterns. Tweed roared with laughter when he saw them, whether
at Casey or seeing Claire, Casey couldn't tell.

"Fast company you're in, Fisk," Tweed shouted as Casey
felt like dying, but Claire was waving her handkerchief while the
crowd behind them listened, fascinated.

"I'm fast company myself," Fisk said. "Will you come aboard?"

"Not tonight. Thanks for the music and fireworks," Tweed
called. And then as he was turning his great body to swing away, he
turned back: "Was it Florence's where we met last?" he called.

Claire poked him and Casey roared: "Yes it was!" He'd not
known his voice would come out like a bull. It must have been the
strain of not knowing what was next. Going round with Fisk and
Claire was like getting caught in a circus aerial act.

"Meet you there Monday night," Tweed said.

In the silence, Casey hesitated to trust his voice, but Claire spoke up clear and sweet across the water: "What time, Mr. Tweed?"

"Nine o'clock!" the big boss called.

His last good-bye was swallowed up in the Erie king's laughter.

♣ 13 ♣

CASEY's head was spinning as they came spilling out onto Houston Street late Monday night, filled with Florence's beefsteak and oysters. He'd been sure Fisk and Tweed wouldn't show, and yet the great man loomed on his right and Fisk's chuckle sounded in his ears. He'd gone slow with Fisk's champagne and yet he felt half drunk despite his caution. He looked up at the moon and it seemed to move, then down at the gas lamps and they seemed unreal like the gas lamps on a stage.

It was that that had upset him. It had seemed too easy, like he only had to wish for a thing to have it, the way he'd daydreamed as a boy turning shantytown to castles and himself the manor lord. He had tried to slow Claire down but she'd only laughed at him.

"That's the way these big men do things," she'd said. "If I'd left it to you, you'd end up doing nothing."

"It worries me. You had no right," he said, but she'd clapped her little hands to her head in her impatience.

"Look at Fisk, up from the circus, running railroads and ships and theaters. And Tweed himself. Wasn't he the same as you, just a slum boy from Cherry Street?"

"Ah, but they didn't do it that way, with a girl staging fake theatricals. It takes knowing the inside, who buys who, and the way the parts fit together."

"Don't you know about all that?" she cried. "Reach out and take it! Look where I've landed you," she said.

It was true, there he was, on a warm moonlit night outside Florence's with the City Boss on one side of him and the Boss tycoon of Wall Street on the other. The trouble was, it had happened so slick and fast he didn't know how to take advantage of it. With a dizzy sense of watching his opportunity slip by, he found he was mainly worried over Claire's plans for herself and Tweed.

When Tweed pointed his stick across the street and said: "Let's drop in at Harry Hill's," she gave a crow of pleasure, though Casey knew her heart must have sunk at wasting her great night at a dance hall. Not that Hill's was really low: rich men went there, judges and leading lawyers, as well as clerks and thieves and pugilists, and though the women all were fast, there were a few perverse schoolgirls, and married women whose husbands didn't know yet what their wives did behind their backs. It wasn't low by what Claire knew when Casey had first met her, but you'd never guess that now. As they passed under the red and blue lantern at the door and went by the bar into the hall upstairs, she had the muted manner of a lady seeing strange and awful sights.

Upstairs, in the dingy hall with its sawdust floors and wooden walls, covered with rhyming house rules that forbade loud talk, drunkenness and profanity, she drew back and looked about her, and it was true Harry Hill's was a heady mixture. It had once been small rooms but wall after wall had been knocked down till the hall was enormous with ceilings all of different heights. In one corner was a stage for farces, and next to it a Punch and Judy box. But the queerest sight was the dancers. Whirling round to the music of the piano, violin and double bass like some company of the damned in fine velvets and rich cloaks, officers' uniforms and top hats, it seemed as if the town elite were on a spree in a waterfront dive.

They stood looking at the dancers a moment, then Tweed turned to Claire. "How do you like it?"

Casey wanted to applaud the dazzling performance she gave. In the space of a second, she managed the effect of a reckless young lady somewhat floored at first look but still gallant and gay.

"It's very odd," she said. "But fascinating. Can we stay and watch awhile?"

Tweed gave her a look of vast amusement. At that look, merry but knowing and informed by long experience, Casey saw she'd not

be twisting the Big Boss about her finger. He knew her worth, and
set her limits, lines to cross and lines to stay behind.

"All right with you?" Tweed said and Casey realized he was having his opinion asked.

"Sure, if you want," Casey said. He sought for words to show his
feelings, that the evening had been an honor, to be with Tweed
and Fisk overhearing what the big dogs said in private to each
other. But nothing came. He felt like a lout. It was only by acting
he could show it. "Can I get a table for you? It looks crowded," he
said.

Tweed's gaze said he knew about that, too. The real workers
weren't glib talkers. He put a hand upon Casey's shoulders. "Good
man," he said and Casey's spirits soared.

He'd thought that night might be the end of it, but next week
they went to Thunderbolt Norton's hotel at Coney Island and the
men went swimming while the ladies strolled up and down the
beach. In July they took the evening boat to Long Branch, making
the promenade past the fine hotels and gaming clubs, watching
the linen-suited swells race their trotters up Ocean Avenue. Tweed
didn't go along for that, but Fisk was almost the king of Long
Branch. They put up at his hotel, the flashy Continental, and Fisk
insisted on picking up their bill.

Back in town, they went driving in his six-in-hand with black and
white horses and two Negro footmen in white livery at the front
and two white footmen in black hanging on behind. That day they
passed Madame Restell out airing her diamonds behind her Cuban
thoroughbreds and Casey thought that Claire might fall from
Fisk's carriage making sure that Restell saw her.

He'd have thought she'd be satisfied with that, an oyster saloon
hooker to have come so far, swanking around hotels in Long
Branch and being drawn through the Park in six-in-hands with the
King of the Erie Railroad. But Claire's ambitions were vaulting.
Nothing would do her but an invitation to Fisk's new Grand
Opera House. And about that, Casey wasn't so sure. It was Jim
Fisk's latest toy and after tricking it up with gilt and frescoed walls,
he was bringing in famous stage acts so that the audience was very

toney with everyone in evening clothes, Judge Barnard and Jay Gould and all that gang. Casey did his best to slow Claire down.

"Don't push your luck too far," he said. "Besides, I don't know we ought to be seeing so much of them. It's expensive keeping up with that mob."

It was, too. Even with Fisk picking up their bar and dinner bills, there were a dozen new dresses for Claire, new clothes for him, tips for the hotel maids, the waiters and such. The whole way of living had gone to her head. She was acting like he was made of money.

But she flew at him when he spoke of it. "Don't be so small about pinching pennies. You'd do better just to press your case. I've seen to it you've got fine connections — it's your business to make some use of them."

"How would you suggest?" he asked with irony.

But she'd not be trapped that way. "That's up to you to figure out." Really she couldn't resist giving advice. "Fisk's a great financier," she said. "He's in railroads and that steamship line and heaven knows what market tips he has. Most men would die to be in your spot."

He had the sense all the time she was pushing him. And the spending went on. He scarcely knew how it had happened before she had him decked out in a white linen suit. When they were invited on Tweed's yacht, he got off the Greenwich coach with Claire, feeling he'd have to be having an inspiration just to recoup their investment.

Fisk and Tweed were aboard by the time they were rowed out in the club's skiff. A colored waiter was serving drinks and one of the ladies was smoking a new cigarette from France while the others were laughing at her. Fisk and Tweed were stretched out in deck chairs, looking to the manor born. You'd never know from their air they were busy all week running the City and the Street.

For all his pleasant look of languor, Tweed was steering huge city orders to his own printing company. He'd just organized a bank — Fisk was a director of that — and he was operating an arms company that sold weapons to the National Guard. He was in real estate too, renovating lofts and stables and renting them to the city for armories.

And Fisk was even busier. Besides managing three theaters and the new Opera, a steamship line and the Erie Railroad, he was fighting a dozen lawsuits from last year's Erie battle, and preparing to swallow up another railway. Lying back in his deck chair he might be, but Casey knew for sure another railroad war was shaping up. He'd lined up Fisk's strong-arm boys himself, most of them from the Arsenal Gang. He'd got Paddy Sullivan and Mose Barry, and Horse Masterson fresh from Sing Sing. Horse had been taken red-handed, and drunk for good measure, in a waterfront warehouse during a newspaper drive to clean up the river pirates. He'd just done two years. But no one would guess to look at Fisk he was mapping battle plans in his mind.

He leaped up when he saw Claire, set her in his chair beside Tweed, pushed cigars on Casey, and had two more deck chairs brought up. It was a lovely thing sitting there as the light talk rose around them. Casey had a drink set in his hand and sat watching it all, the long spars rising overhead, the blue waters of the Sound, the sparkling glasses and fast, pretty women.

But the gang he'd got together for Fisk kept coming back into his head. And that darkened his mood, for it led him to think of Scanlon. Knowing Scanlon always needed extra money, he'd gone to sign him up for Fisk's railroad fight and he'd not believed he was hearing right when Scanlon turned him down.

He had looked about the shabby kitchen at the table that needed paint, the broken rush chair stuffed with a pillow, the children's litter. Two babies were watching him, their lips smeared with crumbs and milk. The second eldest was hanging out the window looking down on the backyard privy — he was the one had been shot in the riots. He'd lost the sight of an eye and had headaches. And Kitty, swelling again with child, was stirring oatmeal on the stove. She was standing in the way of Irish women — her left hand slipping round her waist to press the pains dragging at her back. It drove him wild, that way of standing — it was like an accusation.

"You don't think you will?" Casey said to Scanlon. "Why it's a hundred dollars, man." That was a fortune to Scanlon. He'd always jumped at it before — electioneering, dragging drunks from the sa-

loons to vote, blocking polls in the primaries so only their own
crowd could get in. And going with Fisk was a breeze; it seemed to
Casey a man might go without money changing hands at all. "Ye'll
be at the Delevan House. Expenses paid." Scanlon must know what
that meant — free whiskey from the bar in Fisk's suite, free steaks
when they liked. And Scanlon did. It must have sounded like
heaven to him. His eyes sharpened at it; then he looked down and
shook his head.

"I can't just go haring off," he said. "I've got a family and a
job."

"There'll be no trouble about the job," Casey said. He'd got it
himself for Scanlon as officer in Judge Barnard's court. Sometimes
too, Scanlon picked up work on the docks, poor sort of work, hard
and chancey, but it left him free.

"Ah, didn't I tell you?" Scanlon said, looking so innocent Casey
realized he'd flushed him out. "I just got on the Harlem as a brakeman."

"Did you now?" Casey said, putting steel in his voice. He didn't
like the smell of it. For one thing, it was hard to get, not great pay
but regular. Scanlon wouldn't hook it for himself and Casey cast
about for who had pull. McGlynn, he thought. It was a priest's job,
respectable and steady, the sort they got for family men who came
hanging round the church. Well and good, if Scanlon wanted.
But it seemed to Casey he shouldn't forget the job in Barnard's
court. He drew the pay without work but still there was a *quid pro
quo*. Scanlon had got the quid; the quo was being ready when
Casey wanted.

He'd not say that direct to Scanlon. But the ingratitude rankled;
he tried coming round a different way.

"So you're Vanderbilt's man now," he said with false good
humor.

Scanlon gave him a sick look. He read the papers too and knew
Tweed had left Vanderbilt after the Erie battle; he put it together
with the court job Tammany had got for him.

"Ah sure, those big boys don't care what I do," he said, trying a
grin. "I'm small potatoes."

"You can't carry water on both shoulders," Kitty said, speaking suddenly from her place at the stove. "Either ye've a good honest job or ye hang around the saloons to be at Tammany's beck and call."

So they'd had it out. Casey thought so. And guidance from the priest, too, he'd bet. The word honest reminded him of his sister Mary, and he gave Kitty a hard stare. Gone was the scared, bony girl he'd whistled down from her tenement to take riding when it pleased him. She'd never been what he'd call pretty, so though the bloom was off her, he barely noticed. What he saw was her gaze was different. On the surface it was yielding but in its depths it was bedrock. She'd give up the court job so as to have Scanlon out of the saloons. They were all the same, the Irish women, taking a high moral tone when what they really wanted was to grind a man to death. And the priests behind them always: "Before you marry, make him file fer citizenship. If he drinks too much, see he takes the pledge." He should have known, when he saw Scanlon at the St. Vincent de Paul meeting, that this was coming. The archbishops and that winked at Tammany, being men of the world and knowing how the world ran. But lower down you found fanatics. And that was what he must have sensed about McGlynn. For all his Greek and Latin, the man couldn't bend with the world; he was dangerous.

"You make your bed, then you must lie in it," Casey said to show Scanlon he wasn't fooling. He'd come when he was needed or he'd lose his place with Tammany.

"Ah, Casey, let's not muss," Scanlon said. And to do him justice, Casey knew it wasn't the city payroll he was regretting, but the years of friendship, the fire-fighting, rushing the growler to the Arsenal, the girls they'd met and grand gang brawling.

That was the pull that Kitty feared. She pushed the oatmeal to the stove back so it wouldn't burn.

"He's got a family to raise, and a decent job, so stop pushing him," she said.

Suddenly, Casey felt a fool to be standing in his good clothes in the shabby kitchen being rushed at by a biddy woman as if he was threatening her nest. He threw up his hand and said, "Have it your way. I was just trying to do a favor," turned round on his heel and left.

He thought he'd put it from his mind. There were plenty where Scanlon came from, eager to do any kind of a job for a bit of money, and he'd had no trouble lining up the other boys for the railroad battle Fisk would be having next week up in Albany, so he thought he'd succeeded. Only now, sitting quiet on Tweed's yacht, it crept back to sting him, her acting like his jobs had all been dirt. In a movement of escape, he turned from the sparkling Sound waters to see Fisk. He was in his yachting jacket, his arms folded on his thick chest, his reddish hair crimped above the temples, his great moustaches waxed. His merry eyes dancing with plots spoke of sureness and the barber's scent that enveloped him banished the Scanlon's kitchen like a whiff of dentist's laughing gas.

"I didn't know you cared for opera," he said, smiling at Claire.

My God, Casey thought, she's trying to corner him into the Grand Opera House invitation.

"I know better than that, Mr. Fisk," she laughed back. "You put on plays there."

But Fisk wasn't so easy. Behind the mild air was the sharp operator, railroad thief and watering stock genius. He wasn't going to do anything he didn't want to do.

"You know, Tweed, I don't like the way this boat of yours is bobbing. It's not a good idea for the ladies. I think I'll have a word with your captain. Your pardon, my dear," he said to Claire and rising from his deck chair, made his way forward.

Casey gave her a look that said *You're not so smart*. And she gave him back one that said *Let's see how you do yourself*.

It was that look that reminded him he was lying back wasting his chances. His stock was high, too, having just rounded up Fisk's rough boys for him. A man like Fisk, dealing with tycoons and presidents and making the market rise and fall, might easy enough make him his fortune.

Into his mind jumped a tip he'd had in the Blossom Club that Fisk and Gould were buying gold. It had been in June he'd heard it, when President Grant had gone to Boston in Fisk's steamer.

With an inside tip, a man could get on fast. Suddenly he discovered himself on his feet, strolling forward after Fisk.

He found him standing at the yacht's prow and he leaned on the rail beside him wondering how to bring up the subject of gold.

"It's a funny market," he said, deciding to plunge in.

Fisk shot him a merry glance. "Ain't it always?" he said, reaching inside his yachting jacket for his cigar case. He sprang it open and offered it. "You can always lose as well as win."

"That's true for you," Casey said, taking one. He clipped the end, then they turned from the wind and Casey lighted Fisk's cigar and then his own. As they leaned back against the rail, he dropped it quick and fast. "I was thinking to buy gold."

He knew by the little quiver of Fisk's hand that he'd touched him on the quick. But there were no other signs to read. Fisk's ruddy face just looked mischievous. He put back his cigar case and his chuckle was full of fun.

"Gold's a woman. She's fickle. If I was giving away advice, I'd say stay out of the Gold Room," he said.

"Ah, that's a point now," Casey said, shooting a shrewd look through the smoke streaming by his face. He waited, but Fisk was finished. In another moment, he strolled away and went below deck. Casey stared at the bright blue waters and revolved the tip. There didn't seem much he could do with it and he realized Fisk had given him the slip as neat as he had Claire.

After that, they didn't hear from Fisk again. August dragged on, and early September, and all they knew of Fisk was what they read in the newspapers. He'd gone up to Albany with his gang from the Arsenal to take over the Albany and Susquehanna Railway. But the A&S president had fought back and their doings were reported in the *Herald* and *Tribune* — subpoenas fluttered on both sides from partial judges, the cops locking up first one side and then the other, and finally a pitched battle between Fisk's gang and the A&S men in a tunnel with two engines crashing headlong and Fisk's gang finally worsted. It was the first time Fisk had been beaten grabbing railroads and when Claire started picking on him again about the Grand Opera House, Casey felt himself losing patience.

"That's childish," he said. "The man's been busy. He can't be thinking of us all the time. He's been in trouble up in Albany."

"All that's over now," she said. "He's back in town."

Casey knew that, though he hadn't told her. He had seen Horse Masterson the day before when Horse came dragging back into the Comet with a bullet wound in his arm that he'd got fighting Fisk's battles in the tunnel. Paddy Sullivan had been stunned by a spanner, but the other boys were okay and back at the Arsenal clubhouse again. Horse had been hit the worst and Casey took him to a doctor to have his arm treated. He'd seemed quiet and strange since the two years he'd spent in Sing Sing. As the doctor had him take off his shirt, Casey saw the scars on Horse's neck where he'd worn the yoke, the collar that jutted front and back so a man had to sleep sitting up. It was made of iron and oak and had no padding so it wore the flesh away. There were shady rumors about Sing Sing, the water torture and thumb-string. It gave him a sleazy prison feeling to think of that as Claire was chattering on about the Opera House.

"It's not a good time," he said, clearing his mind of Horse. "I can't be bothering Fisk about theater tickets when he's having financial reverses."

"A big man like Fisk doesn't cry over losses," she threw back.

He gave her a hard look but she was twisting a red curl around a finger and her delicate jaw was set. He ended sighing, seeing that it was useless to reason. When she was fixed on an idea, hell wouldn't stop her.

By the time he got to Fisk's Grand Opera House on Twenty-third Street, the performance had already started. Folk in evening clothes were sweeping past the ticket-takers and Casey felt out of place in his suit and bowler. He was turning to leave when he saw Fisk all black and white and diamonds, moustaches waxed, his flushed face gleaming, and before his courage failed, he strolled over and hailed him.

"Casey!" Fisk beamed, pumping his hand. He was cheery enough but underneath Casey felt he was wary. He was a tricky one, Casey knew, for all his jokes and admiral's uniforms and riding actresses around in carriages.

"I just happened to be going by," he tried.

"Glad you dropped in," Fisk said cheerfully. "Have you seen the new play? It's called *Patrie*."

This is better, Casey thought, seeing an opening. "No. Claire and me have been wanting to see it."

"Here's your chance! Come in now," Fisk laughed. And before Casey could mention Claire again, he swept him past the ticket-takers and by the bronze bust of Shakespeare in the lobby entrance. Hurrying after Fisk to the proscenium box, Casey had a sense he'd been flummoxed out of Claire's tickets but by then they were finding their chairs and sitting down. Fisk leaned across to him and said: "It's still the first act."

"Ah," Casey said, as if it made all the difference to know that. Since it was Fisk's own theater, he gave his attention to the stage. And it wasn't bad at all. He recognized Lucille Western from seeing her with Claire in *East Lynne*, and he was just picking up the story when Fisk rose.

"Stay where you are. I'll just go look in Judge Barnard's box," he said.

Without Fisk beside him he felt exposed. When the lights came on, he studied the famous frescoed walls and ceiling, ran his eye across the gilt, and counted gas globes in the chandeliers while he wished Fisk would come back. But Fisk appeared to be gone for good.

The audience was in evening clothes and they all seemed to be with friends but him. His sense of uneasiness increasing, he rose, and to kill the intermission, took a stroll by the boxes till he found Barnard's.

They were all there, Fisk and Barnard, and Tweed himself, and even tricky little Jay Gould looking prim and smug. Casey tried to catch Tweed's eye but Tweed glanced past like he'd forgotten him. He had the sense that he'd been dropped and wondered why, whether he and Claire had pushed too hard the day on Tweed's yacht or if it was just that their novelty had worn off so they weren't of interest to Tweed and Fisk anymore.

But he couldn't turn tail and slink off. He sidled up to Fisk and though it took more courage than an alley fight, he managed to get out a few words. "Just thought I'd come and find you." He tried for an easy grin.

Fisk glanced about. "There you are," he nodded vaguely. "Having a good time, I hope?"

"Grand," Casey said, waiting to be asked in with the rest.

But Fisk clapped him on the back. "Take a walk about and see it all."

"I'll just do that," Casey said, feeling like he'd been flayed alive. Hardly knowing he was moving, he found himself walking away.

In a strange new kind of pain, he drifted into the marble lobby and up the great staircase to the second floor where the new Erie offices were and wandered by the carved oak doors where Fisk made his decisions beside his sixteen telegraph wires that connected him with every station on the Erie Road. He seemed to be cut in half. Half was coolly watching what he'd read about in the papers. Behind the carved doors, he knew, were the notorious Fisk offices with mirrors and silk hangings, washstands tinted with rose and gold and painted with nymphs, and a blue ceiling that said "Erie." There had been a fearful uproar about railroad offices being in a theater, and half of him was taking it in. But the other half was suffering at the knowledge that Fisk's interest in him had flagged.

An usher began pestering him for his ticket stub.

"I'm Mr. Fisk's guest," he said.

The usher fell back. He must have been used to Mr. Fisk's guests. Then, looking out and down upon the theater, Casey saw a flutter going on in a box above Fisk's box. Tweed was there now, and Barnard, and little Jay Gould, bending above a lady with blue-black hair, and he knew from the cuts in the *Police Gazette* that it was Fisk's mistress, Josie Mansfield. She had her opera box just above his, her brownstone was staffed with servants. She had coaches, furs and jewels. The whole town knew about her, and Fisk with a wife who lived in Boston.

He knew then why Claire wouldn't get her theater tickets. She wasn't good enough to be taken to the Opera House by Fisk, no more than little Peggy Reed. And he himself was just on sufferance, because he'd lined up the gang Fisk had needed. Tonight was his last night, he saw that clearly. More high life he'd have to earn himself.

But how to do that, he thought furiously, looking down at them. Fisk had done it, and Tweed and Gould. They were clever, he admitted, but then he knew a thing or two himself. He picked up rumors and tips at the Blossom Club.

The thought of gold returned to him. He cast his mind back to standing at the prow of Tweed's yacht, trying to recall what Fisk had said and how he'd looked when Casey had pumped him. It was hard to make much of it; Fisk was cagey. But there he was next to Gould, and Gould was buying gold, Casey knew. Gould was a friend of President Grant and Grant's sister, too, and her husband. The government wouldn't sell till they'd all feathered their nests.

The houselights flickered but Casey went on standing in the aisle till the usher bore down on him.

"Time, sir," he said and Casey nodded.

"Second act starting," the usher said, and finally Casey turned and wandered from the mezzanine.

Going past the carved Erie doors, he descended the thick carpeted stairs, his hand touching the velvet rail. From the lobby, he walked past the ticket box into the August night. He barely noticed he was leaving, he was so busy scratching dough together and telling a broker to put him in gold.

❦ 14 ❦

Tʜᴇ cymbals clashed together and with the trumpet lifting the "Star Spangled Banner" into the last September air, the steamer *Drew* headed upriver with the New York and Brooklyn delegates for the Democratic State Convention at Syracuse. The grand saloon was jammed and cigars were already trampled in the thick carpets as Casey pushed past the mob gathered round Big Bill Tweed and stepped out on deck for a breath of air.

For awhile he strolled up and down fighting to control his agitation. It had been bad enough, after his summer's merry-go-round with Fisk, to be cast back to being just one of the crowd. But with the State Senate sessions recessed and Maguire home running the ward from the Comet, he felt pushed into the far shadows. He was an alderman right enough, but with Maguire back in town it was to Maguire men went when they wanted a favor, a gas lamp placed or a watering trough or a job in the courts to support the wife's brother. And attention following power, it was Maguire got the backslapping on board the *Drew* all morning. It was Maguire shook Tilden's hand and traded fake smiles as if the great battle wasn't shaping up between Tweed and Tilden to choose committeemen and draft the platform, and even beyond that, pick the candidate for President three years from now. And it was Maguire was called to meet the Brooklyn delegation's head and help hold together the truce that he and Tweed had made against the Tilden threat.

With the music blaring and the laughter from the grand saloon ringing in his head, Casey leaned on the rail and tried to calm himself by watching the far banks of Jersey pass. The rolling woods went by, and little towns raising up their church steeples. A fast-sailing flat-bottomed scow went skimming by, carrying sugar and molasses on its return trip to the Hudson River farms. It had a Negro skipper with a crew of two who grinned and waved as they sped by and Casey saw how he must seem to them — a lazy rich man with nothing to do but smoke cigars, steaming off to Syracuse to make decisions for the state. And it was true, too. He mightn't have come so far as he might wish, but it was still a grand long way from rolling drunks and fighting to save his eyes in Devlin's ratpit. His spirits lifting, he waved back, and then turned toward the grand saloon to try his luck again at catching Tweed.

But Maguire came stepping over the rim of the sliding saloon door and walked quickly down the deck in the opposite direction. Casey nearly hailed him, but then he stopped. It was hard enough having Maguire back taking over the ward, but ever since Casey returned from the A&S war last month, Maguire had been jumpy as an alley cat. Nothing anybody did was right. He complained there were too many drunks hanging around the Comet, that Casey wasn't on hand enough. Or if he was, then he should have been out checking fires or attending a bartender's wake or looking in at a German wedding. Casey wondered what was chafing him. Being a state senator was fine — it couldn't be his place in life. Perhaps there was trouble at home — they'd just the one child and he a misfortune. Or perhaps it was teetotaling; the last time he was taken drunk was the night he'd been elected senator, and they'd scooped him up firing off his pistol in the Astor bar. They'd squashed the charges and kept it quiet, and he'd climbed back on the wagon.

So Casey stopped himself from calling out. But Maguire came walking back around the deck at last, a black look on his face. He saw Casey and paused, then marched over and exploded.

"The Regency they call it and the Regency it is," he announced.

"Ah now," Casey said, placating him. Only the opposition papers called Tweed's rule the Regency. Maguire must be wild to be talking so aboard the *Drew*. He wondered what had happened.

"This platform we're planning. You'd think they'd want a man's ideas on it," Maguire said. And Casey guessed Maguire must have given some opinion and Tweed had been too busy to listen.

"They'll want ideas. When they've time," Casey said.

"They will not," Maguire said. "I'll tell you what they'll do. Two minutes before we vote, they'll call us in and give us orders. Do this, do that is all you hear. If you want what I think, they're holding this Ring of theirs too close. Three men, four or five — what's that in a great city?"

"Perhaps you're right," Casey said, seeing there was no stemming Maguire's wrath. It was best to let it out to the river wind instead of bottled up to explode God knew when or how, maybe shouted at Tweed himself.

It seemed to work. Maguire leaned on the rail and got down to grumbling comfortably. "They'd not be where they are now if they'd not climbed there on Irish backs."

"True for you," Casey said and Maguire brooded at the current.

"We put them where they are. And we could bring them crashing down again."

"True again."

"It's the attitude I fault. Too close by far. Too high and mighty," Maguire said. "I sided with Tweed at the time but now I see I was wrong about that muss with John Kelly."

"Ah," Casey said noncommittally. Personally, he found Kelly unbending. When he'd fought with Tweed, thrown up his mayor's candidacy and rushed off to the Holy Land, Casey had felt it was good riddance. Tweed's vices were the kind made a man easier to deal with, while Kelly's touring the Holy Land seemed close to religious mania.

"They're all the same. Power drives them mad," he said to calm the waters.

"That's so," Maguire agreed.

"But you've not done so bad at all. State senator, and who knows what comes next. Washington is reasonable."

"That may be," Maguire said, letting himself be placated. Casey'd heard Mrs. Maguire favored Washington. And he did himself, if it came to that, it being even farther than Albany. Not that he wasn't grateful to Maguire, and he'd always back him in a fight. But the ward was getting small to have two leaders try to run it.

"And who knows what a man's troubles are," Casey said, feeling the time had come to excuse Tweed a little. Maguire couldn't stand glowering by the rail forever. "If he was short with you it might be some private worry."

At that, he struck pay dirt. Maguire turned and shot him a look, then turned back to the rail and gave a sigh. He ran a great hand through his black curls and his lined forehead was distracted.

"That's true," he said. "Even myself. If I've seemed a bit sharp lately —"

"A man's allowed some of that," Casey said and held his breath for fear Maguire would stop.

"To be completely honest, it's this thing of Gould's," Maguire blurted. "It seemed all right to me if Gould was in it, and Fisk, too, now by what I hear. Men like that know what they're doing."

"You're not in gold?" Casey said, flabbergasted.

Maguire turned on him. "And why not?" he began, then seeing Casey's face, he stopped. "You're in it too?"

"Up to my ears," Casey said. "I bought at a hundred thirty-five. Just before it dropped."

Maguire nodded. That was ten days before in mid-September. Casey could smile since it had gone back up, but at the time it had been no laughing matter. Just thinking of it brought the fear brushing his stomach, the hot nights lying with the sheet thrown off him, Claire beside him and his not caring. She was silent while he got up and lit the gas jet and paced the little kitchen.

"That's when I got in, too," Maguire said. "Do you think now we were wrong?"

"Not by a damn sight," Casey said. "It's up to a hundred thirty-five again, ain't it? And sure to rise more."

"But if it don't?" Maguire said. "I've bought on margin."

"Everybody buys on margin," Casey said. "It'll rise. Fisk is in it. So is Gould."

"You think Grant's sewn up then."

"Fisk wouldn't jump in if he wasn't."

"But he's President of the United States," Maguire said and trailed off.

Casey gazed in surprise on Maguire's troubled innocence. "How's the country any different from New York City?" he said.

But once he knew Maguire was into gold, Maguire's worry infected him. All during the Convention it was a fever running through his brain and blood. As he walked down the center aisle of Weiting Hall with the five hundred delegates from New York and Brooklyn, he had only a second's satisfaction that they made Syracuse look like the Tammany wigwam. Then the Convention seemed to fade away and he was reminding himself Fisk's brokers were buying like madmen in the Gold Room. He sat through the morning session telling himself that the pall that hung over Weiting Hall was only because the results were so sure that the public hadn't bothered to come. But vaguely he felt that the whole world was in gold and everyone's real concern was what was happening back in Wall Street.

The Convention came to order, the speeches started, then the temporary chairman was elected and addressed them. And after that, Tilden was blasting the Fifteenth Amendment and listing the dangers of Negro suffrage. That was part of Tilden's scheme to grab the party away from Tweed, who backed the moderate Northern position, and ordinarily he'd have listened, but today he felt like rising and shouting from restlessness.

As soon as they were recessed, he ran and found a broker's office and stood watching the gold dial. It stood at 137½ and though he was getting richer every hour, his nerves were growing jumpier too, lest Gould and Fisk be wrong and the President start dumping Treasury gold to force the price down.

That afternoon they had nominations. Nervous as he was, Casey had to admire Tweed's style. When New York County was called, he showed they didn't want to hog it by splitting the vote between the candidates to leave the state ticket to the upstate delegates. Tweed himself called the New York count and so comically split his ticket that the whole Convention roared and burst into applause. He carried the Convention with that. Tilden was finished, it was clear. But in the middle of Casey's flush of admiration, it occurred to him that a man as cool as Tweed wasn't up to his neck in gold. The realization made him sweat as he wondered did Tweed know something that kept him out.

"He don't need to," he told himself. "With his snout right in the trough, why should he gamble." Still, the ice of doubt was trickling in him so he barely could make himself stay in his seat. At the next recess call, he rushed back to the broker and found gold had shot to 141. The final session he scarcely heard, with the naming of the new State Central Committee and the new Platform of Principles — Tweed's platform, not Tilden's. It was adopted without debate, making a clear-cut victory for Tweed.

The two speeches following were a torture, but during them, he looked over at Maguire and took heart from Maguire's misery. As soon as the Convention was dissolved, they jumped up and pushed through the crowd to one another.

"Instead of waiting for the others, let's just catch the midnight train," Maguire said.

"You cut along to the depot," Casey told him. "I'll run by the hotel and get our bags."

The Gold Room was jammed with a shouting mass of men when Casey pushed into it from New Street next day, not brokers and bankers only but merchants and speculators like himself not willing to stay back and let their brokers handle their orders. Still, a man needed a broker. Looking for his, Casey pressed past the messengers clogging the entrance and struggled through the mob staring up at the gold dial as the fluctuations were announced by the ringing of the bell.

The center pit was a bedlam. The bronze cupid-and-dolphin fountain playing near it was almost hidden by the men scrambling to catch the rising figures.

For nearly an hour Casey searched, calling his broker's name and being told he'd been there just that minute, and all the while the crowd was swelling as gold rose a quarter at a time, from 141 to 142. The bears he knew by their sweating faces, for they'd sold what they didn't have, and the bulls like himself were half crazy with hope. But underneath that was a fear and a kind of quivering like his own.

Finally, across the room, he saw his broker's white hair fluffing out beneath his stovepipe. He shouted at him but the bell ringing drowned him out and when he looked up at the gold dial, it had moved again, to 142½. A new sensation gripped him. All night on the train from Syracuse, he'd sworn that if the price only stayed where it was, he'd pull out with his profit. And yet, now that he could, it was strange, but he found it nearly killed him, just the thought of letting go of all the profit he might be missing. Uncertainly, he waited, hanging back with his eye on his broker, watching the bankers surge about him, and the messengers yelling for men inside.

After awhile he took a turn up the street to Maguire's broker and stood with Maguire watching the dial and listening to inside tips that not only Grant but his Cabinet were staking all on a further rise. He stopped in at Delmonico's a few blocks up on Broadway, and that was crowded too with Gold Room overflow. It was there he got the idea to stop by the Treasury offices. He went there on the double to see was there news about the Treasury selling. But he wasn't the first to think of it. The Treasury offices were besieged by a yelling crowd of bears shouting threats and demanding the government step in. But the government stood firm; no bulletins were posted. The Delmonico's whiskey helping, Casey's confidence was growing till suddenly his fear came back and he found himself pushing up New Street again.

He found that by his absence he'd nearly missed seeing Fisk. The great man was just leaving the Gold Room, his diamonds shining, moustaches fierce, his ruddy face wreathed in confidence. He shone so brightly among his brokers Casey nearly missed little Gould creeping quietly behind till all at once they were beset by ruined bears. Hurling curses, a white-faced man grabbed Fisk's coat, and without thought, Casey waded in, tore the man back and hurled him into the messengers jamming the entrance door.

"Thank you," Fisk beamed, and then he stopped as if he was having trouble recognizing him.

At that, Casey's barriers crumbled before the panic rising in him.

He seized hold of Fisk and burst out: "Will it go on up? Or should I sell?"

Fisk smiled at him benignly. "It'll rise. It'll break a hundred forty-five."

Another roar rose from the bears and Casey loosed him. Fisk lit his cigar and strolled off, shepherding little Gould before him. Strangely calmed, Casey fell back, feeling as if he'd downed a dose of laudanum.

As Fisk's confidence slid into him, he went looking for his broker and told him to buy more. After all, there was money to be made every day, and he could collect for switching Scanlon's court job to someone else. Perhaps he'd sell it to Horse Masterson. He pushed the knowledge from him that Horse would pay by slipping into some warehouse, risking Sing Sing and the Yoke again. He skipped on to listing the gamblers who were operating in his ward; perhaps the squeeze could be put on them. He'd never taken dirty graft and even finding himself considering it, he stopped in surprise at the pit yawning before him. Then he remembered what Fisk had said and knew it would never come to that. He'd never have to pay. Gold would rise to 145. And at that figure he'd sell.

Wall and New Streets were already full when Casey arrived next morning, and half the crowd seemed to be drunk. Men with red eyes shouted and pushed against the Gold Room doors. Casey felt drunk himself, though he was only hung over. His mouth was dry and giddiness came and went in his stomach. His palms were sweaty so he rubbed them now and then against his pants. Even his memories of the night before were blurred. Delmonico's came back, with dignified-looking men pounding on the bar. If they'd done it any other night, they'd have landed in the street. After that, he'd been drawn back to see the Gold Room, though it was shut, as if just looking in might help. He saw lights burning still and watched the shadows of the clerks trying to catch up with the day's work. Standing there, regret had seized him that he hadn't sold before the final hammer and he swore he would at opening tomorrow. Then he wandered off, scarcely noticing where he was going, till he came to Claire's.

She was out and he let himself in with his key, drank her brandy, and then suddenly it was dawn and he sitting in his clothes with the gas jets still alight. He looked in her bedroom and saw she'd come home and gone to bed. Suddenly he knew he didn't want to speak to anyone till he was safe out of the market forever. Moving softly not to wake her, he tiptoed to the kitchen, heated water on the stove and shaved at the kitchen table. Then he walked through the sleeping city till it was time to go to the Street.

He was carried in on the first tide as the Gold Room doors were thrown open. In an instant, the brokers were shouting and the center pit looked full of lunatics. He might have sold then but he lingered, scarcely believing as the early sales tipped 145 and went creeping up to 147.

At ten o'clock, the president's hammer announced the formal opening of the Board and Fisk's broker, Albert Speyer, offered 150 for five millions. A shout went up and, here and there, faces froze with terror.

I'll wait, he thought. *Just a bit, till it tips a hundred fifty-five.*

Scarcely breathing, he watched as it rose jumping a quarter of a point, then a half, at last one percent at a time, till at eleven o'clock, the bell rang, and at the roar, Casey whirled to the dial and saw he'd made it — 155.

His shirt sticking to him for the sweat, he felt his legs trembling with relief as he flagged his broker in the pit. Only a fool would stay on after a ten percent rise from yesterday. He'd be out and away and never set foot in the place again.

"Thank God," he heard himself say and stopped to find himself talking out loud. But it was nothing; they were all talking to themselves. Some were even splashing their hot faces with water from the dolphin fountain.

But already his broker was gone. Casey grabbed another one and asked where he'd gone but the brokers were now panicking too, the advance having wiped out all the funds left by their customers. The man tore himself away and Casey lost him in the mob.

The crowd was growing by the second and he guessed from the look of them that the city was slowing to a halt as the word got out.

Bankers and merchants were dashing in, bareheaded, to see the dials.

He made his way to the door and saw New Street was blocked, and at the sea of wild faces staring up at the outdoor dial, he backed off lest he be caught there, and unable to get back. He felt a hand try for his pocket and he whirled but the hand drew away at his move and in the crush he couldn't tell who had done it. But he knew then that the pickpockets had heard too, and drawn like sharks to troubled waters, had come in packs to work the crowd.

He was still looking for his broker when Albert Speyer bid 160 for any part of a million. He stood paralyzed, staggered that he'd nearly sold too soon. But then he shifted into the dream feeling once more that it was all happening like a carnival that he was only watching from the curb. Without sensation, he saw men weeping, and one man fell in a fit or a faint — he saw him go down and the knot gathered around him, but by then he was feeling nothing, only floating aloof and free. He even smiled when he heard 165 to his left while only a few yards over, a man was buying at 161.

The Trinity Church bells were tolling noon when the bell rang again and suddenly, the dial was sinking. It touched 160 and then in seconds, breaking a point at a time, it went down while men shouted and screamed about him and Casey suddenly was in another panic. He rushed to the pit. He caught his broker and roared: "Sell!"

But the dial was dancing up and down in the scramble of the bears to purchase, and it was down to 138 before his broker nodded back. Casey stood stunned amidst the pandemonium. He heard a messenger yell: "The Treasury's dumping gold! They're selling four million!" Of course it had to be that. He'd known it without thinking. Grant was not fixed after all. Fisk and Gould were broken, the gold corner worsted, and the surviving bears were hugging each other as they laughed, capering around him.

Suddenly, it quieted. Brokers hoarse from shouting could only whisper as they gathered together trading notes. Each few moments, the hammer sounded them to order and offered gold to buy or sell. Little Albert Speyer mounted the rostrum, half sobbing in distraction, and cried that all the gold he'd traded was for Fisk or Gould; he'd not even asked for margin. "I did nothing on my own," he repeated, "nothing at all," as Casey shouldered himself through the mob and made his way toward the door.

In a daze, he wandered through the crowds on New Street. Some were openly crying and one drunk man was waving a pistol and threatening revenge on Fisk. At the corner of New and Wall, he thought he saw Maguire but suddenly he didn't want to talk to anyone and he turned away sharply and headed for Delmonico's.

The bar was packed. He put his foot on the rail and when he got the bartender's eye, took his bottle and his glass and tossed down three whiskeys in a row. Gradually the sharp edge wore off his grief and he began listening to the talk that was going on about him. Kimber was ruined, and Speyer and Belden. Old investment houses were washed away, and famous bankers were pulled under. Stocks had crashed too and even winning bears didn't know where they were — if their debtors had gone down, it meant they were ruined, too. The worse the news about the others, the better he felt not having been ruined alone.

As his bottle level sank, his anguish blurred till when the news began to come in about Fisk, he was listening with the rest. And the rumors came thick and fast that a mob of speculators raided his broker's office to murder Fisk but he had fled out the back way, and whipping up his carriage horses, made a dash for the Jersey ferry. A man ran in and said a ruined state senator had shot him. For a second, Casey thought it must have been Maguire, then the man said it was John Morrissey. But by the time they'd all drunk a toast to Morrissey, it turned out to be untrue. Fisk was safe, the next man coming through the doors told them — he was barricaded at the Opera House and Tweed had sent a police platoon to protect him.

"He's done, just the same. Washed up," a banker said.

"Don't believe it," someone answered. "Barnard will sign some fancy writ or other. Tweed will find some way to help him wriggle out of it."

An angry buzz went up the bar. But the thought of Tweed cut

through Casey's whiskey. Picturing Tweed serene and untouched, rich as ever, while he had jumped in and been wiped out, made him feel he was a fool. And fool he must have seemed to them all even when he felt so grand that summer, posing for them in his linen suit. His face burning, he paid up and pushed away from the bar.

On the street, he moved restlessly, neither noticing nor caring where it was his feet were taking him. It was nearly dark and the lamplighter was coming up Houston Street when he found himself near Florence's.

He reached for a cigar and found he was out, then put a hand in his pocket and realized that was empty too. The sight of Florence's sign swinging in the evening breeze put him in mind of steak and oysters and he wondered when he had eaten last. He thought of trying to charge a meal. They knew him in Florence's. The week before, he'd have thought nothing of it, and yet the knowledge he was wiped out drained away his confidence. Drawing in his belly muscles, he headed for Claire's.

As he came running up the stairs past the umbrella shop, he passed a black child carrying a bird cage. Two steps beyond, it struck him the bird cage had looked like Claire's and glancing up, he saw her door was open with the gas light throwing a square on the landing.

"Now what," he said, and went to her door.

The kitchen table was gone and the floor piled with boxes. He saw Claire's sewing machine on a chair and the gauze from her bed curtains wadded up upon another. At first, he couldn't take it in. His mind whirling, he wondered had his creditors moved so fast they'd even uncovered poor Claire and grabbed her furniture for knowing him.

Then Ruby's high-pitched laugh came floating to him, and suddenly wild, he rushed through the kitchen to the parlor. Half the furniture was gone — the little sofa where he'd lie reading the *Herald*, and the piecrust table and his red stuffed chair. But stranger yet, the room was full of boys, some mulatto and some as black as ink, flitting round carrying lamps and pillows and one had a box of bric-a-brac. It struck him he recognized them but he didn't bother about that, for in the center of it was Ruby, her head done up in a bandanna made from Claire's favorite yellow scarf. Her arms were full of blankets and she was laughing till she saw him, then her face stiffened.

She looked at him with a strange expression, half of fear but something else was in it, too. He didn't stop to place it but barred the doorway with his two arms and shouted: "What in hell is going on?"

"Well now," Ruby said. "Mr. Casey." She was playing for time, he saw, and rage overcame him at the thought that she was thieving, clearing Claire out in her absence.

He leaped to her and grabbed the blankets and for an instant, he nearly had them. Then she took heart and whirled away from him, clutching the blankets to her.

"You got no call to do that!" she yelled, and at the outrage in her voice, he hesitated.

"What in hell," he repeated, "are you doing with those blankets? And those boxes? They're all Claire's."

"They was hers," Ruby said with dignity. "She most kindly give them to me."

"She what?" Casey said. Claire had her moments of generosity, but this was wholesale madness. He snatched at a black boy carrying a lamp but the boy melted from him and suddenly he was back in the alley with Fisk, the strange boys darting like birds around them. With a sense of the world reeling, he shouted: "Who are these kids?"

"They my nephews," Ruby said. "Helping me carry."

"Carry what? The whole house?" Casey cried.

But Ruby seemed relieved as if he at last understood. "Now you see. She give it all to me. She said, 'Ruby take it all. I'll not be needing a single thing.' "

"But where is she? What's she doing?" Casey asked and Ruby's gaze fell, then raised again with false candor.

"She's taking a trip I think," Ruby said. "A long trip. I guess it's Europe."

"Where in Europe?" Casey asked.

Ruby shrugged. "France and Paris, all them places."

"On what?" he yelled. He felt his brain might burst. "Where'd she get the money?"

"Now, Mr. Casey, she don't tell me about her business. She's a close one, you know that. She said Europe, take my things, and I just got me these little boys and start doing the way she says."

"My God," Casey said, "I don't believe it."

"Now, Mr. Casey, you just got to," Ruby said gently and at the change in her tone, he caught the other thing her expression held. It was not quite pity but something near it, the kind of shocked staring he'd seen on faces watching accidents.

Not comprehending, he drew back. It gave him a queer feeling to be looked at that way, like he might be wounded bad and not have the sense to know it.

"Ruby, listen. Did she leave a note?" he began and Ruby shook her head.

"Congratulations, Claire!" a voice called from the kitchen, and before Ruby cried a warning, he strode to the kitchen and grabbed hold of Peggy Reed.

She'd been either coming in or going out from her own apartment above. She was wearing a rose-red bonnet and carrying a tasseled parasol which she dropped when he seized her. Her merry little face was screwed with pain but he hung on, drawing her ruffled arm up behind her.

"Congratulations for what?" he asked her.

"Let me go!" she cried but he twisted harder.

"Tell me quick. And tell the truth. Try to lie and I'll break it for you."

She pressed backward to ease her arm, but he shook her and she blurted: "Tweed."

In surprise he loosed her. She tried to run but he caught her, dragged her back, and slammed her against the kitchen wall. Her bonnet slipped to one side and a blonde curl came tumbling down.

"Tweed what?" he asked.

Cornered, her fright changed to tears of fury and she stormed: "She's done a bunk. Gone to Tweed. Don't you see that, you dumb Mick bastard? He's setting her up in a place off Fifth Avenue. With a carriage, the whole thing. If you hurt me, he'll ruin you!"

"Ruin me?" he said, and laughed. It was a strange laugh, low and tearing, as if something were coming loose in him.

He dropped his hands from Peggy's arms, turned, and looked at the little kitchen. He stared at the pile of gauze bed curtains; they needed mending, he noticed vaguely. Ruby stuck her head round the door but she was silent and the boys behind her in the parlor were as still as sleeping birds.

For a long moment, he stared at everything, the metal tub where she'd bathed, his brandy cupboard, the sink where he laid the boiled oysters he brought in at night.

"Mr. Casey," Ruby whispered. "Don't feel too bad. There's other women."

Her voice jogged him. "By God, she really did it," he said aloud in wonder. "She got Tweed."

"A girl has to think of her future," Ruby said softly.

He turned and went out the door.

THE
CONSPIRATOR

♣ 15 ♣

ONE bitter January evening in 1870 a landau was traveling over the snow that lay along lower Fifth Avenue. At Tenth Street it turned and drew up before a quiet restaurant lit by gaslight which struck through the long windows and played over the icy sidewalk like the sparkle of champagne.

A broad-shouldered man got out wearing a silk hat and an overcoat trimmed in beaver. He looked up at his driver shivering on the box, gestured at him to take the landau to the stables round in back, then, stamping on the snow, went down the stone steps and vanished beyond the carved mahogany door.

The landau had just moved off when a clarence rolled up. Its passenger motioned to his driver, too, then descended the stairs and went into the restaurant.

A sleigh came next — a victoria with its wheels replaced by runners and drawn by two horses with two men sitting in back. One was massive with diamond studs shining in his shirt bosom; the other man was even larger.

After that two more arrived. And then over the snow came a shabby hack drawn by a pair of bony horses. A burly young man climbed out wearing a black felt hat and a lightweight overcoat. He fished in his pocket and paid his driver, studied the restaurant and took the stairs. But as soon as he passed through the door, he was stopped by the maître d'hôtel.

"I'm Alderman Casey," he said. "Meeting Senator Maguire."

The wary, lined face eased. He helped Casey check his coat, then led him past the bar and the tables covered with white linen, flung open a door and stepped aside.

At the sight of the crowded private dining room, Casey made a great affair of taking out his cigar case and striking a brimstone match with a show of ease. A mighty group was gathered — Sheriff O'Brien, Prince Hal Genet of the Twelfth Ward, Tom Creamer of the Seventeenth, State Senator John Morrissey, the king of gamblers, and Senator Thunderbolt Norton. The private room was thick with senators and assemblymen. Seeing Maguire by the fireplace, Casey strolled to him so the others wouldn't think he was crashing in beyond his station. And beside Maguire, he felt suddenly composed. He put his palms up to the firelight, turned about and warmed himself well behind, then watched the latecomers filing in. While the waiter went around with whiskey, they arrived stomping snow and holding up their arms in greeting with shouts of "Hello, Hal," and "Well, old Thunderbolt." Diamonds flashed in the firelight and the air grew hazy with dollar Havanas. Three more came in and then another, and all the while the waiter kept going round with the lowering whiskey decanter. Then Thunderbolt raised his head and his shrewd politician's eyes skipped over the faces, but all he said was: "I could eat a horse." That set off a friendly rush and tussle for positions at the table.

Over the Cape Cod oysters and terrapin soup, with the whiskey catching hold, they only joked and rang changes on the Republican they'd nailed up in a Delevan House room with his mulatto girl till he'd had to call the hotel staff. But with the fillet of flounder and even more with the roast wild duck and champagne, they began at last to parry. Prince Hal dropped the rumor of Tweed's new charter and Maguire said: "We'll never get a look at it. Not till it's brought up to Albany."

A kind of growl came from Thunderbolt. "He'd not dare tell us. From what I hear's in it." At that, there was silence as each man fell to considering what the damned thing would do to him.

It was bad enough for Casey. He'd heard that it set up a board of audit to pay all bills against the city, which would do him out of dough for putting in water mains or seeing a saloon got a paved street or a free horse-watering trough out in front. But besides, it gave the mayor all powers of appointment, which meant Casey'd not be making court attendants anymore. Still, men like Thunderbolt and Prince Hal were hit worse, having more to lose, while Sheriff O'Brien had sheriff's fees against the city that ran to nearly three hundred thousand dollars.

With the blancmange and brandied apricots, Thunderbolt came crashing into the open.

"Will you boys stand for it?" he demanded, and Maguire shouted, "Damned if I will!" though the cries were so loud that he was nearly drowned out.

By the coffee, fruit and nuts, they were drafting another charter to push through when they'd beaten Tweed's. They'd go to Tilden, who held a grudge for Tweed's outgeneraling him in the Syracuse Convention, and they figured the *World* would help — they'd need a paper on their side — maybe the *Sun* would come along.

"What about the clergy?" Maguire said.

They turned toward him in surprise.

"There's this talk about Tweed's women. Trotting horses and big diamonds. I'd think the clergy would support reform."

Thunderbolt said slowly, "We're reform surely. That's clear, ain't it? Even our name's reform, don't you think — the Young Democracy?"

"That's what I'm saying," Maguire told him. "We're reform. So we ought to line up the clergy."

"Well now," Thunderbolt said. Prince Hal reached into the bucket near him and made a rattle drawing the champagne bottle from the ice.

"I'll sound out my own ward," Maguire said. "Casey, drop round to St. Stephen's. They've no use for Tweed there. We'll get a statement for the *World*. They're bearcats against vice. You wait and see."

Casey found Dr. McGlynn in the parish house. He came into the library in a rush as he struggled into a seedy coat, not what Casey'd expect on the pastor of a big parish like St. Stephen's. And if it came to that, the library was seedy, too. Books there were. While he waited, he'd been inspecting them — fine big volumes in Greek and Latin and other languages also. But it had not been dusted in a week and it was queerly littered — a plate with the crusts of an old sandwich still on it, a broken glass with the spill where it had dropped. The chairs were battered with the springs sagging, and a pair of worn carpet slippers lay overturned beside the empty coal scuttle. He'd heard McGlynn's old housekeeper drank, and looking round, he'd believe it. He wondered why Mc-Glynn put up with her.

McGlynn caught him wondering. His head came up from shrugging into the old coat and he saw Casey casting another look at the shards of glass.

"My housekeeper has the grippe," McGlynn said.

The grippe, my eye, Casey thought, but he answered: "Poor soul. Not too bad, I hope?" He stuck his hand out and Dr. McGlynn shook it.

"She's coming round. She's old, of course, but when she's well, she's remarkable. We're crowded here — not everyone would put up with us." He stooped and took the slippers. "Father Mahoney's, I believe. Now how do you suppose he got to wandering around without them?"

"I'd not try to guess," Casey said. Father Mahoney, he imagined, would be one of the three assistants. The parish was so big, Mc-Glynn needed them all, but the parish house was small and they were packed in tight, even without the many houseguests.

"You've come about Scanlon?" Dr. McGlynn asked. "I saw him yesterday as they were bringing them into Bellevue." He trailed off as Casey frowned. "You didn't know about it?"

"About what?" Casey said.

"His car jumped the track and plunged over some trestle-work. He was brakeman. There were ten men killed."

"God have mercy," Casey said. "I didn't read the papers yet."

"He'll live, I think. But his ribs were crushed. A construction car, loaded with timbers." There was a crash from the back of the parish house and Dr. McGlynn looked toward it anxiously. Then he turned to Casey, realizing the interview would take longer than he'd figured. "Would you mind talking in the kitchen?" he asked. "With the housekeeper laid up and my assistants out on parish work, it's pretty much up to me."

"Of course, Father," Casey said. His mind was dizzy about Scanlon and he'd a queer, sick pang that it was cutting Scanlon off the court job that had ended with Scanlon in the hospital. It was the other way round, he told himself angrily. The priest had got Scanlon into railroads to save his soul.

McGlynn led the way and Casey followed down the dark hall. A broken doll lay on a table, and a pile of children's shirts.

"The foundling home is just next door, you know," McGlynn called back. "We're having trouble keeping the two households apart."

"More credit to you, Father," Casey said and then stopped as they passed through to the kitchen. An old man sat at the table with strange blue eyes and a halo of gray hair standing up around his head. At his feet lay a teacup with the milk and tea pooling about it.

"Ah now, Father Cooley, you must pay more attention," Dr. McGlynn said. He laid the carpet slippers on the drainboard, took a rag and began mopping up.

But the old priest didn't notice. He said to Casey: "Ye've brought word from the bishop?"

Casey glanced down at McGlynn and Dr. McGlynn sighed. "It's Mr. Casey, Father Cooley. You've not had time yet to hear from the bishop." He looked odd, such a big man to be kneeling with a scrub rag, but he didn't seem aware of that. He only put the cup and saucer back on the table, got up and soaked the rag in the dishpan.

"Father Cooley's from the coal mine country," he told Casey. "Things are hard there. Men out of work and children hungry. He sold his church's silver chalices and candelabra to feed his parishioners."

" 'Feed my sheep,' " Father Cooley told Casey with a sweet, wild smile.

"Yes, of course," Dr. McGlynn said. "Unfortunately, when his own valuables were gone, he rode twenty miles to another church and stripped their altar, too. There was a fuss —"

"The moneychangers in the temple," Father Cooley said, and Casey had a vision of the thin, crazy priest flogging about him in a strange church as he made off with their silverware.

"I see," he said quickly.

"After that, it's a long story," Dr. McGlynn said.

Casey'd bet on that. He'd been erratic before, probably, and warned for it — now he'd be relieved of his parish. And what did a man do who'd been nothing but a priest? They wandered the country, the drunk, the disobedient, the erring priests, waiting word from their bishops that their suspensions were over. And half of them, from what he'd heard, found shelter at St. Stephen's. That's partly what McGlynn had meant by the parish house being crowded. It was kind, but it was foolish, making your home a kind of hotbed for known rebels against the hierarchy.

Still, a reckless man was what he needed, Casey realized, the kind of priest who'd rush into print against the city leaders. He looked more hopefully at McGlynn who was standing by the stove with one big hand upon the kettle.

"Will you have a cup of tea?" McGlynn said.

Casey motioned to ward it off, but Father Cooley smiled acceptance and Dr. McGlynn fixed a pot and brought two cups to the table.

"You'll be wanting to hear of Scanlon," he said. And it was true, he did, though he was eager too to get his business in. To put a check on his impatience, he reached for his cigar case, then remembering where he was, he paused.

"Go ahead and smoke. Here's a saucer for your ash," Dr. McGlynn said.

Relieved, Casey offered him a cigar, but he said: "Not right now. I'll just wait till I've had tea."

As Casey lit up, Dr. McGlynn said: "Well, let's see — there's a cut being covered on the Harlem line, above Yorkville. Yesterday morning, a construction car loaded with timber left Forty-second Street with twenty mechanics going there to work. One car, one

locomotive. As they came to the curve at the end of some trestle-
work — it carried the train over the Third Avenue horsecars —"

"I know the place," Casey said.

"The chain broke that held the brake."

"Sweet Jaysus," Casey said. "Sorry, Father. Had they checked
it?"

"I'll come to that," Dr. McGlynn said. "At the time, the car
raced ahead and jumped the track when they were halfway around
the curve. It crashed over the trestlework —"

Casey whistled. "It's high there."

"Twenty feet," Dr. McGlynn said. "Being loaded, the timbers
showered on the men beneath. Ten were killed outright. The rest
were injured. I saw them brought in myself, broken jaws, crushed
arms and legs. Bellevue looked like Gettysburg."

"But Scanlon, now —"

"He'll pull through, with the grace of God. Even so, he'll be
helpless for months. He'll get no pay. He has five children."

"I'll see to that," Casey said, and stopped. Declaring war on
Tweed, they'd find the Tammany relief funds shut off. He supposed Norton and Maguire had thought of a war chest, but they'd
not be using it for charity. It all came flashing through his mind,
and not wanting to explain, he took out his wallet. He was peeling
off two bills when McGlynn said: "And the others?"

Casey halted.

"What about the ten men killed, and the rest injured. For an
uninspected brake?"

"Ah, it wasn't inspected," Casey said. "They should have done
that."

"The car was borrowed from the Hudson line. They say they
never check the brakes on a car from another road."

"Foreign, was it? That was bad luck." He remembered when
he'd worked in the Harlem shop they only checked their own. Of
course, it was only a technicality, Vanderbilt owning both lines
really; still it was the company ruling. With a wholesale calamity,
he wondered how much the priest was going to hit him for. Half
the men would be just laborers, footloose Irish boys without families, and if McGlynn put on the screws he was going to remind him

of it. Still, he'd come for a favor and he'd no choice but be generous. It was the danger of coming round to make deals with priests.

He added two more bills but Dr. McGlynn said: "Do you know what Mr. Vanderbilt told me?"

"The old Commodore?" Casey said, startled. He stared at Mc-Glynn, realizing McGlynn must have rushed up to the Harlem offices. He suppressed a grin at the thought of the spare old pirate facing the grim young priest. He'd not have got anywhere, but Casey liked his spunk.

"He said the men knew accidents happen. They gambled on that when they went to work for him. They gambled and they lost."

Casey waited. Vanderbilt's exchanges were apt to be salty. But he supposed the old Commodore had checked himself from respect for the cloth. Feeling McGlynn was expectant, Casey searched through the story but he still ended puzzled.

" 'Tis a shocking thing," he offered vaguely.

"Of course the men knew it was dangerous. What work isn't in this city? In the metal works, the converters catch their hands. In the bottling works, the bottles explode in their faces. In the quarries, it's the dust, grinding into their lungs. Lockjaw in brushmaking and feather cleaning. The emery wheels give them consumption; so do the slag works and flour mills. In the dye and wallpaper factories, it's arsenic poisoning. Making salt, they fall into the boiling brine. They have to work just to live and feed their families. They have no choice but to take danger," McGlynn said, his blue eyes bright.

"That's true," Casey said uneasily, feeling something was being indicted that he didn't understand. As he rummaged for a noncommittal phrase or two, he saw Father Cooley had taken up the saucer and was sprinkling cigar ash in his tea.

"Ah now, Father, watch what you're doing," he cried and reached to stop him but Dr. McGlynn motioned him to stop.

"It's a kind of mortification. To take the flavor from his food," he said. "He's been doing it for years and I really think it comforts him."

Casey grunted and drew back. He supposed it was unworldly but spoiling good tea offended him. Lunatic was what he called it and he hoped Father McGlynn was getting an eyeful of where too much concern for the world's misfortunes ended a man — sprinkling cigar ash in his tea and waiting a bishop's word that never came.

But Dr. McGlynn returned to his injured workers fresh as ever. "On this earth, no man is separate. We're part of a great brotherhood. The Fatherhood of God isn't possible without the brotherhood of man."

"Ah well now," Casey said, turning off his hearing with relief it was just the usual priest's blather. For a few minutes, he'd feared he was turning into some queer road. His bills were on the table still and he added another note to it. But that was all — he'd have trouble enough getting that back from Maguire. "I'll tell you what we'll do," he said. "We'll raise a subscription for relief."

"Relief subscriptions!" McGlynn said. "What about the railroad owners? And the quarry owners, and the salt and bottling presidents? They're part of God's world, too."

"Ah now, Father," Casey sighed. It was what made him impatient of religion. It had nothing to do with the facts. It popped back to his mind that had it not been for McGlynn's moralizings, poor Scanlon would not be lying with crushed ribs, but leaning cozy against some bar, drawing his salary from Barnard's court. And if he'd been hurt defending the polls, Tammany'd have taken care of him.

The thought putting his back up, he decided he'd listened enough to be polite and pushed on to his own business.

"Now, Father, I know you don't much like Tammany," he threw out suddenly. "And I'm here to say that I don't blame you."

McGlynn sat up at that, and even poor Father Cooley, who probably didn't know Tammany from a barrel of salt herring, understood well enough that a surprise was being sprung. He stopped stirring cigar ashes and his vague eyes opened wide.

Having taken the plunge, Casey pressed on while he still had McGlynn's full attention. "There's been so much stealing — the court house costs are I don't know how many million, and it's not finished. There's the bills for printing and plastering and papering. And what's it all going for? Rank immorality. Granting we're human, still a man like Tweed, married and with a grown family, flaunting his women in public is something surely must offend you."

"Ah ha, you're after Tweed," McGlynn said. Unaccountably, for a man who had just been stirred up over old Vanderbilt, he leaned back with great composure and took a sip of tea.

"Well, ain't you after him yourself?" Casey said, exasperated.

"Indeed I am. And the Ring. And the way the city's being run," McGlynn said and Casey felt relieved. "I can even make a better case. There's the conditions of the streets, filled with filth and rotting vegetables. Tweed lets the street cleaning contracts."

"One for you," Casey said.

"The thieves are paying him off. No man is safe in his house, much less walking the streets at night."

"True enough," Casey said comfortably. It was what Maguire wanted and would look grand in the *World*. ST. STEPHEN'S CLERGY-MAN ACCUSES, they'd no doubt head it.

"Ships land their cargoes on rotten wharves. The transportation system is antiquated, the public buildings are falling down. The sewage systems don't exist and the poor are dying from it. We've a death rate three times that of other cities."

"And Tweed's gotten rich," Casey pointed out so McGlynn didn't miss it. "You'll join us, then, to fight him?"

"That's a big fight," Dr. McGlynn said. "Who've you got that's brave enough?"

"Ah, fine big men. Don't you worry. We'll not let you down," Casey said, moving in. "The Young Democracy is what we call it. There's Senator Maguire and Senator Norton —"

"Maguire of the Comet saloon and Thunderbolt of Coney Island," McGlynn said.

Casey shot a look at him. He seemed keen enough but there was a humorous undertone that made him queasy. "There's Sheriff O'Brien and Hal Genet —"

"Our honest sheriff, and Prince Hal — I understand he was at

Madame Restell's Open House last New Year's Day," Dr. Mc-
Glynn said.

Casey gave him a blank look. Still, the priest wasn't thundering;
he seemed more worldly than one would think. "Was he now? I
didn't know. Well, we're none of us without sin," Casey said.

"A paraphrase but good enough. Tell me, is Tilden back of
this?"

Casey gazed at him in surprise. He'd not realized the man followed politics so close. "He is," he said at last. "So you see what a
force we have. Would you want to join us, Father, write an article
for the paper. We've got the *World* and maybe the *Sun*. It'll give
you a grand wide audience."

"And what'll you do about my men in the Harlem wreck?" Mc-
Glynn said in the same conversational tone.

Casey thought quickly. A horse could be swapped if it meant that
much. "We'll take care of them. In fact, we'll start a collection
right now." He nodded at the bills. "Take that as first payment."

"And what about the rest?" McGlynn said. "The quarrymen
and the bottling workers, and the men stirring boiling brine?"

Casey gazed at the bills. "Well now, Father, that's a mighty lot,"
he said, playing for time and looking pleasant in case it was some
sort of joke.

"It is. And yet they're being killed and injured every day and
their families forced to thieving and the girl children soliciting
through the streets."

" 'Tis true," Casey said, fixing a sad look on his face. If he could
think of what to do, he'd surely do it, God knew. But it seemed
like the priest was talking as if he should be patching up the natural
condition of the world.

"Will you come out for legislation?" Dr. McGlynn asked. "If
the owners won't help their brothers, what other choice is there
but law? If a man is hurt at work, the factory owner should pay for
it. He's got his property and profits — the worker only has his
labor. Each gives what he has."

"Now, Father," Casey said, smiling to hide that he was stunned
to find a priest of the Church talking like a coal country Molly

Maguire. Still, perhaps he didn't know how his words might be misunderstood. "You can't force a man to give up what he's earned by the sweat of his brow."

"The sweat of Cornelius Vanderbilt's brow?" McGlynn said, smiling back. "And William Astor's?"

"There I have you. William Astor don't own factories to get involved in accidents."

"He owns slum tenement land where they die of disease. How's it different? His tax assessments are ridiculous. If you'd give me legislation, you'd have the money to clean the streets and lay the sewers you're regretting."

"My God, Father," Casey said, forcing himself to laugh a warning. "You'll get a name for a red-hot radical."

But Dr. McGlynn nodded quietly.

It was maddening, the man talking wild when he came to make an honest deal. It crossed his mind McGlynn might be joking still, and to show him that could be dangerous, he rose as if to take him at his word and carry it back as final answer.

Straight-faced, he asked: "Have you any message except raising Mr. Astor's taxes?"

But the big priest didn't blink. "Legislation and tax assessment." He reached over, picked up Father Cooley's cold cup of tea, and carried it to the sink. While he made another, he looked back over his shoulder and said: "You can tell Mr. Tilden his Young Democracy sounds too much like the old one for me."

Casey lay on his belly, the hill of pillows obscuring his view of the Delevan House windows till he raised his head and saw it was full light and the day cold and fair. He groped for his watch that lay beside him on the bedside table and read the time, nearly seven. Then he grunted and sat up, and swung his feet to the thick carpet. When he stood, he found he swayed from all the whiskey he'd put down at last night's victory celebrations. Prince Hal Genet's parlor door had been open wide and such crowds of Young Democrats milling round the walnut sideboard that Maguire had not been able to watch him close, so he'd helped himself at

Genet's, then moved back and forth following the laughter to the other rooms.

The victory itself wouldn't come till today. He stood considering it while he scratched his chest through his nightshirt and looked down at Maguire sprawled out in the other bed. They had the Lower House sewed up by twenty votes and their charter coming up on the Assembly floor that morning. It had been stormy times since Tweed's charter had been introduced and touched off Thunderbolt's attack in the State Senate. After that, they pushed Anti-Ring bills thick and fast but they'd all piled up in Tweed's Committee on Affairs of Cities. Till now they'd got him cornered, with the Young Democracy charter made a special order for the day.

"Hey, Boss," he called and nudged Maguire's foot beneath the blankets.

Maguire came out of sleep fast, his fighter's years making him dangerous, but Casey laughed. He'd figured it and moved away in time.

"Get up!" he said. "It's the big day."

Maguire fell back on one elbow and raked a hand through his springy black hair. "So it is." He reached out and fished his teeth from the water glass. With them in he looked younger, almost the real Cork Champion. "I'm not much on breakfast. Why don't you go down by yourself and I'll meet you later at the Capitol."

"I'll do that," Casey said, pleased by the extension of his freedom. He grabbed his robe up, took his towel and bar of soap. And his razor, too, for the Delevan barbershops charged cruel. Then he ambled down the hall and found an empty washroom for his toilet.

The only jolt of his trip to Albany had been catching sight of Claire in the Delevan House lobby. She was standing by the desk wrapped in a sealskin cape and signing her name to the register. As he stood surprised, she glanced up. She looked the same — the same fragile features. You'd never guess she'd been a Five Points Mission waif. She had the same clear gaze of gentle breeding, more convincing now than ever with the sealskin cape vouching for her. And though the clerk must have known who she was — he was doubtless putting her into the room next to Tweed's suite with its seven rooms filled with liquor sideboards, steel engravings, cut flowers and canaries, she handled both Casey and the clerk with her duchess air. She finished signing her name, replaced the pen with a manner that brooked no knowing smiles, and as for Casey, that was simple. She cut him dead.

Still, even that outrage had its satisfying side, he decided as he lathered his face and bent to the mirror by the gas jet. It would make it more glorious, having her in Albany when Tweed went down in the dust.

Whistling cheerfully, he finished shaving, went back to Maguire's parlor to dress, then rode the grillwork elevator to the Delevan dining room. Usually he had tea and bread for breakfast, but for such a morning he made it grilled trout and mushroom omelette, and as a fillip, he washed down a bowl of hothouse strawberries with coffee from a silver pot.

It was after nine when he finished and dipped his fingers in the fingerbowl. When he strolled to the lobby, he found it filled; the rest of the hotel was already up, too. Knots of men formed and broke up and formed in other knots again. It was a mighty lot of witnesses to enjoy Tweed's debacle. But it made getting a hack difficult. He finally walked to Capitol Hill.

The lobbies and cloakrooms were jammed and the floor of the House was crowded with the shiny-hat brigade and hungry office-seekers rubbing shoulders with famous lobbyists and state officials; even the senators had left their desks to watch the Assembly contest. After pushing through the mob for ten minutes, he made for the gallery to get a seat before the speaker cleared the floor.

And just in time, he found. There was scarcely a place left. The galleries were hardly able to hold the mob packing into them. He pushed onto a bench directly behind the rail and when the end man glowered, he flexed his muscles in his coat and gave him a hard look. But as the speaker banged his gavel they lit cigars and leaned over the rail together.

A great pall of tobacco smoke hung over the Assembly floor, and they watched through it while the sergeant-at-arms and his deputies moved everybody from the floor except the assemblymen and

reporters and visiting state senators. Casey got a glimpse of Maguire huddled with Thunderbolt, then as the floor cleared, he
frowned at a sense of something strange. It took a moment to
know what it was — there were more Republicans in their seats
than he'd ever seen before. And some Young Democrats were
missing. Still, everything today was bound to seem strange with the
great Boss crashing. The Republicans had come to see the fun.
And the Young Democrats had been celebrating so it was in the
cards some would be late.

They began by adopting a resolution to pay a court stenographer's widow the whole salary he'd have got till the close of the
session. Then they got down to real business — the charter, Police
Bill, and the Supervisor's Bill, all Young Democracy measures. The
Police Bill came first and as the clerk started reading it, Casey's
heart gave a leap, for the star performers were coming on the floor
— Prince Hal and Creamer joined Thunderbolt and Maguire and
went striding from desk to desk whispering to their assemblymen
to stand firm. And then finally there came Tweed himself, diamond shining in his bosom, six foot tall, a really huge man. He'd
had to have a chair made special when he'd first taken his seat in
the Senate. At the sight of him so grand and confident, Casey fell
to wondering had he just come from Claire's bed. That set him
wondering what they did there, considering her so small and him so
corpulent. He came to with the start, his face hot from that line of
inquiry and promised himself as soon as he got back to New York,
he'd have a night on Sisters' Row. There were seven houses on
West Twenty-fifth Street run by seven New England sisters. They
cost like hell and certain nights you weren't let in without evening
dress and a bouquet of flowers, but the girls all had style. They
played the piano and talked nicely — it was the nearest thing he'd
found to Claire.

Drawing hard on his cigar, he found that he'd missed something.
Old Mitchell was cursing out the Democrats but he couldn't understand that, Mitchell being one himself.

"You've sold your votes!" Mitchell was yelling, his face the shade
of a turkey's wattle.

"What happened?" Casey asked the man beside him.

The man gave him a look like his wits were wandering, on the bench all the while and still losing track.

"They've struck out the enacting clause."

They'd voted then and he'd missed it, being so deep in Sisters' Row. But striking an enacting clause would kill the bill *in toto*. It wasn't possible.

"The Police Bill?" he asked in disbelief.

"Seventy to forty-two."

"Jaysus," Casey said. He'd caught sight of Maguire shouting to Thunderbolt. He could tell Maguire was mad with rage. He was standing with his fists balled like Samson about to start tearing down the temple. At that, Casey leaped from the bench and made a dash for the gallery stairs.

As he took the last step and shoved into the near lobby, suspicions darted through his mind. As he'd gone back to Maguire's room last night, he'd seen three top Republicans pushing into their leader's parlor. At the time he'd paid no mind to it but now it seemed to him they'd been hatching plots to join Tweed.

The cloakroom was a madhouse. Men were shouting, reporters yelling, and Tweed's chief lobbyist was waving his yellow stick and sending pages running back and forth to the Chamber floor. Casey got as far as the door and hollered to Maguire before a deputy pushed him back.

But Maguire had heard. He came marching out, Thunderbolt hard behind him.

"Come back, man. The fight's not over," Thunderbolt was yelling. "The charter's still to come."

Maguire turned in a black rage. "They'll vote the same and kill the charter. Use your head," Maguire said, waving toward the Chamber. "Half our men are missing. The other half voted against us. Tweed's bought them."

"Ten thousand dollars apiece," the *Sun* reporter said, shoving close. "Five thousand to be absent. Ten thousand to stay and vote."

"You hear that?" Maguire said. "With Harry Smith delivering the rest." Harry Smith was the Republican city police commissioner.

"But you can't quit, man. We need you," Thunderbolt said, and Casey saw he was getting mad himself. With two great bulls losing their tempers, the Assembly cloakroom was too small, and Casey got ready to jump clear. But Maguire shouted: "I'm not quitting!"

"It looks damn like it," Thunderbolt shouted back.

"I say I'm not wasting time here."

"Where you going?" Thunderbolt said, bewildered.

"Where you'd go too, if you had any sense, and Genet and Morrissey — the whole pack of us. To get Tweed where we should have at the start."

"And where's that, my boyo?"

"To New York," Maguire said. "To the Tammany Committee itself!"

Casey was standing at the window of the Jackson Club watching the last of the fierce easterly gale that had been ripping through the city. Rain still slanted on the cobbles, and across Lexington Avenue there was a litter of broken glass where a church had lost its windows. But the storm was passing over. The weather would be fine for the Tammany meeting that night.

"It'll clear," he said, turning, and Maguire shifted in the easy-chair beside the fireplace. He had his black book open on his knee and was making a last check of the votes they counted firm to vote Tweed from the General Committee chairmanship. He frowned and tossed an exasperated look toward the noise that was coming from the bar where Gorry Gorry the Great was on the stick, dispensing cheer.

"I wish they'd ease up on the boozing," he said irascibly. "They'll need their brains, such as they got."

"It's all this rain. It always does that," Casey said soothingly. He clasped his hands behind his back and brushing past Maguire's velvet foot cushion, killed time by studying the champions of democracy staring down from the wall.

But another burst of laughter from the bar brought Maguire's head up. He nearly dashed his cigar on the Brussels carpet, then checked himself, turned and dropped it into the rose-patterned porcelain spittoon.

"I don't like it. They'll need clear heads," he said. "We've no idea what tricks the man's got up his sleeve."

"What tricks could he have?" Casey said, moving from Andrew Jackson to a daguerreotype of Sheriff O'Brien, their candidate for mayor once Tweed had fallen. There'd been a nervous flutter among the city's merchants when their slate had leaked out — O'Brien for the first Irish Catholic mayor, Thunderbolt for the police, Morrissey for city chamberlain. Tweed, at least, had made his haul, while the Young Turks were still hungry. But once Tweed tumbled from power, the businessmen would have to come around. They always did. Business was business, was what they said.

"Who knows what tricks?" Maguire grumbled, raising his voice to be heard above the shouting for "Gorry, Gorry!" that had started. Somebody began singing "Starm along, old Starmy" and men were yelling: "Stand up where we can see ye. Give him the chair now. Up ye go!"

"I don't like it none, the meek way he said yes to our request for the special meeting," Maguire said.

"What else could he do?" Casey asked. "It's in the rules. He's counting on his silver tongue. A few jokes and we'll die laughing."

"Maybe," Maguire said. "Ah God, I wisht they'd stop their foolery. We need cool heads for this night's work." He made a move to get up and fearing he'd make matters worse roaring at them, Casey left the pictures to try to calm him.

But the front door burst open and Thunderbolt came stomping in. They heard him shouting for Genet and Morrissey, and in a second he appeared before them with the old houseman jumping to take his wet coat. But Thunderbolt shook him off and strode in, spattering them with rain and mud.

"By God," he announced. "The crafty bastard!"

"Ah! I knew it!" Maguire said, his hands clutching the carved lions paws of his chair. "What's he done?"

"He's closed Tammany," Thunderbolt said.

There was silence in the bar, then the men came creeping out.

"It's shut up tight, with a notice plastered across it. No meeting in the Hall tonight."

"We'll not stand for that!" Maguire said, starting up. "We'll march downtown and smash the doors in!"

"Will ye now?" Thunderbolt said sarcastically as an answering rumble came from Gorry Gorry's crowd. "Let me tell ye what ye'll find — the whole police force waiting. I saw them as I come up. They was marchin' by the hundreds with drawn clubs, in full uniform — countless platoons, convergin' from every station house in the city."

"By God, Harry Smith," Maguire said, remembering the Republican police commissioner.

"None other," Thunderbolt said with a kind of grim Irish relish in utter catastrophe. "Tweed's bought the House out from under us. Now he's beaten us in Tammany by buying up the police."

Casey leaned forward on the gallery bench that had been roped off for the New York aldermen for the Tweed charter session. He stared down at the Assembly Chamber filled with roughs who'd been riding into Albany on every train since Tammany was closed, capturing the hotel corridors and lounging on the main streets. He recognized half of them — Bowery panel thieves, pimps, and bruisers from Five Points and the waterfront. Tweed had ordered them in case of trouble when his charter came up.

But trouble there'd not be. The Young Democracy supporters were dropping like autumn leaves before a breeze. They'd been vanishing all last night into Tweed's Delevan House parlor, and this morning in the dining room he could tell the ones who'd made deals by the rested look on their faces.

Still, Thunderbolt and Maguire and Prince Hal were fighting on, with Tilden nowhere to be seen, just his shadow falling now and then. And yet there might be a miraculous reprieve if they were able to postpone Tweed's new charter. As the speaker rapped his gavel and the sergeant-at-arms cleared the floor of the roughs, Casey sent a fierce prayer to heaven, and then champing on his cigar, bent forward, locking his hands together between his knees.

And then it all jumped to life, just the way it had been the week earlier when the Young Democracy charter was defeated. Like a stock company performance, every actor was at his old position —

the lobbyists in the cloakroom, sending pages running to the floor, Tweed carrying the battle in the Chamber, moving from desk to desk, and Genet, arms folded, in one corner while Thunderbolt, Morrissey and Maguire glowered like chained titans across the way.

And yet, though the actors were the same, Casey felt there was a difference. The pace had quickened as Tweed's control had grown more sure. When they moved to postpone consideration of the charter, the speaker banged his hammer and asked should a vote be put, and in a flash they were voted down.

They tried a feint next. Old Mitchell jumped to get the floor, but the speaker shouted he was out of order. And before they knew what had happened, Tweed's man had moved to vote the charter without a reading.

"Don't let them do that, man!" Casey burst out, hanging over the rail. It would choke off the hundred amendments they'd thought to fall back on if it came to it.

Already their man was up and yelling, seeing the dodge they'd not anticipated. But the speaker's gavel was hammering and he was shouting: "Out of order!" and threatening the sergeant-at-arms if their man wouldn't sit down.

Numbly, Casey sank to the gallery bench as they prepared to vote. His cigar had gone out and he held it unlighted. He felt so sick, he almost missed the stir on the floor. But then he drew himself to the rail again and hung over to see what was causing Tweed to go sailing to the rear.

Two ladies had come in and were settling on the back sofa. One wore violet and the other a demure forest green with a little fluted bonnet.

"My God," he whispered, recognizing Claire and Peggy Reed.

He couldn't breathe. It was as if he was having apoplexy. But gradually he realized there was to be no cry of outrage. A few reporters moved closer but no one else seemed to notice. And Tweed himself just looked victorious, all diamonds and wide smiles standing by them trading banter.

He barely heard the voting when it started. The charter passed and the gallery was emptying as if the Bowery Theater curtain had rung down before he realized the new charter had stripped him clean.

A brother alderman reached down and held a flame to his cigar. "That does us," he said, and Casey looked up in a daze. The Tweed rule was absolute. He'd seized their aldermanic powers.

♣ 16 ♣

THE rain which had stopped in the early evening began to fall again around nine. Casey heard the driver of the Broadway stage cursing the weather, and through the small window above he could see him wrapping burlap around his legs. Casey kicked at the loose straw and sank his boots in to warm his feet. But it had been raining all day and the straw was wet and muddy. Despair suddenly swept over him at the dirt, the smoking lamps at each end of the car, the driver who was drunk and racing other stages to get passengers. He jumped up and pushed the door to pull the strap tied to the driver's leg.

"By God, ye'll wait till I've made me turn," the driver shouted down. But Casey shoved the door and leaped to the street.

As he caught himself from falling and reached the sidewalk, a blast of band music struck him and the dark wind filled with rocket lights. For blocks ahead it was crowded and beyond the silhouetted heads he could see bonfires leaping above Union Square.

"Well now," he said aloud as if the sight surprised him. But he'd known about the Tammany parade for days. All he hadn't known was he'd be to it. Even when he'd seen the stage and flagged it, he'd only told himself he was doing it to get a breath of air.

Still, as he pressed through the mob, his spirits lifted. The fizz of rockets filled his head and he was jolted by torpedoes exploding beside him. The center of Union Square was full of colored fires burning red and blue and gold, and all over the city, distant flashes lit the sky as the boys set off from the ward clubs. The telegraph wires were hung with Chinese lanterns and Washington's statue was bathed in fireglow. He stopped to watch a fireworks frame spell out Governor Hoffman's name and then, as he neared Fourteenth Street, his heart swelled as he saw the marchers.

They came past Tammany Hall like the sands of the desert or drops of water in the sea, by the thousands upon thousands, carrying fiery torches so a thoroughfare of flame reached back of them toward the East River. To the strains of Grafulla's Seventh Regimental Band blowing themselves purple on the grandstand, a thousand boys in red followed a banner with a portrait of Tom Creamer and the words TAMMANY HALL.

"Ah, the rogue," Casey murmured, but his heart seemed to twist in his chest. Creamer was snugly back in Tweed's good graces. Casey barely saw the stuffed bull that followed on a truck with a transparency above it: low rents, low taxes and plenty of work. But after the next display of Roman candles, he came to himself to see a wagon of painted Indian warriors and after that, the sons of the Fifteenth Ward shooting off rockets and waving torches and dragging a live eagle tied to a golden perch by its crossed legs, supposed to represent democratic liberties.

A three-masted schooner came next, drawn by bruisers dressed as sailors and looking up at the masts where other sailors were pouring fire into cauldrons. Casey laughed aloud to see a pimp he knew. The wind blew a lashing of rain in his face, but he didn't feel it. A temple of liberty passed with a little goddess sitting inside, looking blue with cold. And next came the seventh warders led by General William Tweed, Jr., on a spirited horse with a band of Indians following, whooping and brandishing tomahawks.

As the last Indian raider swept by him, he caught his breath as he saw that Thunderbolt Norton himself was marching. Six foot tall, even more in his silk hat, dignified in sober black with a spotless white cravat, he swung his torch with might and power as if he'd never faltered following Tweed. Before the central balcony of Tammany Hall he saluted the governor and General McClellan and as a cheer went up, the mayor ducked inside and came back with Tweed. The old antagonists waved at one another and as another shower of rockets went up and Grafulla's band played "Yankee Doodle" madly, Thunderbolt stepped out of line and ordered his troopers on. They passed in review before him. Then he gave his torch to the last marcher and strode into Tammany Hall.

"Ah, the rogue," Casey repeated, but a wry smile moved on his lips. They'd all made deals, Prince Hal Genet, Creamer and Norton. Only the diehards still fought on, Maguire, O'Brien and Morrissey, throwing their Young Democracy weight to the Republicans. They'd not quit till they starved. Though they wouldn't starve, he reflected bitterly. Maguire had his saloon, Morrissey his gambling palaces, and O'Brien had put money away. If anybody starved, it would be Casey, chained to their wagon. The spring elections had turned him out as alderman, and he'd been scrimping hand to mouth with whatever Maguire tossed him. Mostly that was the crazy hope they'd win next week's gubernatorial election. They'd built up such hopes that they'd appealed to Washington to protect the polls from Tweed's dirty work Election Day. And Washington had done it. Troops were stationed in the harbor forts and two warships anchored just off shore to support the U. S. Marshal.

Watching the massed columns march by, cheering as they came to Tammany, Casey realized Maguire hadn't a prayer. Tweed would not need violence, not with thirty thousand marchers — he'd seen the figure in today's *World*. The *World*, too, had made its deal. Only he was bound to a kind of lunatic chariot, like poor Anne that summer's day among the blood-red Blackwell's Island roses.

The thought of Anne chilling him, he turned up his coat collar and a gush of rain went down his neck. Cursing, he turned down his collar quickly, and pushed back through the crowds. On Broadway he saw Creamer beneath an awning on a gaslit grandstand, a portrait of the governor rising above him, surmounted by the stars and stripes. In the rear, red and blue lights glared, and the whole was picked out by theatrical limelights. Creamer was bowing and waving at the crowd that surged about the platform banner: ONCE MORE INTO THE BREACH FOR NEW YORK'S FAVORITE SON.

"Ah, the rogues," Casey sighed with yearning. The wind whipped his words away.

By eleven on election night, it was clear Tweed had the city. Standing in Printing House Square, Casey stared up at the *Herald* office bathed in limelight. Behind the windows he glimpsed clerks and reporters grabbing late returns from the telegraph operators. From time to time, a *Herald* clerk climbed out on the narrow ledge that ran along the second story to print the figures on the bulletin board, and the roar that went up blurred the band playing down the street at City Hall Plaza.

The crowd was immense. They'd been gathering since the lamplighters had worked around the Square at dusk. The East River ferries brought them over from Brooklyn, and the omnibuses and coaches had rolled downtown with the rest. They'd lit bonfires and stood about cheering and downing whiskey till the waving torches were a hazard. Casey stepped out of a drunk's way and then saw by his badge he was a deputy city marshal. The marshals had been bad all day. Aside from them, he'd never been in a quieter election.

Since nine that morning he'd been checking the polls for the Young Democracy and he'd seen none of the famous troops. There'd been no soldiers at all, though they were supposed to be planted about the city, waiting to spring out when Tweed got desperate. Thinking of it, he smiled grimly. The way Tweed played the tune, the whole city was dancing for him, even the top financiers. John Jacob Astor had headed a whitewashing committee that came out the day before election with the news they'd examined the city's books and certified they were correct. And one of the committee names was Liggett. Casey wondered what Mary thought of her high-thinking Mr. Liggett endorsing dirty old Tammany. He wondered was it real estate that gave Tweed the hold on him. Perhaps Liggett owned slum property. That's what it was with Astor — whole blocks of six-story tenements with backyard privies, halls reeking with garbage, gutters piled with filth. They kept their hands clean with sub-landlords but they'd not dodge Tweed's tax assessors that easy.

With the millionaires it was taxes, with the whores and gamblers it was keeping open, with the poor it was coal and bread in the winter. Tammany played and the city danced — and Tweed was naming out the tunes to Tammany. All day long Casey'd been seeing how smooth it went, the folks filing to the polls, pushing their ballots in the boxes, so smooth no need to risk it with roughhousing.

It was that merry polka Maguire and O'Brien were trying to stop. As the day passed, they seemed to him more lunatic every hour. When the polls closed at five and the kids came rushing out with their barrels to start bonfires, he dragged himself over to Young Democracy headquarters. By nine, when the returns showed the trend, everybody started to leave.

Maguire asked him home but at the thought of sitting round watching Mrs. Maguire dig her needle into her embroidery, Casey lied: "I must of got a bad oyster," and claimed he was off to bed.

As soon as he was free, he'd gone like a magnet was drawing him down to Mulberry Street to join the mob hanging around the Police Central Office. Tweed was inside with the mayor and governor, and all the big men of the Ring getting election news from the wires. When the clerk announced the figures and the mob gave out a cheer, it must have sounded sweet to Tweed.

At ten-thirty, the great men began to leave. When the governor's carriage came for him and Tweed, Casey was suddenly afraid Tweed might see him and he bent down to give a penny to the organ grinder's monkey that was working the fringe of the crowd. His skin tingling, he peeked up as the carriage pulled away, and then something gave inside him and his eyes filled with grief for himself and the way things might have been. If they'd not bucked Tweed on the charter, or if Maguire had made peace the way Thunderbolt did, it would be Maguire's carriage pulling off next, and himself beside Maguire.

In silk hats and white cravats, they'd be swaggering into Tweed's Metropolitan Hotel suite, filling up on partridges and champagne, and mingling round the board with all the big Democrats. And the Republicans, too, for it was only the Young Democracy that was barred tonight. Creamer would be there, and Thunderbolt and Hal Genet, shaking hands and getting cheers.

He shoved it roughly from his mind. He'd wandered through the carnival crowds from police headquarters to Printing House Square. But outside the *Herald*, the pang came again — he might be celebrating instead of drifting broke and alone, kicking chips back into a bonfire.

He stood immobile at that, the flames blazing in his eyes, as it crushed in on him — the lost alderman's dignity, his sister Mary, frostily pleased, his mother worried for her bit of rent. At least he'd been scraping that together out of his dribblings from Maguire. But his life was crumbling like a city building made up of trash and fill. He thought of the way he'd been dropped by Fisk and the childish hopes he'd had to make his fortune buying gold. The thought of Black Friday in the Gold Room brought back what had followed it and suddenly he was standing stunned again hearing Claire had run off to Tweed.

It was the thought of Claire got him moving. As he pushed through the crowd, he felt first the pain and shock, and then oddly, through the ache, he was reliving the start of it. He'd seemed rich then to them both, lean years though they'd really been. The oyster saloon safely behind, she'd been wild with delight as they'd fitted out the flat on Bleecker Street. He remembered midnight picnics and buying the yellow bonnet she'd worn with him to the races. After that, there was a June day they'd caught the boat to Coney Island, and he smiled at how they'd strolled the deck as if they owned it.

He didn't plan on going by her place. But as the good years floated around him, a Broadway stage came to a stop and barely noticing, he boarded it. For a while, he didn't see the city passing, and then he noticed they were nearing Twenty-seventh Street, and before he knew what he was doing, he'd given the door a shove. When the horses stopped, he got down and looked around him half-surprised. Next he found that he was standing in the gas lamp shadows, gazing up at her house.

It was a three-story brownstone with lamps in front, a formal flight of stone steps, and a rosewood front door. Cream lace curtains fell over the long windows. All was chaste and dignified, with nothing to show the Boss's fancy woman lived inside. Casey wondered did he have the right house. This night he'd have thought there'd be crowds and carriages and there were none, only the street floor lighted like any ordinary evening. Wondering at it, he moved closer till he read on the brass nameplate: *Scofield.* He moved back again at that, deciding she'd gone out to a victory party. Tweed was probably picking her up, on his way from the Metropolitan Hotel. At the sense that the house was empty, he felt suddenly freer and stepping from the shadows, he examined it more closely — the downstairs kitchen was dark, and the second floor bedroom, and the servants' quarters on the top.

Did she still have Ruby with her, he was wondering, when a rooftop movement caught his eye. His first thought was thieves and he nearly stepped back to the shadow. But then he saw the gleam of bare arms and flash of bosom. It was a woman in a ball-gown. As she came to the roof edge and leaned her elbows on the ledge, he saw her delicate face clearly and realized that it was Claire.

He stood paralyzed, knowing there was no chance to get away. When she'd come to the roof edge, she'd seen him and was just leaning quietly, deciding what to do about it. She'd not call for a cop, though in their neighborhood there'd be one close, but that was noisy and meant scandal. And it was not the law anyway that was paining him, but being caught beneath her window. Giving her that satisfaction was like having the skin peeled off him.

But when she spoke, she sounded casual, as if seeing him was no surprise.

"Hello, Casey," she called down. "Lovely night."

He couldn't tell in the dark if she was making sport of him. She'd know Maguire was still lashed to the mast of the Young Democracy and it was a cold night indeed for them.

To turn her words back, he called, "Not so fine as that. You'll be catching your death of cold."

She glanced at her bare shoulders, and then paying them no mind, she looked up at the sky. "I'm watching for fireworks."

"There'll be a lot of them," he cried. It was a queer exchange altogether, one of them on the roof and the other in the street. Disconcerted, he pretended to take a look for election rockets. He saw nothing but the row of brownstones hemming them in, and he was stringing out the looking, not knowing what to say next, when she called, "There goes a beauty! Come on up here and see."

Puzzled, he turned back to find she'd vanished. He stood wondering what plot she was spinning, whether a scheme to make
Tweed jealous, or a deadfall to teach him not to hang around. And
yet, he'd come by on his own. She'd had no part in it. He waited,
hoping she'd return, but she didn't. He moved slowly across the
pavement and climbed the front stairs.

He rang the doorbell and waited, wondering what to tell the
servant, in case Tweed paid to know about strange male callers. It
was her own lookout, he decided. He could not be worse off himself. But as no one came, he understood there was nobody going to
answer. The servants must be out, and she on the roof not coming
down. His face went hot at her leading him on to ring so he stood a
fool at a shut door. He took hold of the knob, gave it a shake, and
when the door swung open, he took an unsure step into the vestibule. He stood looking at the coat tree inlaid with mirror, half
expecting some housemaid to come screaming at him.

"Claire?" he called but there was silence except for a clock ticking and the snap of firewood.

He moved to the parlor threshold and looked in at the dying
hearth, the beaded crystal lampshades, the silk chairs all in yellow,
a champagne bucket with its ice melting. He saw the clock, an
ormolu, ticking away on the mantel.

"Claire?" he called again, but still no answer. Moving cautiously,
he began to climb the stairs.

The next story was a sitting room with silk chaise longues, cream-
colored in the firelight. Leading off it was a bedroom — he could
catch a glow there too, but no other sign of life. The next floor up
was small dark maids' rooms and then a metal ladder to the roof.
She must have had her troubles climbing it in the ball gown. His
spine tingled from the strangeness, the queer silence, the empty
household. Then putting his hands on an iron rung, he swung up
and out to the November night.

At first he missed her, she was standing so still in the chimney-
pot shadow, looking out across the backyards and the houses rising
beyond. Then a Roman candle caught his eye, spewing fireballs
slowly to the north, and he saw her there watching, too. Her back
was toward him and as she moved, the silver pleats glittered down

the back of the white velvet gown. A champagne bottle stood beside her and when she turned, he saw she was holding an empty
champagne glass upside down.

"Hello, Casey," she said softly. "There it is."

"There's what?" he asked.

"The city," she said.

He looked at her sharp, having a shock now he saw her close.
The casualness had been a pose. Her face was keen and bright as if
she was having trouble to keep control. He wondered was she
drunk. Perhaps a bit, yet under the champagne there was something else loosening. He wondered if she were drugging, and then
he put the thought aside. Opium or laudanum wouldn't give the
sense he had of something wild but coiled. Following her gaze, he
saw she was looking hard out at the city.

She began to walk back and forth across the roof. "There's the
Battery and all the ships. And all the money along Wall Street. Up
here's the shops with furs and jewels. And all the rich men's
houses, with their carriages and horses."

He made a cautious noise. At first he'd thought she was watching the glow of bonfires and the night streaming with fireworks,
but now he saw she was straining to see things that were hidden by
the dark.

"He owns it all, you know," she said.

Who? he nearly asked, and then he knew. She meant Tweed.

"And I can have anything I like."

He looked at her in surprise, it was such a childish thing to say.
Then he saw she was looking at him like a child, strained and anxious to be believed.

He said, "That may be," wondering what she was getting at.

She glanced down and saw she was still holding the champagne
glass. "Do you want some?" she asked. "There's lots more."

He shook his head and with an impulsive movement, she tossed
the glass off the rooftop. They heard it shatter against bricks.

"You'll have the cops, you keep doing that," he said.

"Here?" she said and began to laugh. When he thought of what
he'd said, he couldn't help smiling himself. But next second, she
was tossing over the champagne bottle. He jumped for her but too

late. As he caught and pinned her arms, the bottle was shattering downstairs.

"That's stupid. It's a wicked waste," he said to her but she was laughing so hard she didn't hear. Her arms were ice cold to his hands and she was strung up so tight that her body arched against his.

"Why shouldn't I?" she gasped. "I worked for it."

"I guess you did," he said, thinking she meant what she did with Tweed.

But then she said: "It's so cold on the floor. And dark. And always raw there. You get so tired, twisting the wires."

"The wires?" he said, a chill creeping into him.

"The wires and paper," she said irritably. "For two dozen blossoms, we can buy tea and bread."

"Jaysus," he said, wondering what to do next. Making artificial flowers was what she was describing. She must have done it early, at five or six, sitting in a cellar while her mother was on the streets. He'd figured something of the sort, tobacco-stripping or sewing buttons, while the landlord kept threatening to throw them in the gutter. Renting part of the room came next, a corner to a family, the men drinking and the blankets humping in the night to the sound of crying, and finally the time when the child was caught alone and forced down on a pile of dirty rags. It was nothing he hadn't guessed. And there was no one but children made those flowers or did the deft jobs like candy dipping or winding twine. Still, having her caught back in it scared him. His sister Anne returned to him the way she'd huddled in the ship's berth screaming at the devil, and he took hold of Claire and shook her till he was afraid he'd break her neck.

"Goddammit, that's enough! Quit it, hear me?" he shouted.

She gasped as he spun her around and grabbing her bare shoulders, stared down to see had he shaken her out of it. She looked up at him bewildered. Her little face still held its delicate lines; the clear eyes told him nothing.

"What's wrong with you?" he asked.

She seemed confused. And in confusion, fell back on what she knew. She pressed her body to him gently with the air of a child needing to please. He hesitated. The memory of his sister was still chilling him.

"Where are you? Tell me that," he said.

"It's my house," she said carefully.

"Thank God for that."

"And I can have anything I want."

"Stop that nonsense," he said. Still, there was no more talk of wires or cellar floors and that was progress. She'd never drunk much, maybe it was just too much champagne, alone in a great house on the night that the world was out celebrating Tweed's triumph. Feeling better, he began to notice the bare little breasts nestled in white velvet. Then the house seemed so empty except for them that he found his throat going dry.

She swung away from him, and stretching out her arms, she said: "Anything I want."

While he watched her, she began to swing her wide white velvet train till the silver puffs down the back glittered like a mermaid's tail.

"Come here, now," he said. But instead, she began to dance. She danced round the roof while he watched her, then stopping uncertainly, crossed her arms on her chest, and caught her thin fingers in the velvet at her shoulders.

"What do I want?" she asked him, frightened. Without seeming to notice, she was peeling the velvet back, till with a kind of nervous spasm, her hands jerked and she ripped the bodice down.

"By God, that's enough of that!" he cried, and striding over, caught and held her. She struggled with him, trying to free herself from the clinging velvet as if it were something alive and smothering her. They worked against one another till her need changed. She was clinging to him, pleading, trying to draw him down to the roof.

He nearly took her there in a pile of silver fishtails, but at the last, a sense of exposure held him back. Picking her up, he took her down the ladder across his shoulder; she'd not have made it by herself.

He carried her past the maids' floor and at the next floor down, he entered her sitting room and paused by a cream silk chaise

longue. Then a queer sense of excitement urged him on to see
what the bedroom was like.

The fire was nearly out beneath the marble mantel, but even by
the red glow of the hearth, he could see the bed was huge. With
satin coverlid and carved rosewood posts, it carried the stamp
of the great chair made special for the Albany Senate. He crossed
to it and looked down at the shining satin pillows. There was no
embroidered "T" but he was still staring as if he'd find it when she
gave a cry in his arms.

He laid her on the coverlid and she pushed at her skirt. "I can't
breathe with all this on," she said in a fitful child's complaining
voice.

But he liked the crushed velvet in the midst of the cream satin.
It made Tweed's power seem helpless as a white rose with a
cankerworm finding it. He came down to her quickly before she
could loose her skirts and he kept thinking of a rose all the while he
was in the bed.

"Tweed," she said once, starting up in sudden caution.

He paused, listening, but there was no sound from downstairs,
not even the clock ticking. They were too far away for that.

The night had been too much for her, alone with the promise of
riches, and nearly no limit to them. But now in bed with him, nine
years of knowledge were working marvels. As soon as her skin
warmed, she started to threaten him. "If he finds out, he'll ruin
you."

And himself with scarcely two coins left to rub together in his
pocket. He nearly laughed. But he pushed her back on the pillows
instead. "I'd not count on it."

"What does that mean?"

"The man has enemies on every side." he said.

♣ 17 ♣

Iт began like a dark line on an iced pond in the night, splitting, leaping forward, throwing out branches, cracking wider with no one seeing. The first Casey noticed was the change in Maguire's mood. He was quiet but his eyes glistened like a man carrying around a secret. Casey gave him a dozen chances to get it off his mind that February and March, and Maguire almost took them once or twice on dull days around the Comet. But at the last he always drew back, leaving Casey grasping after unrelated hints and phrases having to do with a sudden death, the need for silence, and a glorious Irish victory at the end. There were times Casey thought that Maguire was getting like some old woman reading tea leaves. But then one Sunday night, he let himself into the Comet and surprised a secret meeting — ex-Sheriff O'Brien and Morrissey, and a stranger he didn't know who didn't belong in that fast company, a mousy little man like a smalltime bookkeeper or clerk. Casey got just the one look before Maguire blocked the man from view by leaping between him and the door.

After that, he began to take walks down the Comet's back alley on Sundays when the saloon was closed to see were there carriages hidden there waiting. Throughout April, he saw nothing. But in May there was a flutter — a phaeton and a victoria one Sunday, and the next, he saw Tilden himself going in. Just a glimpse was all he got, the slight body and awkward walk, an unimpressive man to see but there was no denying the brain behind the boyish face. For all his poor health and cowardice in the pinch, he'd crawled up through corporation law to the chairman of the State Democratic Committee. Seeing Tilden, Casey knew they were really onto something big.

But what it was he couldn't guess. Particularly the part about someone's death was puzzling. Till one May morning near City Hall he was standing in the sun by a one-armed Zouave in a faded uniform. He was just buying shoelaces from the wooden tray with the sign I FOUGHT AT GETTYSBURG, when a mousy clerk scrurried by and next second he was following the man he'd surprised in the Comet's back room.

Trying not to stick so close the man would tumble to being followed, Casey chased him through the crowd of minor officeholders across the Plaza and ducked after him into City Hall. Coming in from the sunlight, he had trouble seeing and feared he'd lost him. Then he saw him far away down the long corridor, turning up the stairs. Casey dashed after and was tailing so close, he nearly bumped him going into a room, but he backed up suddenly and as the door closed, Casey read on the frosted glass OFFICE OF THE COUNTY AUDITOR.

For a moment, he stood baffled. Then from the back of his mind, the tarot card of sudden death emerged just as if Maguire had flipped it to him.

One icy night last January, Tweed's old auditor had been killed in a freak sleighing accident. Perhaps, in the confusion, Tilden had slipped a spy into the office to get a look at the comptroller's books. His mind fizzing, he caught a bus and rode uptown.

As he strode into the Comet's back room, he found Maguire deep in spelling out a letter. Maguire slid his arm over it to hide it and there was a ticklish moment as Casey racked his brain for some slick way to ease into the subject of county auditors. They stared at each other till Maguire pushed the letter in his drawer and said, "Take a weight off yer feet."

But Maguire had forgotten the envelope. It was still lying on the desk and as Casey set down his chair, he saw it was from abroad. Another glance brought the word Jerusalem.

"How's John Kelly?" he asked blandly. He'd not have said it except he was suddenly sore at Maguire for keeping secrets. He deserved more, he thought, having stuck with him through thick and thin and being this minute all but pauperized for following blindly after the Young Democracy will-o'-the-wisp. He was so busy counting his wrongs, he barely noticed Maguire was having another of his struggles to be discreet. But this time, Maguire lost. He rose and hollered out to his bartender: "We'll be busy for a bit," locked the door and turned to Casey.

"What I say must go no farther," he said. "The truth is, John Kelly's coming back."

Casey stared at him. There was nothing earthshaking in that. The man was a citizen, after all, and wouldn't be wandering the earth forever. He'd been gone nearly three years since his knock-down fight with Tweed.

"Well now, that'll do him good," he said, "coming back to his own kind. Since he's had so much grief away." He didn't care much for Kelly himself; all the religion put him off, and the pious letters describing the Holy Sepulcher and Mount of Olives kept cropping up reprinted in the newspapers. It embarrassed him for a Tammany man. But you couldn't knock someone who'd lost his family from galloping consumption — a wife, only son, and two daughters, all taken these past few years. The last two had slipped off while he traveled with them looking for a cure. Still, it wasn't the kind of thing he'd expect Maguire to be locking the doors to tell. To have something to say, he dredged up an old rumor.

"Is he taking Holy Orders?"

"He is not," Maguire said, exasperated. "He's coming back to reform Tammany."

"By God, Tweed'll be liking that," Casey said, a grin spreading on his face.

Maguire came back and sat down. "Perhaps I shouldn't be telling you this. But our men are quitting City Hall today. And when they go, they'll be carrying off copies of the Ring's books."

"The auditor's office?" Casey asked, as the pieces slotted into place.

"That. And we've had another planted in the comptroller's office too."

"Jaysus," Casey said, awed by Tilden. While O'Brien and Maguire had been flailing away direct at Tweed's walls, the tricky lawyer's brain had been plotting how to infiltrate. Except for the Astor whitewashing committee, nobody had seen the books.

"We'll have enough dynamite by tonight," Maguire said, "to blast City Hall to the ground."

The fuse was longer than Maguire thought and nearly fizzled out at that. First, O'Brien got the thought he might use the books to pry Tweed loose from the sheriff's money owing to him. But Tweed was too smart to play. He knew that where one copy was there was bound to be another. So O'Brien nearly ended by only getting himself killed. Three plug-uglies jumped his buggy as he came out of the Jackson Club and he was lucky he'd not been drinking and was a big man in condition still. He'd lashed about him with his buggy whip till he forced them back and urged his horse to gallop on.

Then Tilden grew impatient and moved in to print the evidence. But even Tilden couldn't get the *Sun* to touch the stuff and finally they had to give it to the *Times* which wasn't so good a place to show it as the *Times* had already been sniping at Tweed and it looked like a partisan attack. All through July the series ran, and even Casey was surprised by the jaded way the public took it.

Finally, they had a break. Tweed had got so used to being king that one hot day when a reporter baited him, he lost his temper and shouted: "What are you going to do about it?"

Casey got a respect for silence, seeing how much those eight words cost Tweed. It seemed men didn't mind getting robbed nearly so much as being insulted. Next thing that Tweed knew, there were mass meetings formed, demands to repeal Tweed's charter, and the cry was in all the papers: "This is what we're going to do about it!"

But getting repeal through Albany with Tweed buying up the legislators wouldn't be done so easily. It might still have come to nothing without Tilden lurking in the shadow, his clever lawyer's brain scheming to cut Tweed off from the city treasury. He found a way. Neither Maguire nor O'Brien would have thought of it in a million years, but Tilden got a merchant with the honest Irish name of Foley to bring suit as a taxpayer, restraining the city from paying out city funds.

When Casey heard that, he told Maguire: "It's a cute trick. But it's coming up in Barnard's court. He'll never grant it."

Maguire smiled like a cat licking bird's blood from its paws. They were all half-crazed by then from tiptoeing about conspiring.

"You've made a deal?" Casey asked. It was hard to credit. Barnard had been with Tweed for years. Tweed had made his fortune for him. But perhaps it was that was the trouble. Now he was rich enough to suit him, he'd started wanting something else. "What's Tilden promised him?"

"He's taken a fancy to be governor," Maguire said.

"But that's crazy," Casey said.

"Maybe so, but he's swallowed it."

Barnard enjoined the city to stop paying its bills. The injunction was so sweeping, city ditchdiggers couldn't get their wages. From one second to another, Tweed's income vanished.

It filtered to Casey through the grapevine that Tweed couldn't believe Barnard's betrayal. When he grasped it, he had hysterics, threatened suicide, then switched about and had to be talked out of shooting the editor of the *Times* who'd begun the whole thing by baring Tweed's books. But he was hooked fast. His patronage had grown so large, the ruling killed his credit with the banks. All they had to do was reel him in. One Friday in October he was arrested on charges of defrauding the city.

That night Casey was climbing into bed in his hotel room when there was a knock on his door, and before he could call, the knob twisted and a woman came in. For an instant, he thought she was some stranger getting the wrong room. Then she swept off her hat with the veiling and he saw it was Claire.

"What the hell are you doing here?" he said, swinging out of bed in his nightshirt and bare feet. He'd not seen her since last fall's election night. He had tried, but she'd been like granite about that.

But as she threw her hat down he saw it was no time to question her. She'd not done her hair. It was coming down her slender neck in wisps. Her skin was flushed as if she was running a fever, and a vein he'd never noticed was standing out in her throat.

She dropped to a rickety chair and, putting her hands to her face, began rocking back and forth like an Irish biddy at a wake. "By God!" he thought, "she may deny it, but there's the proof it's in the blood. Claire Scofield, me eye, more likely it's O'Grady." The sight swept away his shame that she'd caught him in the shabby room with the gas jet sticking bare out of the wall, the carpet with the mange, and the red rose wallpaper stained from the last tenant squashing mosquitoes in the summer. He went to her and touched her shoulders but she wriggled him off in a fury and returned to rocking.

"It's not so bad," he lied. It was not so bad as it would get, was what he meant. Still, it was no time for truth. "Jay Gould met his bail. He's not in jail yet."

She let out a cry, a kind of wail, then clapped her fingers to her mouth as if she were bottling in the rest.

"And it didn't come as no surprise," he said. "You've had four months of warning."

"My God," she sighed. A little shudder went through her, and remembering the whiskey bottle in the closet, he went and got it, poured a shot in a glass and held it for her. But she waved it off, almost upsetting it. He gave a sigh and drank it himself while he looked down at her clutching her thin arms to her middle as if something in her were breaking.

There was no denying part of him was gloating. Remembering himself standing in her Bleecker Street flat like a fool, hearing she'd thrown him over for Tweed, he felt she'd got what she deserved. But all the same, he had an awed respect for Tweed's misfortune. That a man could rise so high and yet go down as if he was plummeting from a cliff gave him a queer feeling in his stomach. He wondered how Tweed had felt when the sheriff served him with the warrant. Tweed knew it was coming and was sitting at his desk in the Public Works Department when Sheriff Brennan walked in and made the arrest with a great crowd of reporters pushing in. They said he'd taken it like a Roman. Though, of course, Jay Gould was there to put up bail of a million dollars. But though he was free till his trial, the days of high-stepping were over. With the whole city watching, he'd not be strolling up the stairs again to the little brownstone on Twenty-eighth Street. As that thought came, Casey said: "You'll be all right. You're not alone in the world."

She gave a little cry and began to weep.

"You'll be fine." he told her. "You're a pretty woman. Did he provide for you at all?"

She gasped and nodded.

"Ah," he said, feeling relieved. If she'd come to him for money, she'd have been in for a shock.

He found himself wondering what she'd got. Tweed had known he was heading into choppy waters, and he'd had the summer from the start of the *Times* exposure to transfer funds. The main bulk of it would have gone into his sons' names, but there'd have been plenty left to see that Claire was fixed. Gazing down, he tried to think how to bring up the subject. But he couldn't.

He was still standing, thinking, when she made an effort to straighten up. "He's been very generous," she said.

"Ah," he sighed, gratified. "The brownstone, I suppose, furniture, carriage and horses?" And when she nodded: "That'll keep you nicely, if you sell. I guess you'll have to?"

"I may not," she said, dabbing her eyes with her lace handkerchief.

"He's not settled a lump sum too?"

"Mostly stocks and bonds," she said, and fell back to sobbing. "He's been so good. Once the first shock was over — the wickedness, that Barnard!"

"He's a Judas," Casey said. With the Young Democracy, it had been war, both sides knowing it. He hoped she saw the difference. Their stealing copies of the books was only army espionage. He wondered should he point it out. But just then she left her chair, pulling at her hair with her little fists.

"What's going to become of me?" she cried.

"Ah you'll be doing fine," he said, trying to shush her. She could carry on just so far in his hotel. In the rich ones, they made allowances, and in the fly-by-nights, they expected trouble. But at his rates, they'd soon be knocking at the door. She must have strained his credit with the desk already coming up to his room at night for all her veiling and tragic look.

"You'll not be poor," he said, turning her to him so she rested her teary face against his shoulder.

"I'll be alone," she said.

He stroked her back. "What am I here for?"

"I need to marry," she wept.

"Ah now, be sensible," he said. "I'll be coming by to see you. It's almost the same thing."

"It is not! I can't go living in that house by myself. I want a name and respectability. It's not fair, now I have money. There'll be crooks taking it away from me!"

He'd like to see the crook fool enough to try that. He nearly smiled at the way strain had unsettled her. But holding her against him, he stopped feeling like smiling. Beneath the tears and veiling, he began to make out the firm bones of a swap. Me and my money for your name. And your prospects, that was in it, but there they both gambled. Politics was a horse race.

He wondered could he do it. The money made it a temptation. Having money, he could wait to make smart moves. Look at Tilden, he thought; Tilden had made his fortune first in law. Even O'Brien and Maguire had their saloons. Money gave a man dignity. And to have Claire herself was worth something. The nine years he'd been with her, he'd not tired. She might be maddening but since she'd left him, he'd found out how hard it was to find another like her. He felt like groaning. If it hadn't been for her hustling on the waterfront, he thought. And she'd made it even worse by becoming Tweed's woman. He'd not be able to live that down.

"We could start somewhere new," she said. "San Francisco's a good town. You could make your way in California."

And the minute he did, some New Yorker would show up. She took in his silence.

"Or I'll go away and change my looks. Dye my hair and wear plain dresses. I'll come back a Catholic widow —"

"Ah now, that'd never work," he said. But he wondered if it would. With Claire it might, providing nobody saw her too close.

If she ran into Tweed, of course, or even worse, Pretty Boy —. Still, she'd not be moving in that set. He wished he'd time to think. But it wasn't easy with her hanging on his neck. The scent of her perfume was unsettling too. Perhaps, he thought, if he took her, it would help clear his head.

But as he edged her toward the bed, she rushed out with more plans: "Casey, listen. I'll make a lovely widow. I'll take a house and join a church, and make donations to charity."

At that he stiffened. The mention of church invoked the image of John Kelly.

"What's the matter?" she asked doubtfully.

He couldn't tell her. She was in Tweed's camp still, and Kelly's takeover was a secret, though the whole city soon would know it with Kelly sailing into New York harbor tomorrow. But he went chilly at the thought of her playing her tricks on a queer, pious man like Kelly. He'd not react like Tweed and Fisk.

"What is it?" she was saying, giving his nightshirt an impatient tug.

"I'll have to wait."

She pulled away. "What's wrong with you?"

He shook his head. He'd not be able to explain, but the thought of Kelly had cooled his blood.

The St. Patrick's Mutual Alliance Band was blasting "Come Back to Erin" from the pit when Casey and the Maguires took their box. Mrs. Maguire had to be settled first, her skirt safely out of the way of their feet, her fan and opera glasses found, before Casey and Maguire took their chairs and Casey got a look at the night's ordeal.

The Irish associations were all present, from the Knights of St. Patrick to the Catholic Temperance Union, the men scrubbed and shining, packed in the parquets and orchestra seats, while the lawyers, merchants and politicians had filled the boxes with their wives and daughters. As the band bridged into "Minstrel Boy," Casey bowed to Kelly in the next box over. He'd brought a party from the St. Patrick's Cathedral building committee, Casey saw, his heart sinking at the sight of daughters. That meant he'd be stuck with supper after, Kelly being so short of escorts he'd take anything in a cravat, though God help you if your tongue slipped. It was safer not to open your mouth.

Casey sighed as the music died away and a storm of cheers brought his attention to the stage. He took in the line of clergy sitting like blackbirds along a telegraph wire and then Father Burke came flying from the wings, his Dominican habit whipping about his legs, grabbed the lectern and was off, doing "The History of Ireland" tonight.

If he just hung on, Casey told himself, Burke's whirlwind tour was bound to end. It was bad luck John Kelly had taken such a fancy to him he'd not risk missing a golden word, so that Casey'd heard him on "The Pope," "The Christian Man," "The Confessional" and God knew what else. The man never ran out of wind. Half Casey's wages as a city marshal seemed to go on tickets for Burke's benefit lectures for the Irish Dominican order.

For a man like Maguire, it wasn't so bad. He was married, and had had so much trouble with the booze, he couldn't drink. Since he'd had his teeth pulled and wore false ones, his digestion had been going. Maguire was getting on. Besides, he had a sentimental streak about the church, particularly nuns. Sisters of Mercy were forever coming round the Comet tapping the till for charities, and Maguire felt he got his money's worth swapping donations for novenas.

But it was cruel on a man, just the same, following Burke. Even Maguire was starting to chafe. Though part of that might just be resenting Kelly's stiff-necked ways, his domineering rules and orders. Casey didn't mind them like Maguire did. For one thing, it didn't hurt his pride to take an order. Having lived in Maguire's shadow made Kelly easier. Besides, for all his rigidness, Kelly was a simpler man than Maguire. Where Maguire got suspicious at a compliment, Kelly lapped it up without a murmur. Probably he'd got used to the priests flattering him about his piety and donations. He gave the Church money like it was water — oil paintings for St. Patrick's Cathedral, stained windows for his dead family's memory, and he helped untold boys to study for the priesthood.

He glanced to Kelly's box to see did the streak of softness show.

But all he saw was a pug-nosed Irishman with a stubborn jaw and heavy frame, sitting his chair like a sack of lead. He was still examining him when Kelly turned and frowned. Casey thought the frown was for him, not being riveted on Father Burke, till he saw it was for Maguire who'd fallen asleep, his chin resting on his chest. He stuck out his foot to kick Maguire's shoe and Maguire gave a start. Even Kelly smiled at that. And then one of the young girls from Kelly's box looked to see why Kelly was smiling. She glanced puzzled at Maguire and then to Casey. He took in the dark hair, chiseled features, the straight pose as if a rod went up her back, and saw she wasn't as young as he'd thought. She was twenty-nine or thirty. He had the dim sense he had run into her at mass. At St. Patrick's, probably. Maguire had been dragging him there since Kelly got back. And judging from where she sat, she was one of Dan Callahan's daughters. Callahan was on the St. Patrick's building committee. He was in law, Casey thought, but nothing to do with politics, probably corporation law. He wasn't really rich but he must have a brownstone and a carriage. There would have been parochial schools for the boys, convent training for the girls. Trying to place them, Casey decided they were a kind of Irish Liggetts. They'd not come over fleeing the Famine. They must have been here two generations at least, and from moneyed stock at that, younger sons, maybe Dublin College. In the summers, when families like his own had been sleeping on the roofs and keeping the windows shut against the smell of the privies in the back, the Callahans were at the shore. The girls took piano lessons from the nuns and made sweet, romantic retreats, doing the Stations of the Cross around little artificial grottoes. They put on their nightgowns before they undressed, and their drawers were full of frills and ribbons and the kind of embroidered underwear Kitty's mother used to make to feed her hungry family.

The thought of underwear made him think of her naked body. He imagined her struggling to get into her nightgown without seeing her breasts. And at that, he was assaulting her, snaring her in the nightgown like a net and throwing her down on her clean white sheets beneath the crucifix on the wall above her bed. For the instant, she was less a girl than the Liggetts, the shore summers and crocodile lines of clean children promenading to church, and it was less rape than a murder he was performing between her white thighs.

Suddenly he realized she was still staring at him. As she turned her head back to Father Burke, he wondered was she watching him all the time and he felt his face go hot.

Settling back in his chair, he tried to catch up on the History of Ireland. They'd got to Cromwell's invasion, he gathered, and then he slipped away again as he was caught up in a cozy sense of well-being to find himself a city marshal with Christmas coming, the city trimmed with Christmas trees and fir garlands, Tweed indicted by the grand jury, and the rest of the Ring fleeing to France. Even the thought of Claire added to it. She was sitting sullen in her brownstone with no wreath on the door, no Christmas gifts or holiday plans, waiting to see would he break down if she kept to herself. No marriage, no visits. His mind wandered past the parlor fireplace, the yellow silk chairs and ormolu clock and began gliding up the stairs toward the big bed with the satin coverlid, but he pulled himself back roughly. He'd not throw away the years of struggle —the street fights, his lungs bursting, the shame of having Fisk lose interest, the searing memory of sitting on the gallery bench in Albany as Tweed stripped him of his powers as alderman, the eating dirt, the long, hard lessons — just when the grand prizes were coming.

He was suddenly surprised by cheering and looked around to see Burke was finished. He was still holding up his hands to heaven like some old prophet in a stained-glass window. Then as Burke dropped his arms and bowed, the Callahan girl turned in her box and looked back. He nodded and she looked away as if he'd scared her. As well he might, he grinned, if she'd been able to guess what he'd been thinking. It amused him that she'd looked back. Her father wouldn't like her casting eyes at a Tammany bruiser. As he helped Maguire with his wife's sealskin cape, her fan and glasses, and they waited by their door for Kelly's party, his spirits rose. He'd gotten through another night of Burke. Even the supper party didn't seem so bad. He might put his mind to getting a place at the supper table next the Callahan girl.

PART FIVE

1874

&

THE ACCUSED

♣ 18 ♣

". . . and these Thy gifts which we are about to receive from Thy bounty through Christ our Lord. Amen." Young Father Mulcahy finished saying grace, the family crossed themselves and looked expectantly up the table toward Casey who raised his carving knife and began slicing the roast for Sunday dinner.

He didn't do it with the ease of old Daniel Callahan, who was watching with frosty humor, his fingers fairly twitching to take the job over. But Casey hacked doggedly away, avoiding Eileen's face which he knew was arranged to show her family she hadn't noticed her husband's lack of trivial refinements.

Sometimes he thought that look of Eileen's set him on edge more than Dan Callahan's finger-twitching or her two sisters trading glances, or his brother-in-law's impatience to get the job over so he could eat. She had the air of a holy virgin on the gridiron showing no pain but rapt and innocent like she was already entering into heaven.

Estimating he'd carved enough, he sat down at the table's head and began filling plates from the stack before him with cauliflower, cantaloupe pickle and mashed potatoes, sending each plate on its way by the little greenhorn maid. He felt himself relax as the Callahans' attention switched from himself to the maid whose performance was even more doubtful than his own. Last time she'd spilled gravy and fell to scooping it back in the gravy boat before their eyes. He'd enjoyed the way Eileen handled that. She'd nipped from her chair and hustled maid and boat through the pantry door. It was only his own failures brought the look of virgins listening to far-off choirs.

He wondered had she got in the habit of it when they were trying to talk her out of marrying him. For a year and a half she'd resisted Dan Callahan's arguments, and when she'd been banished to Cape May the first summer, she'd written him letters by the yard. He'd been surprised by their heat, as later she surprised him by turning up at his hotel saying that she'd run away. He could have taken her that night. He felt she was asking for it so that she could force her father's hand. But there was something about her fixed blue gaze, her icy fingers, and the wild rose of Erin convent air of her that held him back. He found himself swept along by the girl's dream of romance with a rough politician, and like a figure in a melodrama, he put her cape on her, picked up her carpetbag, and drove her back to her door in a hack and delivered her to Dan Callahan in tears. That spiked Callahan's charge of social climbing. But still, Callahan was a practical man. Melodrama hero or not, a city marshal wouldn't do. It wasn't till Kelly put him on the slate and he was elected a city coroner at $15,000 a year that Callahan gave him a chilly welcome to the parlor and talk began of houses and trousseaus and a June wedding at St. Patrick's.

An uncomfortable feeling still went through him at the memory of those evenings in the parlor with one of her sisters always watching while they turned through the album daguerreotypes of Roman churches and scenes of Irish lakes and castles. He felt a fool, not knowing what to say, and anyway he felt too old at thirty-two for all the formal tarradiddle. Not to mention she was herself nudging thirty in spite of her girl's glow shining through her skin as they waited for her sister to brew the cocoa in the kitchen. But the excursion to the kitchen was part of it too. They flung at each other, keeping an ear out for the sound of pans and china chinking, while he kissed her lips and felt her big, soft breasts, and she begged him to stop before they fell into mortal sin.

That June they married in the Cathedral, Eileen veiled in white and himself in a silk top hat, with Maguire his best man and Kelly and the Tammany bigwigs turned out to stand by Callahan's law partners. Casey's mother was there, overawed, and his brother Frank got the day off from the Second Avenue horsecars. Even his sister Mary appeared. She'd been crippled the year before with rheumatism and not being able to stand the pace at the Liggetts', she'd been forced back to live with their mother. As he paid the rent, she'd had to come to his wedding. But she struck back the best she could, throwing glances of dark foreboding and shaking her head when she looked at the bride. As he leaned from the carriage after the Fifth Avenue Hotel reception, she was standing in the hotel doorway, her fist held tight as if she couldn't bring herself to toss the rice. He grinned and waved his top hat to her and she jerked her fist, still clutching the rice so he knew she'd forgotten it with what she must be feeling to watch him dashing off with his ill-got gains. And yet, her thin face kept returning as they rode to the boat, and after, he kept seeing her all the way to Narrangansett. Like some menacing old fairy woman, she seemed to be hurling curses after their honeymoon.

"May I have the preserves?" young Father Mulcahy was saying.

Casey found his plate was half empty and himself barely knowing he'd been eating. He laid down his fork and as he passed the tomato preserves, the little maid came flying in late with the soda biscuits. In her haste, she left the pantry door ajar and Knob Kerry, his pit bulldog, came slipping into the dining room.

"Ah God!" the maid cried. "The sly beast, he's so cunning. Come with me now," she said, and then cringed at putting her hand to Kerry's studded collar. Kerry gave her a casual look and crept to his usual place at Casey's foot.

For a moment, Casey wondered might he let Kerry get away with it. The dog would come to no harm with his head beneath the chair and if he started moaning for food, Casey'd put a foot on his hindquarters to shush him. He shot a look about the table, but Dan Callahan was getting his "No dogs at table" look and one of Eileen's sisters was already touching her napkin to her lips as if she was losing her appetite. Even Father Mulcahy's soft face was growing peevish as he glanced at poor Kerry. His being a fighting dog didn't help his case either.

So Casey threw down his napkin, pushed back his chair, and

hauled Kerry by his collar to the kitchen. "See he stays here," he told the cook.

She raised her eyes to the kitchen ceiling as if appealing to heaven to judge such finicky ways. She'd been born in a sod house and used to dogs, pigs and geese underfoot. Today he felt she was the only one in the house with sense. He slammed back to the table to find Sunday dinner continuing blandly and everybody pretending that nothing had happened. It was like watching the display behind glass of a wax happy family.

"Ah Jaysus," he breathed as he sat down, and if they flinched inside, not a one betrayed he'd heard. Eileen, looking rapt, offered Father Mulcahy the biscuit basket.

Well, they should see her as he did when they were gone — the blue eyes crazed, the chiseled features frantic as she struggled with him to put out the candle before he got with her into bed. In the dark, it was better. When he found her mouth, her breath was hot and when he'd got her nightgown up, he found her flesh like fire. At first, it hadn't bothered him, all the weeping and praying that went on as he reached his peak. But then it began to make him edgy — like her shuddering at his brass knuckles the day she found them on the bureau, averting her face when he took Kerry out at night to fight in the dogpits, the pale way she kept peeking at Horse Masterson when he stopped by the house. She'd seen the scars on Horse's neck and when Horse left, she kept after him till he told her of the yokes they wore in Sing Sing. "Stop, please don't!" she'd cried, and he was left feeling like dirt for telling her.

The worst was his job as coroner. Now there she wasn't even being sensible, for it was that money was feeding her and putting the clothes on her back. It wasn't as if he handled the bodies either. But just his stopping by the Bellevue dead house was enough. She claimed she smelled it on his clothes, and they couldn't keep a maid for all the cleaning she had her doing. He had the sense he was revolting something deep inside her, and yet she'd wanted the marriage more than he and she'd known about him then. It was that really outraged him. She'd known and chosen and taken it back, like a woman fascinated, jumping into a pit of snakes.

"May I, sir?" the little maid said, and he saw she was trying to take his plate. He jerked his arms out of the way. The floating island came in then, and with dinner so near over, he felt better. When Father Mulcahy asked did he think Tilden would be becoming governor, he put the suspicion from his mind they were offering him a sop, and held forth on the way the city would go as he dished out the dessert.

Afterward, Eileen led them all into the parlor. The maid finished up the table. He could hear her rattling and clinking. And then Eileen went upstairs and brought down the baby, Daniel, and sat him beside her on the sofa. He was a fine baby, Casey'd give her that, and he even felt himself glow as the two sisters gathered round him, poking their fingers and talking nonsense. He had Casey's mouth and chin, Casey thought, though he'd Eileen's eyes. Sometimes it gave him a turn to see her curious, absent listening expression staring out from the baby's face. But he was a great healthy boy, something really to be proud about. Though he tried to look impassive when the sisters started flattering, he soon found himself drawn over and when young Daniel stuck out his fists, he put out his own fist to box with him.

"Please, you'll hurt him!" Eileen said.

"He'll hurt me, more likely."

"No, now, don't," she laughed but he knew the laughing was for her family and he stood up and left the women to their fussing. Eileen was four months gone with child again; he hoped the next would be a girl so they could do their fussing with her. And by then young Dan would be old enough for him to take over and teach him what he'd have to know.

He lit a cigar and strolled over to join the men by the window seats. They made room for him but they'd stopped talking as if they expected him to pick a subject. He looked out the glass for inspiration. And suddenly, he had his self-respect back at being a city official, standing at the window of his own brick house with its stone steps and view of the florist garden opposite. In summer there were carnations. The slaughterhouse was a block up and sometimes they got the smell as well as the sound of cattle lowing in the night, but today the wind was the right way and they heard and smelled nothing.

"A fine day for November," he offered.

"Yes," his father-in-law said.

"Will it hold now, do you think?" he said, and then regretted it. They'd be supposing he was just a politician worrying about elections Tuesday.

But Dan Callahan said he thought it would hold. There was another silence till Father Mulcahy laughed lightly and reminded Callahan of a joke about the weather that they'd heard that summer on their Irish trip. They traveled about a lot together; for all the difference in their ages, they were good company for each other. Casey was damned if he could see why it was, and he stood trying to get the hang of it. But their talk was all historic spots they'd seen mixed in with Cathedral gossip. An hour later, they were deep in a tour through Dublin Castle, arguing which picture hung where, when Casey knew he'd had enough.

"I just remembered," he said too loud so the whole room glanced up, Eileen looking rapt and wide-eyed for her family's sake. But he'd started, so he bulled it through. "I got to drop by and see Mr. Kelly."

In the livery stable down the block, Casey didn't wait for his horse and gig to be brought around, but went in to smell the straw and dung. He sighted Darby, his black gelding, rummaged his pockets for sugar cubes, then helped the colored boy with the harness while another boy brought the light two-wheeled gig down the ramp and hitched Darby to it. The warm mucky scent of the stable and the look and feel of Darby always soothed him. It was like his feeling for Knob Kerry; whatever it was didn't have to be checked by the cautions that seemed to be needed with people. It was simple and direct, man to dog, man to horse. But even apart from that, Darby made him feel good because Darby had once belonged to Jim Fisk.

He was one horse of the matched black and white pairs that had drawn Casey and Claire through Central Park the summer Fisk had taken them up. After Fisk had been shot to death by Josie Mansfield's other lover, Fisk's finances were in a muddle and his property had gone on the block. Casey had showed up at the auction with half New York. It had been strange standing in the welter of porcelain cuspidors, carpets, chandeliers, clawed bath-tubs, two hundred canaries singing in their cages, a stable of horses and silver harness trapping, the whole crazy circus coming under the auctioneer's hammer. Fisk who'd lived so high was dead, struck by a rival's bullet as he entered a Broadway hotel, laid out in his coffin, his moustaches waxed for the last time by his faithful barber, sent to his rest by the Ninth Armory Regiment and the biggest funeral since Lincoln's. The wheel turned so quickly, the mighty were brought so swiftly down, that Casey had been gripped by a need to snatch. Looking around the Ali Baba's cave to see what he'd most envied Fisk, he'd raised his hand, and got Darby with the bid. It was the first use he'd made of his coroner's fees, and the best money he'd ever spent. There wasn't a day went by he wasn't proud of Darby.

Already, not a block beyond the stable, his irritation over family dinner left and between the horse trotting across the cobbles and the brisk November air, he began to feel again he was a man of parts and property. He took a turn around the block to test a new steel wheel he'd had put on the gig, and then straightening out on the Avenue, he came on the Maguires returning from a drive in their buggy, their poor idiot only son between them.

For an instant, he didn't know how to act. It was the first time he'd run into them together since Maguire had been read out of Tammany. If it had been just Maguire alone, he'd have known to look past him, but with Mrs. Maguire he'd a sense that was ill-bred. And to make it worse, there was their boy, thirteen now and a lop-headed call for general compassion. As he wavered, the buggy was coming closer and he had to make a swift decision. Strength went through him as he remembered he was driving Darby and looked like a swell in his gig, so that as they came abreast, he raised his hat and bowed his head. He had an impression of Maguire glowering. The carriage wheels roared going over planks in the street. The boy, of course, didn't notice. But Mrs. Maguire cut him dead.

Flushing, Casey kept his face a blank, replaced his hat, and held the pose of a man out to give his horse some exercise. But inside, his thoughts were molten. He'd not mind, he told himself, if Maguire told the truth about their dustup, that he'd not been able to take orders from Kelly. Casey could sympathize with that. It wasn't everybody saw the need for Kelly's lordly manner, barking orders instead of giving a man the sense he was really swapping favors. O'Brien and Morrissey hadn't stood it either. They'd all been expelled from Tammany as unreliable and insubordinate. But Maguire had mucked it up with a lot of fairy tales about the working man and hurled himself into labor troubles. In last year's Depression, when people were standing on lines by the hundreds to draw their money from the failing banks, he'd joined McGlynn in sneering at Tammany handouts, the coal and bread. Instead of taking wage cuts quietly and riding out the storm, they'd urged strikes. And where were the hotheads now, Casey asked himself rhetorically. They were fired as troublemakers and scraping along on charity. Scanlon was a case in point. With his known connection with McGlynn, he'd have looked like hell getting back with Vanderbilt's railroad when his crushed ribs mended. He'd had to take what work he could on the docks. And he was in trouble there now too, organizing the longshoremen against a stevedore firm that was knocking down wages to get a contract with the shippers. McGlynn would have them both crazy before he was done, Scanlon and Maguire too.

But Maguire had compounded the outrage by going around saying it was Casey was the turncoat and that he'd stuck with Kelly for profit. Going over it again, Casey argued anybody in his right mind would have done the same, left a man quarreling with the world, first with Tweed, then Thunderbolt, then Honest John Kelly. The best answer to Maguire's slanders was that Maguire was going insane.

Halfway to Kelly's house, he realized that its being Sunday, it was wise not to bust in without thinking of a good reason. Reining in, he considered. But all that came to him was some new election posters. It wasn't the best, but it would do. Wheeling Darby about, he rode back to Democratic Headquarters on Thirty-first Street. The posters had come in from the printers the day before. With half a dozen of them across his knee, he rode to Kelly's purposefully.

But when he got to the brownstone standing in the middle of a vacant grassy block in the East Sixties, he saw carriages and liveried coachmen standing about outside waiting.

"Ah ha, some big shindig," he thought, and nearly went right on past. But he slowed to see the horses; and he was curious, too, who was there. He thought he recognized August Belmont's victoria with two men on the box and two horses. Then he thought, "And I've brought posters." Next thing, he tied up Darby and was at the front door pulling on the bell.

The door opened on an old housekeeper dressed in black bombazine with a severe, religious eye that so much as said if she were the Lord, she'd spew him out of her mouth.

"May I see Mr. Kelly," he asked, and lest she remind him it was Sunday, he added quickly: "I've some posters he'll want to look at."

"He's in his study with the archbishop."

That nearly took the wind out of him. But he couldn't retreat so soon down the stairs with the coachmen all watching. "It's Coroner Casey," he said in a dignified way.

"Wait then," she said and went off, leaving him in the vestibule.

He dropped his bowler on the hall table, dipped his fingers in the holy water basin, then switched his bowler to the hatrack bristling with antlers and inlaid with mirrors and mother-of-pearl. After that he inspected his posters and his spirits lifted. Kelly would be glad to see the posters. He was keen on defeating Maguire, who was running for state senator again, this time against Liggett. That was odd, finding himself campaigning for Liggett, though maybe it was even odder, finding Liggett in politics. It was all part of Kelly's plan to dress up Tammany with solid respectable men like August Belmont, Horatio Seymour and Abram Hewitt. Good morals were the order of the new day; whistling softly, he leaned to a mirror and smoothed his hair down.

When a burst of talk came through the sliding parlor doors, he moved to them and took a look inside. He shook his head at how different it was from the old days, the Blossom or the Jackson Club, with Gorry Gorry presiding behind the bar and a drunken tenor raising "Starm along, old Starmy" while a seadog did a jig on the table. There were no diamonds in the shirtfronts, and no checked vests either, only a bunch of quiet gentlemen sitting round like a college board. And yet, the queer order was more truly Irish than the old drunken ways had been. The city was getting to remind Casey of his childhood in a Cork village. Every man in Tammany knew his place and played his part, and everybody knew he'd rise in time. It was that Kelly had brought, the solid, predictable old-country order, spreading up from heelers through county leaders to the Boss, who was Kelly himself, the lay ruler working hand in glove with the archbishop.

The new way, every man got what was owed him. Instead of gambling fortunes on their own campaigns, they gave in a fixed sum for Tammany to wage a general campaign. And after victory, each district leader gave in names for all the vacancies that had come up in the city government. There was none of Tweed's overriding and no wild scramble for places. Those names were appointed to those places. Casey felt it suited something neat and sensible within him. In fact, he was so deep in admiration that Kelly startled him coming up behind.

"What's this?" Kelly said and Casey turned. He took one look and knew he'd got in wrong by coming.

"I thought you'd want to see the posters," he said, sticking them out. But Kelly barely gave them a glance. His square jaw was set and his little eyes were cool and hard.

"I've an office for all this," he said.

"That's so," Casey said. He'd no wasteful suites like Tweed nor Americus Club extravagances, but just two small rooms downtown, and certain hours he kept in the Tammany conference chamber. Casey thought that might be overdoing it. He fancied a bit of richness himself. Still, he'd no time to spare for that now. "I thought since it's to beat Maguire, you'd want to see the posters before we put them up."

"You don't plan to come tomorrow?" Kelly said, answering with a question, Irish-style.

Kelly had him there. They'd be meeting for sure tomorrow; it was Dough Day. Kelly'd be giving out the money for the elections next day. Each district leader got what he needed to hire carriages for the sick and blind to vote, for fireworks and hiring orators, and piecing off the boys for rougher stuff. He could have waited till tomorrow.

The best to do now was to swallow it. "Sorry," he said, and took his hat from the rack. There was no smoothness at all to Kelly, no softening jokes like Tweed. Kelly stood like a lead general as, with his eartips burning, Casey went out the front door and tried to descend with dignity. He glanced up just once, as he told Darby "Giddup." The massive body was still at the door; he could almost feel the gimlet eye.

Barely noticing where he went, Casey headed for the park. It was impossible to go home; he was in no mood for a family Sunday, and he trotted Darby round the curving paths, letting the November air chill his shame. The clean sound of the trotter's hooves, the trees going bare, gradually soothed him. And then, with the coming of dusk, he fell past calm into sadness. It was a queer feeling, not completely unpleasant. He thought of Tweed in the Blackwell's Island penitentiary, Fisk lying in his grave, half the Ring run off to Paris. At the idea of Paris, daguerreotype snatches came to him from Eileen's album. He saw the Arch of Triumph, the Place Vendôme, a little cafe, and he wondered where exactly in Paris Claire was. At that he knew where he was going next. Turning Darby out a park gate, he trotted down Fifth Avenue to get news of Claire from Madame Restell.

For a year, his melancholy moods had been growing on him like a secret vice, first brooding on Tweed and Fisk, the old days at Florence's and Long Branch, recalling Claire and ending with a visit to Madame Restell. Like a vice, it had grown a pattern — waiting till dark to pull up to the mansion opposite St. Patrick's, darting into cover of her stables. In the kerosene-lit gloom with the silver-trimmed mahogany stalls and the carriages and silver trappings gleaming, he tipped the groom and under cover of night, unlike her other patients who slipped through the side entrance to the building, he went round to the front, climbed the marble stairs, and rang the bell.

But tonight he was unlucky. The Negro butler who threw open

the door told him she wasn't home. He stood, feeling oddly empty, not like he'd just been planning a glass of champagne with an old woman, and the careful doling out of news. Last time, Restell had told him Claire planned to return in November. She might have started by now. Anything was possible. At the back of his mind, there'd even been the crazy notion as he'd climbed the steps that he'd find her wearing the new Paris fashions and gossiping in Restell's parlor.

Though the butler was waiting, he couldn't bring himself to turn and go, but stood yearning past the carved entrance to the wide, curving mahogany staircase. And then, as if the strength of his willing had conjured up the wrong spirit, he heard a laugh, the sound of scuffling, and two children ran into view before the staircase.

When they saw him, they halted like surprised deer and he took in their slender bodies and pale hair. They were a boy and a girl, perhaps twelve and thirteen. The girl was dressed in some green stuff that reflected greenish on her skin, giving her an unearthly air. Hesitating between flight and adult manners, she smiled at Casey and approached to the door.

"It's all right, Miss Carrie," the butler told her. "Just an old friend of your grandmother's. He don't know she's not home when he come by."

The boy came up now, behind his sister. They were that, Casey'd seen at once. "Won't you come in?" he said politely and Casey caught the faintest accent.

"Now, Mister Charles, he don't want to come in. She won't be home," the butler said, clearly wishing Casey'd leave and not disturb Madame's instructions. But Casey lingered.

"Charles and Carrie," he said. They were Restell's grandchildren and they'd been brought up in Paris. They'd known Claire. He wanted to ask about her but he couldn't think of how to start, with the black butler looming between them. It might have been a start to ask after their mother, but he didn't dare do that. Restell had tried to fling her to safety beyond her own notoriety by marrying her off early and sending her and the young husband to live in Paris on an allowance. But it hadn't worked. There'd been rumors of trouble, quarreling, maybe drink, Casey thought, another marriage, finally estrangement from Restell. Now the grandchildren had been dumped on Restell, looking like changelings from a fairy barrow. He wondered how Restell would manage to give them a life in New York. The girl looked like Claire at that age. She had the same delicate bones and features, the fair skin and cool look. His heart turned in his chest. He searched his mind for some way to ask how Claire was, what she did, how she looked, where she went in the strange city the children knew.

"Miss Scofield," he began. But it was too late. The butler closed the door before they heard.

Feeling bleak and touched by age, Casey went down the marble steps. He walked to the stables, picked up Darby and drove slowly home in the dark.

✣ 19 ✣

I<small>T</small> was still dark when he woke with a feeling like a great harp string was being plucked in his stomach. He lay listening to Eileen's breathing beside him, heard the birds chattering beyond the window, finally rolled to one elbow, felt the night table for a match and examined the clock. Then he knew what had caused the feeling. It was nearly five on election day.

Maguire came to him — he pictured the black hair, the broken nose, and the gaze cold with accusal of Casey's betraying him. And at that, he was stung so, he moved to throw it off. He flung back the blankets and Eileen stirred, so not wanting her to wake, he held still till she'd settled again on her stomach, her thick dark braid coiled along her back. Gradually, from a dark corner, he heard the sounds of Knob Kerry realizing he was awake earlier than usual. The pit bull grunted as he stretched himself. There was a vague stir in the darkness and he felt Knob Kerry graze his bare leg, as a wet muzzle passed across his foot.

"Sst!" he said, to shut him up. The Kerry breathed heavy as pit bulls did, and if he got to snorting, he'd wake Eileen. There'd been trouble enough about the Kerry's sleeping in their bedroom. Though what she thought that a dog in a dark room made of anything they did, he didn't know. He'd had to put his foot down to keep Kerry, saying he'd not take a chance on servants with a valuable dog; though that was a lie. It was just that having Kerry near, alive and warm, was comforting, like the sense he got in stables.

Getting up, he pulled a robe over his nightshirt, felt for his slippers, and gathering his clothes from a chair, let the Kerry out the door and then felt his way along the hall to the bathroom. He lit the gas in the ceiling globes and tried to be silent as he used the water closet, stropped his razor, and shaved standing at the wood-paneled washstand. But the baby's room was next door and soon he heard young Daniel crowing and then crying and the German nurse creaking out of bed to quiet him. He had an impulse to go in but he suppressed it. Bertha would be in her nightgown, and being a good German girl not off the boat a year, she'd leave them sure if he got ideas of strolling in the nursery at dawn.

Wiping a hot rag across his face, he was struck by the strangeness of having a nurse and nursery, and as he grinned, suddenly the years were gone and he was back in the cottage in Cork with them all sleeping in the one room. Cooking in it, too, and sitting down to table, with the dog and chickens running round, and now and then a pig. There was even once a sick foal. His father had brought it in to keep it warm through a January freeze. They'd thought themselves grand to have the backyard privy instead of going in the fields behind a hedge. And here he was with his brick house, standing in his own bathroom with his water closet bowl shaped like a dolphin and the cabinet-finish cistern above it. He looked around at the iron bathtub sunk in walnut paneling and the marble-top lavatory with hot and cold faucets. Then he laughed and dried his face. He climbed into his clothes and started downstairs with Kerry snuffling after.

But as he reached the landing, Maguire slipped back into his mind accusing him. For an instant, he felt shame, almost as if it was true he had betrayed Maguire. Then rage came rushing back. The real trouble was Maguire thought he was better than anyone else. Too proud to be bossed, and proud of that, too, instead of seeing it made him weak. In a whole city of Maguires, there'd be nothing done at all. There'd be only warring groups, stealing one another's books and running newspaper exposés. For all his high moral pose leading workingmen into calling strikes, it had really been only a shabby trick had helped Maguire bring Tweed down. Looked at cold, it was a theft. And men who stole were usually called thieves.

He was standing by the foot of the stairs working it out again in his head when he heard the kettle start to whistle. He and Kerry went through the hall into the kitchen and found the cook slopping round the range making breakfast in her robe and slippers.

"No need for that," he said. "I didn't expect for you to get up."

Her gray braids swung as she turned. "Well now," she said, "wouldn't that be a fine thing, a great officeholder like yerself off to the wars an' no woman to see yer fed first."

"I'm not so hungry at this hour," he said.

"A cup of tea will bring ye round," she said, putting the towel to the kettle handle. "I'll just bring it to the dining room."

"Maybe tea, then," he said. "It's raw this morning." He pulled a chair from the kitchen table. "I'll just sit here, though, where I'll watch you."

"Dear heart, do what ye like. 'Tis warmer here, there is no doubt." She turned with the tea brewing in the breakfast pot. "So how will yer election be going?"

"We'll win," he said. "Liggett'll carry the district by two thousand."

"Ah," she said, pleased. "It's grand hearin' the inside of things. An' Mr. Tilden fer governor? An' Mr. Wickham for the mayor?"

"They'll all sweep in."

" 'Tis amazin', the way ye know. How about a bite of steak?"

He had to hand it to the woman; old and ugly though she was, he was feeling the stir of hunger. He nearly said he would, but Maguire's face came flashing back and took his appetite. "I must be going."

"But yer tea!" she said.

He was looking through the kitchen window at the gray of morning coming. "I've no time for it. It's nearly light. I got to see what the boys are doing."

He wasn't far from his house before he felt in his bones it was going to be a rough election. The sun hadn't yet risen above the roofs that blocked his view of the East River, but bonfires were already consuming the flour and sugar barrels, and a drunk was threatening to carve up Republicans with a broken bottle. As he stepped into the street, Casey heard the Bellevue ambulance bells and leaped back as the black carriage raced by, its driver flourishing his long whip, a plaid blanket around his knees. He craned his neck to see in the open back end but he only saw the two surgeons and knew they'd not picked up the victim yet. He wondered if it was an electioneering injury. Still, whoever it was, he'd be to the hospital quick now they'd given up commandeering carts and wheelbarrows. If getting there fast was an advantage. He wasn't sure, since they'd started using ether, with the interns holding you down struggling, clamping a cone to your nose and pressing it till you turned blue. He'd kept no count since he'd been coroner, but he had the sense they were piling up corpses from ether collapse.

He passed a contractor he knew who was paving city streets for Kelly. As they nodded, Casey ran his eye across the band of laborers he was marching toward the polls. He counted fifty and he smiled as they reminded him of County Cork. But it had been the gentry did it there, the gentlemen herding their blocs of voting tenants to the polls like sheep they were taking to market. Part of the fine old democratic British system.

Perhaps it was thinking of Cork that made him careless. Too late he saw he'd overshot his street and was walking toward St. Stephen's. It was the last thing he wanted on this morning, and to make matters worse, early mass was letting out. But turn tail he could not; already he'd been sighted. If his luck held, he'd skim by. And then he saw that his luck hadn't. At the church, the side door opened and Dr. McGlynn came strolling down the steps in conversation. Casey knew he'd really tapped out, when he saw the other man was Scanlon.

"Morning, Father," Casey said and tipped his hat. He said neither "Howdedo" nor "How's your cat" to Scanlon, just kept walking on down the block.

On the surface, it had gone well. The new district leader had met his opposition and the watchers who'd been hoping for a fight were disappointed. But as he tried to keep his shoulders loose and easy for all the eyes he knew were boring through them, he had to fight to keep control of some submerged part of his life which seemed to be exploding.

Bits and pieces came up like shell-burst. McGlynn came to him, standing in Scanlon's doorway the day they met. Weedy and innocent he had been then, and yet there'd been the hint of challenge, almost a threat to take the Scanlons. Casey wondered had there been gloating in McGlynn's gaze now. Was there contempt, he wondered, in Scanlon's, the old Arsenal Gang feeling for the boy who'd sold his friend. And then he was back fighting side by side with Scanlon in the Fourth Avenue tunnel, both of them still not full-grown. The Volunteers flashed by with the fires and women screaming and the brick walls collapsing, and he and Scanlon manning the brakes of the old hand-drawn engine. Then it was Maguire's face he saw, the day of the news that Casey'd stuck with Kelly when Maguire was expelled from Tammany.

A reformed thug and a crazy priest, how had they done it. They'd not raised a hand, just stood by the church and watched him, and yet he'd been assaulted, bound and judged. He felt like turning round and shouting, but he made himself walk calmly, even when he thought how Maguire was fooling them all playing the prodigal. After making his pile in the saloon Tammany bought him, being boosted to senator — for all his boozing and his thieving of Tweed's books, Maguire was the martyred hero, done in by a lieutenant. As if Casey was the one who'd sold out not Maguire only but the honest workingman, the widows and orphans, and the Lord knew what else, perhaps the whole Irish race to the corrupt political machine.

McGlynn should know what his fair-haired boy was up to. That was the first thing came to his mind when Horse Masterson met him at the door of district headquarters with the morning's casualty report. Three polling booths hit, ballot boxes overturned, the Tammany tickets taken, three voters assaulted.

"Where the hell were our boys?" he asked.

"Out doin' the same. They just didn't happen to meet," Horse was saying cheerfully, when Casey sighted Mose Barry sitting bleeding by the wall. Paddy Sullivan had put down a revolver he was cleaning and was trying to stanch the blood.

"Where did that happen?" Casey said, cutting off Horse's story,

and striding by two boys who'd dropped in to pick up fireworks
and a blow-hard orator who'd come for instructions and his pay.

Mose grinned at him sheepishly beneath the rag he was holding
to his head. "Sorry, boss," he said. "I was off my timing. It don't
hurt much. Soon as the bleeding stops, I'll go out again."

But Casey cut him off too. "You dumb bastard, let it bleed.
Take it down to the police station."

Mose dropped the rag in surprise, and Casey said slowly:
"You're a member of the Tammany General Committee. Ain't
that so?" And as Mose nodded: "You been assaulted by Independent Democrats. What do you do next?"

"I guess I go to the police station."

"Don't forget it." He turned and raised his voice. "Any more of
you boys get hit, I want that clear. If you're working some kind of a
job or you're a committeeman, remember — an honest citizen goes
to the cops. And be sure the reporters get it. They'll be hanging
round all the stations." He turned back to Mose. "Just to make
sure, I'll take you myself. Wait a minute."

Quickly, he ran through the district business, gave instructions
about the box of fireworks to Paddy who was staying to protect
headquarters, paid the speaker, told him where to talk and when,
and took him out back where the beer wagon was waiting with
bright banners for Liggett, Wickham and Tilden. He checked out
the hired carriages and saw that the men driving them were sober
enough to get the lame, sick and blind to the polls. Then he felt his
hip pocket for his knuckles, and going back past his desk, grabbed
the stack of Liggett posters and gave them to Horse.

"What do I do if we run into Maguire's boys?" Horse protested.

"Give them to some kid to hold."

"They're packin' pistols, did I tell ye?"

"And when have you ever been without one?" Casey said.

It crossed his mind that Fisk always took away his men's pistols
when they went out on railway wars. That was smart, in a way.
Gunwounds sounded bad in the papers. But it was odd, if Fisk was
so smart, he himself was shot to death. The two conflicting trains
of thought collided. Then he leaned across the desk, slid open the

drawer and felt around till he found the spare revolver. He checked the chambers; they were full, and he stuck it in his belt.

"Come on, boys," he called. "All but Paddy," and they hit the street in a body.

With Mose still bleeding as good as they'd want, they marched him to the Thirty-fifth Street station house and saw he made his report right. A *Herald* man had just dropped by and was looking impressed by Mose's blood. When they left, Mose was giving him the story while he waited for the sergeant, and Casey supposed that made up for their being short a man.

From the station, they toured the polls to find Maguire's raiders had been before them, smashing Tammany ballot boxes. The best they could do was smash some Independent boxes themselves and run off Maguire's box tenders. Then they went on putting up posters while they tried to find Maguire.

They wound back and forth picking up news — a Tammany candidate for alderman roughed up, more polls wrecked. Then the rumor that Paddy had been set upon and lost an ear sent them rushing back to headquarters.

But they found Paddy still cleaning his pistol while he doled out firecrackers to the neighborhood boys. He asked after Mose till Horse told him all the reporter had put down while Paddy looked pinched with envy.

"What's it like out?" he asked finally.

"Goddamn rough. More than usual," Casey said. "We can't waste our time here."

He picked up the last of the posters and gave them to Horse. Then they walked to Second Avenue to check the polls in the livery stables. But they'd no more than reached the Avenue when Casey pulled up short.

"What is it?" Horse asked, and Casey nodded toward the men standing round outside the Comet.

Maguire was in their center. His bowler was tilted back on the black curls, beginning to salt with years. His forehead was lined. But he still had the height, the weight and manner of the once famous Cork brawler. He stood like an ancient hero hurling a challenge at all comers. "By God, I'll pitch them out of my ward," he yelled.

And so strong was the man's will, Casey did see it from Maguire's eyes, the cozy handing out of coal and dough and baskets while he voted the poor for Tammany. To Maguire that made it his ward. He'd run it like a chieftain. It was true to a point — even in the Young Democracy muss with Tammany they'd followed him. But that was done now. Casey'd pulled out. And the Arsenal's enforcing arm was gone, too. Maguire was depending on imported muscle, poor thugs from the new Tenderloin, not from the ward at all. Except for Scanlon. That hit Casey, seeing Scanlon. He was the last Arsenal man remaining, and he stood beside Maguire as if he was backing up the story that Casey had betrayed him.

Scanlon stung him into action. He motioned, Horse whistled up a newsboy, and set him to hold their posters. Then, walking slow and easy, Casey led his men up to Maguire's crowd.

There was a silence as Maguire saw them, and a fuse of tension seemed to run down the block. Even the voters and Tammany workers at the polls below the Comet swung round to see what was happening. For a moment, Maguire just stared and Casey eyed him back as hard. Then slowly the crowd swung open, and Casey moved in with Horse close at his elbow.

"This scum don't belong here," Casey said, nodding to the Tenderloin boys. "Get them out of this district or I'll see them sent to the Island."

"Ye'll send no one to the Island," Maguire said. He had the height and used it, appearing to look down with contempt. "Boys," he said, speaking above Casey's head, "stay as long as you like. Pay no mind to this damned Judas."

Casey flushed and knowing he was doing it hurt more than the word itself. "I'm no Judas." Even to himself, his voice sounded thick and not cool like he'd planned.

Maguire gave a grim smile. "You're a damned Judas and a goddamned Judas an' a repeater is what ye are as well."

With the whole mob of them listening and watching to see how he was taking it, Casey grappled for what to say next. But the words wouldn't come — his rage went beyond words. That Maguire threw the repeating in his face after years of paying him to do it drove him wild. All he could think to do was roar: "Ye thief!" And that made no sense to the crowd. He half knew it. They'd not put it together with stealing Tweed's books. And Maguire didn't either. He looked surprised. In choked fury, Casey found he was yelling: "Thief! Yer a thief! It's you belong in the prison!" It was like being in a nightmare — shouting out about Tweed on Blackwell's Island and knowing nobody could tell what it was he was meaning. Maguire stared like he'd gone crazy. Then he shook his head to dismiss the ravings, and blasted out the way he might have years ago in Devlin's ratpit.

"Yer a Judas," he said, coming back to it. "I picked you out of the gutter, dressed and fed you. Without me ye'd be nothing. An' ye go an' sell me out!"

"I did not," Casey muttered.

"He says he did not," Maguire said, addressing the crowd, and again his height was maddening and the smile of contempt was on his mouth. It was the look of a man who could move mobs to laugh and cry; Casey couldn't and he knew it, it was more of the dreamlike struggle, the fighting with his hands tied. "It's strange, if he did not. I ain't in Tammany no more. I don't go visiting Mr. Kelly. But you do, Mr. Judas. All dressed up in yer new swallowtail. If ye didn't sell me out, why ain't you backing me fer senator? Yer not sayin' that ye are?"

Casey gave a short laugh but Maguire's voice rose above it.

"I'll tell ye what yer doin' — yer backing the rich men like Liggett now. Ye've sold out, not me only, but every man in the ward —"

There was a low growl from the crowd and at the sound, a sense of danger brought Casey's senses rushing together. He didn't have to think how to stop him. He moved all of a piece, driving up to the place of danger, and smashed Maguire full in the mouth.

After that, he knew where he was. Maguire was older, but he had the reach and he'd been the old Cork battler. Casey was rocked by a blow on the head before he clinched and tied him up. As they wrestled, the mob exploded, and in the crush of struggling men, Casey clung hard as a pit terrier while Maguire thrashed about, his mouth starting to gush blood. He'd broke his plate, Casey thought, and had no time to spit the pieces. Casey'd not give him the time either. Casey dropped his hold and chopped him quick in the belly, but he could tell that was no use — Maguire's belly felt like iron still. Casey clinched quick again but Maguire had a giant's strength in his anger. He raised up and tossed Casey off, and as Maguire rushed at him, the crowd surged and Casey lost his balance. He got two blows on the temple that made him dizzy, and then another that sent him slipping. If he could hold and wrestle, he could knee and gouge, but Maguire was keeping out of reach and striking in with hammer fists. There was no hope but his brass knuckles. He tried to reach them and was struck again, and as he fell to one knee, Maguire kicked him in the face.

I'm beat, he thought. But then he knew he'd not be that. No matter what it took, he'd not be that. As he rolled over, his arm brushed his belt, and as he came up another kick glanced off his back but he didn't feel it. And there were no more kicks. For he'd come up with his pistol out.

Maguire muttered as the pistol rammed his stomach, but Casey couldn't understand the words. They were lost in blood and the broken plate.

"Spit it out," he said. "And call off your men."

Just then he was grabbed by his shoulder and wrenched about. A dozen things spun in his mind at once: the fear of Maguire striking him from behind, the sounds of shots deafening him, the thrashing arms and bodies of the fighters, the smell of raging sweat, and in the midst of it all was Scanlon's face. It was Scanlon who'd spun him about.

"Murdering Judas," Scanlon said.

He squeezed the pistol to blot out the words and the stinging disbelief they were coming from Scanlon. And then the shooting was all about him. Horse beside him was firing too, as Scanlon sagged against the men's legs and with a red wound blossoming in his head, sat slowly in surprise on the ground.

Suddenly, everything was happening far off, and Casey just watching it through a long tunnel. Even the sounds were distant and nothing that he saw fit together. He heard men shouting "Get a stretcher" and arguing what to do next, but their meaning wasn't clear. Hands began tugging at him. He felt his pistol pulled away and then he himself was being led. The crowd moved. He saw a dog, a little white dog skipping back from the men's feet. He saw the newsboy, clutching their posters, looking grimy, chewing on tobacco plug. Vaguely, he saw they were carrying Scanlon to the drugstore across the street.

After that, the crowd grew thicker. They came from everywhere, the polls in the livery stable, and pouring down out of the tenements. Even Mose turned up from nowhere, his head bandaged so Casey wondered had he shot Mose too till he recollected Mose had been down making charges at the police station. At that thought, the police arrived from every side at once. Wherever he looked, he saw a cop. All at once he heard a scream, and turned his head to see Kitty Scanlon with her brown shawl flying. She flung herself into the drugstore and two cops went rushing after her.

"By God," he said. "By Jaysus God."

He took an uncertain step toward the drugstore, but Horse pulled him back.

"Ye've got no time fer that," Horse said. "Now hear. I've got yer pistol."

He turned to Horse with a frown, and Horse said with queer impatience: "You saw his head yerself. Use yer brains, man. He'll not make it."

It should mean something, he knew. He nodded as if he understood. Then suddenly it opened inside him, Scanlon would die now. He felt nothing but surprise; he even wondered for an instant was it Maguire he'd shot. But his thought steadied — it was surely Scanlon he'd seen slide down the legs to the ground.

"Maguire will crucify you," Horse said and that seemed to make sense or it would soon, he felt. He nodded again to show that he took it in. "Ye'll have to fight fer it. Shall I send Mose to tell Kelly?"

But that made no sense at all. Casey brushed a hand across his face. Horse dug his fingers in his arm.

"By God, ye want to go to Sing Sing? It ain't fun there. I'll tell ye that." And at that Casey saw the scars left from the Yoke. The world swam and then steadied around the white furrows on Horse's neck.

"Kelly," he said, and Horse gestured and Mose appeared beside them.

"Run tell Kelly," Horse told Mose. "An' take these pistols. Better throw them in the river."

"Good as done," Mose said, nodding, and slipped them both inside his pants belt. "Now tell me where'll I find Kelly?"

"Goddammit, I don't know. Try police headquarters. Ain't that where the bigwigs wait? Gettin' the returns off of the telegraph?" he asked Casey.

"Try there first," Casey said and stopped. "Maybe Kelly won't want to mix up in this."

"If he don't, then he don't," Horse said. "You got to try. You'll need all the help ye can get."

Horse broke off as the men came out with the stretcher, and Kitty running along beside them. As they made the turn through the drugstore door, she looked out upon the crowd and stared direct at Casey. He held his breath but she only smiled in a queer distracted way as if she'd picked out a familiar face. They looked up and down for an ambulance, so they must have sent a boy running to Bellevue. But that took time. At last, they began carrying the stretcher down the street with Kitty bending over it as they went.

The three cops that came up looked embarrassed. It took a moment for Casey to see it was a ticklish business arresting the district leader. Knowing that made him feel better, and he dropped his hands and waited, standing easy as he could. But before the cops decided who'd start speaking, Maguire came shouldering from the drugstore, his mouth bleeding and his big face dark and smeared with drying blood. Seeing Casey, he stopped and pointed.

"Arrest that murderin' thug," he said. "He kilt my man."

It was Maguire brought him up, like a diver surfacing. Suddenly, he saw Sing Sing clear, saw the Yoke, the thumb string, the Cage. He saw himself in the Bishop's Mitre, the iron frame a man wore over his head so he had to sleep sitting up.

"Now, Senator," a cop said. "Nobody's kilt yet."

"He's got a ball in his head, ain't he?" Maguire said in fury, not sounding clear without his teeth. "He'll not live."

"We don't know that," the cop said, trying to ease Maguire's wrath, and yet a ball in the head was no light matter. It was hard for the cop, all right, playing two sides of the street. "Still, we might book for assault. Did ye actually see him firin'?"

"By God, as plain as yer face now," Maguire said.

"Well, now, Mr. Casey," the cop said with apology. "I suppose we'll have to see."

Casey slowly raised his hands and as the cop began to pat him gently, Casey met Maguire's gaze.

"I'll have ye locked in a cage like a mad animal," Maguire told him grimly.

A chill ran through him. He thought of the Cage where a man could not sit nor lie down. They kept them there for weeks. He saw Eileen visiting him, Little Dan growing older, asking questions; the fine brick house seemed to melt away; with a pang he thought of his trotter Darby.

"He's got no pistol on him," the cop announced unsurely.

"Ah my God, ye dodging bastard. Where'd ye dump it?" Maguire asked.

Horse said reasonably: "There was a lot of firin'," to the cop. "Who knows what bullet got him?"

"He shot point blank," Maguire said, his voice starting to tremble, he was so angry. He pulled out his handkerchief and held it to his bloody mouth. "If he dies — when he dies —"

"I'd no hand in it," Casey said.

♣ 20 ♣

CASEY lay on his back and looked at the day breaking through his cell window. First the little square washed gray, then it turned rose and grew brighter. Gradually, he made out the armoire, the table, the pitcher, and wash basin, the candlestick and finally his watch and chain laid out beside the stack of yesterday's newspapers.

His robe and nightshirt were twisted about his neck and he pulled about till he got them straight, then lay listening to the Tombs coming to life. Far away, someone was howling. The voice sounded like a woman but the women's prison was on the other side of the building. It must be from the Boy's Hall, some pickpocket lad going into the trimmins or a child witness in safe-keeping till trial, being set upon by the others because he put on airs. The howling stopped abruptly and Casey heard a clank on the gallery, the keeper's keys, a cell door swinging open, and the crash of pails. Breakfast was coming. Vile breakfasts they were too, mush and molasses, or grits and molasses. Whatever arrived, it was swimming in molasses. Thank God, he thought, he still had money to have his steaks and eggs and oysters sent in from the Astor House.

But though he didn't get the Tombs food, the breakfast boy rattled his door just the same and the keeper put his key in the lock, it swung open, and Casey rose to hand out his slops jar. When he was settled back, he heard the whish and slosh begin of the boys scrubbing the gallery floors. They got their value from the boys, he must say. They scrubbed and polished, worked in the kitchen; it was the women, he thought, did the laundry. Though he wasn't sure about the laundry. His own went home twice a week and Eileen's washerwoman did it. At the thought of Eileen, he shifted. He pushed her from his mind and when she tried to get back in, he jumped up and strode to the window. Concentrating on the Centre Street traffic, he counted two boys wheeling oyster carts, a horsecar traveling down the tracks, a dray wagon full of barrels, some poor visitor arriving with her arms full of paper parcels, not knowing the visiting hours didn't start until ten-thirty. The Police Court justice was arriving, climbing the dark stone steps between the dismal Egyptian pillars. Bummers Hall would be emptying now, the tramps and drunks would be shuffling their aches, pains and hangovers into court. At least, he thought, I have the window. He gave a bleak smile at his shrinking list of treasures. Just the same, a window that a man could see from wasn't come by easily. The Tombs cells usually had just a chink placed high up in the wall. Only the ones in front above the entrance had viewing windows; they went mainly to forgers and defaulters, and rich prisoners who could afford them.

The thought of jail expenses made him reach for his cigar case before breakfast. It wasn't just the cell; there were his meals coming in; and the coroner's job lost meant losing $15,000 a year in fees. He'd had to mortgage the brick house and cut his stable cost by selling Darby. As he lit up, he reminded himself that Tammany was furnishing the lawyers. But the thought of lawyers made him queasy; they put him in mind of jury verdicts. As he stared unseeing out the window, he saw himself election morning leaving his house in innocence, not realizing his good fortune, and he let out a groan.

He didn't linger over that morning; he had his story. He only groaned that he'd met Maguire, the crowd started shooting, and Scanlon had caught a ball in his head. And once Scanlon died in Bellevue, the trap snapped shut. The autopsy was performed, the bullet found, next day the coroner's jury was impaneled at the dead house beside the river and for the next four days, Casey sat at the counsel table in the coroner's office while Maguire and ten witnesses confounded each other with conflicting stories. But the verdict was murder by a person unknown. Casey's friends flocked around to shake his hand, and he'd thought he'd skinned off it free. But he'd not counted on the newspapers screaming about violence in politics. A week later the grand jury found a true bill for murder. Then at midnight his bell rang, and with Knob Kerry snuffling at his feet, Casey had poked his head out his bedroom window and seen the dark figure on his doorstep.

"Ah God," he said. He recognized him. It was Captain O'Neil of the detective squad. No need to be shouting out his story in the night. "I'll be right down," he called.

"What is it?" Eileen said. He turned. In the dark, he made out her shape sitting up in bed.

"Hush," he said. "Go to sleep."

But, of course, no woman would. She was groping to light the bedside candle as he picked up his robe and hurried out the door.

In the vestibule he ran into the greenhorn maid, pale and skinned-looking, holding a candle. She'd jumped into her dress but her hair was still streaming down her back and she was stopped before the door, screwing up her courage.

"Go to bed," he told her, reaching up and lighting the vestibule gas jet. From the hall, he saw the old cook peeking through the swinging pantry door. Next he expected to see the German nurse trailing down the stairs. "Go back, the lot of you!" he shouted. "Go to bed, go to sleep! Let me take care of this!"

They lingered while his nerves tightened. But at last they turned unwillingly and withdrew, though he knew they were listening at the door.

Captain O'Neil was still waiting on the doorstep. He was wearing a plain bowler but his air was grave behind his large moustaches. "Coroner Casey?" he said, though of course he knew that well, so Casey knew the warrant had come. As O'Neil reached inside his greatcoat, Casey said hurriedly: "Come in. I'd not expected you tonight."

As he backed up, they both suddenly were staring at his bare feet sticking out beneath his robe. He'd clean forgot about his slippers. Then O'Neil averted his eyes.

"It's just we thought it might be easier without the mobs of newspaper reporters," O'Neil stammered. "But there's no need to go tonight. If ye'll put me up, I'll make out fine till morning."

"Ah now, that's very good of you," Casey said.

"Nothing to it," O'Neil said. "I'm a family man myself." And Casey understood O'Neil was saying it was the sort of thing might happen to anybody — to himself, for instance, the warrant coming to his own doorstep in the night with his own wife listening and the boards creaking about the house.

"Will you have a cup of tea then?" Casey asked, leading him into the parlor and going around lighting gas jets.

"No need for that," O'Neil said, sliding into a chair. "I've my paper and my pipe."

"The boiler's not up," Casey told him.

"My coat's warm," O'Neil said, nodding. "I'll just wish ye good night."

The warrant was served so comfortably that, going up the stairs, Casey nearly forgot that the machinery was grinding that could end him in the Cage or on the gallows. But as he closed his bedroom door, it came rushing back with the sight of Eileen. She was out of bed and in her wrapper, pacing wildly up and down.

"What is it?" she asked and the note in her voice was alarming.

"Ah now, it's not so much. A chap I know from the detectives."

"Is he taking you to jail now?"

He flinched as if he and O'Neil had been applying sticking plaster to a wound and Eileen had ripped it off. " 'Tis not like that. He's very civil." He climbed back in bed hoping that would close the subject, but she stood staring at him till he said unwillingly: "I might go down there in the morning. Come to bed now."

Instead she crossed to the window and peered uneasily out the curtains. "His carriage is waiting." She turned to him. "You've not let him in my house?"

"What do you think?" he flung at her, exasperated. "The man don't want to disarrange me. Should I make him wait in the street?"

"What is this?" she asked, her voice rising. "Where is he?"

"In the parlor," he said, and as she threw her hands to her face and began weeping, he stuck his legs out of the bed.

"Ah my God," he said. "Yer carryin' on fer nothin'."

At that, she began to choke and laugh. "Nothing! I've a husband arrested for murder, detectives in my parlor — you'll be hung yet —"

"Shut up now!" he shouted but she fell to beating her fists against her swelling sides.

"I wish I'd die. I wish we'd both die, me and baby, so he won't have to bear the shame."

"What shame?" he shouted, furious. "It's a misfortune could happen to anyone, a lot of shooting in a crowd —"

"Was it?" she said, raising her head slowly, and with her two braids dangling about her wet face, she looked like an old country witch woman. "Was it just a lot of shooting, Casey?"

"Ah my God!" He jumped up raging, stalked to the closet and began pulling out his clothes to take with him. "If that's how it is, I'll be better off in the Tombs."

She said nothing and he took his carpetbag and slammed to the bureau. He packed while she sat slowly down on the bed and watched him. Knob Kerry whined and brushed against him and he reached down once and rubbed him. As he finished and locked the carpetbag, he glanced over but she was silent, so he took his clothes and went to the bathroom to dress. When he came back, she was lying on her side, staring at the rose wallpaper.

"I'll be leaving," he told her. She nodded slowly. "It's on yer own conscience if I go like this."

She turned and shot him a glinting look through the tears, a look curiously ironic he'd not seen before. He took his carpetbag and went slowly out the door and down the stairs.

"Mr. Kelly, sir, to see you," the keeper said, and Casey found himself at his cell window, the horsecar passing and the police judge vanishing up the Tombs steps between the Egyptian columns. The keys clashed in the lock and as his cell door opened, he had just time to stub his cigar in the table ashtray before Kelly came performing corporal acts of mercy.

But perhaps he was too suspicious of the man's charities, Casey thought, as they exchanged their usual morning greetings, clasped hands, and Kelly lowered his weight onto the chair that Casey offered. There was a warmth in the gray eyes Casey hadn't seen before the shooting and Kelly sounded sincere enough when he asked: "Are ye able to sleep at all here?"

"Not too bad," Casey answered cautiously. Kelly had insomnia himself and relished having fellow sufferers. It would be a blow to the man to go bragging that in the Tombs he still slept like a rock. "Can I give you breakfast? The boy's not come yet; there's time to order," he said, parrying.

But Kelly threw up a hand. "Nothing sets right on me stomach before noon excepting tea an' toast. An' I've had that already. You go ahead," he said. And when Casey shook his head and pulled a chair to the table, Kelly reached across and touched his arm. "I know, me boy. Yer behavin' like a lion. Don't think I miss it." He cleared his throat of the embarrassing note of sympathy and clasped his hands before him on the table. That put him where he had to see the newspapers opened to the headlines: CORONER DENIED BAIL and CASEY'S TRIAL NEARS. "We'll soon have ye out of here," he said. "But it's about that I come this mornin'. I had a talk with yer friend Masterson."

"Ah," Casey said, and struck an air of listening while Kelly looked behind him at the cell grate and gave his chair a jump nearer.

"Ye know, of course, he has — his doubts," Kelly said, lowering his voice, and Casey nodded noncommittally. When Horse had proposed having doubts whether he'd shot Scanlon himself, Casey had not known how Kelly'd take it, having doubts so late in the day. If it struck Kelly as a welch, it could do more harm than good. But already, first crack from the box, he could see Kelly liked the thought fine.

"Still, he's not sure," Casey pointed out.

"Ah, but the clearer things come back," Kelly said. "Now I honor the stand ye been takin' — not to give away a friend."

"I'd not do that," Casey said with abhorrence. Even if Horse had really done it, he couldn't see himself on the stand before the crowd, pointing him out. "And with his record — he told you about Sing Sing —"

"Yes, yes," Kelly said quickly. "I see yer point. They'd be harder on him for that. Still, there's your whole future to consider. Ye've made a start, but unless yer vindicated —"

"Just the same, I couldn't do it."

"My boy, no one's askin' ye to do it. It's just a kind of insurance, in case, God prevent it, the jury brings a hostile verdict —" The words sent a shiver through him. He had to throttle the desire to say to Kelly: "Can't you take out insurance on the jury?" But that he couldn't say, not to Kelly; it would give a false impression. He'd have to make do with the knowledge that in a pinch, Horse would stand up and throw the court into confusion by confessing that he'd done it.

"I honor yer stand," Kelly repeated.

His fears still pulling him every which way, Casey didn't dare to speak and contented himself with nodding.

"I've told yer lawyers," Kelly said. "They'll map it out next time ye see them." He pushed his hands against his thighs and standing up, placed a kindly hand upon Casey's shoulder. "Ye'll be glad to hear, too, another victim of this sad affair is bein' comforted." And as Casey looked up, puzzled, Kelly said: "The poor widow. And Scanlon's orphans."

"Can I help out?" Casey asked quickly.

"Not you, me boy. Ye'll need every bit ye can raise fer yer own family. But Mr. Liggett's been a help, and a few of us rallied round. I suppose Maguire's been active, too. I hope he has," Kelly said sternly. "For his own peace of mind. None of it would have happened but fer his wild Indian raidin' —" He broke off. "But I'll not stir ye up by talking where the blame lies. Keep up yer courage, Casey."

He went to the cell door and shouted and in a moment the keeper was clanking keys in the lock again. Kelly gave Casey a last pat on the shoulder and winked at him more humanly than Casey had seen yet. He must have reached into his old Volunteer fire past for the manner, as he said: "Remember, my boy, yer in Tammany. And Tammany takes care of her own."

"I hope my visit isn't an intrusion."

Charles Liggett stood in the cell entrance, top hat in one hand, a white-wrapped parcel in the other. The light from the cell window played over his blond moustache and beard, his white turned-down collar, the watch chain caught in his vest buttonhole and dangling a bunch of seals. Casey sat staring at the vision. Then he made himself get up deliberately, fit his chair under the table, and come to greet him as easy as he could.

He had the sense he was doing fine, and yet later he couldn't recall how it was the visit started. Liggett must have put the package down — it was cigars like the ones he had made special for himself — and Casey recalled offering him a whiskey; he accepted that, though he said to make it light. By the time they were together at the table, Casey's surprise had worn off enough for him to take in the rest.

"When we last met, we'd no chance to talk," Liggett said and Casey gave a grim smile at the thought of the police station, with Maguire bellowing accusations, the reporters milling round, and all the bigwigs rushing in, Kelly and Wickham, the mayoralty candidate, and Liggett, too, since it was he was running for State Senate against Maguire. Casey had nearly forgotten Liggett had been there; Liggett's presence had been blurred by his relief at seeing Kelly and realizing Kelly wasn't going to cut him off for mixing them all in a shooting.

"I'm sorry my campaign got you involved in all this," Liggett said. "I feel responsible."

"It was an accident," Casey said with rising truculence but Liggett said: "Oh I know that." And Casey felt himself grow easier.

It was hard, as Liggett spoke, not to like him, growing his blond beard to look older. Actually, he was Casey's age or even more. He must be in his mid-thirties, but he had the slight build and fair complexion that made him seem like a boy hiding behind spirit gum and false moustaches trying to impersonate a senator. And his shy manner, talking in spurts, made him seem younger still. As he spurted away about Maguire, Casey found himself almost smiling at the grizzled Cork Goliath brought down by this little David, his fair skin flushing in the cell light.

For though Liggett had sopped up his book knowledge, there was nothing he really knew of politics. He clearly had no sense of how Maguire had come to feel he owned the ward — the years attending wakes, the midnight fires and burned-out widows, electioneering by the boys, and how he'd lost his enforcing arm when Casey'd made off with the Arsenal Gang. All Liggett saw was the raiding parties by outside thugs in the one election; and when he spoke, he sounded like the newspaper editorials, full of words like the people's right to make their free democratic choice. Well, he'd learn about free choice up in Albany, and at the next state convention when Kelly sent in his slate. Meanwhile, Casey liked him — with reservations about the future when Liggett picked up some experience.

His sense of superior knowledge eased him so, a kind of mischief made him want to see what Liggett would do when he said: "Mary sends you her best."

"Mary?" Liggett asked, half-smiling, trying to place what lady was meant.

"My sister, Mary Casey. She was your housemaid," Casey said.

"Yes, of course." At the red that went surging through the fair cheeks, Casey realized Liggett had known it all along, perhaps for years, since Casey'd been an alderman. He'd not have mentioned it himself for fear of embarrassing Casey, but now that Casey brought it up, it made it seem like only Liggett thought it was shameful. Casey felt pleasure glow through him at turning the tables. He let a twinkle creep to his eye as Liggett tried to say that Mary was a grand girl without sounding like he was giving a reference.

On that note of utter victory, Casey saw Liggett to the cell door and shouted for the keeper. He was feeling so expansive, he had no trouble thanking him for the cigars. And feeling like he was tipping a schoolboy, he said: "Thanks for coming, Senator." He could tell by Liggett's quick smile, he wasn't used to the title yet.

It was the title, though, sent him toppling. Liggett was senator, he remembered. Wickham was mayor. The Tammany slate had all slid in. Everyone he'd been backing election day won. The keeper ground the key in the lock, the cell door opened, and Liggett walked out, rich and free.

"You want anything, Coroner?" the keeper asked, and when Casey shook his head, he clanged shut the door and turned the lock.

Casey walked slowly to the cell window and watched till Liggett appeared, tripping down the dark steps between the pillars. He looked up and waved his top hat, but Casey knew he'd not see him in the gloom, so he didn't bother waving back.

♣ 21 ♣

O NE morning in early December Casey descended the Tombs steps between Deputy Sheriff Daley and two men from the City Hall precinct. From Centre Street they began to see crowds and as they turned into Chambers, Casey braced himself to face the mob. Men and boys by the hundred lined the sidewalk and jostled each other on the unfinished stairway of the courthouse that Tweed had built. They seemed curious, almost cheerful, and the holiday mood struck a chord in his memory. As the police formed a wedge to bring him up the courthouse stairs, he suddenly recalled the little boats gay with flags bobbing round Bedloe's Island the day of the Hicks hanging, and his stomach turned over. Trying to keep control of his expression, though he could feel the sweat chilling his forehead, he barely noticed as he was thrust through the lobby and up the staircase till the court officers came flying down to help them past the jam into the Court of Oyer and Terminer.

There were no women among the spectators. He didn't know why he noticed that, but he did. Usually they filled the murder trials. They'd jammed the courtroom over the Fisk shooting, but for him they hadn't come; maybe because Scanlon had died for politics and not for love.

As he went toward the front of the courtroom, he looked for Kelly but though there were politicians he knew — a fellow coroner and his deputy, the Tombs warden and the county clerk, Kelly was absent. He tried not to show that he was looking for him but he felt disappointment touch him. And then, as he reached the counsel table, he saw Maguire at the D.A.'s table. As the blue-eyed, broken-nosed face blazed at him, he felt they were wrestling in the gutter, fingers inching up to rake and gouge. Fear flooded him and his heart began to hammer so his lawyer's words made no sense.

"Sit down, my boy. Don't look about you," Howe was saying and Casey stared at the lion head with the waving hair and walrus moustaches. He smelled of whiskey, though, and that brought Casey round quick to take a sharp look. But Howe wasn't drunk, only drinking himself steady; he looked in champion form this morning, decked out in checked trousers, diamonds glittering in his doeskin waistcoat.

"Perhaps, if he turned about and stared hard at John Maguire," the young partner whispered. Hummel was almost a dwarf, with a large bald head, brilliant eyes and poker face, dressed in black with a diamond-studded death's head dangling from his watch chain. What a pair! Casey thought, but they were the best criminal lawyers in the business. And they handled not just criminals but theater people, the rich seeking out-of-state divorces and Tammany district leaders who got themselves into trouble.

"Why waste it? Wait for the jury," Howe said, giving the D.A. a glorious wave. And then: "Here we go. Here's the clerk. The judge is coming. Display confidence, my boy. Remember you're innocent. There ain't a chance we won't get you off!"

The next few seconds were a whirl for Casey. The court officer announced the opening, Justice Barrett sailed in in his robes, and immediately the jury filed in from their night in the Astor House. They'd been locked up yesterday as soon as they were chosen — commercial travelers, a lumber dealer. They'd picked them fast the day before, discarding only two men opposed to capital punishment. There was no real fear of that, but just the thought of it was unpleasant. Casey had a struggle to scrub out the picture of Hicks swinging above the sun-bright harbor.

"Now you can look at him," Howe was saying. But the words came out scrambled to Casey. His heart had given a warm leap like a young man with a girl, for just as the jury was seated, John Kelly had arrived. As he heaved himself to a counsel chair and reached

over to give Casey's arm a bang, the blood began flowing again in
Casey's veins.

For a while, all he noticed was that Kelly was beside him showing his confidence to the world. He barely heard the judge ordering
the witnesses to retire, and the D.A.'s assistant opening the prosecution's case. A few words came through — a sketch of the shooting,
then a phrase that sounded ominous — "died from a shot fired
from the pistol of an assassin, a cold-blooded and terrible murder."
Then that faded too in the relief of having Kelly beside him. He
lazily studied the wall diagram of the place the shooting occurred
till he came up short at the words: "Who fired the first fatal shot
that killed Dick Scanlon? We have the testimony of the victim that
Casey shot him."

By God, he thought, what's this about? He nudged Howe's arm
and was puzzled by Howe's wink. "What testimony's this?" he
whispered.

"Don't start thinking," Howe said back. "Just try to look like an
honest man."

Maguire took the stand like an avenging angel, raised his hand,
touched the Book, swore the oath, and launched into his story with
a chilling air of truth. He told how he was standing by the Comet
on election morning, Casey's approach, the fight and shooting. At
"I saw Tom Casey shoot Scanlon with my own eyes," a kind of
hum went through the courtroom. Judge Barrett banged with his
gavel and a hush fell, but the D.A. had his point made. He gave
over to Howe with a bow, not breaking the silence.

It was time and past time, Casey felt, for the master's touch, and
he watched while Howe got up, shot his cuffs, hooked his thumbs
in his doeskin waistcoat and sauntered to the witness chair. He
looked Maguire over with amusement, then said in disbelieving
tones: "Tell us more, Senator, about that morning. The Jackson
Club was Independent headquarters. Was Strong-Armed Dan
O'Reilly or the Ape there when you arrived?"

Maguire gave him a look, sensing danger, but before he was sure
just where the danger lay, the assistant D.A. was on his feet pro-

testing to the judge about the nicknames. When that was straightened out, Maguire resumed, but there was new caution in his answers. Like a man playing his hand against a sharper, he answered carefully. So carefully that before he ended, he was denying that he knew if the Tenderloin thugs were at the polls to work for him. A laugh went through the room and Howe turned and gave the jury a glance to be sure they hadn't missed it. Then with an air of getting back to business, he picked up the pointer, poked the diagram of the shooting, and led Maguire back through his story. Relieved to return to ground where he'd done well, Maguire repeated how when Scanlon swung Casey around there'd been just the three of them standing together.

"There was no one else close but Casey. I saw him shoot," he repeated doggedly. "As soon as the cops came, I said 'Arrest them men. Arrest Casey for murder.' "

"Please tell us about that, Senator," Howe said, and Casey saw the jurymen lean forward to catch his low tone. "Concerning the arresting officers. Is it true you solicited the Police Department to get them placed in their jobs?"

"I object," the D.A. said, jumping up, and Judge Barrett made a speech on how he'd allow all reasonable limit to the cross-examination. But Howe made a distasteful gesture as if, after all, it was too sordid to continue.

"Did you ever carry a pistol yourself?" he asked, dropping the "Senator."

"I might have now and then," Maguire admitted.

"Did you not draw a pistol on a man known as Red O'Leary twenty-three years ago?"

My God what's this, Casey thought, leaning forward. They'd been digging, that was clear. Twenty-three years ago would be back in '51, when Maguire had gone to California to make his pile in the gold rush. In his excitement, he reached in his breast pocket but little Hummel put out a hand and flicked his sleeve so Casey let go the cigar case.

Maguire was annoyed. Casey could tell, knowing him so well he could read the signs — the thoughtful silence, the way he put his palms flat on his knees. But when he spoke, it just seemed he was taking a calm interest in getting at the truth.

"Yes I did," he said, considering. "But I didn't shoot at him. He shot at me."

Casey was wondering about the circumstances. And probably half the courtroom was wondering too. Was it when Maguire was a faro gambler, or later when he started fighting for prize money around San Francisco? But apparently Howe's point was made with just mentioning the pistol. Clasping his lapels, he changed position so the jury could see him full and he threw the next question to Maguire across his shoulder.

"Were you not once charged with the pistol murder of a man named Johnny Jackson?"

An astonished sound ran through the court, as if Howe was accusing Maguire of shooting Scanlon himself. Judge Barrett banged his gavel, the D.A. jumped up and objected, and Judge Barrett denied. It all happened in a moment.

"I was not!" Maguire shouted. Casey stared at him in surprise. He'd heard it himself, years ago. Jackson was one of the Native American Bowery butcher boys. Maguire had been had up all right, along with three or four others. Though if he'd done it himself, no one knew. The witnesses had vanished and the case never came to trial. It must have happened back in '53.

"I have a copy of the police blotter," Howe said as if he were bored suddenly with Maguire's lying, and little Hummel trotted up with it.

Maguire's face had gone red. He pushed the blotter copy away and turned in outrage to the judge. "There was nothin' to that at all, yer honor. They might of booked me but no more. I didn't even spend a night in jail."

Slam went the gavel. "Address your answer to counsel," Judge Barrett told him.

Maguire turned back to Howe, his big head lowering dangerously.

"I simply asked were you arrested and charged," Howe said with an air of reason.

"I might of been picked up with a bunch of other boys," Maguire said. "There was a muss —"

"A muss you call it, when a man is murdered?" Howe said swinging to face the jury in pained surprise.

"I'm no scholar," Maguire roared. "I'm just a plain man."

Howe's organ voice swelled out like the voice of God at Judgment. "Oh no, Senator, you're not just a plain man. You're a most unusual man indeed — a man constantly picked up for deadly assault, for murder —"

In the uproar, the D.A. was on his feet objecting, Judge Barrett was hammering his gavel. When the confusion died down, Howe was gently wiping a silk handkerchief across his palms and little Hummel was moving to Judge Barrett, displaying the police blotter.

Howe dropped it there, only saying he might want to call the witness again as if he felt Maguire might flee town. Maguire stepped down, his blue eyes murderous, and the D.A. called the first Tenderloin thug.

The prosecution had bought him a plain suit and scrubbed him up but there was nothing they could do about the jaw, the barrel chest, and the stiff way he sat like the clothes were strangling him. But he was good-humored enough, and a popular witness with the crowd as the D.A. led him through his story of how Casey had come up to Maguire's party in front of the Comet, how they'd fought, and Scanlon fell. He'd seen both Horse and Casey with pistols, though he'd not seen the actual shooting. On cross-examination, Howe struck the light touch, bringing out he was called Strong-Armed Dan, and set him describing a scene in Professor Allen's saloon when he was set upon by a rival gang and mopped them up. Finding himself the center of hilarity, Strong-Armed Dan expanded so quick that when the D.A. tried to stop him, he bulled his way through the rest of the story and stepped down to a scattering of applause.

After Dan, there was Frank (the Ape) Costello. Howe asked where he and Strong-Armed Dan had spent the night before election and though the D.A. got his objection sustained, Howe got his point across that it was an immoral house. Then court was adjourned for the day.

Next morning at eleven the room was less crowded, and they got down to business quickly as soon as Chief Ricketts and his officers brought in the jurors. The prosecution's first witness was a boy who'd seen the shooting, and Casey's heart began to pump till Howe charged in, sneering and hounding, till he had the boy so confused, he identified the D.A. as Casey.

Casey had been worrying about the prosecution's threat that Scanlon's dying words accused him. He had the sense when Dr. Miles was called, the time was coming. And the D.A.'s opening questions had the doctor called to the drugstore, bending over the wounded Scanlon. But at the question: What did he tell you?" Howe was on his feet objecting.

"On what grounds?" Judge Barrett asked, banging his gavel, for the crowd was panting now to hear the victim have his vengeance from the grave.

"Did the doctor tell Scanlon his wound was mortal?" Howe said.

The judge swung his head to look at Dr. Miles.

It was that Casey found so strange — the look of relief on Miles's face. He spoke so quickly, Casey had the sense he'd been waiting days for the question. "No, I did not."

"By God, he did!" the D.A. shouted.

"In that case," Howe said sonorously, "it's not a dying deposition. And it cannot be admitted."

"But he's changed his story!" the D.A. was shouting. He advanced on the old doctor.

"I did not," Miles repeated softly and tossed Howe an odd look of appeal, considering he was the opposition lawyer.

Howe rose to his own. He seemed to grow till he towered, spread his shoulders like the branches of some great oak of justice. He raised his arms in mute protection. "Your honor, I protest the prosecution's attempt to intimidate this witness."

"The court recognizes Mr. Howe's concern for justice," Judge Barrett observed with heavy sarcasm. But the legal point was clear. With Miles refusing to say he'd told Scanlon he was dying, Scanlon's words couldn't be repeated.

At the judge's finding, a soughing noise went through the court, half disappointment, half satisfaction at the spectacle that Howe was making, dispersing the prosecution's case like an old wizard breaking up a brooding storm.

As he left the witness box, Dr. Miles threw Howe another look and Casey said to Hummel, "Did he — ?" But Hummel said "Hst!" and turned away his sharp little face. There was a smile on his lips, though, and he spun the diamond death's head playfully about his crooked finger.

Casey had the sense the winds were calming as the deputy coroner described the postmortem exam. Howe had no questions, and the rest of the prosecution witnesses were discovered to be absent. There was another stir at that, but Judge Barrett hammered again and stopped it.

"Court adjourned until tomorrow."

"These men with significant aliases, men who the night before the crime kept their drunken revels at a place they dare not name, these men with strange names, not one of whom but is a known ruffian or pronounced thief, went through the ward knocking people down, turning over polling boxes, destroying the Tammany tickets," Howe declaimed, while even Casey watched as if he were in a theater. The whole pace and direction of the trial had changed since the prosecution rested and the defense had taken over. Howe had put on different coloring — the checked trousers were replaced, and the diamonds were gone that he had worn while the jury was getting to know him. Now he wore a somber sack suit as he settled down to move them to return Casey to life and freedom.

For nearly an hour, he had drawn dark pictures of the ward as Maguire would run it — criminals running wild, repeaters voting unmolested, innocent men beaten at the polls. It wasn't really untrue, but Casey felt it was overdone and surely the lower wards were even worse. He hoped the D.A. wouldn't think to point out that he himself had been Maguire's right-hand man for fourteen years. But Howe didn't care for defense now; he was carrying the fight to the Independent Democrats.

"Senator Maguire, to give his testimony the stamp of authority,"

he said, "has tried to show he was not with these men that morning. He would have you believe he was a passerby. He would have
you believe that these men with peculiar aliases came there early in
the morning without concert of action, that all met by accident
and had been walking in groups from poll to poll by accident. But
on the morning of the election, this defendant called on the Police
Department and begged their intervention. And when the police
were not able to provide peace and order, the defendant, acting
with the courage of a decent citizen, told both the Ape and Strong-
Armed Dan they weren't residents of that district and should be
ashamed to come there to do their villainous work."

By God, Casey thought, the way Howe was going, it was the
other side was on trial. Having painted in his background, Howe
began calling up his witnesses. One, two, three, four — he had a
dozen, marching up to tell the same story. They saw the fight, neither Maguire nor Casey had a pistol, only Horse Masterson was
firing away. It was astounding where he'd found them — draymen
and carters, liquor dealers, and finally an off-duty barkeep who'd
leaned out his flat window to get a full view of Casey.

Howe acted out a little scene. He took his watch and asked for
perfect silence for a full minute so the jury, court and counsel
might know the space of time it took for all the violence. It didn't
much affect the evidence but gave a general sense of Howe's clear,
scientific frame of mind.

After recess, the defense summed up. For an hour and a half,
Howe told the jury that the only witnesses attacking Casey were
men of notorious low repute, with one exception — here an ironic
bow to Maguire which even fetched a ripple of laughter — and
that one in the middle of a fight, the least likely to see clearly. He
finished up dramatically: "We have proved that another man shot
Scanlon!"

A gasp went through the courtroom. Everybody turned to look
at Horse who sat inspecting his shoe tips with an impassive air.
Casey flushed at Howe's daring to go so far. And yet, looking back
on Howe's witnesses, they'd been saying the same thing. They'd
seen no pistol on Casey, only Horse had been blazing away. He
wondered what Horse was thinking, and then pushed away the

thought. He was as helpless now as Horse. They were both caught in Tammany's machinery, grinding out of their control. On that accusation, Howe ended, daring them to send a man to prison under the guilty party's eyes.

When the district attorney got up, he was as cool as Howe was impassioned so that Casey after all recalled the D.A. was Tammany too.

Still, he gave them all hell on the pistols. "Who was it set out with a band of men armed for bloody deeds?" he said in his opening. "The first man accused was Casey, and the first man on whom the officers laid their hands was he. Why did the officer immediately search him, and search him again at the station? No pistol was found with him but all the witnesses agree that Masterson was shooting, and no pistol was found with him either. There was all the time they needed to pass them on to a confederate while the dying man was in the drugstore."

Casey tensed for whether the D.A. would speak of Horse, but all he said was: "If another man did the crime, why didn't these witnesses cry out: 'The man that did it is standing there!' "

It was a good point, but he didn't press it hard enough to do damage and named no names to force arrests or trials later. The rest of his time he spent exhorting the jury to a firm and fearless discharge of their duty.

They were down at last to Judge Barrett. He folded his hands before him carefully and looked over at the twelve men in the box.

"Gentlemen of the jury," he said. "The first and most important question you have to determine is whether the prisoner at the bar fired the fatal shot that caused the death of Francis Scanlon. Because if he did not fire that shot, he is entitled to acquittal."

That was judicial enough, Casey thought, and settled down to hear the next, which was only a lecture on politics.

"It has been said," Judge Barrett remarked, "that this was a political brawl, a matter difficult to prove and filled with conflicting interests. In my judgment, it is as important to solve the problem of guilt or innocence arising out of a political brawl as any other fracas or disturbance. It tends to lessen not only the general security but the special security of the citizen desiring to express his wishes at the polls."

After that, there was the question of the pistols. "Now there is an immense mass of conflicting testimony. But there are some facts on which there is no conflict. It is an undoubted fact that Maguire, O'Reilly and Costello were unarmed, also an undoubted fact that Masterson, in immediate company of the prisoner, was armed and his pistol was made away with after this occurrence. Because it is an undoubted fact on the testimony that there was a pistol and it is an undoubted fact that none was discovered at the station house."

Casey grunted. It seemed unfair. At the time they couldn't have known Horse should have kept his pistol. God knows, there were plenty of shots. Half the crowd seemed to have been armed that day. An unknown could have done it. But then it had turned out that for safety they needed Horse ready to confess.

"The weight of evidence doesn't depend upon the quantity of witnesses," Judge Barrett said. Casey sat up straight at that. Little Hummel put out his hand to calm him but Casey muttered till Hummel hissed.

"It by no means follows that witnesses commit perjury because they differ. On the contrary, if a host of witnesses should come to court and tell a story which does not deviate a hair in their accounts, it would be a very suspicious circumstance, as tending to show the men had been schooled together."

The assassin! Casey thought, for all he was disguised as a judge. He was wondering if Maguire had got to him when suddenly the worst was over, and perhaps not too much damage done. The old crook was closing.

"If, after the jury have given attention to the case, they as honest, enlightened and intelligent men, should be unable to arrive at a rational conclusion, they are bound to give the prisoner the benefit of reasonable doubt. I leave the case in your hands, trusting that you will arrive at a result satisfactory to yourselves, your consciences, and the public whom we serve." Judge Barrett bowed his head. Casey took out his watch; it was seven o'clock.

"No need to leave, my boy," Howe said. "They'll be right back."

"You think it'll go so quick?" Casey asked and the great criminal lawyer took a bottle labeled Turkey Rhubarb Cough Syrup from his pocket and knocked back a good half. When he lowered it, he let out his breath.

"No doubt of it," he said to Casey. "That little doctor gave us the case."

"Ah, the doctor was sharp as a tack," Casey said, looking wise, hoping Howe would be led to say more. But Howe only lowered a hooded lid and went back at the cough syrup again.

After that, the reporters rushed up but Howe sat Casey back to look confident while he declaimed for them himself and soon little Hummel was handing round pamphlets describing Howe and Hummel's most famous cases. He gave one to Casey, too, and Casey looked it over. Murderers, prostitutes, shoplifters, they'd all got off, it seemed, once they retained Howe and Hummel. Still, cheering as it was, Casey found he couldn't concentrate, but was peeking over the top of the pamphlet to watch the courtroom crowd struggling out while those outside were struggling in.

His friends began to turn up. The Tombs warden, deputy coroner, the county clerk. Not Horse, of course. Howe had told them not to talk together. But Kelly arrived to hear the verdict. Casey waited while he paused to talk to three men lounging around the benches. He supposed they were discussing the case and when Kelly came up, he said, "What do you think?"

But he'd got Kelly feeling pious. The broad, pug-nosed face took on the look of blindfolded Justice. He gave a nod to the reporters and only said: "God protects the innocent."

The next hour was a long time in passing. Howe and Hummel went off to supper, leaving a runner to call them when the jury came back.

"I thought it was supposed to be right over," Casey said and Howe patted his shoulder.

"Just some minor argument. It makes them feel more judicial to haggle," Howe soothed him. Then he swept off to champagne and oysters, and, Casey'd heard, casting up the day's accounts on the restaurant tablecloth — the only bookkeeping they felt was wise.

They'd not been gone ten minutes, when a stir warned Casey something was happening. The court refilled and the judge came back from his chambers, still adjusting his robe, and then the jury returned from the upper floor of the courthouse.

"Where's that runner?" Casey asked but the warden nodded and Casey saw he was already wriggling through the crowds at the door.

After all, it turned out a disappointment. With the judge on the bench, the reporters scribbling, the foreman admitted it wasn't a decision. They only wanted some testimony read — the part where the barkeep leaned out his flat window. Howe's hocus-pocus with the watch must have surrounded him with importance, though he'd told the same story as the others. As the court stenographer droned it off, Casey was suddenly depressed. The gas lights seemed to darken; and the full squad of police that for some reason filed through the doors that moment looked as if they'd appeared to stop a last-minute rescue. With Howe's promise going wrong, Casey took a fearful look at the jury box. They were only commercial travelers, a lumber dealer, a plasterer, but suddenly they seemed shrewd and knowing, and he had a superstitious chill that the corporate jury was blessed by intelligence beyond its separate powers. He struggled against it, clutching Howe's pamphlet about the defendants he'd got off — murderers, pickpockets, thieves, real criminals, not just unfortunate ward leaders caught up in random election troubles. But the stenographer read on, and the jury continued to look transfigured by clear thought. At the end of the reading, Judge Barrett announced they'd be locked up for the night until court opened again next morning.

"Courage, Casey," Kelly told him but the pious voice seemed to come from far away. Deputy Sheriff Daley leaned from behind him and touched his shoulder, to tell him it was time to return to his cell.

As Casey came walking from the Tombs next morning, the steps of the new courthouse were black with men and boys. Captain Petty's police pushed them back, and like the first day, formed a wedge to press him up the steps through the doors. For a few minutes, they were even blocked from the courtroom by politicians demanding entrance. Casey wondered if the jury's delay hadn't got them hoping after all they'd get a hanging. A revulsion against all crowds washed over him. Quick snatches of faces he'd forgot came back — the obscene yelling when the police blocked the view at the Hicks hanging, the mobs firing the Draft offices and shouting up at the Colored Orphanage. Suddenly he hated them. Feeling smothered by his rage, he was shoved and wrestled into the court-room so that when they'd got him clear, he was slippery with sweat. Sitting down at the counsel table, he patted his forehead with his handkerchief, then dried his palms, folded it and stuffed it back in his pocket. Howe arrived, looking cheerful, along with a chuckling Hummel, but even when Kelly showed up too, it didn't ease him.

"Slept, I hope?" Kelly said.

"I slept fine," he answered grimly. But at that, his heart started pounding so he was afraid the reporters would hear it. They had another hour's wait before Judge Barrett finally appeared.

The jury, it seemed, had reached a verdict. The judge was no sooner on the bench than they came filing in and the foreman handed up a sealed envelope to the judge. For a moment, while Barrett opened it and was reading off the paper, Casey had such a roaring in his ears he thought he'd not be able to understand. But when Judge Barrett started to read aloud, it was only the first few words made no sense. Then some queer adjustment took place, and suddenly he was following them all right.

" 'We have to communicate,' " Judge Barrett read, " 'that we stand equally divided with no prospect of arriving at a verdict.' "

A growl went up from the crowd like a dog being teased with a bone. Judge Barrett looked up sharply and the sound subsided. He went on reading.

" 'We have ceased to discuss the question since daylight and we are satisfied that we can never agree.' "

What's this? Casey thought, wondering. Suddenly he couldn't recall what it was happened in such circumstances. Another trial — his stomach roiled. But Judge Barrett was lowering the paper.

"Under the circumstances, gentlemen," he said, addressing the foreman, "with my knowledge of the care you have taken of this case and the evident intelligence of the jury, the fact that you stand equally divided is significant."

Casey leaned over to little Hummel. "What happens now?" he asked.

"He'll dismiss the jury."

"Ah my God," Casey moaned. "I'll not go to trial again?"

"Now, boy, we'll get ye off," Kelly said, but he was shaken too, there was no hiding it. The knowledge hit Casey harder than anything else that had happened. It was as if Kelly himself was doubting. He began to sweat again and he felt light-headed.

By the time the dizzy spell was over, Judge Barrett was dismissing the jury. They stood up and filed out, no doubt to a big feed at the Astor House. Then the court officer was telling them to stand, and steadying himself against the counsel table, Casey got to his feet and they all stood till the judge left.

After that, the reporters pressed around. They threw him questions, but he just shook his head, and after a pull at the Turkey Rhubarb bottle, Howe took them over for him.

"Naturally, we're disappointed. It was a clear case for acquittal."

"What will you do now?" It was the *Herald* man.

"Does he go back to the Tombs?" the *Times* man said and Casey balled his fists. He'd never wanted so to kill a man.

"Now, boys," Howe was saying, smiling. "We have our ways. We're Howe and Hummel, after all. He may go back just for a few hours. But we'll apply for bail. You may be sure he'll be out tomorrow."

"Another trial?" the *Herald* man asked.

Howe smiled. "As for that, I doubt it. Don't put it in the paper. That's just for your information."

Casey turned his head to look at Kelly. It was true, once the limelight glare was over they would have more chance to drag along. With a bit of luck, they'd kill it. The D.A. wouldn't have to push for trial. Casey's breathing began to come back to normal. There were various ways to kill a cat and Kelly knew them. Howe was right. He shouldn't fear another trial. And yet as Deputy Daley led him to the sheriff's office till the crowd would disperse so they could walk quietly back to the Tombs, a sense of depression settled over him.

"Have a drink now?" Daley asked. He saw Daley had closed the door and was reaching for a glass and a bottle.

Casey nodded and Daley poured him a stiff whiskey. When he had drunk it, Daley gave him another.

"Ye'll be all right now, ye'll see," Daley told him. "Bail tomorrow. Ye'll be out. An' that'll be about the end of it."

Casey nodded but he was barely hearing. He was thinking of the verdict. "The bastards," he said.

"It takes all kinds," Daley said philosophically.

Casey stared at his drink, wondering which six men thought he was lying. He ran over the faces. And then he found that was a mistake. He tried to push them from his mind but once he'd let them in, they were bent on staying, six solid citizens of New York, their eyes contemptuous and hard.

It began to snow late on Christmas Eve. By midnight, the ground was white and Casey, standing at the parlor window, watched the soft flakes falling, blanketing the florist gardens opposite his house.

The coal fire in the grate had died down and except for creaks and cracks, the house was silent. The nurse, the maid, the cook were out. And Eileen, too. But at the thought of Eileen, he turned quickly and refilled his glass from the whiskey decanter. Knob Kerry staggered sleepily to his feet and as the dog stared at him, puzzled, Casey toasted him with his glass. There'd been one hell of a row with Eileen, all the worse for no one yelling or crying. It had been about their going to her father's. He'd been giving Eileen money to keep the servants and Eileen felt they had to go to his house Christmas Eve if he wanted. And she had her arguments — with Casey fresh out of the Tombs, they'd had no heart for a tree or family dinners. All that was being done by her father. He had the fir tipped with the candles, the wreath on the door, his daughters and their husbands gathered round him. But it was bad enough trying to find small talk when he was coroner with a house and horse and gig; now stripped of money with a hung jury vouching for his morals, he'd be damned if he'd even try it. So Eileen had gone off with the baby and the new one inside her, looking like he'd turned her out. Her parting shot had been a new one.

"You'll turn up Christmas Day to fetch us?"

For a moment, he'd thought she'd weakened. Her eyes were large, her face was white. But while he hesitated, her pale lips tightened. "I'll tell you something, Casey — you'd just better." And she'd gone straight out the door holding the baby, gone down the steps, and driven off in her father's victoria with the old coachman who'd been sent to fetch her.

"By God, she'll wait till she's old before I turn up," Casey thought. He strolled again to the window and cooled his forehead against the pane, then stepped back and took a pull at his whiskey. And yet he knew he'd pick her up. That had been what she had meant — he had to do it. With the mortgage payments coming due, he'd have to borrow from her father. And to run a household, he'd have to go on borrowing. He'd never do it on John Kelly's dribs and drabs of handouts.

For awhile, he stood wondering if there was a way to shame Kelly into getting him a job. But really he knew he was checkmated. He couldn't go on the city payroll in case the newspapers sniffed it out. If he'd had a clean acquittal, it would be different. But then he could have kept his job as coroner. With a hung jury, he had to count it a blessing to be free on bail while Kelly tried to squash a new trial by pressuring the D.A.'s office. Everything he touched, he stained. Only time and luck could wash the blood off. He couldn't even leave town without Kelly forfeiting bail. And staying, there was Eileen, and the household eating him up, forcing him to borrow more and knuckle under to her father. With money, men escaped their wives and in-laws. There were other ways besides running off. They took up gambling, followed the horses, hung comfortably around the Saratoga casinos. They kept girls who were no better than they had to be. But a man without a dollar had no friend except the bottle.

And that was a dangerous friend to make. He glanced at the dark liquid in his glass, then swung around to look at the decanter with its level lowered four inches. Frank, his brother, came to his mind. He'd been fired from the horsecars finally. It had clearly been coming; Frank had warnings but wouldn't take them. Now he hung around the cheap saloons, coming home at queer hours, having trouble with the steps.

But the thought of his mother's house was too painful. He'd had to hit Kelly to pay their rent and buy them food over Christmas. There'd been no presents. He'd not had the heart to visit. He knew what he'd find. They'd be sitting glumly in the kitchen, Mary doctoring her rheumatism with patent oils and flannel, his mother reading the tea leaves or clinking away on her rosary beads while they listened to find out how much drink Frank had been able to cadge by whether he'd come walking to the door or stumbling. Next month would be worse. He'd no idea how he'd keep them going. Coal he'd get, that was sure, from Tammany. And even, if it came to it, food baskets. But Kelly had had to remove him for the time as district leader, so every penny he got he'd have to beg for.

Feeling hot, he set down his drink, and then to wipe the whole thing from him, he strode to the vestibule, took down his coat, and pulled on his boots. Knob Kerry followed him, jumping up at his knees to go with him, but he said: "Kerry, go back!" Then he let himself out the door without admitting why he left him.

He walked through the snow across Thirty-first Street raising his face to let the great flakes wet his lips. He took draughts of iced air to drown the whiskey and tromped his boots against the pavement as if he could shake off the house that way. On Fifth Avenue, he headed south, and by then the thought of Claire had floated to the surface of his mind. It was just a walk, he told himself, a nostalgic trip to remember his youth. She was probably still away. Though at that, he knew very well Restell had said she'd be back in November.

Even if she were home, he told himself, he wouldn't ring. He'd not want to be seeing her now with his fortunes at a low ebb. He'd best wait for conditions to change. Still, the chance he'd find her windows lit set a queer excitement spiraling through his gut. Her face flashed before him almost as clear as if he saw her — the gleam of gaslight on her hair, the way she held her lips, the delicate line of her jaw. He found himself walking fast.

When he turned into Twenty-eighth Street, he saw her windows were dark. Walking slowly to her street light, though, the excitement began in him again. It was late; she might be home; she might simply have gone to bed. Then he saw the Christmas wreath on the door. A woman still in France wouldn't decorate a New York house. He stood, hardly able to catch his breath. And then, as he moved toward the steps, part of him was shouting not to ring. But he moved on just the same, placing his prints in the white sheets of snow, till he was on the top step before the wreath.

He was reaching out to ring when he saw the changed nameplate. For a moment, he didn't take in the new name, he only saw the brass plate was different. He stared, uncomprehending, then took one end of his scarf, wiped it free of snow, and read: *Thompson*.

"By God," he thought, "what's going on here?"

Wondering if he had the wrong house, he stepped back to look up the block. But there was no mistake. It was Claire's house all right, only now that he looked close, he saw the curtains were changed and the shutters painted gray instead of black. There were people living in it, too, but the feeling of them was different. Then he knew what it was — Claire had sold. She wasn't coming back at all. She was gone as surely as if she had died.

He was startled by the blow of the knowledge. It was like the last punch a man gets before he goes down. All the others had only angered him — Eileen, her father, the loss of his job, his own family's troubles, mortgages to pay off, the sting of handouts. But this was different; it came from nowhere when he was weakened. Standing defenseless, he thought irrelevantly of Scanlon as he'd been election morning. He heard the shot exploding, saw Scanlon sinking down with a look of surprise. A secret compartment in him seemed to open and an acid guilt came welling out. He felt as if it were dissolving him.

As he clung to the railing on Claire's steps, he thought of Kitty and Scanlon's children with a kind of horror, saw them broke and hungry, going down to a life in the streets, and it came to him it was his doing.

As he sickened, the crimes of his life came back to him, not so much the drunks rolled while he ran with the Arsenal Gang, or even his dealings with Restell, but the crimes of devouring and destroying. He felt as if a tiger was inside him lurking till he found a chance to take its prey. It had been there with Maguire. He'd stalked him, jumped, and taken him over. Hanley had sensed the danger from the start, and without Hanley's dying he'd not have had his chance. Perhaps he had betrayed Maguire as Maguire claimed. God knew he'd left him for Kelly. He felt as if one more crime would be nothing. He felt uncaring, as if he'd not defend himself anymore, just stay till he froze and the snow covered him up.

But then a movement in the house quickened him. A step, a gleam of light behind the shutters, someone aware there was a presence on the doorstep. All the years of his forming reacted for him and he turned and sprang down the steps and was away up the snowy street.

As he came to Fifth Avenue, he heard bells jingling on horses' harnesses and he looked up as an omnibus loomed out of the snow falling heavily now. Without thought, he hailed it, jumped on and fumbled with his numb fingers for the fare.

No one else was riding late at night on Christmas Eve and he had the pot stove to himself, stuck his wet boots in the straw and sat warming his feet.

The next thirty blocks he didn't move, only stared at the flame flickering in the stove and his eyes were wide and staring like a cat's. In a vague way he was thinking, seeing the way he'd taken over Maguire; he'd not done it by planning, then. Only tonight in his despair did he really see it, the stalking and capture. For just a moment, he had reeled, considered letting go and sinking. But then the noise inside the house, the sense of danger, had warned the other deep within him and it had come bounding back to protect him.

At Sixty-ninth Street he jumped up, pulled the strap, and leaped down lightly. In the snow, his tread was noiseless, as he moved through the dark streets.

John Kelly's house was dark except for a window on the second floor. He stood looking up at it, then picked up a paving brick and sent it crashing into a vacant lot where it struck and broke a bottle.

In a moment, Kelly's girth came toward the window. The curtain moved and Kelly looked out. As Casey showed himself beneath the street light, Kelly hesitated, surprised. Then he pulled up the window and called out: "Casey!" His voice seemed unsure and as Casey stepped, Kelly went away and came back wearing his eyeglasses.

"What are you doing here on Christmas Eve?"

Casey raised his arms and let them fall. He didn't speak. For another moment, Kelly paused. Then the lone figure took its effect.

"Come," he said. "I'll let you in."

As the window slammed again, Casey lowered his face against the snow. Head thrust forward, he crossed the street and sprang lightly up the dark steps to Kelly's house.

PART SIX

1886

♣

THE BOSS

♣ 22 ♣

Outside it was May again, with the trees in fresh leaf, the lilacs pressing against the panes. But in John Kelly's library, there was no longer any season. The windows were always shut, the weather stuffy from the coal fire smoldering in the grate, the time perpetual dusk, and in the air there hung a mustiness mingling with the smell of laudanum.

It was the opium was getting him, Casey thought, as he watched the old Boss drowsing in his armchair. The doctors said his condition caused his mental lapses but that had only been indigestion and bouts of the insomnia before they had started giving him the stuff. Now they called it nervous prostration and said he couldn't sustain mental effort though they added to the newspapers that his mind was clear.

But this time when his young wife looked in to see if Casey was tiring him, Kelly came to himself quickly and waved her off.

"I'm fine, Mrs. Kelly," he told her. "We've still some business to discuss."

She lingered, taking an unhappy view of Casey. It was as if she felt he was holding the old man a captive and she ought to precipitate a rescue. But how she'd do it still puzzled her. She was a pale, religious girl, niece of the Cardinal; Kelly had married her when he was fifty-four. After they had two children, she found herself turned into his nurse. The strong Boss of the city, the old firefighter, grew vague, sighed and lapsed, dreamed in his armchair and complained of his stomach. Her ship drifted without a captain.

Worse, a strange fo'c'sle hand was always sitting in the captain's cabin. She grew to wear an air of apprehension as she popped in with custards, milk and egg, spooned-out medicines; and when she could announce another one of the visiting hordes of priests, she seemed relieved as if authority would be brought to bear at last.

But there were no priests today yet. Kelly motioned her out and returned to where he'd been before he'd drowsed.

"Pay no mind to what the crowd says, and less when you hear them cheering," he told Casey. "There'd be a bigger crowd to see you hanged."

"Ah, it's true," Casey said, settling back and wishing he could light a cigar. But it was best not to fill the room with smoke, no windows being open. Kelly had always been strong with advice but lately as he'd gone floating off from life's details, he seemed to be seeing the bigger picture clear. Or perhaps the opium was just loosening his grip on the bitter truths he'd locked up. Some of them were grim enough, Casey found to his surprise. Not that he disagreed, but it was strange to find Kelly knew that much.

"Say 'No' ten times before you say 'Yes.' It gives yer 'Yes' its worth. Make a payoff with fine phrases if ye can. If the man won't be satisfied with that, then pay him with a scare. But if he's strong and dangerous and sly and won't settle for praise or a scare, ye want to make friends with him fast."

"I'll remember it," Casey said. It was all tough, sound advice. Though sometimes it was uncomfortably close to the bone, like Kelly's saying twenty captains were safer than two, so before they cut your throat they'll start a fight between themselves. He hoped Kelly wasn't listening too close to himself saying that. But then, words were one thing, acts another. For all Kelly sounded like he saw the world so clear, he had his blind spots — pride and vengeance. They had cost him nearly all he'd gained for Tammany.

Fingering the tidies on his chair arms and nodding at the old man's maxims, Casey burned at how much those feuds of Kelly's had cost. In the fight with Tilden in '78, Kelly had ordered the Tammany delegates to bolt the Democratic State Convention. He got the revenge he was thirsting for. When the Democrats split their ticket, the Republicans had been elected. But Tilden's

County Democracy was declared the regular party, and when they took over in the last mayoralty, they grabbed the boodle. Their elected board of aldermen had the railroad franchises in their pockets. Kelly's fight had beggared Tammany.

Still after that, he took on Cleveland. Blind to the nation's sudden fad for reform, he sent the Tammany delegates into the National Convention to stop the liberal Cleveland on the floor. They fought a losing battle with dogged loyalty, but there it was, the fight was lost. And when Cleveland swept the nation, that was when Kelly cracked at last. He couldn't eat nor sleep, and the doctors started him on the laudanum. For the past year he'd retired to his house.

None too soon, Casey thought, to let Tammany save itself. For it was only with Kelly's breakdown that he'd been able to start moving cautiously. Acting as Kelly's link with the world, he came in, took his orders, and went out. At first he'd been careful how he changed those orders, but his confidence increased fast. Now it looked like they might have a chance.

Last November they had picked up a few offices. Casey himself had become fire commissioner and Casey's man had got in as sheriff. That was a big piece in the city game; the sheriff's office was worth real money. He charged the city for the care of prisoners, for carrying them back and forth from Blackwell's Island, and he appointed his own official auctioneers. Tammany also elected some aldermen and a few state assemblymen. That meant money flowing to oil the slick organizational machine Kelly had put together. And he'd really left them that — wheels within wheels, working together, so that orders moved along smoothly from the Boss, through the district leaders, to each lowly captain, one to each block in the city.

As Kelly mused at the glowing coals in the grate before him, Casey sneaked a look at his pocket watch, and then rose to make his escape. But Kelly was hard to leave. He fought like a child at bedtime.

Sitting up, he grasped at the old authority. "I've another piece of business fer ye to attend to," he said with a fussy air. He looked around at his desk and dropped back helpless. There was nothing for Casey to do but help him with it. Crushing back his impatience, he strolled to the inlaid mahogany desk and stood waiting for instructions.

" 'Tis a letter from some poor woman. Her man has lost his arm," Kelly said. "He caught his hand in a set of factory cogwheels and they had to amputate his right arm. He has five children to feed."

Casey pushed through the mess of papers. There was thanks from the Sisters of Charity, letters from the St. Patrick's Board and the American College in Rome. There was one from the mining country where Kelly had raised a fund some years back to build a church. They were having graduation at the church school and inviting him to attend.

"I've found it," Casey said, just as Kelly tried to struggle from his chair. "It's on blue paper."

"That's the one," Kelly said, sinking back. "They're from the Eighth Ward. I think she says they have a son of twenty. See he gets appointed to the Island penitentiary."

"We'll do that easy," Casey soothed him. At least they had that bit of patronage now they'd elected Hugh Grant to sheriff. He was pleased about Hugh Grant; Grant was his own man and not Kelly's. Casey had raised him up himself.

"Ye could get the boy made a keeper," Kelly said. "That way, he'll help support the family. We can see they get coal too, if they need it."

"It's May now, but I'll look into it. Maybe they could use a hundred to tide them over till the boy starts getting his wages."

"That's the way to do it," Kelly said, his features softening. There was no denying he was a saint for charity. Charitable he really was, and surely honest. Though looking at him, Casey wondered how much good the honesty and charity had done him. He sat in his leather armchair, his fingers trembling, the skin hanging from his big face, his hard eyes timid now in flashes, an old man at sixty-four, sipping his custards, milk and sherries, drugging what was left of his brain to sleep. A lot of good the Church's gratitude would be doing his wife when he died. She had two children to support, a boy of seven, a girl of four. They'd not be eating gratitude from the Sisters of Charity, nor dressing up in letters from St. Patrick's and the schools he'd started.

There was a ringing at the doorbell.

"You have guests, so I'll be leaving," Casey said, grasping his opportunity.

"I wonder now," Kelly said, like the dog eyeing the meat reflected in the river water. He didn't like to let loose of Casey till he knew he was getting something better.

But better it was — two Dominican fathers from the Church of St. Vincent Ferrer a few blocks over. Kelly's face lit when he saw them. And Casey bolted from the musty library and escaped to the fresh May afternoon.

As he entered the Hoffman House bar, his spirits were rising. He stood looking at the nude oil paintings in their gilt frames, the alabaster statues, the velvet drapes. Enjoying a sense of opulence, he strolled to his usual table, greeting old friends on the way, as his regular waiter came running with his usual order of Vichy water.

The Tammany crowd soon began to gather. Horse Masterson and Paddy Carroll came for the day's orders. He sent Horse off to see the Eighth Ward district leader about Kelly's charity case.

"Tell him to give them a hundred dollars," Casey said.

"I'll do that," Masterson said, nodding sharp. Lately Horse had picked up new manners. He looked bright; he had stopped slouching. He'd even bought a small black notebook and though he didn't know how to write beyond signing his name when he had to, he'd worked out some pencil signs to jog his memory. Prosperity suited him well. He watched himself and never got drunk; he'd given up his loud clothes without a murmur when Kelly had passed the word along that diamonds and loud vests went out with Tweed. He'd taken to wearing a square beard that hid the Yoke marks. When the time was ripe, Casey thought he would be able to spirit away the records and raise Horse to replace him as fire commissioner.

"Lost his arm in a factory accident," Casey explained. "So he

won't be working," He brought out the blue-colored letter. "Here's
the name and address. The son's name is Patrick. I'll see Sheriff
Grant about putting him on the Island payroll."

"He could be a keeper. At the penitentiary," Horse said and as
Casey nodded, Horse made a pencil mark and shut the notebook.
"What else?"

There was another job to be got, with the New Haven Railroad.
Casey almost gave it to Paddy Carroll to take care of, but then he
decided it was too complicated. With Tammany still weak, they'd
best handle it through the Republicans, swapping favors against
the day Tammany would come back to power. He saved it to do
himself and sent Paddy off instead to explore a rumor that the city
was going to repave a street and had old granite blocks to sell. By
having Paddy drop by the city auction on the right day, he might
turn a tidy profit, selling the blocks to a contractor he knew who
needed them.

When Masterson and Carroll left, he bought a drink for the
Third Ward leader, had his own glass refilled with Vichy, and then
a hardware company president appeared to drop the hint it would
be worth something to have the Tammany assemblymen block a
bill putting safeguards on factory machinery. Somewhere dimly
and far away, the blue-colored letter came back to him as he recalled it was in a factory that Kelly's man had lost his arm. For an
instant he saw the cogwheels, saw them connecting the two shafts,
the vicious wheels whirling away with no guard, and he frowned at
the oil nudes, the gilt frames and the alabaster. But just then the
hardware president rose. He let it go, drank down his Vichy, and
looked around for an excuse to take out his irritation. At the sight
of one of Vanderbilt's lawyers standing against the bar, he signaled
his waiter.

"Tell Mr. Stewart I'd like to see him."

They'd not rung the bell on Vanderbilt lately. It might be time
to threaten an overhaul of railroad accident legislation. The Doctrine of Assumed Risk was a phrase that sent their hands slipping
to their pockets. If it wasn't for the Doctrine — the workman waiv-
ing his right to damages because he knew the risk he ran when he

took dangerous employment — the courts would fill up with suits. The companies had been buying off for years; just the words started money flowing.

But even as the waiter reached him and the lawyer turned and smiled, Scanlon came to his mind. He suddenly was sitting in Mc-Glynn's kitchen the day after Scanlon had his ribs crushed in the railroad accident. It had been Assumed Risk that time had saved Vanderbilt — Scanlon knew a brakeman's job was dangerous when he took it. He couldn't sue; he'd lived on charity till he was well enough to work again and feed his family.

The thought of Scanlon brought a blackness crushing down on him. It spread out staining the Hoffman bar, the sitting rich and easy at his table, having his Vichy trotted to him by a smiling colored waiter. As the railroad lawyer crossed to him, he thought: "I don't like this at all. I wish I could keep out of it."

He wished with a passion that Tammany was in again so he could make do with just the most honest graft, trading city contracts for stock in ice and gas companies and the like. If he were at the County Democracy headquarters today, he'd be seeing plenty of that. Railroad executives, companies after city bonding deals, construction presidents and gas vice-presidents wanting city contracts to put in streetlamps — they were all hanging about Tilden's followers. That was where the clean graft had gone to, and they could thank John Kelly for that.

But by the time the railroad lawyer pulled up his chair, he began to feel more sanguine. After all, he thought, the tide was turning. With Kelly house-ridden and safely cordoned off from feuding, they had made a start. Hugh Grant was in as sheriff; they had four aldermen and five judges, Superior, Supreme, and Common Pleas. One of these election days they would be strong enough to make Grant mayor and with the mayoralty they'd seize the heavy patronage appointments. When they'd got a commissioner of public works appointed, the city contracts were sure to follow.

At the thought of Hugh Grant, he remembered he had a four o'clock appointment with him. He took out his watch and saw it was that already.

"Have a drink with me before I leave," he smiled to the lawyer. He had no time for Assumed Risk. He raised his hand and brought the colored waiter running.

Hugh Grant's carriage was standing before Casey's new house on Seventy-fourth Street when Casey got there, but he paid off his hack and paused to watch the gardeners dragging young trees off the city dray wagon and setting their roots safe in holes before the brownstone. The marble steps looked fine, he thought; he'd picked them up cheap from a downtown mansion being demolished to build the new telephone exchange. The stained-glass windows were from a city auction; his new streetlamp was a favor from the board of aldermen. Even so, he was up to his neck in loans and mortgages. Tammany had better sweep in next election; he was already in debt over this year's income.

The little maid who let him in was new, another green girl off the boat. They had only had her a few days and she was clumsy with the hats and coats so he took his time to calm her down.

"I see Mr. Grant has come," he said.

"Ah yes, he's in the parlor. With yer missus."

"You'll call her Mrs. Casey," he said, reminding her, and she slapped her palm against her forehead.

"I keep fergettin'. I'm that sorry, Commissioner," she said. "But there's so much new to me. It's such a fine place with telephones and the gas lights blazin' like a fairy palace. It's got me crazy."

In spite of knowing she was slathering it on, he felt the glow of pride. "Sweet Christ, remember Kelly," he told himself. "Beware of flattery."

"You'll hang the hats there on the antlers," he said dourly and continued to the parlor.

But as he crossed the parlor threshold, he wished he was still back with the maid. Eileen was sitting like a ramrod, a social smile pinned to her lips, and he could tell she was icy with anger for his embroiling her in his politics. Not that Hugh Grant was like Horse Masterson or Paddy Carroll; there she might have a point, having to entertain gorillas. But Hugh Grant knew how to talk and act. If it came to that, he'd been to college, though trying to pass him off as a gentleman might be stretching it a bit. The family money came from liquor and a pawnbroker had brought him up after his father died. There'd been money enough left for that. And since Grant had entered politics, his old guardian had been financing him. Now that Grant was sheriff, he was paying back.

But Eileen's disapproval of Hugh Grant was over morals. Good Catholic he might be, but she felt that he was fast. Though how she knew, Casey couldn't guess. He was amused at how a convent-bred girl took one glance at a man and told that.

Fortunately, Grant wasn't quick to pick up slights. Bent over in the tufted chair beside the mantel, he was playing he was a bear and raising his paws while the baby shrieked with delight, ran to hide and rushed back to strike at his leg.

"Now, Mr. Grant, don't let her do that," Eileen told him.

But Grant just chuckled. He raised his paws again and gave a growl and Betty crowed and darted at him.

Eileen sat up straighter. "You'll make her rough," she told him coldly. Seeing how the land lay, Casey strode in saying loudly: "Hello, Hugh!"

"Casey!" Grant beamed. He seemed good-humored enough about waiting. But as he rose, Betty hurled herself at him and before Eileen could get any chillier, Casey scooped up Betty, and sat her astride his shoulders, drawing her little legs down on his chest.

"Careful," Eileen said. "She'll fall backwards."

"For that she'll have to stop pulling my hair," he said, smiling easy for Grant's benefit, though in truth he was getting sore himself. She had no call to play the Ice Queen before his friends. And though he had created Hugh Grant himself, he was still the high sheriff of New York.

But to avoid trouble, he gave in, lowered Betty from his shoulders, and set her down on the Turkish rug. Betty gave a high-pitched scream and made a rush at Grant but Eileen grabbed her hand.

"Come, dear," she said, "and say good-bye. We'll leave the gentlemen alone."

He felt easier as she turned toward the door, pulling Betty who didn't want to go.

"Sit down, Hugh," he said. "Have a whiskey?"

But Hugh Grant said: "Wait a second!" He said to Eileen: "I haven't had a chance to give Betty her present."

Eileen turned and tried to look gracious, though it was clear to Casey she didn't like Grant giving the children gifts.

"Ah now, Hugh," he said. "You shouldn't."

But Grant was grinning with an air of mystery. He sat down on the sofa and beckoned to Betty. Unwillingly, Eileen loosed her hand and as Betty looked in wonder at them all, Grant motioned to her again and slid his hand in his inside breast pocket. As Betty approached, he took out a thick white envelope.

Ah my God, Casey thought, he shouldn't do that. Eileen was still standing by the door trying to decide what kind of child's present came in a white envelope. Betty was puzzled. She stretched out her fingers and Hugh laughed aloud, caught and turned her, steadied her between his knees, and put her other hand on the envelope to hold it safe.

"What is it?" Eileen said, and to Betty: "Come to Mama."

Betty turned all around, plucking at the unstuck flap, and Casey bent down.

"Come to Papa!" he said urgently. But the urgency was a mistake. It put Betty off and she backed from him, then laughed and ran across to Eileen.

As Eileen touched the envelope and saw the money, her face stiffened.

"I'll take it, Betty," he said, rising. To put an end to dangerous nonsense, he strode across the room, swept her up and took the envelope, sticking it away inside his pocket.

"You better count it. It's the whole ten thousand," Grant laughed.

It was better than he'd thought — Grant was only elected last November and he was paying off already. He was a fool to do it like this, but then he couldn't know Eileen despised him. And if it came to that, why should she — it was Grant's money would build her new conservatory and help educate her children. But at that moment, he had his hands full. Betty was starting to whimper at losing the envelope and to stop her, he laughed and whirled her round the way she liked. It was Eileen put the cap on it.

"I'll take the child now," she said and her tone even got through to Grant. He watched Casey hand Betty over, and though he beamed the same as always when Eileen said: "Good afternoon," as soon as she'd swept out, he turned to Casey.

"Tell me, old man, did I do something wrong?"

"Ten thousand bucks is never wrong," Casey told him. "It's just that my wife don't understand politics."

"I will not have it in my house around my children," Eileen was saying. She was standing by the mantel, her hand clenched on it, and Casey could tell by the set of her thin shoulders that her face would be red and the veins in her temples starting to swell. Still, the advantage of a house full of servants was it acted as a brake on family scenes. As long as she was able to control herself, she'd keep her voice low. But she couldn't always do it. Lately, she'd flung herself into a state of real hysterics, smashing knickknacks, tearing at a bolster, and once she'd tried to claw him. That time he'd knocked her across the room, and young Dan had run in to find his mother on the bedroom floor. The memory of his son's face still made Casey uneasy, and now he tried to calm her down by using reason.

"What harm could it do the child to take an envelope? Hugh's a clown but there's no harm in him. Anyway, he owed me the money."

She gave a harsh laugh. "He owed you for electing him sheriff. He bought his job."

"What's wrong with that? It's a business I'm in like any other. The butcher wants dough for his steaks. The doctor sends his bill. Your own father gets paid for writing his briefs."

"That's different altogether."

"How's it different? Every time he tells a corporation how to weasel through a loophole —"

"Stop!" she screamed and began sobbing, pressing her forehead against the marble. "It's dirty money, got from thieves and murderers and loose women. I won't have it soiling little Betty's fingers."

"Ah my God," he breathed in outrage. "You've been living on it fine, paying your dressmaker and driving out in a carriage. But whenever poor Hugh comes to see me —"

"I won't have that man in my house! And Masterson and Paddy Carroll! How can I explain it to my children? They're getting old enough to notice. Masterson is just a jailbird!"

"Now watch yourself, spreading dirty stories," he said to her dangerously. A lot of good it would do him, destroying Masterson's records to make him fire commissioner if his own wife went around reminding the world about Sing Sing.

She began to laugh at that, throwing her face back with the tears glistening on it, and this time it was he who feared the servants.

"Stop it now!" he said but she went on laughing wildly till they heard the back door slam and the sound of their sons running.

She wiped at her eyes quickly so that when Dan came in, the tears were gone, but there was no hiding that she'd been crying. Dan took that in at a glance but he arranged his face politely and gave no sign. He was a tall, slender boy at thirteen with gray-green eyes the same as Casey, but all the rest of him was fine-boned like Eileen. Behind him Peter was poised, a year younger, with more hell in his eyes, but still delicate. They were handsome boys, it was true, but ah my God, Casey thought, those clothes of Eileen's! He saw they'd come from their riding lesson. Full white sleeves and braided vests, stripes down their pants legs, red semi-military caps, like organ grinders' monkeys. He wondered they weren't set upon in the street.

"Well," he said, trying to work out of his embarrassment at their blundering in on Eileen's dramatics, "How is the riding going?"

Peter shot him a look of mischief. If he wasn't far too young for it, Casey would have thought the boy saw through him perfectly and was having his fun watching him struggle out of it. But Dan was another matter. He leaped in to help all too quickly. His face keen and polite, he babbled on about their ride. A twitch of exasperation caught Casey's face at the way Dan had picked up Eileen's social manner. Jesus God, he thought, Eileen had better let him teach the kid how to fight. With those girly manners he was going to need it.

Still, he knew the boy was trying. He forced back his irritation and tried to help smooth the situation.

"That's good," he said to stem the flood of the riding description. They went to a riding master in Central Park. "I've been thinking now we have our own stables, perhaps the time has come to buy you each your own horse."

Having hurled that into their midst, he stood to wait results. It was a master stroke, he felt, making the announcement at this moment when Eileen was still sore about Grant's money. Her sons' excitement would be a lesson on the emotional negotiability of money.

It took a moment before he realized that he wasn't getting the results he'd expected.

"Why, Papa," Dan cried. "That's daisy!" And somehow, although the words were there, they came out in the same bright tone he'd used before, as if he still only cared to put a gloss over the picture of his mother's face swollen from crying. But to force the pleasant mood up, he had clapped both his hands together. It was the gesture of a boy much younger, and it triggered Casey's old distaste for Eileen's teaching them to call him by the Frenchified Papa.

As for Peter, he said nothing. He only lingered behind his brother and his quick blue eyes were dancing. It was that look of mischief that punctured Casey's hope. It was as if Peter thought he was trying to buy them. He knew he was being fanciful. The kids hadn't heard of Grant's white envelope. And even if they should, what difference would it make. It was only Eileen's crazy moral prissiness that saw harm in a man paying back a favor.

"Thank you, Papa," Dan was saying.

"Yes, thank you, sir," Peter murmured, moved to say a few words at last. But the look of amusement, almost malice, was still there; either that or, Casey felt, he was losing his mind.

"Well then, we've settled that," Casey heard himself say. It seemed impossible that such a gift to two young boys should fall so flat. Bitterly, he saw himself at their age, wolfing down his potatoes and tea, fighting to make a few pennies in the streets. It was as if they lived behind a glass pane where he watched them without knowing what made them act.

At that point of their impasse, Eileen stirred. "Boys, it's time to change your clothes. Your piano teacher will be arriving." She turned to Casey courteously: "Shall I tell Norah you'll be with us tonight for dinner?"

"No," he said, surprised by his voice's thickness. He had supposed till that minute that he'd be home for dinner. His answer wasn't really to her question but was his way of lashing back in disappointment at the boys' reaction to the horses. It was a great No about Daniel saying "Papa," about the tricky riding suits, Dan's keen, bright, false expression, Peter's malice, a great aversion to piano lessons. Jesus God, he thought, piano lessons. No wonder he'd never dared to take them visiting his old ward.

But already Eileen had taken him at his word. Gently patting her two sons before her, she shepherded them out of the parlor and proceeded down the hall to tell the cook there'd be one less to dinner.

Striking his foot against a black enamel table, he nearly turned it over. Then he caught a bowl of straw flowers from falling, and set them back. In a rage, he moved into the hallway, looked about and went to the telephone box. Giving Liggett's number to the operator, he took a grim pleasure in ordering him to join him for an unexpected dinner at the Hoffman House.

Liggett had scarcely changed in the twelve years since he had strolled into Casey's cell in the Tombs prison. He had the same patrician airs and gingerly care not to insult his inferiors. His blond moustache and beard were graying but it was still the same boyish face; the white collar and linen were snowy, the seals dangled from his watch in the same offhanded rich way. A stranger watching them wouldn't know who it was gave out the orders. It was Liggett suggested the terrapin, discussed the tenderness of the asparagus, had his own wine fetched from his private bin in the cellar of the Hoffman House.

"I'll stick to Vichy," Casey said dourly.

"It's a lovely wine, the right side of the hill, a perfect season for the grapes."

"I don't like wine," Casey said, and as the waiter retreated, he put his elbows on the linen tablecloth and got back to railroad risk legislation.

Liggett responded to direction so gracefully; it was no trouble to save his dignity. Casey had barely hinted how Liggett should vote in Albany, before Liggett was seeing the point and agreeing entirely. Casey didn't even have to split with him. That was the advantage to silver spoon candidates — Liggett's interest in office was just sweet ambition. After his years in the State Senate, he was hoping for Tammany's backing to run for governor. After that — with the man's overweening vanity — Casey had his suspicion Liggett was daydreaming of the White House.

But tonight everything Liggett did rubbed him wrong. The light way he laughed, his quickness with words, kept reminding Casey unpleasantly of his disappointment in Daniel. The manners that once seemed so right in the rich dining room with its plush carpet, crystal chandeliers, gilt pier mirrors and velvet, appeared a fancy covering for weak character. His courtesy was only irritating innocence. The man, he decided, was an ass, and suddenly he was at no pains to save Liggett his dignity anymore.

"You have it then," he said shortly across the terrapin. "You'll leave for Albany tonight. Anyway, you shouldn't be down here so much in the middle of the session." That he knew was unfair; half the Senate was usually absent. They only showed up to push their own bills. Well, let Liggett push his. He'd be introducing reform so railroad men could collect on injuries due to dangerous work conditions. Tammany hadn't rung the railroads' bell recently; Liggett would find half the Senate keen to help him shake up Vanderbilt and set the dough jingling from his pockets. Everybody would be richer for defeating it, and it would give Liggett the workout that he needed.

But he'd put it to Liggett more roughly than usual. And instead of saying Yes, Liggett took his time as if he was thinking. He speared asparagus with his fork and frowned at its dab of Hollandaise.

"I wonder is it wise to pass such a bill in a climate of labor crisis," Liggett said finally.

"Pass? Who spoke of passing it?" Casey asked. Normally, he'd have gone along with letting Liggett pretend the bill was real; but tonight Dan's polite pretenses had left his nerves on edge.

But deals like that Liggett never faced directly. He weaved and ducked and waved his arms and spouted, but to call a spade by its right name was congenitally beyond him. Besides, Casey's mood had made him nervous. He ended by backing away altogether.

"Is it the time for me to put my name to a radical bill? The railroad strikes aren't long over — Chicago, Pittsburgh, remember the attacks on railroad property? And Hayes sending the troops into Pennsylvania. They may have hanged a few Molly Maguires but you know as well as I that they're still everywhere in the coal fields. If workmen started collecting on their suits, the courts would be flooded and the railroads beggared. Every man who broke a fingernail would be living on a pension."

"I never knew you was such an orator," Casey said dryly. What he meant was he'd not realized how frightened Liggett was. In another moment, he'd be giving figures on the Almshouse and if it wasn't Casey opposite, probably dropping the number of Irish who were living on City charity. Liggett's class had not forgot the Draft Riots. Scratch their surface and they started screaming about burning, looting and murder.

As he cut into his terrapin, Casey considered Liggett's plans to be governor. Decorative he was, but he lacked the common touch, the rough geniality a New York politician needed. He might carry the Swallowtail districts, but he'd not do well downtown in the crowded Bowery and waterfront. And a Tammany candidate was worth nothing if he could not deliver the whole city. They'd need that to overcome the upstate vote which was Republican. So Liggett's hopes would come to nothing. As Liggett spouted on about the radicals, Casey flagged the waiter to refill his water glass. His gaze began cruising round the dining room for distraction.

On the far side against the velvet drapes, he spotted Thunderbolt Norton. The old rascal was looking fat and ruddy. His Coney Island properties were booming; his East Side saloons were minting money. Of all that gang who'd ridden high with Tweed, it was only Tweed had been the scapegoat. Connolly was living on his loot in France. No suit had been brought against Mayor Hall; even Sweeney got out of it by pinning his own guilt on his dead brother. None of the respectable bankers and contractors who'd made fortunes had had their names made public. It was Tweed alone had been brought down, jailed and muzzled with promises that he'd get out if he'd keep quiet and not disclose too much.

The time had passed wearily for the old rake in his chambers at Ludlow Street Jail. It wasn't, of course, a dungeon. He had two rooms, a grand piano, his windows full of potted geraniums, the jail walls covered with engravings. Cretonne curtains disguised the bars and he was tended by a Negro servant. Still, gradually the hope went out of him. He grew diabetic; his heart went bad. He died at last, abandoned by everyone he'd made rich, but till the end he'd been philosophical and wry. After all, he'd always been a realist.

Maguire was dead by then, four months before his old enemy. He'd got a cold and then pneumonia stamping around town addressing voters in the elections of '77. The irony was that he died the champion of the poor against Tammany. And there were plenty of poor who believed it. Casey had watched his funeral pass. He'd been mourned like a martyr, fifteen thousand following his casket — Father McGlynn's parishioners, railroad agitators, dock strikers and union leaders, all crying for the workers to take their fate in their own hands.

"Ah my God, it's unfair, the man a hero," Casey thought. Even after nine years, a groan almost escaped him above the terrapin. Turning his head from the sight of Thunderbolt sucking meat from a lobster claw, Casey dropped his knife on his plate, and Liggett stopped talking in surprise. With a tic of annoyance, Casey sought a way to rend him.

But Horse Masterson had entered the dining room. In his high collar and dark sack suit, he looked like any other gentleman hoping to find a friend to dine with. Casey was struck by the power of clothes to change a burglar into a candidate for fire commissioner.

Suddenly dropping his annoyance with Liggett, Casey raised his hand and when the waiter came, he said, "I'm leaving."

Liggett frowned in dismay, seeing the ground beneath him quivering. But breeding still counted for something. All he said was: "Won't you have dessert?"

Casey didn't bother to answer directly. Waving Horse he'd be right with him, he threw down a tip, and signaled the waiter to put the check on his tab. Only as he got up, he told Liggett: "I want some air."

Horse didn't protest though he'd missed supper. He followed Casey to the street and stood taciturnly staring at the park across the way till Casey's carriage was brought round. The driver was a wizened little Corkman who'd been a keeper at the Tombs during Casey's trial for murder. When the County Democrats threw him out, he'd come to Casey who fancied him for his silence and hired him. And silent he was; he saw it all and gave out nothing. Now he just gave a questioning grunt and Casey said: "Drive through Central Park."

Rattling up Fifth Avenue, Casey stared moodily at the crimson fittings of the clarence. Horse gave him a look but when he'd offered his case of Reina Victorias and been refused, he lit his own cigar and held his peace. They ended with each brooding out his own window at the gas lamps before the brownstones.

Opposite St. Patrick's, they jogged past Restell's mansion, cut up now into apartments. Nobody would buy it as a residence after the way Madame Restell had died. With Kelly outraged by her flaunting herself across from the Cathedral, her years of fixing cops and judges had ended. The Vice Society had her arraigned — it was the first time in thirty years that had happened. But she made her trip to court in one of her silver-trimmed barouches, and pleaded not guilty to procuring abortion. Her trial was set for the next Monday but that night she cut her throat in her bath.

The old vixen, run to ground, had saved her cubs, too. The two changeling children could not be found. Rumor went the girl had married and with her brother and her young bridegroom lived in a chateau outside Paris. Madame had sent them off herself with her converted cash and diamonds. The money from the house, stables and horses, the marble busts of Washington and Franklin, the rosewood tables, chairs and pictures, was filtered to them through the wiles of Howe and Hummel.

They were dead, Casey thought as the clarence swayed over the cobbles, all dead — Tweed and Maguire, Fisk the joker, and Madame Restell. Flashy wicked they'd lived and died as flashy — Tweed jailed, Maguire a hero, Fisk shot to death, and Restell killed by her own hand like an old Roman. The Flash Age was dead; wickedness walked respectably veiled now so a man couldn't tell a pimp from a church warden. Sighing, he shifted against a cushion, and Horse took a quick look out Casey's window. He saw what they'd passed and guessed the rest.

"Sometimes a man needs a lively girl," he said softly.

They were drawing near the Park and Casey gazed at the dark ailanthus trees stirring the evening wind before the brownstones. For a moment, he was tempted. He swept across the chasm of the past to when he'd first broken with Claire, when he was alderman, and he showed up in evening dress with his bouquet at Sisters' Row to make his night's choice from the ladies playing the guitar in the front parlor. But there had been other nights much wilder when he'd joined the throng pushing along the Tenderloin past the saloons, brothels and dance halls. He'd ducked in past the lights blazing from the Haymarket to take his pick from the women dancing the cancan in the haze of smoke and whiskey fumes. He had vague memories of masked balls at the Buckingham in Twenty-seventh Street, peculiar exhibitions in the back boxes, and even a few disjointed memories of the Cremorne basement that brought a flush to his face.

Perhaps, he thought, with his blood rising, if he could go like some Baghdad prince disguised in rags, he might shake off the death and sadness. But it had been years since he'd risked it. Times had changed with Tweed's downfall; Kelly had set a new mold for politicians. It was Vichy now instead of champagne, and a bitter wife in a dark bed instead of tipsy laughter at the French Madame's. The best Horse could do was set him up in a rented room in one of the assignation houses off Sixth Avenue. A closed carriage would bring him there to a brief encounter with a girl too green yet to recognize him. It was the surest way to avoid blackmail. But

with so much need for caution, there was no giving way or forgetting. He was just a middle-aged man drinking Vichy, and he would
leave the house drained but sad.

It wasn't worth all the setting up and trouble. When Horse
pressed: "What do ye say?" he shook his head, knocked his stick
against the trap and when the Corkman's face poked into view, he
shouted: "Take a turn to Coney Island. To the racetrack."

The little Corkman never questioned. It didn't concern him it
was night and a strange hour to go to a racetrack.

"Ye want the ferry or the new bridge by way of Brooklyn?"

"Take the bridge," Casey said. And to Horse: "There's a trainer
there I want to look up. He'll tell me where I'll get two saddle
horses for my boys."

The Coney Island season hadn't started and though the hotels
were newly painted, the amusements weren't yet going, nor band
concerts nor night fireworks. The iron piers glided by them where
the steamers from New York would be tying up with the racing
crowds, but there were no drags on the road filled with pretty
women in spring toilets, no hucksters selling peanuts, beer and toy
balloons between the trains and track. And the track itself loomed
strangely empty, its grandstands bare and clubhouse balconies
gleaming by moonlight. They drove by the watchman at the gate
who tipped his hat at their driver's cry of "Fire Commissioner,"
and wound past the colored stablehands and exercise boys till they
saw the kerosene lantern hanging outside the stables. Casey and
Horse got out and stood listening as a mascot cock began crowing.
A horse whinnied and one of their carriage horses answered.

"Where do I find George Couch?" Casey called to a stablehand
and the boy pointed ahead to the stalls. The years and the sadness
lifting, Casey strode ahead with an odd quickness.

They came on Couch overseeing a big bay with its head ducked
to a trough, a wiry, sun-browned man of sixty with a bright, sardonic eye. For years he'd helped Restell buy her horses and given
her tips when she drove out to Jerome Park, Coney Island or Rock-
away. Tonight, he dropped his heel from the stall side and shook
hands with Casey and then Horse, his weather-browned face smil-

ing in the lantern light, his glance amused as he waited to see what had brought them out so late.

"I've a mind to have two saddle horses. Nothing rough. They're for my boys," Casey said. "Know where I'd go to pick them up?"

"I might," Couch said. "But if you want a buy, let me ask around a bit."

Casey nodded and offered his cigar case.

"Not in the stalls," Couch said and led them out into the moonlight beside a line of lilac bushes. They lit up and stood gazing at the empty paddock ring.

"We passed Restell's old place tonight," Casey said with an air of irrelevance.

Couch gave him a quick look. "Those were the days," he answered, understanding.

"Poor Tweed," Casey said.

"And Fisk." They exchanged the words in set response.

Casey said: "Have you heard anything from the old crowd?"

Couch sighed and shook his head, for he knew that Casey was asking if anyone in the racing world had seen Claire. For twelve years no one had come across her. The nets were flung wide from San Francisco to Saratoga, as far south as New Orleans and Havana. Stranger fish than she had been sighted — a vanished witness to Fisk's murder bought off by Howe and Hummel; a bank embezzler turned up in Denver; Fisk's old mistress on a poor farm in South Dakota. But of Claire there was no word.

The trail had petered out in France when the letters to Restell stopped shortly after she'd sold her house. There were rumors that came to nothing — she was mistress of the city boss in San Francisco; she had taken religious orders; she had married a Western farmer. Casey had thought once he'd stumbled on her track himself.

It was when he'd moved his sister Anne from Blackwell's to a private lunatic asylum up by Tarrytown. Coming indoors from the rose arbor where Anne spent the fine days, he'd caught sight of red hair, the curious shade of a good setter. The straight carriage was the same, the little bones and head held high. But when he cried out and she turned, he saw the ravaged face and drew back.

"Sorry," he said, feeling foolish, to an attendant who was watching. "I thought I knew her."

"And so you might," the attendant said.

She was a famous Bowery Theater actress who'd taken to the drink, kept here now for ten years by a well-known shipping magnate.

"Every time he takes her out, he has to go looking for her on the waterfront," the attendant said. "She must of banged half the crew that sails his own ships."

"It wasn't who I thought it was," Casey said, hurrying to cut off confidences. For nearly a year after, he was haunted by the idea Claire was in some place like it.

But she was gone. Gradually, he came to know it, gone like Restell, Fisk and Tweed. And even Pretty Boy had joined them. He'd been found beaten and drowned, recognized by his clothes when he was fished out of the East River. The bloody sixth Ward gave him a wild funeral with twenty carriages and two of his girls dressed in widow's weeds each trying to crowd the other's carriage out of line. It ended with them catfighting at the cemetery so they had to be pulled apart before Pretty Boy could be laid in his grave. It was the kind of scandalous way to go that Pretty Boy would have enjoyed.

"How's Mr. Kelly?" Couch was asking. Casey came back with a start, and as he threw away his cigar, they turned and strolled again to the stalls.

"He's not well and that's a fact," Casey said. "The illness is wearing him down." His tone was formally funereal, but as they entered the big bay's stall and found the horse finished at the trough, Casey found a sugar cube in his pocket, gave it to him and stroked his head. The warm feel of the animal soothed him. As he lingered smelling the hot dung, the straw and animal sweat, the knot of sadness finally loosened in his chest.

"I'm sorry to hear it," Couch said. "But the world moves on. There's always changes."

"True for you," Casey murmured.

"How's prospects for the fall?" Couch asked him. "Tammany is stronger every day, I hear."

"No doubt about it." Casey ran his hand down the bay's withers. "I'd like to race fine fellows like this."

Couch shot him a sharp, merry look. "The sport of kings? Well, why not, if you want it."

Casey gave him a slight smile, clapped the bay and said: "We have to go. Let me hear about the saddle horses. You can drop me a line at the Hall."

"I'll do that," Couch said. "Good luck to you, Commissioner." It was hard to tell if he meant Claire or Tammany. The brown-lined face was shrewd, pleasant and enigmatic. He waved beneath the lantern light and Casey and Horse crunched back across the gravel to their carriage.

♣ 23 ♣

The calcium lights were blazing in the vast Tammany auditorium so that from where he sat on the platform, Casey looked out on the posters with flaming headlines, the American flags, banners and bunting anchored to the gold pillars, the red, white and blue streamers falling from the lofty domed ceiling painted with roses, naked goddesses and cherubs. To accommodate the crowd, the seats had been taken out and the galleries and stairways were packed with men standing — Irish mostly, but some Germans, here and there spiced with Italians and a few Jews from the tides of new immigration crashing each year on the Battery. The noise of them made Casey's head throb. Every time the band struck up a new tune, they fell to cheering and hurrahing, and squeezed together in their overcoats, the stench of sweat was drifting to the platform where the chiefs of the Order of St. Tammany were sitting.

Still, Casey told himself, they were his legions. Next week on election eve they would spread out over the city. On gusty street corners and under the flaring gas lights of cheap saloons, they'd fight the good fight for him. All through the November night they would be weaving back and forth through the singing, arguing drinkers, past the yellow pine ticket booths posted like sentries on the corners, while the ticket handlers scurried about delivering their flour sacks full of ballots.

At dawn the hushed snow of votes would start falling. The

workmen first, dropping in with their dinner cans and tools, then the tenements would empty, the hired Tammany carriages drawing up with the lame and blind, while the Prince Albert and black-cravat Democrats loitered about the corridors of the Hoffman House making wagers as the odds changed at the special telegraph dispatches, and across the street at the uptown *Herald* offices the transparency frames were put on canvas and exposed before the building. By that night when the bonfires were lit on the side streets and the electric light radiance lit up the *Herald*'s front, his legions would have won his victory — Hewitt for mayor, nine Tammany congressmen, aldermanic candidates and, if everything went smoothly, three assemblymen as well.

As he stared out at the sweating faces, he felt a tap on his shoulder and turned to see Horse Masterson who had come up behind him on the platform.

"Hewitt ain't showed up yet," Horse informed him.

Casey swung to inspect the platform as if he might find the mayoralty candidate. But it was true. Daly was there, Belmont, and Travers, but not Abram Hewitt. Goddamn all rich men, he thought, they never saw you had to take politics just as seriously as they took their business. Unless Hewitt fell in line when he was mayor, he'd find himself dumped hard and fast, just the same as Liggett had been.

Still, bad temper now would gain him nothing. He forced his irritation behind the phlegmatic public mask he was developing the way Kelly had formed his air of military severity.

"Send a man to see is he still at that German rally at Cooper Union," he said. And squinting past the calcium lights to the Seventh Regiment Band playing in the gallery, he added: "Tell them to keep going."

"Right, Boss," Horse said briskly, and as he turned to leave, Casey saw the necktie drawn through a seal ring at his throat and he smiled at how fancy Horse was getting. With his memo book filled with tricky pigeon tracks, his dark suits and squared-off beard, Horse had taken to aping the Prince of Wales with four-in-hands pulled down through seal rings. But while the smile lingered on his mouth, he recognized the ring with a pang. It was the one he'd brought to Horse himself from his European jaunt that summer, and the trip still left him with a hollow feeling.

After Kelly's death, and the funeral done, he'd made a trip across to buy good English horses. As long as he was going into racing, he made up his mind to show the Belmonts, Oelrichs, Lorillards and Roosevelts he'd race the best. But as soon as his boat docked, he'd found he was still in time for the Grand Prix de Paris at Longchamp. It was too good a chance to miss. He took the next ship across the Channel.

Paris had been beautiful in June with chestnuts in leaf along the boulevards, the winding Seine, the scudding clouds changing to showers, ladies of fashion in open carriages passing the bright disorder of the shop signs. His first morning, he bought the ring for Horse in a jeweler's store piled with gold ornaments, and the rest of the day he bought presents for Eileen and the children, inspecting the stationers filled with paperweights, the chocolate dealers and perfumers. That night after supper he went to a variety theater but he couldn't follow it properly, not knowing the language, and he walked slowly back to his hotel over the cobbles feeling queer and lonely beneath the lines of gas jets on the dark, slowly emptying boulevards, a sedate, middle-aged American, till suddenly he was tired and hailed a cab. Paris was about what he'd expected and yet he was let down and disappointed.

Next day was Sunday. He rested in his room till past noon, then dressed and hailed a cab, shouting "Longchamp" till the driver understood he must be taken to the races.

The Bois de Boulogne was filled with carriages when they entered the gate to Longchamp and jostled their way through the omnibuses, the elegant landaus and victorias, nearly running down the crowd on foot. Casey's cab drew up among the cabs four rows deep along the barriers and he looked around him at the strange scene, the bookmakers standing in open broughams with their odds chalked on boards beside them, the drinking booths set up beneath gray canvas.

For the first races he stayed near his cab, getting the hang of it. The field behind him looked like a country fair. Picnics were spread out on the grass and all about him champagne baskets were being handed down from the carriages by liveried coachmen. The holiday air eased him of his stranger's feeling, and after the City of Paris race had been run, he was craning his neck to see the central pavilion, its balcony fitted up with scarlet armchairs. Finally he walked toward the enclosure and stared about at the scattered chairs, the children running free, the stands rising in tiers above the green fresh lawns and young horse chestnut trees. He was stopped by the gate attendant and he was turning over what he knew of French money, when suddenly he realized he was staring at Claire.

She looked the same — the same fair skin, red setter hair and delicate frame. She was wearing a simple black silk edged with braid, a large lace hat and parasol. There was no doubt that it was Claire. His heart pounding, he stood frozen, a classic figure of the middle-aged rich American, not knowing the tongue and unable to push past a foreign gateman. But then as Claire turned her head and their gaze met, it was as if he'd been released from a spell. He took out a fistful of franc notes, pushed them at the gate-man and rushed by him. With the man trying to catch his arm, he kept on walking into the enclosure and then the gateman seemed to sense it was something unusual and beyond him. Perhaps Casey's black derby and dark suit, though peculiar amongst the patent leathers, crimson neckties and silk hats, struck him as de-cently expensive. He loosed Casey's arm and stood back when Casey stopped before Claire's party.

For it was a party. He saw that finally. Beside Claire an old man was sitting dressed in black with a lorgnette dangling down his pleated shirtfront. On the chair next to them lay a pair of field glasses as if their owner were visiting the bookmakers' section but would soon be returning. All at once Casey felt feverish. He knew it was Claire and yet he felt so confused, he could think of no words but just stood looking down at her. She'd changed a bit after all, he noticed irrelevantly — the fair skin was cleverly pow-dered. There were lines etched at the eyes. But the clean chin line was still there — she kept her face held high, of course. It came to him she must be nearing forty.

"Monsieur?" she said in a stranger's voice. But instead of making him more unsure, the tone struck away the years and he saw a young, ruined girl with braided chignon tumbling down her back as she lay against the wall in the back room of a saloon.

"Victoria Livingston?" he asked with a grin spreading across his face.

But that name she really didn't recall. Hearing it threw her off and as she paused, the old man stirred and fumbled with his lorgnette. "Monsieur is American too?" he asked. He had a strong accent but it wasn't French.

Before Casey could place it exactly, she had recovered herself and was speaking quickly to the old man in Italian. He blinked back at her like an old lizard. He looked as if he'd seen everything, that old man. Casey took in the long white fingers, the costume out of date but rich, the Marechal rose in his lapel, and realized he'd never seen an Italian like him, certainly not around Tammany Hall.

"I have just explained to my husband," Claire was saying in English, "that though you are American, I do not know you."

He hesitated. And then it seemed to him there was a plea in her eyes. His heart softened. After all, he didn't know what she'd got into. There was no need for him to ruin her setup. He bowed and said: "It's my mistake, then. Just the same, it was nice to meet you."

He gave her a chance to give her new name but she was too canny. She kept her little chin raised and stayed silent. Nodding at the old man who had finally got his lorgnette lifted, he sauntered back past an ice vendor and departed through the gate.

But doggedness set in then and made him stop there. He'd be damned if he'd throw her back into mystery so easily. Reaching into his trousers pocket, he peeled off a fifty franc note and held it up before the gateman.

"Speak English?" he asked. "Who was I just talking to?"

The gateman gazed at the fifty francs, then he reached and took it. "The Count and Countess . . ." There was a long string of Italian names after that Casey knew he'd never follow. "They come from Italy once a year to see the Grand Prix de Paris."

That was it, then, Casey realized. The lines between France and
New York were good — he would have heard if she'd been living
in France. He turned for another look at the count. An old rake-
hell, by the look of him, willfulness blossomed into eccentricity.
God knew who he thought she was. An American heiress, most
likely, whose funds were frozen year after year. Still, he likely had
enough for both. Well, life didn't look so lively for her, though he
granted a title was worth something. She'd done all right for a
mission girl.

He was still watching when the man strolled to them. "By God,"
he said in disbelief. Surely it was Pretty Boy. He had the same
disdainful manner, the same movements as he lifted the field
glasses and sat down on the chair beside Claire. But Pretty Boy was
drowned, Casey remembered, fished out of the East River, dead
and buried at a riotous funeral, and he realized the man was too
young, too. He looked like Pretty Boy but it was just the type he'd
always hated, the fair, the elegant young whoremaster.

"The countess's nephew," the gatekeeper murmured.

Casey looked down at him quickly, and it seemed to him he
caught a quiver in the little gateman's eye.

"That's so," he said. "I recognize him."

Shaken, he went back to his cab and watched the race run without really seeing it. He left Paris that night still feeling hollow, as
if she'd managed with her tricks to strip him even of his memories.

Casey's attention drifted back to the auditorium, to the flags and
bunting and the huge portrait emblazoned HEWITT FOR MAYOR. The
gallery band was playing selections from *The Mikado* and in the
back a drunken crocodile was forming as the audience tired of waiting and were making their own plans for the evening. They were
going to have to start without Hewitt, Casey saw. But instead of
nodding to the chairman, he lingered, hands on knees, gazing out
on the sea of brilliantly lit faces. It looked like a Cork county fair,
he decided.

For a moment, he had the queer sensation they were all staring
directly at him, thousands of eager Irish faces, waiting for orders he
alone could give them about something important, abstract and

vague, such as what they were to do with the city now they had it. He felt he was in a nightmare and had forgotten what it was he had to tell them.

Then a man jumped up in back and shouted: "Solid for George!" It was the opposition's battle cry. Casey's eye flickered to him. He was a big shambling man, a bit drunk, dressed in the coarse checked blouse longshoremen wore. He waved his arms and fought fiercely as the crocodile boiled over him and threw him out.

He was one of the workingmen's party that had surged up to follow the radical Henry George, who promised them the earth. No man in his right mind would expect paradise for nothing, and yet the workers were flocking to him, forming groups and unions, the Printers' Legion, Cigarmakers, the Horseshoers, Progressive Painters, the Fruit Handlers, the Marble Cutters. Every night he spoke to packed houses, and by day he roved about the city shouting from the back end of a truck. Casey had seen him himself at an open air meeting at the Battery, a short man with a bright smile, ruddy skin, Prince Albert and a slouch hat, shouting hoarsely at the crowd. And such a crowd! Standing under the blue sky, the harbor rippling with wind behind them and the telegraph wires festooned from the buildings all around, were longshoremen with their dinner pails, hooks sticking in their belts, carters, draymen, cattle drovers, ferrymen. Dirty street girls hung on the crowd's fringe, looking like they'd just escaped the Tombs, grimy match peddlers sold their wares while filthy child thieves ran about and sharp shopgirls paused before they hurried back to work from lunch. The real shock was seeing Father McGlynn. He was standing on the truckbed following every word George said. His face was stern and he looked to Casey like a desperate radical for all the trappings of his priest's collar and hat. When George cried: "The land belongs to the people!" McGlynn nodded, and at "All men have an equal right to apply their labor to the nation's resources," McGlynn held his hands up and applauded while cheers rocketed from the crowd.

Every day the man was getting more lunatic. Archbishop Corrigan was furious but McGlynn kept bulling ahead, carrying his Irish parishioners with him. Even Casey's mother and acid Mary, gnarled and crippled as she was with rheumatism, were wrapping pamphlets urging the workmen's revolution, and every time Frank Casey sobered up, he put on his clean collar and good suit and trotted round distributing fliers on how Tammany kept the poor in chains.

The man's own charitable past made him more dangerous. After the Battery meeting, the archbishop had ordered him off George's platform, and more orders were coming through suspending him from his duties at St. Stephen's. He'd be summoned to Rome to explain his support of strange, radical positions. Casey wondered if he'd be so foolish as to refuse to go. It was possible he would. His back was up on workingmen's rights. Well, if he did, he'd find himself excommunicated. Either way, his use to George with the Irish was ended. And with McGlynn's help cut off, Henry George's fight was lost. Already Tammany and the County Democracy had joined their uneasy forces to defeat him. And to make doubly sure, the Republicans would sell out young Teddy Roosevelt, who was running on their ticket. Defeat George they would surely. The rumors were already flying that he was secretly anti-Irish. The trick that elected Fernando Wood was doing duty again. Between the archdiocese, the rich merchants, the County Democracy and Tammany alliance, the threat the Irish vote would go radical was ended. Staring out from the platform, Casey told himself it would be the last time they'd face that danger. Bread, coal and charity baskets, Kelly dead so they'd have no more of his feuding, and the Tammany machine would grind on forever. The city would be stable and sure as an Irish village.

A weariness swept over him as he stared out at the gleaming faces. As they were, so he'd been, he supposed — and worse, street fighting, rolling drunks, gambling his life on nothing at all, carried out of himself by their same passions. And yet, somewhere deeper there'd been the dreamer, the young Casey lying on his dirty blanket thinking back to Sir James and Cork, the gleaming hunters, the thoroughbred dogs, the green rolling demesne, the quiet dignity of the squire. For an instant, he teetered between the two identities, the surly villager rebelling against the landlord's arrogance, and the figure of Sir James that he felt he was just a breath now from becoming. Vertigo spun him around. Then he grabbed the chair arms hard and forced himself back to common sense.

He frowned out at the crowd to see them clear. They weren't the meek and saintly oppressed masses the radicals painted. They were just what he saw now, venal and grasping, rough-and-tumble men in an alley. Give them drink and they'd swill it down, then go back to their cold flats and turn their fists against their families. Half of them couldn't write and were proud of it. In the riots, they'd burned, looted and murdered. They were the mob, and the mob went on forever. It was endless, forever poor, boiling with passion, faceless and always dangerous. Only the gleam of brass and helmets controlled it. A dark channel of blue uniforms constantly had to course through it.

For just a second, he felt he'd missed something. A street child's keen face came to his mind, but it connected with nothing. He put it from him as a cheer went up. Hats began waving and he saw Hewitt was coming in, already drawing off his overcoat. With two policemen opening a passage, he stepped smartly down the aisle and the chairman helped him up on the platform. The band crashed into "America" and Casey nodded to the chairman.

He moved wearily on his chair as the chairman strode to the stand and pounded with his gavel. There was more cheering and hat-waving. Someone let off a firecracker. But at last the Hall settled down.

Casey composed his face in respectful lines and the first speaker cleared his throat and was off.